AARON'S ROD

AARON'S ROD

Michael Baum

Matador
9 Priory Business Park,
Wistow Road, Kibworth Beauchamp,
Leicestershire. LE8 0RX
Tel: 0116 279 2299
Email: books@troubador.co.uk
Web: www.troubador.co.uk/matador
Twitter: @matadorbooks

ISBN 978 1788033 435

British Library Cataloguing in Publication Data.
A catalogue record for this book is available from the British Library.

Printed and bound by CPI Group (UK) Ltd, Croydon, CR0 4YY
Typeset in 11pt Aldine401 BT by Troubador Publishing Ltd, Leicester, UK

Matador is an imprint of Troubador Publishing Ltd

I dedicate this book to my long suffering wife who has supported me through thick and thin for more than 50 years, I was thin when we first met and now I'm "thick".

Lebanon

Syria

Tyre

TEL DAN

Golan
Heights

Daraa

Akko
Haifa

Nazareth

Afula

Irbid

Netanya

Nablus

West
Bank

The route from
Amman to Bethlehem

Amman

Tel Aviv

Mediterranean
Sea

Ramallah
Ramla

Jericho

Ashdod

Jerusalem

Madaba

Bethlehem

LACHISH

Gaza

Hebron

Jordan

Gaza

QUMRAN

Dead Sea

Khan Yunis

Beersheba

Israel

Al Arish

Egypt

0   60km

40mi

Eilat

Taba

Aqaba

Red Sea

Prologue

London 2038

Olive Hathaway was a sprightly sparrow of an old lady whose age was a closely guarded secret but judged to be well into her nineties. She belied her age and whatever the weather she would walk round the bridle path of the Hampstead Heath extension two or three times a week. She claimed this was in order to clarify her thoughts, yet her neighbours and family members, were of the opinion that her cognitive functions were alarmingly clear and often outperformed theirs. Perhaps it was her reading material that helped feed her brain rather than her regular walks.

Next to her comfortable armchair in her cozy cottage, was a table of books and magazines that were organized like a ziggurat according to size. She always had one book of fiction and one book of non-fiction on the go; the work of fiction was usually from the short list for the Booker prize whilst the topics of the non-fiction books were reflected in the weekly or quarterly magazines that formed the base of the pyramid that in turn reflected the surprisingly esoteric interests of this unusual old lady.

Embedded in the collection of magazines could be found the latest editions of "Smart Computing" and "PC world" together with "Biblical Archaeology Review" and "The Palestine Exploration Quarterly (PEQ)".

It was a chilly early winter evening with the wind blowing across the Heath from the northeast, when Olive settled in her reading chair, switched on her reading light, swapped her bifocals for reading glasses and picked up the as yet unopened copy of the PEQ.

She nearly spilled her tot of brandy when she started reading the first paper in the journal that was entitled, "The murder of James Leslie Starkey near Lachish 1938". This event 100 years in the past had come back to haunt her. The reports of James Starkey's murder, as they appeared in the newspapers of that time, appeared in the annex of the publication. One from the Palestine Post was so vivid it was if she had been involved in the investigation from the start, yet the ripples in the pond provoked by this outrage didn't reach out to her until nearly 70 years after the event.

The Palestine Post January 11ᵗʰ 1938
Murder of British Archaeologist, J.L. Starkey killed in cold blood.
Discoverer of 'Lachish Letters' shot by Arabs

Mr. John Llewellyn Starkey, one of the most distinguished among archaeologists working in Palestine, was shot and killed at 5 o'clock yesterday afternoon by a gang of Arab brigands on the Beit Jibrin track, north west of Hebron. Mr. Starkey, who was 50 years old was the director of the field expedition of the Wellcome Foundation at Tell ed Duweir, the site of ancient Lachish, where some years ago he made the discovery of inscribed tablets dating back from the period of Jeremiah.

Mr. Starkey was on his way from Tell ed Duweir to Jerusalem today at a preview arranged at the Palestine Archaeological museum. The car in which he was travelling was on the Beit Jibrin track some two kilometres from the main Hebron-Jerusalem highway when it was stopped by a band of armed Arabs. The driver was questioned and, it is said, Mr Starkey was asked who he was. He answered that he was British. He was then ordered to leave the car and the driver was told to drive on to Hebron. Mr Starkey was made to march on. As the driver made off, he heard shots and, turning his head, saw the archaeologist fall. The driver went on to Hebron and informed the police.

A large party of constables, later reinforced by troops, set out for the scene where they found the body of Mr Starkey on the track. He had been shot eleven times in the back and some other unofficial accounts suggest that his body had been mutilated.

Mr. Starkey leaves a widow and three children who, it is believed, are at present in England.

In one sense the murder of the Director of the Wellcome Expedition typifies the struggle between civilisation and primitive savagery of which we have experienced so many unfortunate examples recently.

★★★

January 12ᵗʰ

Police dogs were brought to the scene of the murder of Mr. Starkey, some two or three kilometres west of the Hebron-Jerusalem road on the Beit Jibrin, at dawn yesterday morning at took up a trail that led them across the hills in the direction of the coast.

Detachments of the British Palestine police, fully armed and equipped with Lewis-guns, proceeded to the scene of the murder. Many villagers are reported to have been arrested.

Mr. Starkey was not robbed nor was the body removed until the police arrived from Hebron.

A particular tragic aspect of the murder is that Mr. Starkey had always been on the best of terms with the Arab peasantry in the district, and that during the past 5 years he had engaged hundreds of them in the diggings, thus pouring thousands of pounds into the district in the form of wages. He could also converse fluently in Arabic and was a keen student of Arab folklore and customs.

★★★

As Olive read the full publication, she made copious notes and didn't stop until she had completed and inwardly digested the contents of the long scholarly report. Suddenly the memory of her adventures came flooding back and as she read on, missing pieces in the jigsaw fell into place.

She then sat back and thought hard about those words "Mr. Starkey was not robbed". She accepted that her life was drawing to a close and she also accepted that much of her covert knowledge was still covered by the Official Secrets Act 1989 and couldn't be disclosed for another 10 years. She there and then determined to complete a full written narrative account of the events between 2015 and 2018 that could be held in a secure place and in her will there would be a note to the executors to release the material in 2048. She also conceded that this was a task beyond the skills or for that matter, the memory, of one old lady so she would need the help of at least one of the surviving members of her team of amateur investigators.

She looked at her watch and decided that 8.00 pm on a Sunday evening might be a good time to call so without pausing for further thought activated an audio-visual link on her i-Phone 12S to contact her old friend Professor Sanjay Manchandra.

★★★

PART 1

The Hanging Man

Chapter 1

Sanjay Manchandra

Sanjay Manchandra was born in 1978 precisely at the moment when the Sun, Moon, Mars and Venus were in exact alignment, that in astrological terms was called a conjunction at the first degree of Virgo. The place of his birth was the village of Aymanam in the State of Kerala in southwest India. To the delight of his parents the village astrologer concluded that there had not been a more harmonious or auspicious time to be born in the last 50 years and great things were expected from this little boy.

Because of consanguineous marriages and pollution of the backwaters there was a high incidence of congenital abnormalities in the village and Sanjay was no exception. However in his case the abnormality was advantageous, as the little brown and bubbly baby was born with an intelligence that had to be the gift of the Hindu Goddess of knowledge, Saraswati. There could be no other explanation, as his father was an illiterate humble fisherman and his mother was a simple woman who helped tend the rice paddy fields belonging to the village. His intelligence became apparent as he rapidly passed his milestones walking and talking intelligibly at the age of 18 months. At the same time his sense of humor became apparent as he found much pleasure in hiding his father's flip-flops and his mother's necklaces. His motor skills and cognitive skills developed in parallel and by the age of three he was joining the big boys on the village maidan in playing cricket. Although his parents only spoke Malayalam by the age of 5 he had picked up some English words from the tourists staying at the nearby

Coconut Beach holiday resort. As a result of this he dreamed up a number of scams that won him much street credibility and a stache of cash that he hid behind a loose mud brick in the back wall of his hovel, just behind his head where he slept on a rush mat covering the beaten mud and straw floor. The first scam was to wait by the multi-colored fishing boats that were pulled up every morning on the beach facing lake Vembandu, to off load their morning catch of herrings. In the cool of the mornings in the high season of October to January after the monsoons, many guests at the neighboring resort would enjoy an early morning walk. Sanjay and his toothy gang of friends in their colorful shirts and dresses would provide wonderful photo opportunities. First he learnt to ask for "school pens" and the seasoned travelers, who would always be carrying collection of cheap ballpoint pens, were happy to show off their understanding of the native customs, and always happy to oblige. These he would bind together, into clusters of 5, with elastic bands and sell them in the local street market for fifty paise a time. Later, emboldened by his success he would ask 5 rupees, before posing with his gang of juvenile delinquents. His charming grin, when he said, "My name is Sanjay 5 rupees pliss" would often work on the naïve jet lagged English tourist, who had no idea what 5 rupees was worth in buying power in this neck of the wood.

In the evenings of the high season he had two other scams that played out on the east side of the village next to the backwaters. The first was to run alongside the converted tea barges, that were now hired as houseboats for the tourists, as they drifted along the narrows, singing "Rude Britannia, Britannia rudes de wabes", picked up from the Last Night of the Proms on the BBC news channel much favored by the visiting British. This would earn him a few rupees but his best wheeze was the cricket bat scam. The Indians, as a legacy from the last days of the Raj, loved cricket as much as the English and were rather good at the game. The boys and even some of the girls would play the game on what passed as the maidan or village green in a cleared patch of jungle, adjacent to the last paddy field on the eastern side, before and after the monsoon season. Every village had a team that competed with their neighbors and the village elders made sure their boys were adequately equipped. However Sanjay spotted that during the high season, almost all Englishmen who fancied their hand at the game, would want to impress his wife or girl friend by bowling an over at the village boys.

He then hatched a plan of genius by hiding the village bats when they saw tourists walking towards them, especially if the men were wearing panama hats, replacing them with rotting lengths of fencing slats crudely shaped to look like bats. After the English gentleman was allowed to bowl out the little brown batsman or catch the ball in flight after a hit, Sanjay would cry out in a sad voice with a trembling lower lip; "Oh pliss sirs if only we could buy a proper bat we might one day play for India". With a 60% rate of success, the accompanying young lady would say words to the effect, "Oh darling how sweet, do be a pet and give the boys 10 rupees towards buying a real bat." And so by fair means or foul, at the age of 6, young Sanjay went to school already speaking passable English and had enough money hidden in a cavity in the wall of his hovel, not only to buy a couple of cricket bats, but also pads and stumps, yet such was his thirst for knowledge he was already saving it to buy school books.

Sanjay had an older brother who he idolized and an eccentric uncle. His brother Ashok, tall and handsome with a neat Clark Gabel moustache, was a fearsome fast bowler. His education stopped at the age of 16 and although perfectly literate and reasonably fluent in English, he lacked ambition and was content to work with his father as a shallow water fisherman in the morning, selling the village produce at the local market twice a week and drinking Kingfisher beer or chasing the local girls every evening. His uncle, Vijay, had early in life decided to dedicate his life to the pantheon of Hindu Gods as a sàdhu, yet never wandered far from his spiritual home in the nearby Pandavam Sree Darmashasta temple. He was a useful wicket keeper and handy with the bat at number 4 in the batting order, incongruous in his saffron robes tucked in to his breeches. The white vertical stripe running down the centre of his forehead was an irresistible target for a "Yorker" bowled by the neighboring villages' fast bowlers, yet as if to compensate for that vulnerability, he was immune to being given out "leg before wicket", as the umpires were afraid of his reputation for summoning up divine retribution. Because the family had traditionally earned their living as fishermen, they belonged to the third highest caste of *vaishyas,* but as the Sate of Kerala was ruled by a tolerant and enlightened communist government, this was of no consequence and certainly no impediment to Sanjay's education, although there might come a time that this could limit his parent's choice of a suitable girl in the matrimonial stakes.

Sanjay scorched a path of intellectual achievement from 1st to 10th grade at the government high school at the neighboring village of Kudanaloor, where the entire community was taught regardless of any social divisions. The teaching staff was divided in their attitude to this rising star. Half considered him too big for his boots, insolent and too quick to raise his hand in class piping out, "Me Sir, please, me Sir". The other half recognized his nascent genius and by giving him extra tuition and tolerating his knight's move way of thinking, were hoping to bask in his reflected glory as a small way of compensating them for their own low level of self-esteem.

The village children of Aymanam were also very fortunate to live close to Kottayam, the city that acted as one of the main educational hubs of the State. The Kottayam District of Kerala was the first district to achieve full literacy rate in the whole of India. Mahatma Gandhi University and Medical College were also situated in Kottayam. He graduated high school ranking 8th in the State and entered medical college at the age of 17 having been in the accelerated stream at school. Although years ahead of his peers in intellectual maturity, he lagged behind in developing social skills and couldn't understand why the whole world didn't love him and admire his cleverness, like his family and cricketing friends in his village. Most of his classmates lacked the sophistication you might come to expect from medical students in the UK or USA and had no way of coping with this ebullient, man-boy who outranked them in every exam, as they clambered up the slippery pole of pre-clinical and clinical studies. To tell the truth he was lonely at college and spent most of his leisure hours in the village studying his books, with the occasional release of playing cricket when the ground was dry. At the age of 22 in the year 2000 he graduated top of his class with a MB BS honors, the Ernest Borges prize in surgery and the gold medal.

Following this success he was appointed at Kottayam Medical College Hospital for a rotating internship and after 12 months, embarked on his career in surgery at the grade of senior house officer. After two more years of clinical practice and intense study he took the MS exam locally and then went up to Mumbai to sit the intercollegiate exam for the British MRCS. Both of which he passed with distinction.

After this his ambitions were too grand to be contained in a backwater of medical mediocrity like Kottayam, so he applied and was accepted for a three-year rotation in surgical oncology at the world famous Tata Memorial Hospital in Mumbai, a specialist cancer treatment and research centre. Sanjay's motor skills, first evident on the maidan of his village, served him well as a surgeon. He rapidly mastered the craft and with dexterous movements of wrists and fingers, an eagle eye and a perfect knowledge of anatomy. Within three years he was capable of performing meticulous radical excisions of cancers of the head and neck, breast, oesophagus, stomach and large bowel. But although mastering his craft he was not content. His enquiring mind and capacity to think outside the box convinced him that surgery alone was not the answer to cancer, however perfectly cut away. Furthermore he was sensitive enough and sufficiently empathetic, to become aware that however triumphant was the operation, patients were left with enormous burdens to bear for the rest of their lives. The colostomy after a radical abdomino-perineal excision of a rectal cancer and the mutilation of the chest wall after a Halsted radical mastectomy truly appalled him. He therefore found time for training in onco-plastic surgery to learn if it was possible to mitigate these deformities and studied the principles of radiotherapy and medical oncology, to see if better combinations of the three modalities might further reduce the scope of surgery. With few friends and no social life to speak of he would spend most evenings and weekends in the pathology laboratory, driving the on call pathologist mad with his unbridled enthusiasm. All that changed dramatically when he was tagging on to the back of a group of medical residents as they were being taken on a teaching round of the pediatric oncology wards. As many of these sick children were immuno-compromised, all the residents were wearing masks. He happened to look across the huddle of residents and was suddenly captivated by a pair of large, luminous and long lashed brown eyes looking back at him, from a face almost hidden by a green mask.

It was love at first sight because the eyes weren't just beautiful, but sparkled with intelligence and mischief. Abandoning his studies in the pathology labs his next major project therefore involved research of a different kind. "Who was this lovely lady and what must I do to impress her?" The project was completed in no time thanks to his brilliant powers of deduction, aided by the list of residents posted on the notice boards outside each of their wards. Yet the result of his enquiries left him feeling hopeless and helpless. The young lady was Dr. Savita Deobagkar, the niece of Professor Dileep Deobagkar, Vice-Chancellor Goa University-and a member of a very distinguished Goanese Brahmin family. He was not a "suitable boy", so he aborted his quest but had not taken account of the fact that Savita had spotted him at the time he had spotted her. She did her own homework and discovered that he was already acknowledged as a brilliant scholar and as far as she was concerned, whatever his caste he was a "suitable boy". Sanjay was very shy of girls and furthermore his cultural background frowned upon the dating system of the west, so he was overcome with confusion when Dr Savita Deobagkar sat down next to him in the hospital canteen a few days after setting eyes on him and introduced herself. His shyness rapidly evaporated once she had engaged him in a discussion on the role of chemotherapy in the management of early breast cancer. Little did he know that this young woman had already learnt the art of seduction, with the quickest way to a man's heart was through his IQ; well at least for a man like Sanjay who she had already profiled. They immediately hit it off and in the frequent retelling of this story Sanjay rather unromantically, likened their attachment to that of oestradiol binding with great avidity to the oestrogen receptor.

Within a few months the dreaded invitation arrived for this very unsuitable boy to meet the parents of this high caste girl, when he was invited to spend a weekend off duty at the Deobagkar ancestral home in Panaji overlooking the Mandovi River.

★★★

He had been dreading this meeting but as with all his other examinations he trusted that adequate preparation would get him through the ordeal. Savita met him at the airport and commented favorably on his choice of smart casual attire that was modest in appearance yet carried subtle logos of expensive brands. They were of course counterfeit.

The Deobagkar compound was intimidating; although the gardens overlooking the river were so beautiful that they helped him to arrive at the front door in a state of nirvana. Savita's father greeted him warmly at the door and conducted him to a veranda overlooking the gardens and brusquely ordered a servant to fetch chi and fruit. He had clearly been well briefed about Sanjay's scholarship by his daughter and engaged him in a cross examination on his career so far and future prospects, whilst retaining a twinkle in his eye. But when his future mother-in-law strolled in, night fell. However, he was well prepared for this and strode over made a deep and respectful *Namaste* and uttered the words, "Oh you must be Savita's sister, you look so alike". The oldest trick it the game, yet it seldom fails. The sun broke through the darkness when he expressed convincing surprise that this was indeed Savita's mother and proffered, as a gift, a beautifully illustrated antique copy of the Ramayana. The portly middle-aged woman had to smile, but clearly was reserving judgment. It is perhaps worth noting that Sanjay's brother had a nice little sideline in marketing perfect facsimiles of ancient manuscripts, produced by the latest photocopying equipment in Cochi, bound in genuine antique leather harvested from the second hand bookshops in the back streets of Mumbai.

The weekend was a great success and Sanjay was accepted as a suitable boy and the *Sakharpuda,* or betrothal ceremony, was arranged for December, when the weather would be at its best. The wedding would occur shortly afterwards but first they had to consult the bridegroom's family priest and astrologer to agree on the most auspicious date.

Fortunately the sun, the moon and the planets were lined up perfectly at a date shortly after the betrothal ceremony that allowed for all the out of town guests to stay for a full week to accommodate the sequence of complex rituals.

Savita's father had hired the grounds and most of the freestanding villas at the luxurious Taj Exotica hotel for the duration. The wedding itself took place in a huge and totally convincing Hindu Temple, built as a façade in grounds of the hotel overlooking the Indian Ocean, from which balmy winds blew in to help the younger dancers over-heating in their frenzy later that evening.

Once the 700 guests were seated in front of the Bollywood stage setting, the bridegroom's procession entered to the sound of drums and trumpets. Sanjay felt an idiot in his elaborate brocade costume and pantomime turban but carried himself with dignity.

Once the rituals were complete, the bridegroom, with a croaky voice burst into a traditional Sanskrit song. The bride then put her right hand on top of the bridegroom's and the mother of the bride put her right hand below both hands. Then the father of the bride poured holy water onto the stacked hands, symbolizing giving away his daughter.

Once the wedding ceremony was complete all the dignity and solemnity came to an abrupt end and things went "mental". The dancing, the singing and the feasting went on until midnight, all this exuberance being fuelled by love rather than alcohol, although a few bottles of the finest single malt whisky were kept at hand for the western guests and the lapsed members of the Hindu faith. At the close of the festivities, a million fireworks, that would have done the closing ceremony of the Olympics proud, lighted the sky.

The couple's honeymoon was postponed until the Spring to allow them time to complete their contracts and collect their visas so as to be able to enjoy two weeks of freedom in London before Sanjay settled down to work as a research fellow at University College.

★★★

Their arrival in London in early May 2007 after a 9-hour flight from Mumbai to terminal 4 at Heathrow was followed by a multi-layered culture shock for both of them. This was their first visit to the western world and they were "hard wired" for stereotypic images of England as a country of cricket played on village greens and London populated by white men in top hats, bowler hats or deer stalkers, bumping into each other in a "pea-souper" fog, while ragamuffin children and arch villains exploiting the fog by picking a pocket or two. For a start the long line of arrivals passing through immigration were mostly Indians as was the immigration officer checking their passport and visa, who wore a Sikh turban. The baggage retrieval hall was quiet and well organized unlike the feeding frenzy on arrival at any airport in India. The taxi taking them into town was clean and modern with a friendly West Indian driver and most of the pedestrians they saw from the M4 passing through west London had black or dark brown faces. As they approached the Chiswick flyover and appeared to be entering the great city for real, they were amazed to see that all the tall buildings were clean and in good repair, unlike Marine drive in Mumbai were one in every three tall buildings looked like a case of advanced dental caries. This good impression was sustained all the way along the West Way until it dipped down into the Marylebone Road. Now at pavement level another culture shock took over. Not only were the buildings well maintained, but also the side walks. In all the cities in India they had visited, pedestrians had to walk at the edge of the road because either the pavement was full of pot holes bridged by unstable planks of wood, or else they were occupied by sleeping itinerant villagers or traders. Here people walked on the pavements, cars and taxis drove on the road and there were no wandering cows or beggar children to be seen. The air was free of fog and relatively free of pollution apart from that of the exhausts of passing heavy good's lorries. In fact the first honest to God stereotype English gentleman they met wearing a top hat, was the door man at the White House hotel on the east side of Regent's Park. They were to spend the first week of their honeymoon at the hotel before moving into rented accommodation in Camden town, arranged by Savita's dad through the good offices of a not too distant cousin.

The White House hotel had the superficial glamour that one would expect from a central London hotel, but then that's what you would expect from one of the Taj or Oberoi hotels in India. But what made this experience rather special was the view from their 6th floor window overlooking Regents Park to the west of the hotel. They had never seen such ordered and colorful beauty, with the spring flowerbeds at their best and the avenues running between the flowerbeds free of litter and homeless people. The nearest you could get to this were the tea plantations of the western Ghats in Kerala, but apart from the tea pickers no one was allowed to stroll around the avenues.

They thereupon determined to explore the park the following morning after a good nights sleep as their biological clocks had now reached 1.00am.

They slept well and woke early hungry for their breakfast at which point another layer of culture shock awaited them. The buffet allowed for one's plate to be filled to overflowing with a "full English" breakfast; a nauseating concoction of fat and fried porcine meat or kippers, an alien species of fish that smelt like the lavatories at Mumbai airport. They settled for the "continental" that was simply coffee and doughy pastries. At 8.30am they strolled out of the hotel and turned right to encounter the full force of the London rush hour. Sure there were lots of cars, black taxis and iconic double-decker red buses but the traffic seemed to ebb and flow to the rhythm of the lights at the junction between the Marylebone Road and the outer circle round the park. Furthermore this was achieved without the sounding of horns or furious gesticulating policemen. Just as they crossed the road at the flashing of a little green man on the traffic signal, Sanjay was distracted by the appearance of a beautiful, modern, white marble clad building, that on closer inspection revealed itself as the Royal College of Physicians. Savita whooped with excitement, as one of her ambitions was to take the exams to qualify as MRCP whilst Sanjay was studying to gain his FRCS.

The park was breathtaking on this crystalline fine spring morning. As well as the Technicolor flower beds, there were giant urns overflowing with exotic flowers unknown to those who lived in tropical latitudes. Yet they were the only ones to stop and stare as everyone else was striding purposefully to work. They were very lucky with the weather and eventually had to come to terms with the fact that for most of the year London was monochromatic even when not raining. The rain itself was alien, as it came as a drizzle or a damp mist rather than the torrential downpour they were acclimatized to in the monsoon season. Having enjoyed an hour or two walking round the park they picked up an open top double-decker tourist bus for a hop on hop off tour of the capital. The bus took them past the grand shops on Oxford Street and then turned south along the even grander shops of the graceful crescent of Regent street, and then round the statue of Cupid at Piccadilly Circus turning south again along Haymarket to Trafalgar Square.

At Trafalgar square they dismounted and stared slack jawed in wonder at Nelson's column, surrounded by four enormous granite lions. Looking straight down Whitehall they could just make out the Palace of Westminster, "Big Ben" and the "London Eye". The square was animated with pedestrians and pigeons competing for space and all the surrounding white stucco neo-classical buildings reflected back the late spring sunshine. Turning round they faced the great staircase and classical colonnade with Corinthian ornamentation. They had no idea that this was the National Gallery but curiosity drew them in following behind a daisy chain of primary school children wearing green uniforms. This was the first time in their life they had visited an art gallery and they were at a loss as to the protocol for entering such hallowed halls.

In answer to their enquiry the uniformed attendant assured them that there was no entrance charge and invited them to explore the gallery and come and go as they wished. They also learnt that it was not the convention to remove one's shoes.

From the main lobby they were faced with three choices, turn right, turn left or go straight ahead through the huge and intimidating doors facing them. They chose to turn right into the east wing of the gallery and as a result saw the whole collection in reverse chronological order. In a way that was an advantage, as they were at least familiar with one of Van Gogh's sunflower paintings, but as far as the rest of the collection was concerned they simply did not know how to react and until the end of their visit had no real point of reference with their own culture. Savita enjoyed admiring the ladies dresses in the Victorian and Georgian periods but Sanjay used the whole tour as if it were a ward round at the Tata memorial looking for tell tale signs of pathology.

They enjoyed the temple like hush of the great Baroque arcades but only felt at home in the last set of rooms, the earliest in the chronology of the history of art, with the jewel like brilliantly painted small works by Cimabue and Duccio, where the liberal use of gold leaf and the heavenly blue of lapis lazuli, reminded them of Mughal illuminated manuscripts. They left the gallery via the Sainsbury wing, somewhat chastened, turned east across the northern esplanade of the square and leaving the exploration of Parliament Square for the afternoon, turned around the south east corner of the gallery into St Martin's Place and Charing Cross road, looking for a light lunch.

What they encountered was of little nutritional value but yet another layer of cultural divide as symbolized by their host city-palace's of entertainment known as "West End" theatres. By any Indian standards Sanjay and Savita were cultured people. They were knowledgeable about all the labyrinthine details of the Mahabharata and Ramayana. They both could recite ancient Sanskrit poems and had an excellent knowledge of English literature although that was limited to Bronte, Austin, Thackeray and Dickens. They also loved the Jungle Book and the poetry of Rudyard Kipling, yet had never read modern Indian literature by such luminaries as VS Naipal, Vikram Seth and Salman Rushdie. So when the moment arrived for them to be immersed in the vibrant culture of a great western capital city, it is in no way patronizing to claim they found themselves all at sea.

Although in all the dazzle, glamour and excitement of

entering London at "the deep end", these currents of cultural dislocation remained subconscious, yet they were to remain a source of embarrassment as they climbed the professional ladder and entered the circles of London's intelligentsia and sophisticates.

★★★

The second week of their honeymoon was spent settling in their rented flat on the third floor of an old Georgian terrace house in Hawley Crescent just off Camden High Street. In spite of the rather down at heel appearance from the outside, their flat had been recently redecorated and equipped with a modern kitchen and bathroom. In fact compared with their humble accommodation as junior residents in Mumbai this was almost luxury. Their distant kinship with the landlord helped in many ways and by chance it was an inspired location for both their professional and social life in London. There were a number of young middle class Indian families and students living nearby and an excellent Indian vegetarian restaurant on the High Street. Camden Lock market just across the High Street enjoyed the same intensity and touches of insanity that they were used to in any Indian market or bazaar. The prices of all the clothes and electric consumer goods were so low one would think they had fallen off the back of a lorry, which might have been close to the truth. This way their rather Spartan flat was rapidly and colorfully kitted out in no time.

The tribes and gangs that roamed the local streets accentuated the apparent lunacy of their neighborhood. Although rather threatening at the start, they soon learned that they were not at risk from the spiked haired tattooed and pierced Punks with their zips, chains and tartan trews or the glum looking black clad black-eyed Goths. The muscular pumped up leather clad Bikers were only a threat to members of other chapters, whilst the ragged filthy old men and women muttering to themselves as they pushed shopping trolleys full of rubbish, were merely burnt out schizophrenics who meant no harm.

The other advantage of living in Camden town was their proximity to the Northern Line of the underground. Taking the route south towards Charing Cross would get them to Warren Street station in about 10 minutes, very close to University College London and its hospital, whereas taking the tube north towards Edgware would have them in no time at Belsize Park, next door to the Royal Free Hospital and the Hampstead Campus of the University. So all in all Sanjay was nicely placed to start work on his research for his PhD whilst studying for his FRCS at the same time, and by now was itching to get started. On the last day of their holiday they decided to take a trip on the narrow boat "Jenny Wren" along the Regent's Canal. They broke their journey at London's Zoological Gardens at the north of Regent's Park and were overjoyed to see tigers and elephants from their homeland. As if on cue, their holiday ended as the cumulus nimbus clouds gathered and the London weather switched to normal service ensuring that they got soaked to the skin on the short boat trip back home.

★ ★ ★

Chapter 2

"This is your life Professor Black"

May 31ˢᵗ 2009

Joshua Black set out for work that morning at 7.00am, light of heart and with a spring in his step, enjoying the early morning light and fresh chilled air, as he began his steep walk up Wildwood Road before entering the dark woodland of Sandy Heath on the southern perimeter road of the Hampstead Heath extension. Today was his fiftieth birthday and that night, together with his wife and two boys, he was going to Covent Garden for a performance of La Traviata, with Rene Fleming in the role of Violetta. He was also looking forward to the weekly clinical pathological meeting of the department of surgery at the Royal Free Hospital in Hampstead, where he would hold sway and mischievously provoke animated debate between his senior colleagues. He was a bit of a showman and today was also the first chance he had for meeting his three new PhD students, giving himself a new audience to impress alongside his fresh group of young medical students, who these days almost always included one or two attractive young women. Although he was utterly devoted to his adorable wife Rachel and had no intention ever of being unfaithful, he was nevertheless a bit of a flirt and paid careful attention to his appearance.

He stepped off the pavement and entered the heavily wooded section of Sandy Heath at a spot where there was no evidence of a path yet gave access to a secret land just like the children in C.S. Lewis' book, "the Lion, the Witch and the Wardrobe", who would push aside a rack of old coats in an old wardrobe to enter Narnia. In fact C.S. Lewis was inspired to write that book whilst taking a walk across the Heath after a heavy snowfall. Joshua knew the Heath like the contours of his face and although this stretch of woodland looked featureless, there were ancient paths to be found if you knew where to look. William Blake's beautifully restored farm house was hidden deep in the woods on his right hand, whilst all that remained of the 18C Prime Minister's house, William Pitt the Younger, was a derelict gateway with a faded blue plaque at the end of a barely defined footpath on his left. Half way up the hill towards Spaniards Road was a plateau with a peaceful sun dappled glade and a small lake with no name. This was his favorite place and he almost always had it to himself at this time of day, apart from the occasional early morning dog walker. The pond was one of Hampstead's many flooded gravel pits. This pond had the magical gift of changing its appearance completely four times a year. In the spring on a still day like this, the pond was a perfect mirror reflecting the bull-rush covered banks, the floating waterfowl, the trees and the cloudy sky upside down, in such a way that you might become disorientated if you stared for too long. In the summer the pond's surface would be completely covered by a thick layer of green algae that looked like a closely cut lawn that might tempt the unwary to step off the path and sink in up to their waists. In the autumn the algae would clear and the pond would reflect the russet tones of the leaves above and those floating on its surface, like a cubist collage. In the winter the pond would always freeze over as if with malign intent to invite an innocent little boy to his untimely death by drowning, when he foolishly attempted to skate across. At those times of year large white notice boards carrying warnings in large red letters, appeared in the glade, yet over the years the pond with no name had taken its toll.

After a pause to enjoy this sylvan solitude he would continue on his way uphill in the gaps between waist high prickly gorse bushes and then onto the road through a narrow gap in the wooden barrier marking the route between the Spaniards Inn and Jack Straw's Castle, two of the oldest pubs in London. Turning right towards Whitestone pond at north London's highest elevation, it was then straight downhill along East Heath Road to the Royal Free Hospital. The department of surgery was on the ninth floor, but rather than waiting for the overcrowded lift he kept himself fit by jogging up the stairs. He always paced himself in order to arrive in the seminar room precisely at 08.00 to maintain his reputation for obsessive punctuality, whether for the start of the weekly clinical pathological conference, an out patient clinic, or the operating list. Others were forced to follow his example or suffer from one of his withering put downs such as, "London traffic bad this morning?" or "Mummy forgot to wake you on time?" That aside he was greatly respected for his leadership skills and academic achievements. It was therefore no surprise, that apart from the three new PhD students, the room was full and the undergraduates, and the junior staff on his firm. As the duty registrar was presenting the first case, two sheepish late comers slipped in at the back, one chubby and Indian in appearance and the second lean, hawk nosed and Middle Eastern in appearance. Professor Black stopped the show to welcome them, "Ah, Dr. Sanjay Manchandra and Dr. Ishmael Nadir I presume, kind of you to honor us with your presence, do take a pew for now and report to my office at 09.30 on the dot. Where is your colleague Dr. Ibn Sharif?" The newcomers shrugged their shoulders and shook their heads and Professor Black indicated that the show could restart.

At 9.00am on the dot Professor Black returned to his office, checked with his PA if there were any urgent messages and had a quick glance at his e-mail in box, before preparing himself to greet his new PhD students. He loved teaching at any level and enjoyed his responsibilities in mentoring bright young men and women with academic ambitions. He had high hopes for at least two of his new postgraduate students but had serious doubts about the third. Sanjay Manchandra was of humble origins but had a brilliant career up until this point and was strongly recommended to him by his old friend the director of the Tata Memorial Hospital in Mumbai, professor Rajan Lakhani.

Ishmael Sultan was even more exotic having been born the 7th son of a Bedouin family, herding goats south of Beersheba in the land of Israel. His extraordinary intelligence was recognized at an early age by his schoolteachers at a kibbutz in the northern Negev and he went on to study medicine at the at Ben Gurion university. He had been strongly recommended by the Dean of the medical faculty there, another old friend, professor Yosi Ben Yosef. The third was the joker in the pack. He had been strongly recommended by his old friend Sir Manfred Hoffbrand, the Dean of his medical school, on the strength of the fact that the young man's father, a minor but very wealthy Saudi prince, had promised a £5M endowment towards the building of a research institute of bio-engineering. Although this was not overtly stated there was some kind of understanding that accepting the young Ibn Sharif for a postgraduate studentship was a pre-condition. In other words the third PhD student had been foisted upon professor Black in spite of his fierce protestations. Now although a vain man and secure in the knowledge of his own brilliance, Joshua Black was of humble origins and had a strong sense of fair play and an aversion to any kind of racial or religious discrimination. He even took pride in the multi-racialism of his department and was naïve enough to think that bringing Arabs and Israelis, Hindus and Muslims to work together in the name of science, would contribute to world peace.

At 9.30am on the dot he buzzed his long serving, long suffering and loyal PA, Christine O'Reilly, to ask her to show in the three new members of the department.

The Indian and the Bedouin walked in and stood to

21

attention before him but he had to wait another 10 minutes for the Saudi princeling to show up. The latecomer breezed in on the dot of 09.40 full of smiles, floating along in an alarmingly white *thobe,* from neck to toes with a red chequered headdress; whilst a lackey carried in a long brown paper wrapped cylinder that was ceremoniously opened and rolled out in front of the professor's desk. The beautifully woven silk Persian carpet was offered up as a gift from the young man's father.

Joshua for once was at a loss for words. Abdulla Ibn Sharif sat himself down and invited the others who were still standing to join him. Swallowing hard and biting his tongue professor Black accepted the offer to sit down in his own office. The carpet carrier was dismissed and the three new postgraduates looked expectantly at their new professor.

Joshua cleared his throat and launched into his set piece. "Gentlemen, you are here at great expense to do some science under my guidance but first do any of you have the faintest idea what science is?" Expecting blank stares of surprise he was delighted when Sanjay fired back at him without a pause, "Science is the formulating of a testable hypothesis followed by systematic attempts at its refutation." Without changing his expression he then turned to the Bedouin and asked, "How do you test the hypothesis?" "By controlled experiments" came the prompt reply. Still looking stern he turned to the man in the white robe and asked, "How do you determine whether screening for cancer saves lives?" After a moment or two of thought followed by a wide and endearing smile Abdulla responded, " I would randomly allocate a large population of men or women at risk to be screened or left to nature then after say 10 years count up the dead in each arm of the trial; now ask me a difficult question" At this point professor Black relaxed his stern expression and burst out laughing and said, "Either you've been briefed by Miss O'Reilly or you really knew the answers that would please me either way; gentlemen we are off to a good start".

Then turning serious again he challenged them with the

next question, "If what you say is correct then why is scientific fraud futile?" None of them could find the answer and raised their eyebrows whilst shaking their heads in unison, although the young Indian gentleman shook his head by moving his neck side to side in a most disturbing manner. "Scientific fraud is futile because firstly there is never a right answer merely a refutation of what others may think is right and secondly you will always be found out because all good science must be reproducible. Right, with those principles established let's talk about your projects." At this point he buzzed Christine to bring in 4 cups of coffee.

They chatted amiably over coffee as the three younger men started to feel more at ease after which professor Black got down to business. "OK let's start talking about your projects and how to get started. Sanjay and Ishmael have already produced provisional protocols but so far I've had nothing from you Abdulla, and to be honest I only learnt that you were to join the team a week ago." Joshua expected nothing back from the man in white, still assuming that he was a spoilt rich boy who would expect others to do the thinking and working on his behalf, but was again pleasantly surprised by the response he received. "Well sir in my part of the world we see terrible breast cancers. They appear at a much earlier age than in northern Europe and the USA, they tend to be advanced on presentation and are usually of an aggressive phenotype on light microscopy. We have no adequate cancer registry in Saudi Arabia, but what we do have is much consanguineous marriage between cousins. I'm one of many who suspect that these cancers are linked to a low penetrance mutation linked to a DNA repair mechanism. For a start I would like to study your cancer registries here and in Sweden, then through our ministry of health try and set up something similar in our country. Our health minister happens to be one of my uncles. Next I would like to compare the genetic fingerprints of our cancers with those in the UK after which…." At which point professor Black raised his hand to stop the flow. "Abdulla, enough already! I have seriously misjudged you and apologize. You have obviously thought deeply about what you wish to achieve and if you are prepared to work hard I will expect great things of you. Please draft me a protocol but before starting make appointments to see Professor Coleman at the London cancer registry and Professor Latchman head of the department of pathology. They, I'm sure, would be delighted to help you. Miss O'Reilly will provide the contact details. In addition I would like you to sit in with me at my outpatient clinics and operating theatre to learn about the disease we commonly encounter in the south east of England, and to collect fresh frozen material at the time of surgery for your genetic work. One last thing, *please* wear western style clothes in the clinic so as not to frighten the Jewish women who live in NW3!"

"Now Ishmael, you've produced an excellent protocol and here are my revisions in red print. For the animal work you'll need to get a license from the Home Office so please go and see Miss Olajemedi our chief technician for help with that, but in the meantime, as with Abdulla, I would welcome your attendance in the OPD and the OR."

"Finally Sanjay, please seek out Professor Jonathan Tobias, head of the department of radiotherapy and Stavros Metaxas, chief physicist, as we will have to work very closely with them to realize your dream for intra-operative radiotherapy for the benefit of the Indian women living in rural areas, who are denied the prospect of breast conservation. Again, as with the others, I will expect you to help out in the clinic and operating theatre as our NHS junior staff always seem to be on study leave or maternity leave." At that they all burst out laughing and were ushered out of the office by a beaming professor.

Joshua sat back in his chair with a sigh but then the smile left his face as he realized that something was missing. It was his 50th birthday, there were no cards and no presents from his PA or others in his department, it had been ignored or forgotten. Well at least he had the evening to look forward to. He finished up his work on the correspondence he'd opened first thing and replied to the most urgent of his e-mails and was just about to leave for a lunch time faculty meeting, when Christine popped her head round the door. "Sorry to disturb you Prof but the Dean needs to see you urgently in his office, something about the department's submission for the university's quinquenniel grant." Cursing under his breath professor Black threw on his jacket stormed out the office and jogged down nine flights of stairs and strode off in the direction of the medical school's administration offices.

He threw open the door to the Dean's secretary's office and demanded of his startled PA what could possibly be so urgent. Very meekly she replied, "So sorry to disturb you Professor Black but it looks as if we have an unscheduled inspection and they are now awaiting you in the Board Room." Joshua grunted, turned on his heel and burst into the boardroom that to his surprise seemed full of vaguely familiar faces wearing large grins. Before he could register what was going on, Manny Hoffbrand popped up from behind the Cathedra at the end of the long mahogany boardroom table, bearing a large red bound volume crying out, "Joshua Black, this is your life!" The room erupted with applause from the audience of his students and junior staff, whilst Joshua sank into the nearest chair in total confusion, having been taken completely by surprise.

At this point Amy Oladjemedi turned on the projector whilst the Dean read from the big leather bound book, the illustrated story of Joshua' life. There had to have been collusion with his family, as the exquisitely embarrassing pictures of his childhood appeared on the screen, including one of him as a chubby little boy in his first suit with long trousers, wearing a *tallis* at his bar mitzvah. Next they showed a picture of his graduation from medical school flanked by his proud parents. At which point his father's voice boomed out of the speaker system wishing him a happy 50th birthday and saying how sorry he was that his late wife couldn't be there for this happy occasion (she had in fact died from malignant myeloma two years earlier). At this point the celebrant

25

could hardly hold back his tears. Next the double doors to the boardroom burst open and Joshua and his father fell into each other's arms. Old Dr. Samuel Black was rumored to be a survivor from the *kindertransport* arriving in London in 1937 or thereabouts. He was a sprightly 80 year old and had spent most of his working life as a GP in Whitechapel, catering for the needs of impoverished émigrés starting life afresh in the east end of London. Next they showed a picture of the victim's wedding with the young and handsome Joshua looking bewildered in a top hat, alongside his glamorous bride Rachel Adelman, who he stolen from the corps de ballet at Covent Garden. Her sweet tones came over the sound system wishing him a happy birthday and begging forgiveness for her involvement in this subterfuge. She entered the room demurely, looking gorgeous in a little black dress and Joshua's heart swelled with joy and pride as they hugged in front of a delighted audience. His sons and senior colleagues followed in quick succession and there were even video recording sent in from professor Lakhani in Mumbai and professor Ben Yosef in Beersheba. All in all this represented a remarkable well-organized conspiracy involving his family and staff that must have been a long time in planning. At the end when the Dean handed over the leather-bound volume of "his life" Joshua could barely hold back his tears of joy as he suddenly realized what an extraordinary token of love and respect this represented. After the applause died down the gathered throng were invited to lunch next door in the private dining room reserved for special occasions.

★★★

Chapter 3

The death of Dr. Samuel Black

August 2014

The five years following his 50th birthday were amongst the happiest of his life.

This period of professional success and domestic contentment reached its zenith on the evening Rachel and he celebrated their silver wedding in the large private dining room upstairs at "Rules" in Covent Garden, the oldest restaurant in London and amongst their favorite places for eating out. Their firstborn, William, had just qualified as a doctor so this was really a double celebration whilst their second son, Jeremy, was in his third year at medical school and doing well.

In addition to his father the guest list included a couple of maternal aunts, three cousins and their partners and six couples who counted as their closest friends. Also included were three members of his department who had bonded closely with him over the last five years, Sanjay, Ishmael and Abdulla. The first was accompanied by his delightful wife whilst the third, as had come to expected, turned up with a sensational, exotic, doe eyed and heavily bejeweled young lady, wearing a rather revealing gown from a famous and stupendously expensive couturier, together with six inch heels with bright red soles that announced, according to Rachel, were by Christian Louboutin. These three young men had lived up to their promise and had all completed their PhDs whilst gaining their FRCS at the same time. Their combined talent and complementary characters had been an asset to the department and Joshua had urged them to stay on. Sanjay, the most experienced was now a senior lecturer with consultant status in the NHS, whilst the other two were lecturers with excellent prospects of promotion in the near future.

His father, although very frail and bent, stood up and made a short speech followed by a toast to Joshua and Rachel. Joshua then stood up and made a very long speech that was full of scholarship, erudite humor and romantic love. He started by reminding everyone that as he had paid for dinner they were his captive audience, so he could speak for as long as he liked. He concluded his speech with a song of praise for his wife, before passing her a slim, dark blue and gold leather case. Rachel loudly expressed her delight to find it contained a braided silver chain, with what looked like a 2 ct diamond pendant set in platinum. His wife had long lustrous black hair, a long neck, white skin and was wearing a simple cobalt blue silk dress by Chanel, with a low neckline, all of which showed off the diamond pendant to perfection. Joshua earned himself a long and embarrassingly passionate kiss for his trouble; mind you by this time Rachel had polished off a couple of generous balloon glasses of Chateau Petrus 2000. After a round of applause Sanjay, Ishmael and Abdulla stood up and sang, in far from perfect close harmony, there own words to a tune of their invention that started something like this; *"The Hindu, The Bedu, The Sunni all agreed, that with Joshua Black's your PhD is almost guaranteed…."*. Almost no one could follow the words because of the collision of thick accents, not helped by the fact that Sanjay was off key, but the performance and little dance steps were so obviously well rehearsed, that the audience almost wet themselves with laughter. In fact one elderly maternal aunt had to excuse herself. The evening was a riotous success but the following day his father died and as an indirect consequence Joshua' life went into reverse.

Joshua loved and respected his father but when the phone call with the bad news came from the care home on The Bishop's Avenue at 5.00am the next morning, he was deeply saddened yet not surprised. He had watched his father slip into advanced old age rapidly over the last three years. He could no longer care for himself, shuffled around on a Zimmer frame and was losing his edge as a member of the star bridge pair at Hammerson House. As a medical man of some experience, Joshua understood and had witnessed the loss of dignity in extreme old age and believed that, just as there was a time to be born, there was also a time to die. Joshua would mourn and miss his father, yet his final appearance at the silver wedding party the night before must have exhausted the old man, who then allowed himself to slip into a sleep so profound that he wouldn't be woken until the *shofer* sounded on the Day of Judgment. In other words the rituals of burial and the *shiva* had to be endured but were an occasion for the gathering of the clan and a celebration of Dr Samuel Black's long and richly woven life.

It was not the fact of his father's death that destroyed the peaceful equilibrium of his life but the contents of a letter handed over to him, by his late father's lawyer, at the first meeting to discuss probate and his father's will, four weeks later. His father's estate was modest and there were no unforeseen problems in administering his will, but the thick foxed vellum envelope, bearing his name in his father's characteristic spidery black ink, was destined to change and ultimately shorten his life. Along with the envelope, was an old fashioned black leather document case with a brass lock, bearing the initials in gothic lettering embossed in gold; **E.B.**

The vellum envelope was dated 31/05/1957, the day of Joshua' birth. Scribbled across the seal at the back were the words, "not to be opened until after my death".

He decided to open the envelope and the box in the privacy of his study at home that evening, without letting his wife into his confidence, until he had learnt of the contents of them both.

At 8.00pm that evening after dinner he retired to his office with a glass of Talisker, informing Rachel that he had a host of e-mails that he had to deal with. With a sense of foreboding he slit open the envelope and withdrew a letter in his father's handwriting, a two page typewritten script together with a little brass key, designed to unlatch the document case. His father's letter read as follows:

My Dear Son,

By the time you read this I will have shuffled off my mortal coil and I hope and pray that by then you will be a successful man in his middle years with a family of your own, please God. You must now learn of a guilty deception that I have planned to protect you from some unsavory facts about your grandfather and the shame you might have felt in your years as a young man.

I have put it about that I was one of the "kindertransport" children sent out of Germany in 1938 and that your paternal grandparents died in the holocaust. That is not true, your grandfather Eduard Bloch and your grandmother Emilie, arrived in this country in 1943 with me as a young man of 15. The circumstances of his escape from the jaws of the Nazi extermination machine were quite extraordinary and probably unique.

Your grandfather was born in Frauenberg and studied medicine in Prague and then served as a medical officer in the Austrian army. In 1899 he was stationed in Linz. After his discharge from the army in 1901, he opened a private clinic in his house at 12 Landstrasse, where he also lived with his wife, Emilie (née Kafka) and my sister Trude. I was born in 1925 when your grandfather was 53. Dr. Eduard Bloch was held in high regard, particularly among the lower social classes. It was generally known that at any time at night he was willing to call on patients. He used to go on visits in his hansom, wearing a conspicuous broad brimmed hat.

30

In 1904 your grandfather became the doctor favored by the Hitler family whose son Adolf, later achieved (how shall I put it?) high office and notoriety.

After the Third Reich 's annexing of Austria in 1938 life became hard for Austrian Jews. My father's medical practice was closed on October 1st 1938. His daughter and son-in-law, your grandfather's young colleague Dr. Franz Kren, fled overseas to the USA.

Your grandfather then sixty-six-year-old wrote a letter to Adolf Hitler asking for help and was as a consequence put under special protection by the Gestapo. He was the only Jew in Linz with the status of an "Edeljude" or noble Jew. He stayed in his house with his wife undisturbed until the formalities for his emigration were completed. He was allowed to take only the equivalent of 16 Reichsmark out of Austria and made it to the east end of London in 1943. Plagued by guilt and shame he could never disclose his true identity and I was pledged to secrecy. He died in 1945 within a month of that monster Herr Hitler. Although my mother and I were left penniless some support came from my sister Trude in Brooklyn and I was fortunate enough to win a scholarship to study medicine at the London Hospital in Whitechapel. My father left me his diaries that I pass on to you. I started translating them into English in case they gave some original insight into the psychopathology of Adolf Hitler. I gave up leaving the task incomplete with a sense of being stigmatized simply by reading about the early years of the architect of the "final solution" and leave it to you to decide whether to burn the books or finish my work of translation. Please try not to share my disgust of being the son of the man entrusted with the healthcare of the most evil monster of the 20thC. Although the bible says that the iniquity of the fathers are visited on their sons to the third and fourth generation, I believe my father acted in good faith at the start and in desperation for the wellbeing and survival of his family at the end.

Be strong and of good courage,
Your loving father,
Samuel Black (Bloch)

Joshua knocked back the remainder of his glass of scotch trying hard to control his shaking hands and turbulent emotions. Yet if he thought hard and retained his rational state of mind, nothing had really changed and the events described in his father's letter were ancient history as far as most people were concerned. Unfortunately Joshua was not "most people", he was a Jew with a strong sense of his identity and folk memories and he had an insatiable enquiring mind. So without hesitation he turned to his father's translation of his grandfather's diary.

★★★

Extracts from the diary of Dr Samuel Bloch
April 1ˢᵗ 1904

A poor recently widowed woman, Mrs Klara Hitler knocked on my door at 8.00am and begged me to come and visit her son who seemed seriously ill. Once I'd finished my morning surgery I took the hansom and drove to her frugal apartment on the third floor on the east side of Linz. When I was let in the poor woman seemed distraught and explained that she had already lost three children, two with diphtheria and one with measles. Her 4ᵗʰ born Adolf was 15 years old and she thought he had also acquired diphtheria. The polite young man was indeed feverish but I had no difficulty in diagnosing tonsillitis and advised antiseptic mouthwashes and a liquid diet. Mrs Hitler was greatly relieved and reached for her purse. I waved it aside as I could judge that the family of three, there was a little girl named Paula who hid behind her mother's skirts whilst I was there, were penniless. I then made a mental note to overcharge Baron von Trapp's widowed mother, double my usual fee to compensate for my generosity to the Hitler family. This way I can maintain my reputation with the poor of this town as well as with the rich, the paradox being that the rich think more highly of you the greater your fees. How I can live with my own chicanery is another question.

Two days later whilst making my rounds amongst the sick in the east end of Linz I went to check on the wellbeing of young Adolf Hitler. I was delighted to note that he was out of bed fully dressed in short lederhosen. He greeted me politely with a bow and thanked me for my care and generosity. He still looked pale and I couldn't help but notice that he had inherited his mother's startling blue melancholy eyes.

★★★

Februrary 27ᵗʰ 1907

The last patient in this morning was Mrs Klara Hitler accompanied by her son. It had been a very busy surgery and I believe that the Hitlers had been waiting patiently to be seen for nearly two hours. Young Adolf, a handsome youth, did the talking and explained that his mother had a painful sore on her chest. Apparently it had been getting worse for nearly 6 months. I asked my nurse to take Mrs Hitler into the examination room and help her to disrobe. As I entered the room the smell almost knocked me off my feet and one look at the purulent dinner plate sized ulcer that had replaced her right breast, left no doubts in my mind. This was a very advanced and completely neglected breast cancer.

I examined her all over and noted an enlarged liver and knew that the poor woman had less than a year to live. I asked my nurse to clean the wound with hydrogen peroxide and then I did my best to cauterize the ulcer with silver nitrate.

Whilst Mrs Hitler was having a fresh linen dressing and chest bandage applied, I slipped out of the room and explained my diagnosis and prognosis to Adolf. He was clearly shocked and expressed disbelief but I couldn't really offer any comfort, I did however promise to look in every other day to change the dressings and cauterize the ulcer. As this was a painful procedure I gave the young man a bottle of laudanum to dose his mother in anticipation of my visits. I also explained that I would take no money and made another mental note to myself to exploit the Von Trapp family once more. Adolf stood up straight and gave me a stiff bow struggling to hold back his tears and declaimed, "Dr Bloch, yes we are a very poor family but I have my dignity, if you wont accept our money then I will insist that you accept hand made gifts from me in return for your services" Having no idea what he meant, I returned his bow and thanked him.

December 21ˢᵗ 1907

Certified the death of Mrs Klara Hitler. Poor woman had suffered terribly over the last few months of her life and required ever-increasing doses of morphine sulphate to control her pain. For my troubles I had acquired four watercolour paintings from her son and although I am no connoisseur, I think the young man shows some talent and who knows one day these paintings might be worth something.

January 30ᵗʰ 1908

Today I received a large canvas painted with a pretty landscape signed, A. HITLER.

This was accompanied with a short note that read, "Ich werde Ihnen ewig dankbar sein".

★★★

34

Having read the two pages of his father's typescript translation of extracts from his grandfather's diaries Joshua then reached for the little brass key and opened the old leather document case. On opening the lid, the musky smell of old paper escaped and the gathered dust made him sneeze. Inside, neatly stacked, were 36 diaries spanning the years 1900 to 1936. Opening one or two at random, Joshua noted that they contained densely written pages covered in very neat copper plate hand written text in German. His heart sank at the enormity of the task involved in completing the translation. First he had no knowledge of German, although he knew a smattering of words in Yiddish, learnt by eavesdropping on his parent's conversations. Secondly to employ someone for the task, would involve breaching his father's wish for confidentiality. He was about to abandon the task before it had even begun, when he had a flash of inspiration. He and Rachel kept an eye on an elderly Viennese couple who lived in an apartment at Belmoor just by Whitestone pond, Otto and Lisa Grossmark. They were childless and had more or less adopted the Blacks as a surrogate family. Like many of that lost generation, they were very cultured and in earlier years would often take Joshua and Rachel to concerts at the Royal Festival Hall or the Wigmore Hall. Now in their early 90s they didn't go out much but had both preserved sharp minds and a wicked sense of humor. Lisa's family had got out of Austria in 1935 but Otto remembered the *Anschluss* and escaped deportation to Buchenwald, but refused to talk about his escape from the grip of the Nazis. Otto and Lisa could be relied upon to keep his dark secret and between them they might look upon it as an interesting and perhaps a historically important task, to occupy their declining years as they became more and more housebound. Somehow he would have to approach them without letting Rachel into his secret. Having made that decision he crept into bed without disturbing his wife and was plagued by frightful dreams all night.

★★★

Chapter 4

Dr. Samuel Bloch's diary translated

January 2015

It took the best part of 6 months before Lisa and Otto Grossmark had completed the translation of Samuel Bloch's diary. Although they welcomed the challenge one or other them was frequently sick or even hospitalized. Once the task was complete they realized that what they had been working on was of enormous historical interest for two reasons.

Number one it acted as a first hand account of the decline and fall of the Austrian Jewish intelligentsia under the jackboot of the Nazis, and secondly it was a first hand account of the rise of young Adolf Hitler from callow youth to ruler of the third Reich. Incidentally it also allowed insights into the practice of medicine in Austria in the early years of the 20thC, at a time when Vienna was considered the medical capital of the world. The Grossmarks thought it was a great pity that it would never be published but fully sympathized with Joshua Black's reluctance.

Joshua wasn't sure how to reward his old friends for completing this task, knew they wouldn't accept money and in any case they were quite well off, so instead he went to an auction at Christie's and ended up by paying more than he intended, for an exquisite pen and ink drawing by Egon Schiele that would guarantee their delight.

Joshua's opinion on the contents of his Samuel Bloch's

diary was identical to that of the Old Viennese couple but he felt the pain of his grandfather's humiliation as if it were his own. It was bad enough to be stigmatized by wearing a yellow star on his jacket whenever he dared venture out of doors, but the forcible sale of his medical practice and his art collection, was almost too much to bear, although the confiscation of an original work by Hitler was no great loss. In the end the poor old man eked out a living by selling his services for trivial sums amongst the equally desperate local Jewish community, and venturing further out to the slums, were he used to treat the poorest of the poor for free, only to be patronized and insulted by families he had looked after for decades, in exchange for a handful of pfennigs. He now understood why his grandfather threw himself at the mercy of the Fuehrer for the sake of his family.

It was the consequence of Samuel Black's letter to Adolf Hitler that led to the last and by far the most interesting entry in his diary.

★★★

April 8ᵗʰ 1937

My letter to Herr Hitler had born fruit and I had been summoned to his presence at the Reichstag in Berlin. I confess to have been terrified of my first face-to-face meeting since Adolf had been elected as chancellor and I was a sorry sight. I arrived an hour early and as a result I was kept waiting for nearly two hours in the large anti-room to the Fuehrer's office. My best dark suit was shabby and threadbare, my white shirt grey and my yellow star all the more prominent as a result. I sat huddled in a corner with my head bowed frightened in case I made inadvertent eye contact with one of the praetorian guards, in their magnificent uniforms, who were standing like statues on either side of the huge mahogany double doors that led to the private rooms of the most powerful and ruthless man in Germany. I was hungry and thirsty but worst of all desperate for some reading-matter to distract me from my obsessive thoughts, but my newspapers and journals had been confiscated when I was searched at the entrance to the building. The only way I could retain my sanity was by counting the marble tiles on the floor, imagining a chessboard and replaying some of the most famous games of the chess grandmasters of the era, in my head.

I had no idea who was with the Fuehrer at the time but after about 90 minutes I heard voices raised and before long I could recognize the rhetorical style of Herr Hitler and imagined him pacing up and down whilst addressing a cowering group of supplicants.

After about another 30 minutes the double doors were thrown open by a matching pair of guards from the inside and Hitler's private secretary showed five men out. The double doors were sealed again awaiting my summons. In the meantime I studied the five men who had just exited as they continued in animated conversation but I was so inconspicuous that they were clearly unaware of my presence. To my surprise they were talking in English. One of the men was instantly recognizable as his picture had been in yesterday's newspapers shaking hands with Adolf Hitler. He had a neatly cut grey beard and wore a long black robe and a curious white flat-topped headdress. This was of course Haj Amin al- Husseini, the Grand Mufti of Jerusalem. A tall dark handsome man who appeared deferential to the Grand Mufti accompanied him. The third I also recognized from pictures in recent editions of Zeitschrift für Krebsforschung. He was professor Eugen Fischer, director of the Kaiser Wilhelm Institute of Anthropology, Human Heredity, and Eugenics, who had been writing letters suggesting purification of the German race by mass sterilization of the Jews. The other two looked like Englishmen but couldn't have been more different in their appearance. One was a mousy little man with a tight black suit, wing collared white shirt and dark tie. The other was a large barrel shaped man about 30 years his senior. He wore a flamboyant and rather old-fashioned assembly of morning suit, cravat and cloak. He was red in the face and had a large bushy moustache with a long grey beard. He was clearly angry with the mouse-like second Englishman and spoke with a loud booming voice. My English wasn't good enough to follow the conversation in detail but the word Palestine kept coming up. They seemed to be talking about Archäologie and a place name like Lucheich or Lachetch. Eventually the old Englishman turned away in disgust and strode out of the waiting room along with the Grand Mufti and professor Fischer with the timid second Englishman running after them pleading for I know not what. The tall dark Arab looking man was last to leave but as he turned to survey the empty room he caught sight of me and we locked eyes for an instant.

Shortly after that I was lead into the inner sanctum by Hitler's secretary. I needn't have worried as I was warmly welcomed by the Fuehrer and offered coffee. He asked after my health and the well being of my family and of course I said things couldn't be better. He then reassured me that my plea for a visa to leave the country would be looked into in due course, but for the time being I was being granted the status of Edeljude and the Gestapo had been instructed to protect me until I left the country. I left the Reichstag greatly relieved yet with a sense of shame that I was being granted special status whilst the rest of my tribe were being persecuted like the bondage of the ancient Israelites in Egypt.

★★★

His grandfather's description of Hitler's meeting with the Grand Mufti, a notorious Nazi doctor and two anonymous Englishmen intrigued Joshua. He knew enough of the history of the Middle East to remember that al-Hussenei was a Nazi sympathizer and had eventually raised an Arab brigade to fight alongside the Germans in the Balkans, with the hope that they might be in the vanguard of the attack on the British mandated territory of Palestine, in order to liberate Jerusalem. The third most holy shrine in Islam was on the Temple Mount in the old city where the Dome of the Rock protected the site where an angel had stayed the hand of Moses after God ordered him to sacrifice his son Isaac. Two clicks on his computer mouse revealed the repulsive ideology of professor Fischer. He therefore suspected that the meeting described in his grandfather's diary must have involved English anti-Semites or proto-Nazis, who were thick on the ground in the years leading up to the Second World War. He then decided that it might make an amusing exercise in research and detection to try and track down the identities of these two mysterious Englishmen and perhaps write a scholarly paper on the subject without disclosing the original source material. He put that thought in the back of his mind as he had more urgent matters to attend to, but a chance meeting over lunch at his club, the Athenaeum, set him off on the hunt.

★★★

The Athenaeum club is housed in a beautiful neo-Georgian pile at the corner of Pall Mall and Wellington Place. The membership of the club consists of the meritocracy of the London scene. In other words you are not elected as a result of whom you know but what you know. Membership was granted only to scholars of high achievement in the Arts, science or humanities but also includes bishops, archbishops and Ambassadors to the court of St James. One of the most charming consequences of membership was the chance to dine at the member's table, a long highly polished mahogany Victorian affair, overlooking Pall Mall. You sat down in order of appearance and with any luck you might find yourself next to a famous author, a Nobel Prize winning scientist or a senior judge. If you were not so lucky it might be a sanctimonious bishop although in their favor they certainly knew which wines to order. On this occasion about 6 weeks after he'd finished reading his grandfather's diaries, he found himself seated next to a jolly old talkative gentleman named Arthur Templeton, who was professor emeritus of archaeology at University College London, and was just back from a dig on Elephantine Island in Upper Egypt, just downstream of the first cataract of the Nile. His work involved further research into the foundation of the Temple to Yahweh established by ancient Israelites who were expelled from Judea after the Babylonian conquest and the sacking of the first Temple in Jerusalem. At this point Joshua interrupted professor Templeton and with a tone of deep skepticism blurted out, "Professor, I'm a Jew and quite knowledgeable about the history of my people but this is the first time I've heard about a Jewish Temple in the land of Egypt, how can this be?" "My dear professor Black you are not alone. For reasons that are unclear to me, I find that very few Jewish or for that matter gentile folk are aware of this ancient Jewish community and the Elephantine papyri that were unearthed in the late 19thC. This subject has been the focus of most of my research over the last 30 years and even now as an emeritus professor at our university I am often asked out as a consultant to the Egyptian department of antiquities to help with the authentication and possible provenance, of new finds dating from the 5th C BCE. If you are interested let's have coffee together after lunch and I'll tell you more." At this point although totally captivated by the conversation, Joshua glanced at his watch and noted with horror that he was going to be late in starting his lecture to the undergraduates waiting at the Gower Street branch of the medical school. He apologized and explained his rush but begged Professor Templeton for his card and promised to pay him a visit to learn about the ancient Israelite colony on Elephantine island and also to enquire about another archaeological puzzle that had recently been troubling him.

★★★

Chapter 5

Olive Hathaway

Olive Hathaway at the fine old age of 72 had perfected the art of invisibility.

She started to become invisible after her husband died suddenly from a heart attack ten years earlier. He was a GP working in a group practice in Belsize Park northwest London. An expert in providing risk assessment and risk management for men worried about coronary heart disease, he prided himself in managing his weight, blood pressure and serum lipids. It went without saying that he never smoked and he kept himself lean and fit cycling to and from work up and over the hills of Hampstead village to his comfortable home in Wildwood Road overlooking the heath extension of Hampstead Garden Suburb. As he lay dying with excruciating chest pain half way up Heath Street, a passer by overheard his last words; "it's bloody well not fair".

Unlike her husband, Olive did not believe in fair play but accepted life in a philosophical manner and was adept at managing the slings and arrows of outrageous fortune. After her retirement party at the age of 65, celebrated in the functional surroundings of the department of social work of the London Borough of Barnet, she made her second move towards a state of invisibility accelerated somewhat when the new head of her department addressed her as Myrtle when presenting her with a porcelain figurine and a large card signed by all the department. She bore no grudges and understood how easy it was to mix up Olive branches and Myrtle sprigs.

Although left comfortably off with her own pension

and half the NHS pension of her husband, she set about downsizing. She no longer needed a five-bedroom house as her three grandchildren had long since given up on sleepovers in granny's and she was never one for "entertaining" in the style of her Jewish neighbors. Instead she sold her house on Wildwood Road and moved across to the west side of the heath extension into a charming little one bedroom home in an "arts and crafts" cloistered development built in 1912, part of the vision of Dame Henrietta Barnett, one of the original "champagne socialists". Dame Henrietta's idea at the time was that the female domestic staff serving the grand folk in the big houses could live nearby safe from molestation, very much like in a convent, but with the freedom to walk out with suitable young male artisans, who could safely make the perilous journey into the suburb from the stews of the east end of town. Of course it never worked out that way as transport was too difficult and young women of this class not destined for a nunnery preferred the dangers and dirt of the east end rather than living cheek by jowl with the toffs.

These days, such charming little cloistered homes, were favored by quiet and invisible elderly gentlefolk and changed hands at about £850,000. As a result of this downsizing, Olive progressed from merely being comfortably off to the status of a millionairess. As she chose to walk most places and was only ten minutes away from the tube at Golders Green, she had no need of a car and, apart from private health insurance; her cost of living was so modest that even her pension income began to accumulate. Her only extravagance was the quality of her fine cloak of invisibility.

To achieve this she would always wear a tailored suit of the finest Harris Tweed, the density of the weave varying according to the season. Her sensible shoes were foolishly priced. Her high-necked blouses were of the finest silk. The cameo broach at her neck was genuine 18th C Wedgwood and the selection of pieces of costume jewellery worn on the left lapel of her jacket, were golden antiques inset with either rubies or amethysts. So bold and beautiful were these ornamentations that any passing mugger on the tube from Golders Green to Harvey Nicholls in Knightsbridge via Charring Cross, would assume they were paste.

Olive wore her grey hair in a tight bun held in place by a lacquered Japanese hair-grip, a silver wedding gift from her late husband bought at auction at Sotheby's in Bond Street. She wore round steel rimmed spectacles to complete the picture or in her own mind secure her invisibility. Unlike most of her kind she chose to make a virtue out of necessity and relished her role as the "invisible woman". Her only vulnerability or Achilles' heel was in her eyes. Not so much the cornflower blue of the iris but the spark of intelligence and enquiry, the so-called twinkle. Added to that a truly astute observer might have noted the "crows feet" of mischievous humor at the corners of her eyes. However as the rather thick lenses of her glasses made it difficult to spot such give away details she felt confident about entering and leaving a crowded room without being noticed.

She occupied herself doing good works. She acted as a Church Warden at nearby St Jude's in Central Square, arranging the flowers, editing the Church magazine and sitting on the Church council. She also acted as a volunteer at the local hostel for physically abused women on the Finchley Road. She was one of four invisible women amongst the churchwardens and it amused her that the vicar could never tell them apart. Yet her greatest delight was to take part in the church's council meetings and be subjected to the patronizing treatment by the self-important male laity. After about an hour of such gentle abuse she would quietly and with great dignity provide an elegant solution to whatever problem they were debating whether it be organizational, financial, ethical or even ecclesiastical. The pompous men on the council would then bluster or claim they thought of it first. The vicar was full of admiration for her whatever her name was and often ended up by offering sincere thanks to Mrs Hemingway or even sometimes Mrs Meadway the name of the main street cutting through the suburb.

There were only five people in the world who could see through Olive's cloak of invisibility. Her daughter Christobel, her three grandchildren, Alice aged 15, the twins Sam and Leo aged 11 and her brother Arthur. Her daughter had married well to a City lawyer and lived on the north side of the North Circular Road only three miles away but a nightmare journey for someone without a car which meant that as the grandchildren grew older and had multiple after school activities and enjoyed sleep over with friends at the week end she saw them less and less. Her brother Arthur was the professor emeritus of Egyptology at University College London. He lived in St Johns Wood but even in retirement was often involved in field trips to hot and dangerous places. You might therefore reasonably assume that she was lonely but such was not the case. In spite of external appearances she was skilled at information technology, a prerequisite for her employment as a social worker and enjoyed her social network on line that kept her in touch with the activities of her grandchildren. She could even make audio-visual contact with her brother on "Facetime" somewhere in Upper Egypt. Sometimes to her amusement she would note the postings of Alice who clearly had forgotten that her granny was also one of her "friends" on Facebook.

Olive's carefully cultivated invisibility spiced up her life but she would never have guessed in a million years just how spicy life might get for an elderly widow following a chance encounter at the collection counter of John Lewis at the Brent Cross shopping mall on Sunday morning in late June 2015.

★★★

Olive was really looking forward to her outing with Christobel and the children. Firstly she was excited about buying her first smart TV that would allow her to stream both TV programs, e-mails and web pages onto a high definition, slim built, 30 inch monitor. This she rationalized would be better for her eyesight and the comfort of reclining in an easy chair whilst surfing. Although in truth she was a bit of a geek when it came to IT equipment and apart from her clothes and costume jewellery, "boy's toys" were her secret luxuries. The other pleasure she was anticipating was a morning with the grandchildren. They loved browsing round the mall on a Sunday morning with granny, knowing full well that this would include ice cream sundae's at Kool for Kids and new books from Waterstons. She also intended to treat her daughter to a new cocktail dress at Fenwicks and all she wanted in return was a lift to and from the mall plus help in carrying the smart TV from John Lewis to Hampstead Way. This way everyone was a winner. All five were laughing happily as they moved Christobel's hatch back A class Mercedes, from the main car park to the small parking area reserved for clients picking up heavy items purchased at John Lewis. Leaving Alice and the twins in the car happily reading their new books, Olive and her daughter walked into the reception area where she handed in her docket. There were two other customers in the line ahead of them and whilst they waited Olive indulged in her private game of deductive logic in working out who or what these people were.

The first in line was a distinguished looking gentleman of about 50 years of age and the second was a most undistinguished young woman in her mid twenties trying to control a snotty nosed little boy aged about 3.

The gentleman's face looked familiar but it took a moment or two to place him but in that time she was able to satisfy herself that he was a medical man. His designer jeans and a pink cashmere V necked jumper, his meticulous manicure and self confident bearing, reminded Olive of her late husband. However, the carefully crafted wings of rather too long silver grey hair that were combed back over his ears, suggested the affectation of a consultant surgeon rather than a GP. The final clue was a glimpse of an FRCS after his name on the docket he handed over the counter.

At this point she remembered seeing him at the St Jude's Prom concert two nights before when she was acting as an usher for the performance of Carl Orff's Carmina Burana.

The young woman was easier to place. She wore a dirty pink shell suit with her pierced navel bulging through the gap between top and bottom. As she turned her back a tattoo of a blue bird was displayed just above the cleft of her buttocks. The give away sign though was a fading bruise below the young woman's left eye. This had to be a poor mother from a sink estate battered by a drunken husband and shortly to be seeking refuge in the safe house on the Finchley Road. Both characters looked right through her, the first to flash a brilliant smile at Olive's attractive daughter, clearly a lady's man, and the second to scream profanities at her little boy who was growing impatient and trying to climb over the counter. She then tried to predict the nature of their purchases and was not surprised to see the young woman collect a baby buggy but the parcel for the consultant surgeon was not the golfing equipment she had predicted but a rather elegant set of matching leather luggage. These and Olive's new smart TV were delivered from the shop floor at about the same time by men in brown warehouse coats, one of whom gallantly offered to help Christobel with the large cardboard box so that there was a bit of a scrum as they emerged from the depot. Mr Consultant surgeon got away first and dropped his cases in the boot of a silver grey E series Mercedes whilst battered young mother dragging snotty child made for a battered old Ford Prefect. At that point something strange and alarming occurred. The distinguished looking medical man's mobile phone rang and, as he answered it, he went white in the face and started shouting. He then jumped in his car turned sharp right across the neighboring battered old Ford Prefect tearing the front bumper off from its nearside bracket and sped off. As he disappeared Olive registered his number plate and was not surprised to note that

47

this egotistical medical man had chosen to announce to the whole world that this smart Mercedes was being driven by J. Black as deduced by the non standard arrangement of letters and numbers, J13LACK. Battered mother screamed after him an unrepeatable profanity whilst Olive tried to offer comfort and advise. "Young lady, I witnessed what happened and I took note of his number plate so he will easily be tracked down by the police for not reporting an accident. I would be happy to attend the police station with you when you report him". She was then rewarded by a stream of abuse that contained the following sequence; "...why don't you piss off and mind your own fucking business a fat lot of good that'll do as I ain't got no fucking insurance have I? Stupid old cow. Damien come back here you bleeder and get in the fucking car or else I'll bloody well kill yer!" Christobel was horrified and wanted to intervene but Olive cautioned her off.

Paradoxically Mrs Hathaway felt nothing but pity for this young woman and could easily envisage her life of quiet desperation, smoking to stave off her hunger in order to feed her kids, drinking to numb the pain of her pointless life, married too young, with Damien probably the youngest of three, living in a tower block of council flats stinking of urine with a brutal, unemployed and useless husband. She had seen it all over and over again through her work in the London borough of Barnet and since retirement via her charitable work at the refuge on the Finchley Road. Although she appeared to let the matter drop, such was the sense of injustice she felt about the damage to the car of the damaged young woman, she was determined to take the matter up with Mr. J. Black.

Her daughter dropped her off outside Olive's little secular retreat and helped her in with the large cardboard box containing the new TV and the three grandchildren lifted their noses from the new books to kiss granny goodbye. The boxed set would remain unopened until the little man from the little electronics shop in Golders Green came round the next day to help set up the new integrated system. Once her daughter had left and she'd eaten a frugal lunch Olive walked up to central square to help arrange flowers and set up the stage and the stalls for that evening's "last night of the Proms".

Although only a humble simulacrum of the world famous "last night at the Proms" at the Royal Albert Hall, St Jude's was really proud of what they had achieved. They always had a decent if relatively small symphony orchestra and a famous violinist or clarinetist would volunteer their time for free in aid of the worthy charities supported by the proms. They also found favor with one or other of the famous mezzo sopranos who lived nearby, to belt out "Land of Hope and Glory" in an over-the top dress created in such a way as to embody the Union flag of the United Kingdom. The local residents and northwest Londoners in general loved the Proms at St Jude's and the last night was always a sell out weeks in advance. The exterior architecture of St Jude's was hideous and was a blot on the skyline when approaching the suburb across the Heath from the south. The gabled steep sloping roof was grossly disproportionate to the height of the walls. There was a square tower slapped dead centre in the roof crowed with a comical lead clad steeple that looked like a witch's hat. However ugly the exterior, the interior was an unexpected visual and spiritual delight. What Olive loved most of all about these events was to see the nave filled to capacity with the lighting of the interior setting off to perfection the early 20th century frescos on the walls and ceiling. No one in this audience was a dyed in the wool jingoist but they all loved the self-conscious ironic waving of the flag whilst singing "Rule Britannia" and Blake's "Jerusalem" at the end. What with this and the excitement of her new smart TV she completely forgot about the event in the car park at Brent Cross until reminded of it a week later following a phone call from her daughter. With nothing better to do at the time she set out to discover the identity and whereabouts of Mr. Black. It turned out to be remarkably easy. Having remembered the brief encounter with the man at the St. Jude's concert the week before, she retrieved the program from her archival files and searched through the list of "friends" of St Jude's Proms and sure enough there he was in the silver list having donated £95.00 to secure priority booking and the best seats. He was listed together with his wife as Professor and Mrs. Joshua Black. The telephone directory then provided an address on Wildwood Road just a few doors down from where she used to live on the other side of the Heath extension. The fact that they had never met was not so surprising in that the folk in the grand houses on the east side of the Heath kept themselves to themselves and never stopped for a gossip over the high hedges, the treasured, distinctive and mandated feature of the area governed by the Hampstead Garden Suburb Trust. She determined to beard Professor Black in his den after dinner on the Wednesday evening full ten days after the event.

★★★

At 8 o'clock on the Wednesday evening the 3rd of July, dressed in her suit of invisibility she strode forth in her sensible but expensive shoes across the Heath. The Heath looked at its best as the sun set behind her cottage and long purple shadows crept across the newly mown grass of the meadow. The purple shadows and the emerald green of the grass in the oblique rays of the sun were an enchanting combination entirely appropriate for Wimbledon fortnight. The broom and the wildflowers framed this canvas in a tumult of vibrant colors. The blackbirds were singing their hearts out, the magpies were hopping about like happily married couples and the woodpeckers could be heard but not seen clacking away like typist on an old-fashioned keyboard. For some reason she felt uplifted, like a knight errant off to help a maiden in distress, relishing the forthcoming confrontation as a little excitement in her otherwise ordered life. The moment she stepped onto the pavement of Wildwood Road she noticed something odd. On both sides of the thoroughfare cars were parked as far as the eye could see.

Usually you only saw this in the days when popular

symphony concerts were held at the lakeside concert bowl at Kenwood but this year they wouldn't start until Late July.

She then guessed it might be some kind of Jewish family celebration in one of the many houses in the area carrying a badge of Judaism in the form of a *mezuzah,* on the doorpost. Her local Jewish neighbors seemed to have very big families that were forever celebrating weddings, bar mitzvahs or high holy days that tended to involve marquees, catering vans and road congestion in the area. She bore them neither grudges nor anti-Semitic feelings. In fact she was quite envious of their gregarious nature and family commitment in contrast to the rather understated and frugal nature of family affairs and church events in her own community. Of course if it wasn't for the large Jewish community in the suburb who were passionate about classical music, the Proms at St Jude's could hardly continue as almost all the names in the silver and bronze list of "friends" sounded Jewish. Still mulling this over in her mind and trying hard to deduce a rational explanation for all the parked cars she found the Black's house, mounted the steps between pretty terracotta pots overfull with scarlet geranium and stood in the porch of a neo-Georgian doorway with an elaborate *mezuzah* on the right hand door post. She was about to ring the bell when she noticed the door was ajar so she gently pushed it open to find the entrance hall packed with women wearing shawls over their hair. An elderly woman wearing a large wig put her finger to her lips and handed over a thin black bound book bearing the words "Prayers in the House of Mourning". This obviously explained the parking problem on Wildwood Road but now she was stuck, as it would have appeared disrespectful to back out at this juncture. The chanting of male voices from within a large reception room on her left resonated round the house as some kind of religious ceremony seemed to be taking place. This went on for about thirty minutes and after it finished she found herself trapped as two large bearded men in large black hats and long black coats barged past her from the west looking bay window in the front of the reception room. The crush of the crowd started

51

to creep forward in an anticlockwise direction so that with little choice poor Olive was swept along. Eventually she was carried by the flow through a doorway deep in the house at the eastern end of a huge reception room that seemed full with over 100 people, men at the front and women at the back. To add to the macabre experience she noted that all the mirrors were covered in white sheets whilst along the northern wall of the room a middle aged woman and two young men were seated in little chairs like school children. With mounting horror she realized that she was being pushed along to offer some kind of greeting to those she supposed were the principle mourners. Just before panic overtook her she overheard the two women in front of her murmur "I wish you a long life". Once again she was glad of her invisibility as she reached the mourners and mouthed what seemed to be a ritualistic greeting. She passed that hurdle without any problem and on the way out politely declined a cup of tea and biscuit. Just as she reached the doorway with a sigh of relief her cloak of invisibility dropped when a large and heavily bejeweled triple chinned elderly woman stopped her and asked, "Aren't you Levi Herschon's *machatainister*?" Not having a clue what the question meant she politely answered in the negative but still couldn't get away as Mrs Triplechin grabbed her arm by way of support as she waddled down the steps to the road. "Oy, what a tragedy, what could have made him do it, he had so much to live for, poor Rachel Black what will she do now?" With that the fat old woman waddled off to her waiting car leaving Olive to deduce that Professor Joshua Black had just committed suicide. Yet something about that realization didn't ring true.

She learnt more about the event in the report of the inquest into the death of professor Black in Friday's copy of the "Ham and High" the local newspaper carrying stories about events and news in Hampstead and neighboring Highgate.

Distinguished local man found hanging on Sandy Heath
Report from the North London Coroner's court.

On Monday morning the 23rd of June at 8.00am Mrs Angela Moody aged 47, a professional dog walker, was leading three poodles on a leash through the glade in the centre of Sandy Heath, mid way between Spaniards Road and North End road, when she came across a grisly scene of a middle aged man hanging from a branch of an old oak tree just to the east of the pond. With great presence of mind she called the ambulance and the police. Within 5 minutes the emergency services were there but it was obvious that he had been dead for some time. The body was that of the renowned professor of surgery at the Royal Free Hospital and University College London, Joshua Black. At the inquest this week the police forensic medical officer concluded that the cause of death was strangulation by hanging with the time of death at approximately 02.00am on the morning of the same day. The police then presented a suicide note that was found pinned to his sweater wherein Prof Black had confessed to scientific misconduct and fraud, stating that he could no longer live with this guilt. They also produced a three-legged stool that was found at the site tipped over below the professor's free-swinging feet. The Coroner, Dr. David Middleton, also noted that Professor Black had a past history of acute depressive illness and concluded that the death was from suicide and released the body to the family for burial the next day according to Jewish custom. Professor Black leaves his wife Rachel aged 47 and two sons aged 19 and 22. A full obituary will appear in next week's edition of the "Ham and High".

"A man who buys expensive leather luggage and gave my daughter a smile like that was most certainly not contemplating suicide at the time. It must have been something he learnt on his mobile phone just before he rushed off, that precipitated his decision. I better contact the police with this information," Olive thought to herself after reading the short news item. With that she put on her sensible shoes and strode off to the police station on Finchley Road a mere 15 minutes walk away. The station looked very run down and sad reflecting the London's Mayor's plans for rationalizing the Metropolitan Police force and its imminent closure. The desk sergeant was lethargic and overweight as if in anticipation of an imminent redundancy notice.

He asked her to complete some forms after which she was invited into the down-at-heel back office to meet the local CID officer. The man from the CID who gave off an aroma of stale tobacco and damp tweed and was also clearly beyond his sell by date, introduced himself politely as detective inspector Ramsay and invited Mrs. Hathaway to take a seat and even offered her a cup of Nescafe that was politely declined. After thirty minutes of cross-examination by inspector Ramsay, who was well acquainted with the episode having been the first member of the CID to arrive at the scene of the misadventure, drew the interview to a close. Olive was sincerely thanked for her trouble and, as there was absolutely no evidence of foul play and as the coroner was satisfied with suicide as the cause of death, the case was closed. As she was ushered out of the interview room Olive turned her head and asked "By the way were you able to trace the last call he received on his mobile phone?" "Funny you should ask but we never found his mobile, but suspect it is at the bottom of 'No Name' pond on Sandy Heath along with his brief case and research papers referred to in his suicide note and we ain't risking the lives of any of our frog men to dredge the bottomless gravel pit of that death trap"

Once Mrs. Hathaway was out the door D.I. Ramsay shook his head with a deep sigh and thought to himself, "well there goes the peaceful count down to my retirement. I always suspected there was something dodgy about that so called suicide." He then summoned in his desk clerk and asked him kindly to take the burger out of his fat face, pull out his finger, shift his fat ass and fetch him the file on the suicide of that professor what done himself in on Hampstead Heath last month.

★★★

Chapter 6

Winter 2015

About 5 months after her little adventure linked to the death of Professor Black, Olive Hathaway woke up one morning and felt a lump that shouldn't have been there.

Like most women of her age and education she went into a state of denial and wished it away. This state of mind only persisted for 24 hours, so after a restless night she checked herself again and confirmed that there was indeed a lump about the shape and size of a cherry, in the upper outer part of her left breast. Being an eminently sensible woman she controlled her panic and phoned up her GP practice on the dot of 08.30am. Her doctor saw her as an emergency later that morning and confirmed the findings, and as Olive had private insurance referred her to a specialist he trusted, a young surgeon from the Indian subcontinent, who saw private patients on a Wednesday afternoon at the Princess Grace hospital, just off Marylebone High Street. She so wished that her husband was still alive to accompany her to the specialist and know what questions to ask, but at least she had a devoted daughter to drive her there and back and make notes of the consultation.

She and Christobel arrived in good time at the clinic, completed the formalities and at 5 minutes past the time of her appointment the nurse showed her into Mr. Sanjay Manchandra's presence. He leapt to his feet with a wide smile and greeted mother and daughter warmly immediately putting Olive at her ease. Very efficiently he took a history of her presenting complaint and noted her past medical history and enquired about any family history of breast disease. He then invited her to go behind the curtains and strip down to the waist, where the clinic nurse was waiting to act as chaperone and if needs be as counselor. Mr. Manchadra completed a very thorough clinical examination that included feeling under her armpits and palpating her abdomen and once again smiled at her in a reassuring way. "I'm now going to do an ultrasound examination on you, it wont hurt but please just wait a few minutes before asking my opinion, as I can fully sense your anxiety although you are hiding it very well." The nurse then wheeled in a machine looking like a lap top computer and the specialist squirted jelly from a warmed up tube on to her breast, just above the lump, turned the screen so that Olive could see what was going on, and then gently stroked a flat faced probe over the area of concern. After just a minute or two, during which time the patient couldn't make head nor tail of the fleeting images on the screen, Mr Manchadra turned to her with a broad smile of genuine pleasure, " Oh, yes indeed, this is very very good finding, because of your age I assumed we were dealing with a cancer, but goodness gracious me it is just a simple cyst. See here this circular black hole is fluid and this bright patch at the back of the hole, indicates that the sound waves are passing through the cyst fluid faster than through the surrounding fat. Now watch very carefully I am about to do famous Indian fakir magic trick and make it disappear. He reached out a hand towards his nurse who passed over an empty 50-millilitre syringe with needle attached. Swabbing the skin just below the probe he inserted the needle with such skill that Olive felt nothing whilst she watched in awe, as the black hole shrunk to nothing in front of her eyes, the needle was swiftly withdrawn and the maestro waved a syringe, full translucent yellowish fluid, with a flourish and a "Voila!" At that Olive didn't know whether to laugh or cry but chose the latter route. Mr Manchandra returned to his desk and offered instant reassurance to Christobel who also started crying and gave her mother a huge hug, after the patient emerged from behind the curtains dressed and once more in control of herself.

The surgeon then explained as follows; "Well Mrs Hathaway I'm happy to confirm that the lump was a simple cyst that is in no way premalignant. I will send you for a mammogram as a routine and see you once more in a month in case the cyst refills. Is there anything more you would like to ask?" The question that followed took him unawares. "Thank you very much doctor. May I ask if you ever knew Professor Joshua Black?" "Of course I did! I worked under his guidance since 2005. He was my mentor and supervisor for my PhD. Since his untimely death I miss him very much. It is as if a light has gone off in my life. Why do you ask?" "I don't believe that his death was suicide" Olive replied. There was a shocked silence in the room and Mr Manchandra open and closed his mouth like a goldfish in a bowl but no sound emerged. It was left to Christobel to intervene, "Mother what on earth are you saying? You've shocked the poor man. I'm really sorry Sir I think the relief following your good news has sent her head spinning after a sleepless night." Olive then apologized for speaking out of turn and mother and daughter left the consulting room with the latter scolding the former.

Sanjay slumped down on his chair and dismissed his clinic nurse, as Mrs Hathaway was the last patient of the day, but his nurse couldn't help but notice a thin film of sweat on her boss's forehead and an expression of anguish she had never seen on his face before.

Once he had completed dictating his clinic notes he made a couple of discrete phone-calls and then took out Mrs Hathaway's notes to see if she had left an e-mail address.

Fortunately for him this nice elderly lady appeared to be IT literate and there it was on the front sheet: olive.hathaway3z@ gmail.com. He then composed a short note:

Dear Mrs Hathaway,
It was a pleasure to see you in my clinic this afternoon and I'm delighted that it just turned out to be a simple

cyst. I was surprised by your last question and I would like to know why you suspected that Joshua Black's death was not suicide? I wonder if you would be kind enough to visit me and a couple of my colleagues in the department of surgery on the 9th floor of the Royal Free Hospital on this Friday afternoon at 3.00pm? We share your suspicions and I think we need to compare notes.
Best wishes, Sanjay Manchandra MS, FRCS, PhD

★★★

With extraordinary synchronicity DI Ramsay made up his mind to act on his suspicions, after carefully going through the photographs taken by forensics at the scene of professor Black's death. He then saw what he had previously blanked out in anticipation of a peaceful end to his career, with early retirement and redundancy payout, that would allow him and his wife to realize an ambition in setting up a sandwich franchise in a shop that was to let in Hampstead village. It was so bloody obvious that he could kick himself and actually felt ashamed for such lack of professionalism, even though it was the end of his career. It was that thought that accounted for nearly 6 months of delay.

It was the knot in the noose that kept troubling him. Instead of a slipknot the close up photographs showed a simple granny knot, a professor of surgery would have known better. He then put through a call to one of his old mates, who had climbed to the rank of detective superintendent in the Metropolitan Police, with an office at New Scotland Yard. " How yer doing Alan, care for a swift pint this evening at the Old Bull and Bush?"

★★★

Chapter 7

December 2015

Olive meets the three wise men

Olive arrived at the 9th floor of the Royal Free Hospital at the appointed hour slightly out of breath and wearing her smartest outfit as if she was about to be interviewed for a new job. Mr. Manchandra's secretary welcomed her and offered a cup of tea before she was ushered into the inner office. As if pulled by a puppet master in the sky, three brown men leaped to their feet with broad welcoming smiles. The brownest, with the skin color of a chestnut, was the one she had met earlier in the week who then introduced her to the other two. The first of these with the skin color of burnt umber was lean with a hawk like expression, went by the name of Ishmael Nadir and he greeted her with a solemn bow. The second, went by the name of Abdulla Ibn Sharif, was extremely handsome, with beautiful white teeth, an Omar Sharif like moustache and a skin almost the hue of yellow ochre. He greeted her effusively and complimented her on the lovely Chanel suit she was wearing and the prefect ruby set in gold on her lapel. She then realized that in the presence of these three wise men of the East, her cloak of invisibility had slipped and blushed with delight at their undoubted interest in her as a person rather than a cipher. Olive's cup of tea was then brought in and they all sat down in a crowded office full of books and manuscripts dominated by a 23-inch screen of an Apple Mac.

To make room for her a stack of journals was lifted off a chair and failing to find any other flat surface to store it, Sanjay Manchandra elected to put it on his own chair and perch on the pile like a benevolent wise owl. He then took charge of the proceedings.

"Mrs Hathaway, you said something very surprising when I met you in my clinic on Wednesday afternoon. Would you kindly repeat it for the benefit of my colleagues" "With pleasure" Olive replied, "I never knew the man but for all that I don't believe that professor Black committed suicide!" There was a sharp intake of breath all round, Sanjay nodded his head as if vindicated in some way and then Ishmael joined in. "Dear lady, you claim never to have known the man and yet you have the courage to challenge the verdict of the coroner, please enlighten us". With that Olive launched into the narrative exactly as described to DI Ramsay last August. The three wise men listened intently and once the story was complete went into a huddle excluding Olive from their whispered comments, after a few moments she heard Sanjay say, "All right then, it's agreed" he then turned to her and continued, "Mrs Hathaway or Olive if I may?" Olive nodded agreement. "What you described reflects that you have extraordinary powers of observation and deduction and you are not easily deterred from following things through. We would therefore like to take you into our confidence and invite you to join our team. Like you we are convinced that professor Black did not take his own life and what you just described strongly supports our own suspicions. There are three reasons why we suspect foul play. Firstly, even though we learnt that he had a past history of clinical depression, he was most certainly not depressed in the weeks leading up to his death. As doctors dealing with cancer we are experts in diagnosing depression as it affects 30% of our patients. Lay people assume that depression is simply a dark mood but it's much more than that. It usually expresses itself with insomnia, agitation and lethargy and the loss of a sense of humour. Right up until the day before his death

Professor Black exuded confidence and frenetic energy and his expression was always animated. Furthermore when we went round to offer his wife our condolences she was as expected in a state of shock but had good reason to be taken by surprise, as they were planning to leave for a cruise in the Black Sea the week after his death. You were probably one of the last to see him alive and he was obviously buying a new set of luggage for their holiday. The second reason for our suspicions is that we learnt from Rachel Black that in his suicide note he confessed to scientific fraud and provided a specific example. When the three of us here were first inducted into the department and briefed by professor Black, he went out of his way to condemn scientific fraud explaining it was stupid and futile for a number of reasons, most important of all being that the best results were the unexpected results, so that fabricating data to provide the expected results would paradoxically, fail to promote your career. Apparently he lived through a couple of bad experiences in the past that heightened his sensitivity to the matter. The third and most compelling reason has just come to light and I'll let Ishmael take over at this point. Ishmael is really a Bedouin goatherd playing at being a surgeon in his spare time but his daytime job in the hills of the northern Negev made him very sharp eyed" he concluded with a grin. Ishmael played along with this friendly banter and bowed to Sanjay and in mock humility replied, "Thank you Effendi for calling upon your humble servant to give witness in front of this Memsahib." Then turning to Olive responded in a far from frivolous tone of voice, " Dear Lady, if professor Black was guilty of scientific misconduct then so am I. A man of his seniority supervises research and seldom gets his hands wet, let alone enters results of experiments into laboratory logbooks. My PhD thesis involved the immune response to cancer and the search for cancer specific epitopes that are localized regions on the cell surface, carrying an antigen capable of eliciting an immune response and of combining with a specific antibody to counter that response"

Olive raised her hand as if to seeking permission to ask a question but Ishmael continued, "The details aren't important Mrs. Hathaway, it is sufficient for you to understand that we were doing research on nude mice bearing cultures of human cancers," Seeing that Olive was rapidly losing the plot he apologized, "I'm sorry for all this unnecessary scientific detail Mrs. Hathaway so perhaps I should explain that nude mice are bred with a genetic defect that allows for the transplant of foreign tissue and incidentally are completely hairless from birth. Again the details are not important but it's the way the results are recorded that is important. Having had his fingers burnt in the past, professor Black insisted that all experiments and their results were logged in duplicate, and in this case, as well as myself, there was also the laboratory technician in the animal house, Hazel Mumford, who shadowed me. The hand written data was then uploaded onto a password-protected database where an algorithm, written by this self proclaimed IT genius, Mr. Sanjay Manchandra, alerted us to any inconsistencies between the double accounting of the data. For each research project there was a unique reference number and password and in my case there were only three people who knew the password, myself, Hazel and Professor Black. The set of experiments that I described were in some way a failure, as we could not identify any cancer specific epitopes, but by chance we did discover that a number of epitopes found in normal tissue, were grossly amplified in cancers arising from those tissues. This redirected our research along a more fertile path and we think we now have treatments that might exploit this amplification phenomenon that are now in phase I trials. As the results of the first set of experiments weren't very interesting, none of the highly regarded journals were interested in publishing them, but as these experiments were important simply for being negative, Professor Black insisted that we published on line in the web-based journal 'Annals of the cellular and molecular biology of tumour-host interaction'. Because I was implicated as a co-author in this supposed fraud, I've already had a visit from representatives of COPE, the Committee of Publication Ethics and an interview with the Dean. It has not been a happy time for me but fortunately I had access to my own set of data that were duplicated by Hazel Mumford's set. Yet in spite of that, the paper that appeared in Annals showed positive results and I could confirm that this had been tampered with on line because I had made a pdf file when the paper first appeared. I have therefore been exonerated. In the meantime, Sanjay, our IT genius, was able to deduce the number of times our paper had been accessed and without asking permission, hacked into professor Black's set of results. There is no doubt that someone with extraordinary computing skills, those that you might associate with national security agencies, have tampered with the professor's log book and altered the on line paper". Olive couldn't contain herself any longer and spluttered, " but surely that might have been the professor himself?"

At this point Abdullah chipped in, "Very good point Olive except for two facts. Firstly scientific fraud for self-aggrandizement would require that a paper be published in a journal with a high citation index like 'Nature' or the 'New England Journal of Medicine', whereas this web-based journal is a dustbin of negative results. Secondly our self-proclaimed computer genius, Mr. Manchandra, was able to confirm that the journal and professor Black's log book were both hacked into on the same date that happened to be Rosh Hashanah, the Jewish New Year, a day when the professor was guaranteed to be out of the department." There was a deathly hush until Olive once again could contain herself no longer, "Then we must go to the police immediately! The poor man was murdered and his reputation ruined." Sanjay once again took charge, "That was our first reaction; but think for a moment. What was the motive for this murder and what kind of people are we dealing with who had the skills and resources to carry out this complicated plot? If news of what we have found out reached their ears our own safety might be at risk." After another long pause for thought Olive spoke up again, "Well you've hacked into Joshua Black's computer hard drive once, then what's to stop you doing it again, search his files especially those that might be encrypted, assuming you have the skills to build the appropriate Rossetta stone algorithm, and in particular look out for the fingerprints of any spyware cookies or worms; they might provide you with clues to the motive and identity of his murderers."

The three wise men gawped with respect at this computer literate grandmother and nodded with approval. "Exactly what we had in mind Mrs. Hathaway and welcome to the team" said Sanjay.

★ ★ ★

Chapter 8

Breaking the code

Following the death of professor Black, Sanjay was appointed acting head of the department whilst the appointment was advertised in the British Medical Journal. The then Dean set up a search committee to look out for suitable applicants, and perhaps entice someone of distinction already holding a chair at a provisional university, by offering start up funds for establishing their own line of research. Unfortunately this stratagem rarely worked because university salaries were fixed all over the country and the cost of buying a house in London was twice that of any provincial town or city. Sanjay never seriously considered himself for the job as at the age of 37 he was only just ripe enough, but as an outsider he never thought he stood a chance. In spite of that he enjoyed being acting head and was popular with everyone including that dragon Catherine O'Reilly, who was in deep mourning for the loss of her old boss. As a result Sanjay had the run of the department with easy access to professor Black's computer. It took him about a week working in the evenings when the department was empty, to hack deep enough to find and disable the spyware and malware, before he could even start on searching the professor's files for clues to the motive and identity of his killers. In spite of frequent entreaties from his junior staff, who were all members of the Apple Mac appreciation club, Joshua Black remained loyal to his Microsoft Windows computer still being run on Windows professional 7 software. As a result it was vulnerable to attack from all number of rapidly evolving malicious viruses. To begin with, Sanjay disconnected the computer from the Internet in case there was a "keylogger" virus operating in the background, and some person or persons unknown were still monitoring the activity of the machine. He had already deduced Professor Black's password to gain access to his desktop and as expected, like many of the naïve and innocent users of the web, he had chosen his wife's name and birthday. He used CDs to upload three different spyware search and destroy programs, bought at the local branch of Curry's on Tottenham Court Road, in order to avoid downloading anything from the Internet. Each of these was left to run for 24 hours but even so he nearly missed the two bugs. One was acting as a portal for corrupting the content of files and the other was for logging keystrokes whilst the computer was in use.

The sophistication of this viral attack was terrifying, as it required cutting edge technology and the work of a team of hackers that suggested, as he guessed, the security services of some multi-national corporation or Nation State. Apart from the spyware detection programs, Sanjay had to use all his skills of deduction and observation before he could crack it. The commonest portal for these malicious vectors was when downloading free software programs or videos and music for entertainment. Social websites were a nightmare as well. So in addition to letting the anti-virus software run through all the files and programs on the hard drive, Sanjay looked carefully at the professor's desktop to see if he could detect some kind of preference or pattern of usage.

He also looked up from the screen at the contents of the office and the clutter on the desk, remembering the teachings of a wise old clinician who was on the staff of the Tata Memorial Hospital, Professor Sunil Patel. "When you approach a new patient in his bed, stand back a little and look at the whole person AND the contents of his bedside locker. The collection of drugs, inhalers and sputum pots will give you clues to his ailments whilst the collection of greeting cards and photographs will give you clues to his social history." Sanjay scanned the room and noted one thing for sure, Joshua Black adored his wife and two sons; there were pictures of them on every surface and on every wall. With that in mind he studied the software that his late boss was using for uploading and storing his collection of photographs. To his surprise he found Picasa rather than XP Windows and immediately guessed he was on to something. The software was state of the art but took at least 5 minutes to download during which time the computer was vulnerable. He then remembered that some malware sequences could be hidden in high-resolution images so he thought the best bet might be searching the professor's collection of digital photographs. He next opened the files of photographs and noted as expected thousands of pictures of the Black family on holiday in far away places. Professor Black obviously had an expensive camera and all of his pictures were stored at high resolution. You could blow up any one of his pictures to the size of a wall without it becoming pixilated. This offered millions of lacunae for viruses to nest. At this point the last of the search programs that were running confirmed his suspicions that Picasa was the vector, but to find and destroy the viruses in the high resolution pictures needed another approach. In the end, after working through the night at writing his own program that piggy backed on the commercial package, he could start scanning all the pictures pixel by pixel. Having run his new program for 48 hours he found the two bugs. One was in a family photograph on holiday in Venice and the other was a picture of his wife Rachel in a bikini on a yacht off what looked like a Greek island. By magnifying these images by a factor of 10^6 he could see a square panel measuring about 1000 x1000 pixels carrying the malicious codes. He was now in a position to search through professor Black's private files.

Unlike the professionals who had infected the computer Joshua Black was a complete novice at hiding or encrypting his secret files. Three clicks of the mouse on drop down menus starting at "Faculty Board minutes" moving on to

"Agendas 2009-2010" and finally "My eyes only", took him to a 10 MB file that was password protected. He tried the names and birthdays of the professor's sons kindly made available in his contacts file and that didn't work. He tried again with the first names and birthdays of the senior staff in the department and again nothing. Given pause for thought, Sanjay closed his eyes and imagined his mentor at the time and the topic that was most on his mind on the date logging the creation of the file and Bingo! It came to him in a flash. HOMEOPATHY was the magic word that opened the file and Sanjay couldn't help laughing and indulging in a short passage of self-congratulation.

In the last two years of his life Joshua Black had lead the successful campaign to close down the Royal London Homeopathic Hospital, that for some obscure historical reason was included in the group of hospitals managed by the University College Hospitals Foundation Trust. Homeopathy was an affront to his fundamental concept of scientific integrity and intellectual honesty, with as much relation to the practice of modern medicine as astrology is related to modern cosmology. This of course made him many enemies but it was highly unlikely that the plot to kill him was stage managed by the homeopathy lobby even with the help and funding of the Prince of Wales. In any case the homoeopathist's approach to sabotaging a computer would have involved sprinkling the machine with an extract of an apple diluted in water to the power of 10^{-20} but that wouldn't work on this Microsoft Windows contraption.

Within the "My eyes only" file were multiple sub-files none of which were password protected so Sanjay decided to read them according to the date order of when they were last modified starting with the earliest dated March 1st 2012 entitled, "The diaries of Dr. Eduard Black translated from the German by Lisa and Otto Grossmark". This was such a large file that he decided to read at home at his leisure and considered it no disrespect or abuse of trust, to send it encrypted via "Drop

Box" to his home address. After all he now had proof positive that Joshua Black was a victim of a well-orchestrated plot. With that he very much wanted to show off his findings to his partners in cyber-crime, Ishmael, Abdullah and Olive. His sent them all an e-mail bearing their operational code name, "Olive and the three brown men" with a password protected Word document bearing the following message: <u>Code cracked, conspiracy confirmed, meet me at close of play this evening.</u>

On the dot of 6.00pm the gang of four convened in the late professor Black's office at a time when all other members of staff had left for the evening. Olive brought some biscuits she'd baked and Sanjay provided fruit juice as apart from Olive, who enjoyed the odd tipple, no one had adjusted to the British tradition of sundowners at 6.00pm.

Once they had settled down, Sanjay with the manner of a vaudeville magician conducted them down through the strata of the hard drive into the darkest recesses of Joshua Black's Microsoft desktop. When his audience finally saw the viral sequences embedded in the magnified jpeg pictures, there was a synchronized sharp inhalation of breath. Ishmael and Abdullah applauded whilst Sanjay took his bow, leaving Olive to state the obvious.

"That means when you hacked in to examine professor Black's log book, whoever is monitoring this computer would have logged the keystrokes and deduced that their plot had become uncovered. For all we know their agents might already be watching the department." She looked around the room as if searching for a hidden CCTV camera. The applause died down and for once Sanjay felt himself blindsided in the game. Then he remembered with a deep sigh of relief that he had disconnected the computer from its server at the time he searched the log books, having anticipated something like this might have happened, so he was able to reassure the audience and this time Olive clapped hands as well.

"What next?" asked Abdullah. "The next task is for us to read through all the secret files in Joshua Black's 'my eyes only' files and see if we can come up with a plausible hypothesis for the motive and a lead on the possible culprits" replied Sanjay. "I have uncovered the following files in date order: 'Dr. Eduard Bloch's diary', 'Meeting with professor Templeton', 'Flinders Petrie' and 'The Lachish letters'. I will make a start with the first as it might provide the key to the others." Olive then interrupted, "Did you say professor Templeton? Is it by any chance Arthur Templeton?" Sanjay consulted his notes. "Yes, how did you guess?" "Arthur is my brother and is professor emeritus of Egyptology at UCL, I think I'd better have first crack at that file," replied Olive to the stunned gathering. "I'll take the Lachish letters," said Ishmael, "as I used to graze goats near Tel Lachish when I was a boy. It's an archaeological site about 30 miles south west of Jerusalem". "Well by the process of elimination that leaves me with Flinders Petrie, whoever that maybe," chimed in Abdullah. "Flinders Petrie was the first person to hold the chair of Egyptology at UCL and in fact Arthur's proper title was the Flinders Petrie professor. I think he died about 60 years ago. How on earth can Arthur be involved in all this?" "I'll think you'll soon find out Olive," concluded Sanjay. At that point he handed out three USB memory sticks to his co-investigators and they agreed to read their allotted files and reconvene the following week.

★★★

Chapter 9

The Templeton File

The material I've collected over the last few months is so extraordinary that I think it is worth publishing in a paper for say, the Journal of the Royal Society of Medicine or even expanded into a book. For now, as I'm so busy with clinical and academic responsibility, I've decided to record my findings by way of a journal. I've never kept a diary but inspired by my grandfather's writings I might as well start now although I very much doubt that any of my patients will one day turn out to be tyrants like Adolf Hitler, although I suspect one to be a member of a notorious Russian Mafia gang living in The Bishops Avenue. Following up on professor Templeton's invitation I went to visit him for coffee on the 8th April 2014. He'd promised Danish pastries as well as freshly ground coffee as his office was on the Bloomsbury campus just off Gower Street. It happened that I was lecturing that morning at the medical school and didn't have a clinic until 2.00pm that afternoon on the Hampstead campus so I thought it would fill in the time nicely. My first surprise was the location of his office. If you walk down Gower Street to Waterstones, the best bookshop in town, then turn left into Malet Street, you will then find a narrow pedestrian alley on your left hand called Malet Place. This leads down into the deepest recesses of the original buildings that made up University College London at the time of it's founder, Jeremy Bentham, about 150 years ago.

I was told to look for the Petrie Museum half way down the lane on the left. It would have been very easy to miss the anonymous old door if it hadn't been for a plaque bearing the face mask of an Egyptian Mummy and a notice reading, "Petrie Museum of Egyptology, Open to the public 13.00-17.00 Monday to Friday". I had no idea that my University housed a museum of Egyptology but that is not really surprising as UCL is one of the largest Universities in Europe, organized on three campuses with only one senior common room just off the main quadrangle in Gower Street. Us clinical academics are usually far too busy to indulge ourselves in leisurely lunches in the senior common room, that is usually full of professors and senior lecturers from the faculty of Arts, who teach maybe 7 hours a week and spend the rest of their time in dusty libraries, or these days browsing "Wikipedia" to gather material for their books. However we probably earn twice what they do so I'm not the least bit envious. But I digress.

I pushed open the non-descript door and entered a small dark vestibule leading to two steep flights of stairs, whose walls carried copies of old black and white photographs of men and women in Edwardian garb at archaeological digs, in what presumably was Egypt; accompanied by a grinning native or two in flowing robes and heads topped off with a fez. At the top of the stairs another tired looking door invited me to push and at last I was in the museum. I was greeted by a charming young woman sitting behind a desk in what I suppose was the reception lobby, although it looked more like a 1950s sub post-office. I explained that I had an appointment for professor Templeton and gave my name. Shortly after that a bear like man came bursting through the inner door to the museum with a huge smile on his face. When I first met the man he was sitting at the member's dining table at the Athenaeum and I hadn't realized how big he was. He must have been six foot two and 18 stone but he was one of those men who carried his weight well and his bearing and warm smile conjured up the cliché impression of the "gentle giant", but I also put good money on the fact that he must have been fearsome as a wing forward in the varsity first XV. His neatly trimmed beard and moustache and his hand shake that nearly ended my career as a surgeon, added to the image of a very friendly bear who shouldn't be let loose in a china shop. Yet as he ushered me through a set of double doors I found myself in what must have been the oldest china shop in northern Europe.

I had entered the most bizarre museum I'd ever seen: an Edwardian time warp, with rows and rows of very long and narrow glass fronted cabinets filled with pottery dating back three or four thousand years. Each of these mahogany cabinets had six sets of drawers with brass fittings below the displays. "Welcome to the Petrie museum!" boomed the bear with an expansive gesture and a mock bow. "If you've got time I'll show you round later but first coffee and croissants in my little office backstage". His office at the back of the museum was indeed little and his looming figure seemed to fill it yet he found space for me to sit and went off to bring in a tray of pastries and cardboard cups bearing the logo "Costa". In his short absence I noted that all four walls were fitted with bookshelves that held countless textbooks on archaeology, bound volumes of learned journals and clusters of little figurines of the ancient Egyptian deities. He backed into the office carrying the tray, daintily carried out a pirouette and gently placed the tray on a clear corner of his surprisingly tidy desk. "Please call me Arthur," the kindly ursine character suggested and in return I offered him my first name. "Well Joshua we have two agenda items if I remember correctly, first you want to learn about the ancient Israelites of Elephantine Island at Aswan and secondly you had some kind of personal request where you thought I could help you." I nodded vigorously with my mouthful with a fresh croissant. He then launched into an extraordinary monologue that must have been refined after much repetition to his students but for all that had me captivated.

" From my time as a young postgraduate I have been interested in the archaeological sites near Aswan at the junction of upper and lower Egypt just north of the first cataract of the Nile. I had argued that this geological feature that impeded migration and trade, might have provided a rich seam to mine, to learn about the Old Kingdom in the early Bronze Age. Yet what we had never expected to uncover was an archaeological site linked to the history of the ancient Israelites, dated about 600 years later than the estimated epoch of the Exodus from Egypt, round about the reign of Ramses II in the New Kingdom approximately 1300BCE. We discovered historical evidence that, during the reign of Manasseh in Israel who succeeded Hezekiah in 687, a colony of Jews – including Levitical priests – migrated from Israel and founded a colony on Elephantine Island in Egypt. This Island, so called because of its shape that vaguely resembles an elephant or more likely because it became the hub in ivory trade, sits in the Nile close to Aswan. It is strongly possible, if not probable, that the Elephantine Jews were escaping the desecration of the Temple and the persecution of King Manasseh. In our first season of excavations on Elephantine Island, we thoroughly investigated ruins of a replica Jewish temple that had been built around 650 BCE, which precisely matched the dimensions of Solomon's temple in Jerusalem as described in the Torah. Of course, the practice of building temples outside of Jerusalem was strictly forbidden by Deuteronomic Law, so only the direst of circumstances would have compelled a group of Jewish refugees to undertake such a project. Nearby we also discovered a number of ancient Papyri that seemed to confirm the existence of a Jewish Temple at Elephantine. Egypt, or at least certain districts of Egypt, would have been a safe haven for Jewish refugees, as we see from King Neco's friendly appeal to Josiah in 2 Chronicles 35:20-21, less than a generation later. One then has to ask oneself what would have provoked these ancient Israelites into such an extraordinary enterprise. My theory was that it was to escape the wrath of God at the time of the Assyrian destruction of the Northern Kingdom of Israel, early in the reign of King Manasseh and the punishment they might expect as a result of Israel turning against the Ten Commandments. Let me illustrate this by reading a passage from the Torah." At that he turned his chair, reached up and much to my surprise brought down a copy of the Artscroll edition of the Chumash and confidently leafing through pages, pounced upon a section by jabbing his index finger. " If we turn to Deuteronomy 28 verses 15 onwards we learn of God's admonitions for disobedience of the holy laws, I will read you some excerpts in order to understand the terror of those people who believed absolutely in prophesies of the Old Testament whilst witnessing the depravity and corruption of the Israelites under the leadership of Manasseh."

He then started reading the ancient Hebrew in a rather comical plumy English accent and translating paragraphs back into English.

"If you do not hearken to the voice of your God, to observe all His commandments and His decrees then all these curses will come upon you and overtake you:

Accursed will you be in the city and accursed will you be in the field. Accursed will be the fruit of your womb and the fruit of your ground. The Lord, Hashem, will attach a plague upon you. He will strike you with swelling lesions, with fever, with burning thirst and with sword. Hashem will cause you to be struck down before your enemies. Your carcass will be food for all the birds of the sky. Hashem will strike you with the boils of Egypt, with heamorrhoids, madness and with blindness".

At this point he stopped to take a sip of his coffee that allowed me to express my surprise and awe at his command of ancient Hebrew. Modestly he responded, "Well dear boy, to become a professor of Egyptology you have to have a passing knowledge of the ancient languages of the Levant as well as Egyptian hieroglyphics and their hieratic and demotic forms, I also can read and translate Aramaic that was pretty much the lingua franca of the period in question. Anyway Deuteronomy 28 carries on like that for a full 40 verses of your holy book and concludes that the Jews will be scattered among all peoples across the four corners of the earth if they failed to obey the law handed down to Moses at Mount Sinai. Now you can interpret this in two ways, either the founders of the Israelite community on Elephantine island took these prophesies literally or else like the Jewish refugees, who fled Nazi Germany in 1936 until the shutters came down in 1938, they were capable of understanding the political upheavals going on around them that would over the next century transform the hegemony of the Levant twice over. Firstly through the actions of the Assyrians led by Sennacherib that lead to the deportation of the ten lost tribes of the northern kingdom of Israel, and finally by the destruction of the Kingdom of Judea at the time of Nebuchadnezzar in 587 BCE during the reign of Zedekiah. So over a period of about 100 years both the ancient Kingdoms of the Israelites were destroyed and the wise amongst those peoples took refuge far afield before the storm-troopers got their hands on them, and many set up a safe haven back in Egypt about 600 years after the estimated date of their epic exodus."

I had to admit my total ignorance of this slice of our history but I was so fascinated by his eloquent and masterly way he delivered his private tutorial, I begged him to continue.

" If you insist," he continued with a mischievous smile. "Although the Temple Mount in Jerusalem was the last known location of the Ark of the Covenant, its date of departure from the Temple is a topic of much debate. The last known reference alluding to the Ark's presence in the Temple dates from 701 B.C., when the Assyrian king Sennacherib surrounded Hezekiah's forces in Jerusalem. Isaiah 37:14-16 states,

'..and Hezekiah received the letter from the hand of the messengers, and read it; and Hezekiah went up to the house of the Lord, and spread it before the Lord. Then Hezekiah prayed to the Lord, saying: 'O Lord of hosts, God of Israel, the One who dwells between the cherubim . . .' This I take as a reference to the presence of God's Glory abiding on the Ark of the Covenant, between the cherubim sculpted on the lid of the Ark, and seems to confirm that the Ark was still located in the Holy of Holies in 701 B.C.

It appears that the villain in the drama of the Ark was the next king, Manasseh, and that the Ark most probably was taken out of the Temple during his reign. The extent of Manasseh's evil is summarized in the Bible noting that he placed pagan idols in the Holy of Holies. I believe that an uncorrupted Levitical priesthood, left over from the days of Hezekiah, would not have tolerated the degrading and polluting of the Temple containing the Ark of the Covenant and clandestinely removed it to a safe place. Whatever the reason that the Ark was removed, it is interesting to note that just a short time after King Manasseh died in 642 BCE, the Judean King Josiah mentions the Ark's absence from the Temple. In 2 Chronicles 35:3 we read": At this point Arthur Templeton paused and leafed through the scriptures again until he found his place and continued. " Then he said to the Levites who taught all Israel, who were holy to the Lord: 'put the Holy Ark in the house which Solomon the Son of David, king of Israel, built. It shall no longer be a burden on your shoulders.' This appears to confirm that the Ark had been removed temporarily from the Temple. Where it sat in the meantime is a subject of much learned speculation as well as the fevered imagination of relic hunters over the years. However we do have a papyrus amongst the bundles we found on Elephantine Island that contains a request for the Arc of the Covenant to be transported to safe keeping in the facsimile Temple of Solomon we discovered on the Island. Let's see if I can find it". He then returned to his bookshelf and rummaged around for a while until he pulled out a file containing a sheaf of photocopies of brown ancient inscriptions. He pulled out one with a look of satisfaction claiming it was written in Aramaic and proceeded to translate its contents.

"Greetings, the Temple of YWH in Elephantine.
To my brother Shelomem from your brother Osea.
Blessings of welfare and strength, now blessed be you
by YWH that he may hold your face in peace.

We learn with great sorrow of the times of destruction and threats to our holy city of Yerushalom from the mighty hordes of the idol worshipers from the north and the east. We learn from your messengers that the Holy Ark of the covenant has been transported for safe keeping by the faithful Levites of Lachish."

At this point I sat up with a start but decided to hold my peace until it was my turn to pose the question about my grandfather's diary. He continued, having failed to notice my sudden interest.

"Now that the wolf has descended on the fold and slavering at your gates I beseech you in the name of YWH to transport the Ark and the rod of Aaron, the first High Priest, to the sanctuary of the Temple we have built on Elelephantine, let it sojourn with us until YWH witnesses that the evil decreed by the King Manasseh, may his name be stricken from the book of life, is washed away in the blood of our enemies and the sanctuary in the Holy city of Yerushalom is restored and the Holy Ark and the rod of Aaron will be restored with great dignity and celebration to their original seat at the centre of the earth bathed in the Glory of HASHEM.

Your mother and the children are well.

Greetings to your house and your children until the HASHEM beholds your face in peace.

Your brother Osea"

Arthur Templeton turned to me with a look of satisfaction on his beaming face beaded with sweat as he had clearly got carried away by his recitation almost as if he had carried himself back in time 2,500 years. He continued:

" Unless they kept copies of their correspondence this suggests the letter was never sent but it provides dramatic evidence that at the time the Assyrians were carving up the northern Kingdom and then threatening Judea, the Ark of the covenant and the rod of Aaron were transported to Lachish for safe keeping and then about 100 years later when Judea was about to fall to the Babylonians, the exiled Israelites in Egypt built a Temple in anticipation of providing temporary sanctuary for the holiest objects of the Jewish faith, until God saw fit to drive out the barbarians and rebuild the Temple in Jerusalem. What in fact happened to these objects remain a mystery, the subject of scholarly debate and the story of a great film starring Harrison Ford, 'The Raiders of the lost Ark'. The Temple on the Nile fell into disuse eventually in the middle of the 4th C BCE ".

I was totally absorbed by this narrative and could hardly believe that I'd never encountered it before. I then asked him to explain the significance of Aaron's rod mentioned twice in the Elephantine papyrus.

"Well there are many legends and apocryphal beliefs about Aaron's rod amongst the three Abrahamic faiths but for a start I suggest you read a copy of the Sarajevo Haggadah. Muslims also venerate Aaron's rod and it is one of their beliefs that their Messiah, the Mahdi, will be recognized by possession of this holy relic." Once again I was astonished by his knowledge of the history and language of my people but he dismissed my compliments with a shrug and confessed that his first degree was a DD or Doctor of Divinity. He then changed the subject and asked me about the subject my own enquiry.

I then started to recount the episode in my grandfather's diary whilst waiting in Hitler's anti-chamber slightly modifying the story about my relationship to the author of the journal. When I came to the altercation between the two English archaeologists Arthur Templeton slapped his thigh and fell about laughing. When he could catch his breath again he explained his mirth. "I can easily guess who those two gentlemen were from your account. The meek one must have been J.L. Starkey who excavated Tel Lachish and uncovered the 'Lachish letters' and the second was none other than his immediate superior Flinders Petrie. They were always at each other's throat because of scientific disputation and ideology, but what that had to do with the Grand Mufti of Jerusalem is beyond my understanding." "Flinders Petrie as in the name of this museum" I burst out.

"Indeed" he replied. It was then apparent that he was about to embark on another long monologue when I glanced at my wristwatch and noted with horror that I had been so engaged by this erudite and articulate man that I hadn't noted the passage of time. I indicated that I needed to rush off; otherwise I would be late for the start of my clinic for the first time in my life. As I stood up and thanked him for his hospitality and suggested we meet again for lunch at the Athenaeum he gave me a final bone-crushing handshake and sent me on my way with the following advice. "If you are interested to learn more about Flinders Petrie I suggest you explore the archives at the Royal College of Surgeons, that should give you a head start!" At that he burst out laughing and I could still hear his guffaws as I left the building and entered Malet Place.

★★★

Chapter 10

The Flinders Petrie File

After I reached my office at the end of my afternoon clinic on the day of my visit to the Petrie museum, I went on-line and visited the Royal College of Surgeons' website. As a FRCS I could access the archive of the college library and search for files related to Flinders Petrie. There was only one in the catalogue and I was able, through an exchange of e-mails to make an appointment to view the file under the supervision of the archivist and after completing an on-line proforma giving my details. The following day I received confirmation that the file would be available for me to search the following Wednesday afternoon. I then searched Amazon books on-line and found a second hand copy of a facsimile of the Sarajevo Hagaddah available for £13.00. With it's usual magic the brown cardboard box from Amazon appeared on my doorstep 24 hours later.

The book was beautifully illustrated and I thought it would serve me well at our next Passover celebration. It didn't take me long to find details about Aaron's rod amongst the copious footnotes.

"Legend has still more to say concerning this rod. God created it in the twilight of the sixth day of Creation, and delivered it to Adam when the latter was driven from paradise. After it had passed through the hands of Shem, Enoch, Abraham, Isaac, and Jacob successively, it came into the possession of Joseph. On Joseph's death the Egyptian nobles stole some of his belongings, and, among them, Jethro appropriated the staff. Jethro planted the staff in his garden, when its marvelous virtue was revealed by the fact that nobody could withdraw it from the ground; even to touch it was fraught with danger to life. This was because the Ineffable Name of God was engraved upon it. When Moses entered Jethro's household he read the Name, and by means of it was able to draw up the rod, for which service Zipporah, Jethro's daughter, was given to him in marriage. Her father had sworn that she should become the wife of the man who should be able to master the miraculous rod and of no other. It must, however, be remarked that the Mishnah as yet knew nothing of the miraculous creation of Aaron's Rod. This supposed fact of the supernatural origin of the rod explains the statement in the New Testament, that Aaron's Rod, together with its blossoms and fruit, was preserved in the Ark. King Josiah, who foresaw the impending national catastrophe, concealed the Ark and its contents; and their whereabouts will remain unknown until, in the Messianic age, the prophet Elijah shall reveal them."

Amongst the endnotes provided by the publisher of this facsimile was also a mention of the importance of the rod amongst those of the Moslem faith.

"The rod is likewise glorified in Mohammedan legend, which, as is usually the case with the Biblical accounts of the Mohammedans, is plainly derived from Jewish sources. The following passage from Hadith al-Bukhari will serve as an illustration:

'Moses flung his staff upon the ground, and instantly it was changed into a serpent as huge as the largest camel. It glared at Pharaoh with fire-darting eyes, and lifted his throne to the ceiling. Opening its jaws, it cried aloud, 'If it pleased Allah, I could not only swallow up the throne with thee and all that are here present, but even thy palace and all that it contains, without any one perceiving the slightest change in me'.

From this a tradition has emerged in certain Islamic

countries that whoever can control the rod of Aaron can control the world.'

I found that all very interesting but concluded that it was of no relevance to the meeting between the two English archaeologists in 1936.

The following week I arrived precisely on time at the neo-classical façade of the Royal College of Surgeons in Lincolns Inn Square and made my way up the grand staircase that lead to the Hunterian museum and the College library. The senior archivist greeted me with suspicion for reasons beyond my ken and drummed into me that the papers in the file had to be replaced in strict order, no photographs were to be taken and notes could only be written by pencil. She conducted me to a library corral and handed over a slim portfolio with a look of disdain. Leaving a chill in the air she flounced out whilst I shrugged off my jacket and set to work.

The first letter in the file nearly made me fall off my chair in shock whilst at the same time making me laugh out loud. I was shushed crossly by other library users and mouthed "sorry" to all around. I copied the whole letter out in long hand in pencil although the original was typed by an old fashioned Remington by the look of it. I deduced from the other contents of the file that the recipient was Sir Arthur Keith, Hunterian Professor and conservator of the Hunterian Museum of the Royal College of Surgeons in London.

Government Hospital, Department of Health
Government of Palestine, Jerusalem
9/10/44
Dear Sir Arthur,
When Sir Flinders Petrie was admitted to the British section of this hospital on 27/10/40 with B.T. malaria at the age of 87, one of the very earliest requests he made in case he should not survive the attack, was that his skull should be sent to the museum of the Royal College

of Surgeons under your care as a specimen of a typical British skull...

As you know he died on the 28/7/42 and he had more than once reiterated his wish to preserve his skull for you. The night he died, Dr. Krikorian and I removed the head after injecting Muller's solution and to be sure that the solution had been effective in the brain tissue the vault was taken off. It was found that to be well infiltrated and the brain is now preserved in formalin and is available for transfer to you when the occasion is possible....to be sent at some future date along with archaeological material when the war is over... The willing and even anxious cooperation of Lady Petrie in this matter forestalled any feelings of desecration.

Yours Faithfully
Dr. W .E. Thompson (specialist)

Now I understood what Arthur Templeton found so funny about giving me a head start! So the pickled head of this old guy was now somewhere in the cupboards of the museum next door. By way of endorsement of this legacy were two postcards from Lady Petrie bearing the home address in Cannon Drive Hampstead NW3, a short walk from my place of work. But if that wasn't sufficiently bizarre the remaining contents of the file were more than enough to make me think that I had unearthed a hornet's nest and I now think I understand the archivist's attitude to me.

Here is the next letter in the file:

Department of Applied Statistics
University of London, University College
The Francis Galton Eugenics Laboratory The Biometric Laboratory
To Sir Arthur Keith Royal College of Surgeons 19/11/32
Dear Sir Arthur,
Many thanks for your kind letter of congratulations. I

admire the generosity of the Germans to an alien enemy
more than their wisdom in selecting myself...
  Karl Pearson

An academic department of Eugenics at my University? This must be a shameful and closely guarded secret of the past. The rest of the file contained a three-way exchange of correspondence between Flinders Petrie, Karl Pearson and Sir Arthur Keith, discussing "Biometrics" and the statistical proof behind the racist theory that encouraged the pseudo-science of Eugenics. Much of the material from Petrie was written by hand and difficult to read, but there was no denying from this evidence that institutionalized racism nested in the very heart of the academic aristocracy in London, infesting my University and my College. This I needed to expose in a paper to some learned journal but first I needed to learn more about the three main players.

I tidied up the file and handed it back to a junior archivist, as her boss was apparently far too busy to pop out to answer any questions. Having exited the library I walked a few steps along the thickly carpeted corridor and turned left into the Hunterian museum. Unlike the Petrie museum with its Edwardian gloom, the Hunterian had enjoyed a recent makeover and was state of the art. Although the contents of the exhibit were macabre, the environment was bright and welcoming and it fact had just won a prize for the best small museum in the land. The contents on display were an extraordinary and eclectic array of specimens collected by the famous 18thC surgeon and anatomist, John Hunter. John and his brother William lived in Soho Square, where they had the best school of anatomy in the Kingdom. They were never short of cadavers and when the supply of executed prisoners dried up, they could always rely on the assistance of the "resurrection men" to defile a graveyard by digging up a recently buried corpse. William Hunter was a gifted dissector and preserver of anatomical specimens, whilst John was the first true clinical scientist in the country. One of my favorite exhibits in the museum is a bisected femur of a chicken used by Hunter to prove that long bones lay down new bone and grow in length at the epiphysial junctions. Probably the most famous exhibit of all is the skeleton of Charles Byrne, the 7 ft 7in "Irish Giant", who suffered from acromegaly caused by a pituitary tumour. When my boys were younger they loved coming to see the giant and his companion the tiny skeleton of the dwarf, Tom Thumb. They also enjoyed browsing round the pots of pickled dissection specimens, freaks and skeletons of rare or extinct creatures.

I stopped at the desk and gave the attendant my card asking if by any chance Alistair Murray was in his office. The current Hunterian professor was a crusty old Scot who taught me anatomy when I was studying for my primary FRCS and was still going strong in his late seventies. My luck was in and the old boy welcomed me warmly.

After the usual pleasantries I enquired if he knew the whereabouts of the preserved head of Sir Flinders Petrie. He went quiet for a while then ushered me into his office and began talking in his delightful soft Scottish burr.

"Aye laddie it is good to see you but I have to admit that your interest might be very embarrassing for the RCS and me in particular. In August 2012 the Israeli Antiquities Authority conducted a memorial service, to mark the 70th anniversary of the death of Flinders Petrie. One of the people who attended the ceremony at the Protestant Cemetery on Jerusalem's Mount Zion, was an Israeli archaeologist Shimon Gibson, the only one to have ever met the deceased – or at least his head. In 1989, shortly after I was appointed here, I discovered a human head, in a sealed glass bell jar in the basement storerooms of the college, with no means of identification. After searching the archives of our collection I suspected that the head belonged to Petrie. I then approached Gibson, with whom I had passing acquaintance and was then working at the Palestine Exploration Fund in London. I asked him if he could help me identify the head preserved in the jar.

He arrived armed with photographs of Petrie and in our downstairs laboratory; I broke the seal on the jar, drained the formalin and placed the grisly specimen on a plate in front of him. He asked me to open the eyelids and we both noted that the perfectly preserved irises were bright blue. Although we had little doubt that the head was that of Petrie in spite of the nose being flattened by having it pressed against the wall of the jar for 70 years, he was surprised to note that the hair was black and not white as shown in all the photographs of Petrie as an old man. I was able to explain that phenomenon by reference to the fact that the white fur of our collection of preserved primate specimens turned black after a few months exposure to formaldehyde. You can now understand why the college might be embarrassed by journalists if this story got out and also it wouldn't please our Israeli friends to learn that they were honoring a died in the wool racist and anti-Semite!" Everything now seemed to slip into place; I thanked my old friend, reassured him that I would not make my findings public and left the museum. On my way out of the college I nodded at the famous painting of John Hunter by Sir Joshua Reynolds hung nearby, noting for the first time that part of Charles Byrne skeleton was to be seen lurking darkly in the background. As I entered the sunlight and fresh air of Lincolns Inn Fields I took a deep breath and determined to find out more about the racist triad, Petrie, Keith and Pearson.

★★★

The next time I enjoyed an hour or two of leisure free from professional and domestic affairs, I made a start in finding out more about these three proponents of eugenics. I thought I might as well continue with Flinders Petrie as he seemed the central figure in the search that began with my reading of the last entry in my grandfather's diary.

For a start I wasn't interested in the man as a famous archaeologist or pioneer in the field of Egyptology- that was a given. I was searching for more evidence about his ideology and support for eugenics. Much of this could be discovered only two or three clicks away in a search of the Internet. Of the latter there was no doubt, although some of his ideas were bizarre and ridiculed at the time.

Petrie was a close friend of Francis Galton, the founder of the eugenic school of thought, and worked closely with him to provide skulls and long bones from his archaeological digs with the hope of corroborating the teachings of Galton. Petrie claimed that that there was a "Dynastic Race", that was of pure Caucasian blood_that entered Egypt from the south, conquered the "inferior" mixed race then inhabiting Egypt, and slowly introduced the finer Dynastic civilization as they interbred with the inferior indigenous people. "Racial Photographs from the Egyptian Monuments" was the first work Petrie completed for Galton that provided a series of 190 Photographs of the various races conquered or visited by the Egyptians. After this he continued working for the Galton Laboratory, collecting, measuring, and delivering skeletal remains. In fact, the Laboratory requested so much from Petrie that, in 1895, there was no more room for the skulls and skeletons. As a result, the Anthropometric Lab was expanded. Petrie was also affiliated with a variety of far right-wing groups in England and was a dedicated believer in the superiority of the Northern peoples over the Latinate and Southern peoples. Petrie did not stop his eugenic mission there but presented ideas about social change that reflected deep-seated eugenic influence. In Janus, a book he published in1907, he argued that if a state is successful, it is because a majority of its people, or at least a majority of the people who were in positions of power, were of good character. Thus, in order to create or maintain a society's integrity, that the state must support the 'best stocks' and 'tax down the worst stocks.' To achieve this vision of utopia it would be necessary to 'carefully segregate fine races and prohibit continued mixture, until they have a distinct type which will start a new civilization when transplanted.' The segregation of 'fine' races would be done through state-monitored marriages and reproduction as well as state-monitored abstinence and sterilization. He objected to reforms on child welfare that favored nurture over nature as a way of overcoming poverty and low expectations of life. His most repugnant view was to dismiss the poor being the "worst stock" and the urban poor almost looked upon as separate race, using the expression "weeding out inferior stock". Left to him I would not be here as a professor of surgery at Petrie's own university. In short this repulsive man was promoting an ideology that guided the barbaric application of racist theory by Adolf Hitler 30 years before he came to power. At last I had a clue as to why he might have been invited to meet the Fuehrer as described in my grandfather's diary.

Next I turned my attention to Sir Arthur Keith, the Hunterian Professor and conservator of the Hunterian museum of the Royal College of Surgeons in London. He too was a proponent of eugenics. Where others had postulated that physical separation could provide a barrier to interbreeding, allowing groups to evolve along different lines, Keith introduced the idea of cultural differences as providing a mental barrier, emphasizing territorial behaviour, and the concept of the 'in-group' and 'out-group'. Man had evolved; he claimed, through his tendency to live in small competing communities, a tendency, which was at root determined by racial differences in his 'genetic substrate'. Writing just after *World War II he particularly emphasized the racial origins of anti-Semitism*, and in 'A New Theory of Evolution' he devoted a chapter to the topics of anti-Semitism and Zionism in which he argued that Jews live by a 'dual code'. He clearly had a grudging sympathy for Adolf Hitler as expressed in this quote from his book.

"The German Fuehrer, as I have consistently maintained, is an evolutionist; he has consciously sought to make the practice of Germany conform to the theory of evolution. He has failed, not because the theory of evolution is false, but because he has made three fatal blunders in its application."

Finally Karl Pearson FRS. The first thing I realized on searching the net, was that I already knew the name but in a different context. I have often used the Pearson coefficient in my statistical calculations to explore linear correlations between two biological variables. In fact Pearson pretty much established the discipline of biometric statistics and in 1911 he founded the world's first university statistics department at *University College London*. He was indeed a proponent of *eugenics*, and a protégé and *biographer of Sir Francis Galton*. In 1905 he published this assertion:

"History shows me one way, and one way only, in which a high state of civilization has been produced, namely, the struggle of race with race, and the survival of the physically and mentally fitter race. If you want to know whether the lower races of man can evolve a higher type, I fear the only course is to leave them to fight it out among themselves, and even then the struggle for existence between individual and individual, between tribe and tribe, may not be supported by that physical selection due to a particular climate on which probably so much of the Aryan's success depended…"

He even construed that the genocide of the Tasmanian aborigines by white settlers, was a corroboration of this theory. Furthermore he was an overt and unapologetic anti-Semite as judged by this quotation from a paper he published in the Annals of Eugenics in 1925 describing his opposition to Jewish immigration to Britain. "…these immigrants will develop into a parasitic race, taken on the average, and regarding both sexes, this alien Jewish population is somewhat inferior physically and mentally to the native population". He obviously had an emotional attachment to Germany as he studied in Heidelberg and changed his name from Carl to Karl and went on to receive a prestigious academic award in Berlin probably related to the "thank you" letter I uncovered in the college archive. He owned a "haarfarbentafel", a gauge for measuring hair color and texture, that was bought from Eugen Fischer, the Director of the Institute of Racial Hygiene in Berlin, later appointed by Adolf Hitler as rector of the Frederik Wilhem

University in 1933. So, at once, the circle was complete, Galton, Pearson, Petrie and some unspeakable eugenicists in Hitler's inner circle. As Pearson died in 1936 he could have had no direct link to the events described in the last entry in my grandfather's diary but if one is allowed to judge a man by the company he keeps we can start to believe that in some way Petrie had some common purpose with Adolf Hitler.

This then brings us to consider the last three characters who accompanied Petrie in Hitler's anti-room: The Grand Mufti of Jerusalem and, if Arthur Templeton's guess was correct, James Leslie Starkey and the last, a minor player, probably an acolyte of the Grand Mufti.

To ask whether Al-Husseini, the Grand Mufti of Jerusalem, was an anti-Semite and a fellow traveler with the Nazi party would be like asking if the Pope was a Catholic who tended to believe in the virgin birth. Al-Husseini took it upon himself to raise a militia of 20,000 Muslim sympathizers in the Balkans to aid and abet the final solution in Croatia and ended up seeking refuge in Berlin when the war in North Africa and the Middle East turned against the Axis in 1942.

James Leslie Starkey seemed to be the odd one out in this "hall of infamy" but before describing my findings about him I need to try and deduce where the archaeological site of Lachish fits into the equation.

★★★

Chapter 11

The Lachish File

I began my search in the British Museum. For a start I purchased a slim and copiously illustrated volume in their bookstore entitled "The Bible in the British Museum: interpreting the evidence" by T.C. Mitchell, and read the sections relating to Lachish, sitting in their coffee bar before checking out the exhibits for myself. Apparently during the reign of *Rehoboam*, Lachish became the second most important city of the Kingdom of Judea. After the fall of the northern kingdom in Samaria to the Assyrians in 722 BCE the Kingdom of Judea effectively became a satrap of the invaders by paying tributes. In 688 BCE, during the Judean revolt against Assyria, Sennacherib captured Lachish that was at the extreme southwestern border of Judea and the Assyrian Empire, despite determined resistance. The archaeological site contains the remains of an Assyrian siege ramp to this day. Sennacherib later devoted a whole room in his palace for artistic representations of the siege on stone that is on view in the British Museum. The town later reverted to Judean control, only to fall again to Nebuchadnezzar in his campaign against Judah in 588-587 BCE during the reign of Hezekiah. During Old Testament times Lachish served an important protective function in defending Jerusalem and the interior of Judea because the easiest way to get a large attacking army up to Jerusalem was to approach from the coast. In order to lay siege to Jerusalem an invading army would first have to take Lachish, which guarded the mountain pass. In January 588 BCE the Babylonian army placed Jerusalem under blockade and began the destruction of outlying strong points, taking them one by one until finally only Lachish and Azekah were left standing. The fall of Azekah was movingly illustrated in one of the "Lachish letters", in which an officer in charge of an observation post writes to the garrison commander in Lachish that the fire signals of Azekah can no longer be seen.

"And let my lord know that we are watching for the signals of Lachish, according to all the indications which my lord hath given, for we cannot see Azekah."

The city that once occupied an area of 20 acres was finally razed to the ground shortly before the conquest of Jerusalem leaving a huge mound of rubble that until the early 20thC was known as Tell el-Duweir. The Wellcome-Marston Archaeological Research Expedition led by James Leslie Starkey excavated the site of Tell el-Duweir in 4 seasons between 1932 and 1938 during which time the "Lachish letters" were uncovered.

Armed with this information I then went to inspect the exhibits for myself.

I love the British Museum. The huge domed great court glassed over in triangular panes, an act of sheer genius by the architect Lord Foster, provides the most beautiful internal public space in London. The central rotunda that once housed the British Library where Karl Marx wrote "Das Kapital" now provides exhibition space but also carries a serpentine broad stairway on its outer wall that allowed me direct access to the upper floors carrying exhibits from the ancient Levant in room 57 of the Sackler galleries.

Having inspected the drama of the ancient Assyrian engraved graphic narrative of the siege and conquest of Lachish, I strolled past the crowds of foreign visitors to a quiet gallery holding artifacts from the period of the fall of the first Temple. There I found four humble pieces of cracked terracotta pottery covered with very clear ink inscriptions in paleo-Hebrew. Next to the Rosetta stone, these non-descript objects had to be considered the most important specimens of ancient text in the British Museum's collection. These are the oldest specimens of classical Hebrew writing in existence and the first archaeological evidence that verified the historical truth of the section of the Old Testament describing the reign of Hezekiah at the time of the prophet Isaiah and the Babylonian conquest of Judea over 2,500 years in the past. 18 of these inscribed pottery fragments, known as ostraca, were unearthed by J.L. Starkey and his colleagues between 1935 and 1938. Just as I was about to leave the room, a flash of gold to the left of the ostraca caught my attention. My heart skipped a beat as I read the label, "Gold Pectoral 7th C BCE, Tel Jemmeh, Fliders Petrie". Here was the first connection although more was to follow. After leaving the museum I walked to my next commitment, a boring meeting of the faculty in the medical school on Gower Street, determined to learn more about J.L.Starkey when time allowed.

★★★

J.L. Starkey was born in London, the son of a surveyor. As a child he was not much interested in formal education but spent much of his spare time reading about archaeology and visiting the British Museum. During World War I, he served in the Royal Air Force and at one time was posted to a lighthouse for some months on coastal reconnaissance, where he continued to read books on archaeology that were sent to him.

After the war he attended evening classes in Egyptology at University College, London, where he came in contact with Flinders Petrie and started studying Egyptian hieroglyphs. In 1923 he committed himself to an archaeological career, working with Petrie at Qau in Upper Egypt for the British School of Archaeology in Egypt (BSAE).

When the BSAE transferred their work to Palestine in 1926, Starkey joined Petrie as his first assistant at Tell Jemmeh, near Gaza, applying his experience with workmen in Egypt to the newly engaged and untrained Bedouin.

In 1932 Starkey left Petrie to lead his own expedition, financed by Sir Henry Wellcome, Sir Charles Marston and Sir Robert Mond. The chosen site was Tell el-Duweir, identified as Biblical Lachish. In January 1938, at the age of 43, Starkey's career was tragically cut short. He was buried in the Protestant cemetery on Mount Zion, Jerusalem, his funeral attended by hundreds of mourners. His close friend and colleague, Gerald Lankester Harding, one of the men responsible for acquiring and preserving the "Dead Sea Scrolls", gave tribute to Starkey's outstanding contribution to Palestinian archaeology and his personal qualities through the Palestine Broadcasting Service just a few days later. Fifty years later a memorial service for him was held in Jerusalem attended by his son John and grandsons.

He was clearly an honorable and well-liked man and I could find no hint whatsoever of any linkage to the eugenic movement of the time. However on searching one of the archives linked to the British Mandate government of Palestine in 1938 I came across a couple of lines describing his death that chilled my blood:

REPORT by His Majesty's Government in the United Kingdom of Great Britain and Northern Ireland to the Council of the League of Nations on the Administration of PALESTINE AND TRANS JORDAN for the year 1938

…On the 10th January, Mr. J. L. Starkey, the well-known archaeologist, was murdered by a party of armed Arabs on the track leading from Beit Jibrin to Hebron en route to the opening of the new Palestine Archaeological Museum in Jerusalem.

This story now had all the makings of an Agatha Christie murder mystery perhaps entitled, "Death on the Road to Hebron".

Putting all the pieces together one might speculate that J.L. Starkey had made another extraordinary discovery at Lachish of such importance that if it came to the attention of Adolf Hitler it could change the sphere of influence in Palestine just before the outbreak of the Second World War. Perhaps the most charitable interpretation was that Flinders Petrie

95

unintentionally shared the secrets of this find with some of his right wing sympathizers and one of these had the ear of a member of the Nazi archaeological eugenics group, possibly Eugen Fischer, who then passed it on to Hitler. The presence of the Grand Mufti at the fracas witnessed by my grandfather suggests that this find was either of unwelcome significance by way of refuting eugenic ideology and/or something of great importance for the future of Palestinian Arab Nationalism. To keep that secret may well have been the motive for Starkey's murder.

★★★

Chapter 12

Olive and the three wise men reconvene

The Gang of Four reconvened at the appointed hour in the late professor Black's office bringing highlighted printouts of the files they were instructed to study and proceeded to brief each other. There were four pieces of the jigsaw to fit in place, Eduard Bloch's diary, the Templeton file, the Flinders Petrie file and the Lachish papers. Sanjay had to fast forward to the last entry in Eduard Black's diary to make sense of the whole picture. Ishmael was able to add some footnotes to the Lachish file as he had recall of herding his goats up the grassy inclined plane of the Assyrian siege ramp. Olive was amused and intrigued by her brother's involvement and was excited at the prospect of confronting him with the evidence of this putative conspiracy.

Finally Abdullah expressed disgust at the viper's nest of eugenicists at UCL in the interwar years and a little embarrassed that Joshua Black's suspicion of conspiracy had involved Islamic fanatics, yet agreed with the others that Professor Black's analysis of the events was plausible. The puzzle that remained was why, after 75 years, this conspiracy was of sufficient relevance today as to justify the murder of a distinguished professor and how on earth did he trigger an alert to draw attention to his findings. Eugenics had for a long time been debunked as a pseudoscience but Islamic extremism was perhaps even more active today than in 1938. The so called "Arab spring" turned into deep midwinter with civil wars in Syria, Afghanistan and Lebanon whilst there were constant murderous insurgencies in North Africa, Egypt,

Sinai, Iraq and Yemen, not to mention the spread of the so called Islamic State with its barbarous ideology, in Syria and Iraq. The murder of Joshua Black by exclusion, had to be linked in some way to the unrest in the Middle East.

That then left the problem as to how the modern day equivalents of the conspirators learnt of his research. There was a silent pause as four very high IQs, switched into top gear. Olive broke the silence by quietly saying, "I know how it was done." There were looks of disbelief as she continued, "I bank with Coutts & Co and last year they discovered that my credit card had been cloned, alerted me immediately and temporarily stopped all transactions on my card. I asked them how they got on to it so quickly and they replied that they had a special algorithm. They have thousands of customers around the world and for each one they build up a profile or fingerprint of their transactions. Once there are two or more departures from this pattern and the customer hadn't warned them in advance, the mainframe bank computer alerts the staff and shuts down the account. I think that somewhere in the world there is a very large and very powerful computer that is silently monitoring all the billions of hits on search engines like Google and if a certain sequence of hits is detected that is beyond any possible random pattern, the algorithm wakes up a sleeping cell of terrorists. That sequence must contain some if not all searches for Eugenics, Flinders Petrie, Karl Pearson, J.L.Starkey, Lachish, Eugen Fischer, the Grand Mufti of Jerusalem and Adolf Hitler. Imagine how unlikely it would be for any permutation of that sequence to occur out of random curiosity." The silence that followed was so profound one could hear the traffic in Pond Street nine floors below and was only broken when Abdullah burst into the song from "My Fair Lady" that opens with, "My God she's got it" and Olive blushed with pleasure whilst Sanjay cursed himself for allowing her to get there first. At the same time he was delighted and in awe of meeting someone with a quicker brain than his. Waking out of this reverie he continued the discussion. "I think you are right Olive, but that technology is only about seven years old. The secret must have been passed by word of mouth or coded text for three or four generations so why did the conspirator's descendants suddenly and at great expense, set up this global electronic surveillance unless their own intelligence hinted that another agency had stumbled on the legend of Lachish. This suggests that we have witnessed collateral damage of cyber-warfare that could only be conducted by those with the resources of a national intelligence service like the CIA, or Mossad. If my guess is correct then we are way out of our depth and we should take the intelligence we have gathered by chance to MI5." "I think you are right Sanjay," replied Ishmael, "but how in practice does one do that?" To which Olive replied, "As I'm the only one known to the authorities I suppose I could contact the member of the CID I spoke to when I reported my suspicions and I'd better do that right away whilst we are here all together". With that Olive pulled out her mobile phone and dialed the number she stored for DI Ramsay.

The one side of the conversation the others heard was as follows:

" May I speak to detective inspector Ramsay please?"

" When did he retire?"

" Do you by any chance have his home number?"

" Oh dear-when did this happen?"

"Thank you for your help"

On putting her phone back in her handbag, Olive, her face drained of blood, explained.

"It appears that DI Ramsay was killed by a hit and run driver a week after I met him. What a tragic coincidence, who should we try next?" Sanjay was the first to respond. "What if it wasn't a coincidence? Consider this hypothetical scenario. Ramsay reflects on your evidence and this supports some concerns of his own that for professional reasons he doesn't want to share with you. He then takes it to a higher authority in the Met. This higher authority starts making waves and a mole in the organization leaks these suspicions to the conspirators who then choose to bump off the detective inspector."

Abdullah then leapt upon Sanjay's musings.

"If that is indeed the case, DI Ramsay's file would include Olive's statement which then puts her at risk!"

"That's kind of you to think that way but firstly I'm invisible to most folk and secondly I subscribe to a private security firm that patrols the Suburb to pre-empt or prevent burglaries but I suppose I could increase my subscription for their meet and greet service on the rare occasions I go out at night". In truth Olive had already anticipated Abdullah's concerns and had determined to look both ways when crossing the road and to keep her front door double locked and on a chain.

"There is something else I don't understand," said Ishmael, "Why has there been no follow up to the visit by the Dean and SCOPE once I'd been cleared of wrongdoing? They must also have reported this to a higher authority and where does that leave me? Is there no one we can trust?"

"We could of course discuss this with Joshua Black's family but that might put them in harms way" suggested Sanjay. It was then Olive's turn to chip in. "I trust my brother Arthur more than anyone in the world. He is well connected and would in any case be able to help us follow up on the archives that might lead to an understanding of the relationship between Petrie and Starkey and the likely content of an archaeological find in the late 1930 that still resonates to this day. I suggest we set up a meeting with him."

The next to speak was Abdullah and what he had to say was so outrageous that it almost led to a falling out between friends. " I have to agree with all that's been said so far but I would now like to make a suggestion that might advance our cause and also help our protection if indeed we put ourselves at risk in pursuing this subject. My uncle Ali who lives in Jeddah and claims to be a senior executive in Exxon Oil Saudi Arabia, does in reality hold high office in the Mabahith Saudi secret police. He might prove to be a vital ally."

"Are you mad!" came back three voices in perfect synchrony. "No, I've been giving this serious thought as we've been talking. I have a personal stake in my pride as, being a minor member of the Saudi Royal family, I would hate to think that somehow my country would be involved in a conspiracy like this. So I argue as follows: my country values its links with the Western world and in particular with the USA and the UK. Most of our officer class has trained at Sandhurst Military academy. You may not like our form of government or the way women are treated as second-class citizens but out of enlightened self-interest we are loyal allies. So I ask myself, if this plot is linked to ideological fascism, then who has the most to gain in keeping it secret until the time they could use these ancient archaeological finds, whatever they may be, to advance a contemporary campaign such as the establishment of a new global Islamic hegemony? I can only come up with two suggestions: ISIS and or the Muslim Brotherhood." In spite of increasing agitation expressed by his small group of friends he continued. " Saudi Arabia has nothing to gain as ISIS destabilizes the troubled region and the Muslim Brotherhood is no friend of my country. The danger perceived by the Al-Saud family from the Muslim Brotherhood remained remote, as long as the movement was in opposition. Its brief tenure in power in Egypt and Tunisia has completely changed the situation. Riyadh fears that the rise to power of the Brotherhood encourages Islamist opposition inspired by that movement, to resume activities within our kingdom. The Saudi ruling family perceives the Brotherhood and its doctrine as an ideological rival to Wahhabism, which may spread and sow discord in the kingdom and threaten the monarchy. The perception of this danger also has a regional dimension, as some of our leaders fear that the rise of an alliance between Egypt, Turkey and Qatar, the only Gulf state to maintain close ties with the Muslim Brotherhood, may reduce the dominant regional influence of Saudi Arabia." Having overcome his shock Sanjay finally interrupted Abdullah's flow. "I'm very impressed with

101

your political knowledge about the Middle East but how on earth could your infamous secret service help our cause?" With a wolverine smile Abdullah responded. " True, my friends and family who covertly work for or with the Mabahith are not afraid of getting their hands dirty in the cesspit of Middle East politics but I'm not here to defend their methods but to consider if we have common cause and if so exploit their access to the global intelligence concerning the activities of the Muslim Brotherhood. You mentioned the capacity of the CIA and Mossad for espionage to protect their national interests; they have nothing to compare with the resources of the Mabahith in Jeddah. Now even I'm not supposed to know this, but every time one of our citizens takes a shit its recorded and anytime one of our women puts on makeup it's noted. A sneeze in the mosque at a timed judged disrespectful by the Mullah goes down in your file whilst the covert use of alcohol or call girls amongst our diplomats all round the world is kept on file for future use if required. If anyone has an algorithm for monitoring poor professor Black's keystrokes on his PC then the Mabahith could in no time at all develop an algorithm to monitor the algorithm and for all I know the fingerprints of the perpetrator on the keyboard. Furthermore my uncle Ali owes me a favor or two because he knows that I know stuff about him that even the surveillance by his own peers hasn't been noted. You remember that young woman I brought to professor Black's Silver wedding anniversary?" Ishmael groaned at the thought. "Well I was teasing you all. She wasn't a young lady: *he* was uncle Ali's catamite who happened to be on a shopping expedition in the West-End and: well never mind, some secrets I must keep even from you. I think if it came to it my uncle might be persuaded to help us if I convinced him it was in our National interest."

After a pause for thought Sanjay responded, "Every time I think to myself that we are exaggerating or dramatizing our findings, I have to remind myself of the extreme sophistication of the corruption of professor Black's hard drive. As I've already suggested only a large multi-national corporation or national surveillance agency would have expertise and capacity to do that, so I am slowly coming round to considering Abdullah's offer of help as long as we can in no way be linked with his approach to his uncle. How would you set about it Abdullah?"

"Well, first of all I have a perfect excuse for a visit to Jeddah and secondly all I would need to say was that from some reliable source I have by chance learnt of the presence of a sleeping cell of conspirators in London who are enemies of Saudi-Arabia. That alone together with 'calling in a favor' from uncle Ali, should be sufficient."

"And what is your perfect excuse for visiting Jeddah?" asked Olive.

" Simple, I wish to propose marriage to his youngest daughter!"

"You what?!" was the synchronous response. With a wide smile Abdullah continued:

" I know everyone thinks I'm a rich playboy prince and I enjoy playing that role but for two years I've been secretly engaged to Fatimah the loveliest girl on the planet. We have delayed our plans for marriage for two reasons. To begin with, she required that her two older sisters married first and my visit to Jeddah will officially be the invitation to the wedding of the second sister. Secondly, my pride determined that I should be independently sufficiently well off to care for a wife and children without relying on hand me downs from my father or future father-in-law. As I am close to being promoted to consultant senior lecturer in this department, I think it can now all come together nicely."

"I'm delighted by your news Abdullah but, as acting head of the department, I can't see how you can be so sure of this promotion now that you have lost the patronage of Joshua Black."

"Ah but there's where you're wrong Sanjay, when you are promoted to the chair I'm sure I'll enjoy your patronage." In spite of Sanjay's protestations Abdullah continued. "You are far and away the best candidate for the job, you have all the academic requirements, as acting professor you have made yourself very popular within the medical school as a whole and yes, there is another factor if I can remember: of course, I nearly forgot, my father has been in touch with the Dean and expressed a passing interest in funding a new facility research in surgical-oncology to the tune of £5M."

At that point everyone except Sanjay fell about laughing. Sanjay did his impersonation of a goldfish again and his blush was sufficient to show through the walnut color of his skin.

"Well that's settled," said Olive, "Perhaps while you are away the three of us should take lunch somewhere private with my brother Arthur."

"Just one moment Olive, I think we've forgotten something." Sanjay said as an afterthought just as they were about to leave, "What about the phone call professor Black received that started you on this mission". Without another word all three turned round and trooped back to their seats and looked expectantly to hear what Sanjay had to offer. "The phone call he received in the car park appeared to have induced his rapid and careless departure. Whoever was at the other end of the call must have provoked or frightened him to speed off and in some way fall into a trap. At the moment I can only come up with two suggestions. Knowing how much he doted on his family, the first suggestion is that the caller was someone he trusted alerting him to the fact that either his wife or one of his sons had been admitted urgently to the hospital. The second might have been a stranger threatening a member of his family or even suggesting they had been taken as hostage. Any further suggestions or ideas on how to proceed?"

After a short pause Olive was the first to respond. "Where was his car found after the time of his death?" The question was so obvious that the other three mentally kicked themselves for not thinking of it first. "If the car was found parked somewhere in the Royal Free car park then Sanjay's first proposition holds up but if it was parked near the scene of the crime or never even discovered then that would support the second proposition."

"Goodness gracious me, Olive, you have missed your vocation. Is it too late for you to retrain for the CID," joked Sanjay but then he turned serious. "You are absolutely right: the key to his abduction and murder might be the whereabouts of his car. If we are to proceed any further then we have no choice but to bring Rachel Black into our confidence." "I think you are right Sanjay, I'm going to have to bite that bullet", said Olive in a tone of fierce determination.

★★★

Chapter 13

Tea with Rachel Black

'Twas easier said than done and in the cool light of the day, Olive couldn't at first bring herself to phone Rachel Black to arrange a visit by saying she had something to communicate relating to the suspicious circumstances of her husband's death. There was no difficulty in finding out the telephone number as it was recorded in the files of the major donors to the Prom concerts at her church but she couldn't initially dream up the words to explain the reason for her visit. After a couple of days of introspection she hit upon the idea of a half-truth that her visit would be somehow related to Joshua Black's generosity in support of the Proms and her wish to place a death notice in the church Gazette in memoriam of this great and generous man. Having made the call she found herself invited to Sunday afternoon tea in the rather grand house on Wildwood Road the other side of the Heath extension to where she lived.

When the time arrived she repeated her walk across the little patch of woodland and meadow to the front door that had been ajar on her last visit in order to let mourners in for the service of ritual mourning. As she arrived she was startled to note a large silver Mercedes with the number plate J 13LACK brooding half hidden behind tall privet hedges. She didn't even have time to crank up her powers of deduction to interpret the significance of this observation, when the door opened to let out an earlier visitor leaving Rachel Black on the doorstep to invite her in. Rachel was a petite, slim and beautiful woman probably in her late 40s, very elegantly dressed in somber colors. Her hair was carefully coifed and she wore a touch of make up. Taken all together she looked about 20 years younger than at Olive's first visit to the house of mourning.

Olive was greeted with a genuine smile of welcome and conducted into a cozy parlor cum television room where a tray of teacups, teapot and biscuits was already set out. They were obviously not alone in the house as loud music and footsteps could be heard from the room directly above where they sat.

After the conventional chit chat about local issues and the Proms and the drinking of tea with the polite refusal of a second biscuit, Olive describe her wish to add an *in-memoriam* note in the church magazine and the program for the next Proms. She had every intention of carrying out these tasks even though the idea was an expedient to allow her to pursue the real agenda. Rachel graciously accepted the offer providing she could have the final say in the wording of the announcements. At that point the door burst open and a handsome, tall dark haired young man in his twenties, obviously one of Rachel's sons, entered and quickly apologized for interrupting and was about to back out when his mother insisted he stayed put and introduced him. "Mrs. Hathaway this is my younger son Matthew, he makes a lot of noise but is really a nice young man and is studying medicine to follow in his father's footsteps." After a firm handshake and a muttered apology, Matthew again started to back out when Olive realized that this was the perfect opportunity to break the news of the secret behind her visit with the young man present as witness and to provide psychological support.

"Mrs. Black, or Rachel if I may, I have something else to talk to you about and it might be for the best if your son was a witness to what I have to say." Looking very surprised and turning very pale, Rachel urged her son to take a seat. " Please forgive my intrusion into your grief and period of mourning but I believe I have some information that might in a small way help to relieve your suffering." Mathew's face turned red and holding his mother's hand he angrily spoke out, "Mrs.

Hathaway, if you think that Jesus can save us through prayer and are trying to convert us to Christianity you've come to the wrong house." Rachel tried to stop his flow but Olive raised her hands as in surrender. "Young man, I know this is a Jewish house and I can assure you that I am not an evangelical Christian promising you salvation in the world to come. You need to understand that this is my second visit to this house but you wont remember my first visit." In response to the raising of two sets of eyebrows Olive continued. "On my first visit I blundered in on one of your evenings of prayer shortly after your father was buried. I was carried along in a tide of visitors and wished you both a long life at a time I hadn't got a clue about what was going on. Over the last few weeks I've learnt a lot about professor Black's death and I thought it might be of some comfort to you that I have evidence to show that your father was not guilty of scientific misconduct and that his death was not suicide it was murder!" Mathew now got very angry and made as if to throw Olive out of the house shouting, "How can you be so cruel, hasn't my mother suffered enough, are you another of these conspiracy theory cranks?" Olive thought it was about time to drop her cloak of invisibility and show the cross young man that she possessed a rod of steel in her spine and changed the tone of her voice in order to express her determination.

"Matthew I suggest you think very carefully before you open your mouth again and listen carefully to what I have to say. I am not in the habit of making up stories and I do not subscribe to conspiracy theories. So before you go any further I suggest you call Mr. Sanjay Manchandra on his mobile phone, I have his number, and I think you will find that he can vouch for me." "Do you mean Mr. Manchandra, the senior lecturer in surgery at the Royal Free?" Olive nodded and dialed Sanjay's number and passed her mobile phone to Matthew noting with wry amusement when the young man stood at attention to take the call. It didn't take long for him to be convinced and as he sat down and returned Olive's phone he turned to his mother and said, "She appears to be kosher Mum."

Quick as a flash Olive responded, "I'm glad I'm kosher but I'm not here to be eaten I'm here to be listened to." That comment broke the ice and was rewarded by a brief chuckle from Matthew and a look of strained concentration from Rachel. "Now that I have your full attention," Olive continued, "I want to ask you a simple question after which you will receive a full account of a remarkable story that even I have difficulty in believing, and as you may judge, like it or not, I also have a stake in the events that may follow our meeting today. Now for my question; I assume that the black Mercedes J13LACK belonged to your late husband. Rachel, where was it found after the discovery of his body?" "It was found in the ambulance bay outside the A&E department of the Royal Free, illegally parked and clamped, but what on earth is the relevance of that?" Rachel promptly responded. With a wise nod of her head Olive launched into her story.

With frequent interruptions for clarification, it took almost an hour for the tale to be told.

Olive then wrapped up as follows; "The fact that the professor's car was found outside the accident unit at the hospital supports our theory, that on the day before your dear husband's body was found, I witnessed him taking a call from someone who he had reason to trust, claiming that one of his closest family members had been admitted with severe injuries. I would go even further and suggest that his assailants were waiting for him to arrive and as he climbed out of his car they must have bundled him into a waiting vehicle that was perhaps disguised as an ambulance. So, Rachel and Matthew, who might have been on the other end of the phone?" Rachel was the first to speak, "As far as I know the only ones he would trust sufficiently to make such a desperate journey in such haste would have been his PA Christine O'Reilly, his senior lecturer Mr. Manchandra or one of his lecturers Mr. Nadir and Mr. Ibn Sharif." Mathew then butted in, "There might be one other-the senior surgical registrar who was on duty that day."

Olive thought to herself that it was highly unlikely that one of her new friends might be guilty and welcomed the final suggestion but determined to trust no one for the time being. Rachel then spoke again, "Before we go any further may we bring my oldest son into the picture, I think we will have to act as one in the future and I think I aught to get my family lawyer involved as well." Olive had more or less expected that response and so needed to play for time until she had thought further about the probable identity of the individual who had lured professor Black into the trap. "Of course Rachel, I might have done the same if our roles were reversed, but could you hold off for a short while to allow me to brief my friends and my brother with this latest development and then perhaps we could all convene in the offices of your lawyer as the outcome of all this will require much expert legal advice for us all. I already have a meeting arranged for next week at the RSM to bring my brother up to date as the putative threat to my well-being is a concern he needs to share." Mother and son nodded agreement and just as Olive stood up to leave Mathew held out his hand to say goodbye. "Mrs. Hathaway, please forgive my doubt and rudeness at the start but you can understand my skepticism. Mum, when you come to think of it, Olive has done us a favor. Nothing can bring back my father but if this is all true and he was murdered, we will have rescued his reputation by proving he was never guilty of scientific misconduct and we would have lifted the Jewish stigma that is associated with suicide. After all that, the University might reconsider holding a memorial service in his honor." Olive smiled at Matthew by way of accepting his apology and Rachel nodded agreement to her son and whispered proudly to her guest on the way out, "I told you he really is a nice boy just like his older brother and I am very lucky to have such sons who carry the very finest characteristics of their late father."

★★★

As soon as Olive got home she phoned Sanjay again who was of course anxious to learn the upshot of her meeting with the Blacks. Instead of responding to his enquiry she merely inflamed his curiosity by asking this question. "Sanjay, before I go any further it is important I find out the name of the senior surgical registrar who was on duty at the hospital the night Joshua Black died." She refused to budge on this and for the first time caught a note of irritation in his voice however in the end he agreed to search through the duty roster once he got back to his office the following morning. At 9.00 am on the dot on the Monday morning she received a brief e-mail from Sanjay that read:

PURCHASE DISPOSABLE MOBILE PHONE AND CALL ME ON THIS NUMBER 07775267778

ALL CALLS BETWEEN US MIGHT BE MONITORED IN FUTURE

Alarmed an intrigued in equal measure Olive popped down to the local phone shop on the Finchley Road and bought a cheap Nokia mobile with a prepaid SIM card.

On returning home she called his new number and Sanjay picked up the phone immediately. Without even enquiring who was calling he started talking. "Olive I know this is you as for the time being you are the only one who has this number. When I put the phone down I want you to use your new phone to call Ishmael and Abdullah and ask them to also buy new phones like I just instructed you. The senior registrar on duty the night Joshua Black died was a locum named Selah Al Mazri. He left the hospital with little warning two days after the body was found without leaving a forwarding address. I think we now know the *modus operandi* of Joshua Black's murderers and I think we should call a meeting with the Black family and their lawyers as there seems to be little doubt as to what went on in spite of us having only the wildest idea about the motive." "Is it alright for me to talk now whilst you

111

catch your breath?" Olive interjected. "I think there is more than enough evidence now to interest the Crown Prosecution Service whatever the motive might be and I'll set this up at a time to suit the four of us as well as the Blacks and their lawyer. Now what's all this cloak and dagger stuff with the mobile phones?"

"If our suspicions are correct and detective Ramsay's death was not accidental then indirectly you will have been implicated by his reports on file. We have secured all our computers but you are still vulnerable to eavesdropping by the spy in the sky. If your calls to us are detected then we are all implicated and lose our one big advantage of hiding below their radar. See you on Thursday at the RSM."

★★★

Chapter 14

Lunch with Arthur Templeton

A few days later, Abdullah set off for Saudi-Arabia to seek the hand in marriage of uncle Ali's youngest daughter, Fatimah, as well as calling in a favor from his ambidextrous uncle. That same day, Olive, Sanjay and Ishmael sat down with Arthur Templeton for lunch at the clubhouse of the Royal Society of Medicine, No 1 Wimpole Street, where Sanjay was a fellow. Olive had "set up" her brother by suggesting that this was a celebratory lunch at her expense to thank her two doctors for saving her life. How they had saved her life was left as an enigma for Arthur to solve.

They enjoyed terrine of duck and a hearty steak, whilst Sanjay made do with the vegetarian options. Arthur, more or less on his own, polished off a bottle of the finest club claret and insisted that he paid for the sauterne to go with the pudding. By this time they were all in a jovial mood as Arthur had regaled them with stories about his adventures in Upper Egypt whilst Sanjay tried to compete with stories about his adventures exploring the lower gastro-intestinal tract. This somewhat put Olive off her pudding. At that point, Arthur, who was no fool, turned on his sister and said, "OK Olive me dear, what's this really all about? Have you got some bad news to break to me?" Sanjay then answered on her behalf. "Professor Templeton, we three have a mystery to solve that depends on your expertise and is all highly sensitive." "My expertise? How on earth can the papyri of Elephantine Island be of any value to you? Unless you have in mind to exploit my expertise about the best vintages of Bordeaux wine to lay down."

"It is your expertise on Egyptology and Flinders Petrie that we require but to discuss this in private I've taken the liberty of booking a small conference room adjacent to the library here where we can take our coffee and speak without fear of eavesdroppers." With Arthur looking none the wiser, Sanjay then summoned the waiter to settle the account and lead them upstairs to a quiet room where a jug of coffee awaited them.

Once the room was secured and the coffee handed out Olive began the story by recounting he experience in the car park at the Brent Cross mall and its consequences.

She also explained how she had got to meet Sanjay and to reassure her brother that she had nothing to hide concerning her health. Sanjay took over and explained how he hacked into professor Black's computer, uncovered the elaborate way the hard drive had been infiltrated and the recovery of the professor's secret files. Meanwhile Arthur listened carefully with his expressive face registering the full gamut of emotions from amusement to horror. Sanjay then went on to describe the final entry in Eduard Bloch's diary, Joshua Black's two meetings with Arthur himself and finally the results of his research into the strange tale regarding Flinders Petrie's head. At that point professor Templeton couldn't contain himself any longer, fell about laughing and used a few juicy expletives to describe the character of the otherwise revered pioneer of the science of Egyptology.

Sanjay then cautioned him as to the very sensitive and to some extent dangerous nature of this knowledge before calling upon Ishmael to tell him about the contents of the Lachish file. In fairness to Arthur Templeton he listened closely to everything that was said, making notes on a pad provided by the club and only occasionally asking for clarification. Finally Olive explained her mission to Mrs. Black and her sons and how she deduced that the phone call that succeeded in leading professor Black into a trap must have come from someone he trusted on the staff of his hospital and his possible identity. As Olive ended her account, they all turned expectantly to learn what Arthur thought of their story. He thought long and hard whilst doodling on his pad and then looked up and simply stated, "I think your analysis of these extraordinary events is correct and I also think that your lives are in danger." There was a sharp intake of breath from Olive and the two surgeons as Arthur continued. "I have spent many years of my life in the Middle East and North Africa. Although my expertise is in the archaeology of Upper Egypt I have followed up my enquiries on sites linked to Assyrian, Babylonian and Palestinian ancient history. I have been arrested as a suspected spy in three countries and shared cells with many unsavory types. I have often bribed or befriended senior members of the police or security services in these countries in order to gain the permits that allowed me to explore ancient sites and export licenses to take our finds to the laboratories at UCL. Along the way I've learnt much about the politics above and beneath the surface of this troubled part of the world. What you describe has all the trademarks of an organization something like the Muslim Brotherhood and they will not tolerate any interference with their long-term plans for a global *ummat al-Islamiyah* or Caliphate. The various offshoots of Al Qaeda and ISIS have the same objectives and experience as para-military groups, but I doubt they have the resources or savvy to carry out this level of sophisticated espionage.

The meeting between the Grand Mufti and Adolf Hitler was an early part of this grand plan for the rebirth of a Caliphate and is of course public knowledge. It does not surprise me that Flinders Petrie was comfortable in this company but clearly Starkey was the odd man out. If I remember correctly there was no love lost between him and they fell out when Starkey took his team and several of the local Arab workers with him to Lachish leaving Flinders and his wife Hilda, pretty much to their own resources. Furthermore Petrie and Starkey certainly did not agree with the eugenic way of thinking. I need to check this, but if my memory serves me well, Starkey's group discovered skulls in proximity to the famous ostraca that clearly

115

belonged to ancient Israelites that went a long way in refuting Petrie's prejudices about Jews being an inferior race as judged by measurements of the cranial volume. If Starkey had made a find that might change the course of history I've no idea what it might be. As a start I will try and gain access to Starkey's archive that I think is shared by the Wellcome Institute and Olga Tufnell's archive at the Palestine Exploration Fund, as she was the archivist of the Lachish dig and in fact published their findings after Starkey's death. I'll also search the Flinders Petrie archives for clues as they are close to hand either in the museum or the department of archaeology at UCL. If I find anything of value I'll contact you three by e-mail but I also suggest we arrange to meet up again in a week's time to review the fruits of my research and plan what to do next. I've got a good friend who is also a member of the Athenaeum who happens to be a senior civil servant in the Home Office who I might tactfully sound out about this matter without implicating any of you as I truly worry about my sister's safety. Finally I would be happy to join you at the meeting with the Black family and their lawyers."

Before they broke up Sanjay offered this warning; "Please Arthur whatever you do, avoid searching on line for web pages linked to the leading protagonists in this plot and in any case carry out an antiviral sweep of your hard drive at your first opportunity. I also think that from now on all communications between us by e-mail should be coded or password protected and we must assume that Olive's original mobile number has left us vulnerable so in future we should use her disposable phone."

Once again Olive had the last word, "Coutts & Co allows me on line banking with a six number numeric code that is constantly changing and is accessed by a credit card sized device. I suggest that Mr. IT genius here," nodding at Sanjay, "set this up for us and acquires five such devices." "Who is the fifth person in the group?" asked Arthur. "Oh he is a rich Saudi Prince who is on a secret mission for us in Jeddah at this time," replied his sister. "Well that's OK then!" concluded Arthur with heavy irony.

★ ★ ★

After leaving the Wimpole Street exit of the Royal Society of Medicine Arthur turned left and walked west for six blocks enjoying the buzz and glitter of the West End all lit up in anticipation of the Christmas festivities only seven days off, before turning left into a narrow pedestrian alley and left again into an unremarkable cobble stoned cul-de-sac before stopping in front of a steel riveted door where a yellow plaque bearing the initials PEF announced that he had arrived at the entrance to the library and archives of the Palestine Exploration Fund. The modest and slightly sinister looking front door did little justice to this remarkable organization that was founded in the mid 19th Century to support Biblical archeology in the Middle East with the poorly disguised prejudice of discovering unequivocal evidence in support of the veracity of the Biblical narrative. He pressed the intercom and the steel door clicked open. He then climbed a short narrow flight of stairs to be warmly welcomed by the office staff on the mezzanine floor of the narrow building. Here a group of three bubbly ladies headed up by the archaeologist in residence, controlled access to the library above and the archives in the basement. Furthermore this office was responsible for the editing and production of the much-respected scholarly journal, the Palestine Exploration Quarterly. After some friendly joshing and an offer of a cup of coffee, professor Templeton eventually returned to the task in hand and requested permission to study the Olga Tufnell archives.

There were 12 box files but he decided to focus on the ones covering the years 1937-38. He was asked to sign the register recording all documents leaving or being returned to the cavernous archive room in the basement that stretched in darkness into the cellars of the neighboring property. He noticed in passing that the last time these files had been signed out and back in, was in May that year. He took the files into the library and dropped them on the leather top of the long single table that occupied the full length of the room. He had the place to himself and set to work methodically examining each handwritten letter all of which were carefully embalmed in transparent greaseproof paper. Olga Tufnell was a prolific correspondent and most of her letters were addressed to her mother, a few went to her father and the minority that were typewritten, were addressed to professional organizations and the patrons of the archaeological dig. Amongst the latter he noted with amusement was a formal letter of complaint against the interference and bullying of Lady Petrie who held no official role in the running of the excavations in the zone of the British Palestine Mandate, yet abused her status as the consort of Flinders Petrie to try and influence the direction of the exploration and the management of the team. This clash of personalities explained why she, together with the foreman of the native staff of laborers, Sultan Al Mazri, decided to leave Petrie in Gaza and chose to work under the charge of Starkey at Lachish. In contrast, her personal letters were beautifully written and easily read and acted as a detailed diary of her experiences in Palestine. Eventually he reached a letter dated January 12th 1938 that like many were written on stationary bearing the name Hotel Fast and an image of the "Dome of the Rock" Jerusalem. This was the letter he was hoping to find and the more he read the faster beat his heart whilst the other epiphenomena of adrenaline release caused him to loosen his collar as if to let out steam. Anyone observing his appearance would have worried about an impending apoplexy but old professor Templeton was in fact in fine fettle enjoying the excitement rarely experienced when his autonomic nervous system told him he was on to a very important historical find. The letter read as follows:

Hotel Fast Jerusalem
January 12th 1938

Dearest Ma,

Terrible news! James Starkey was murdered two days ago. I begged him not to travel to Hebron at night. Its all bandit country round here. He seemed a bit overwrought before he left because of a remarkable new find at the bottom of the mountain of skulls that I mentioned in one of my letters last year. Anyway this particular find, that I'm honor bound not to disclose to anyone, he judged to be of extreme historical importance as well as being particularly sensitive in the current political climate. However he hinted that it had something to do with the 19th "Lachish letter" that Flinders had elected to add to his private collection. Only James, Sultan Al Mazri, our foreman, and myself know of its existence and James was suspicious that he couldn't trust Sultan any more and suspected he was in cahoots with Flinders. Anyway he told Sultan that he was taking it to the new museum in Jerusalem but confided in me that he was going to hide it until the political crisis in the Middle East and the threat of war with Germany was over. So on Sunday evening he suddenly declared that he was off and refused to listen to my words of caution. His mutilated body with bullet holes in his back was found the following morning on the road to Hebron. Just before he left he slipped a note into my hand that was supposed to give me a clue to the hiding place that only I would be able to decode. I can't make head nor tail of it at the moment but I enclose a copy for you for safekeeping.

We are all very downcast and I've given everyone a week's leave. He will be buried in the Methodist churchyard in Jerusalem after the inquest sometime next week.

I'm too upset to write any more just now but I'll describe the outcome of the inquest in my next letter.

Very much love to you and Daddy,

Ever yours

Olga

After reading and copying this out in his notebook Arthur took a deep breath and picked the buff colored envelope that accompanied the letter. It was addressed to Mrs. B Tufnell, 14 Queensbury Place, London, S.W.7 and carried a red postage stamp of the Palestine Mandate bearing the profile head of King George VI. He slipped his finger inside in the faint hope that it might contain Starkey's cryptogram but was hardly surprised to find it empty. He was just about to pack up and closed the files when the franking mark over the stamp caught his eye. Although the mark was faded by age there was no doubt that it did not correspond to the date on the letter in fact it appeared to have been misfiled from the year 1937. He went back to the box carrying the 1937 archive and sure enough there was a near identical envelope with the King's head defaced by the franking mark 13/01/1938. As he gingerly slipped his finger inside his heart skipped a beat. Almost adherent to the front surface of the envelope was a thin slip of what looked like rice paper. He pulled out the delicate slip of paper with a pair of forceps that he used for handling scraps of papyrus or parchment that he always carried along with pens and pencils in the breast pocket of his jacket and carefully smoothed it out on the flat surface of the 1938 box file. It was indeed some kind of coded message in very fine writing that at some points had perforated the paper. Taking out a small magnifying glass from amongst the tools of his trade that he carried amongst his bulky person he set about transcribing the message to his notebook.

~ Complex 21
System B
E wall
QB6

He had no idea what that meant but he had spent his life decoding runes and hieroglyphics from ancient times so why should an inscription from merely 77 years in the past cause him too much trouble. He then deftly returned the scrap of paper to the envelope, tidied up and carried the box files back to the office. On signing out to confirm the return of the files his eyes wandered up to the line above and he nearly passed out on reading the name above his signature, Saleh Ibn Abdullah Al Mazri. "Has someone walked over your grave?" Asked Felicity the young lady who was gathering up the files with genuine concern in her voice, as once again professor Templeton's labile autonomic system flagged up his emotions. "No" replied Arthur " but I certainly think that I've disturbed someone else's burial place". With that enigmatic response he staggered to the door and made his way back to his office welcoming the blast of arctic air blowing down Wigmore Street from the east.

Chapter 15

Lunch at the Athenaeum and
Tea with the Blacks

January 2016

After professor Templeton arrived back at his office and calmed down a bit he decided that he should share his new discoveries with his sister and then perhaps convene a meeting with his co-conspirators before their meeting with the Black's family lawyers. Unfortunately, what with Christmas and the New Year festive season when London ground to a halt for the best part of two weeks, that meeting had been postponed until January 3rd in the New Year. He therefore had the idea of inviting Olive and her new friends for lunch at the Athenaeum the same day for a briefing session before the scheduled meeting with Rachel Black and her sons at Barnet, Peacock and Schecter's offices on the Strand, next door to Charing Cross station a short walk across Trafalgar Square from his club on Pall Mall. Using his disposable mobile phone he contacted Olive, briefly sketched out his remarkable new discoveries and agreed on the date for lunch by which time Abdullah would be back in town. The two of them agreed that the appearance of the name Al Mazri as the last person to search the Tufnell archive was too much of a coincidence and served as the "smoking gun" linking Joshua Black's death indirectly to events in Palestine 77 years ago. Olive then went on to point out that the date when the archive had last been accessed was just a few days before professor Black's body was discovered on Hampstead Heath. In the downtime between then and the New Year it was agreed that they should all keep a low profile although Arthur did intend to contact his friend from the home office. Olive then reminded her brother that they were both meeting up again for Christmas lunch at the home of Christobel and her family and that would provide another opportunity for a quiet chat. With that reminder Arthur completely forgot about calling his friend at the Home Office and once more joined the crowds admiring the spectacular Christmas illuminations along Oxford Street in a last minute rush to buy gifts for Olive, Christobel and his great niece and nephews. Feeling in a generous mood he turned south into Regent Street at Oxford Circus then into the gigantic atrium of the biggest Apple store in the land and spent a small fortune on i-pods, i-pads and associated gizmos for all. Without question he would be the most popular uncle in town on Christmas day. But then he had no children of his own and loved indulging Christobel's lot and also knowing that Olive was a covert gadget geek, he felt sure that the latest remote touch pad and keyboard would complement the new love of her life, the smart TV she had bought at John Lewis that summer.

★★★

At 12.15 on January 3rd 2016 Arthur Templeton arrived at the grand Portico of the Athenaeum club. Although the address given to the club was Pall Mall, the long side of this glistening white neo-classical rectangular building with its imposing front entrance, faced Waterloo place – one of the prettiest squares in London. It was a freezing cold day with a cornflower blue sky and a centimeter dusting of snow on the ground. Looking straight ahead he saw the only man in the street suitably equipped for this weather as embodied in the memorial statue to captain Scott of the Antarctic looking heroic in his rather primitive parka and snow boots. Captain Scott finished second in the race to the Antarctic and froze to death for his efforts. There was something endearing about the English who made heroes out of such failures, Arthur thought to himself as he mounted the steps and entered the grand vestibule of his club. He strode across the lobby and hung his heavy coat and muffler on a brass hook in the far right hand corner and ambled back to glance at the headlines in that day's copy of the Times conveniently set up on a tall lectern at the foot of the grand staircase.

On the stroke of 12.30 he turned to see his old friend professor Martin Tanner waddle down the stairs in the direction of the dining room. They greeted each other warmly. Professor Tanner was a rather disheveled old man in his early 80s who was dwarfed by professor Templeton. The old man was an emeritus professor of surgery at his university and was famous in someway for discoveries in the epidemiology of cancer the details of which Arthur had never really grasped. That aside they had a common interest in biblical archaeology with professor Tanner having had something to do with discoveries linked to the fall of the second Temple in 70 CE. These days the old man spent most of his time writing his memoires in the south library upstairs in the good company of the ghosts of Charles Dickens, Thomas Huxley and Charles Darwin. The chat was interrupted as a gust of cold wind announced the entry of another guest. A smartly dressed woman of exceptional beauty and startling green eyes embraced the old man. Professor Tanner proudly introduced his daughter to a speechless and blushing Arthur Templeton before ushering her into the member's dining room. Arthur had the fleeting impression that he had met that handsome young woman before but no sooner than that thought sprang to mind, another gust of arctic wind announced the arrival of Olive, Sanjay, Ishmael and Abdullah. Olive introduced Abdullah to her brother who was immediately disarmed by the natural charm of the Saudi princeling. Once they were unburdened of their heavy overcoats, Arthur guided them into the ornate members dining room. He was greeted with genuine affection by the *maitre d'hotel,* Philipe, who directed them to a pre-booked round table by the eastern wall overlooking Waterloo place that was set for a party of five.

Once the guests had been provided with menus Arthur busied himself taking their orders and writing them down on a docket according to the traditions of the club, before handing it to a waiter hovering discretely nearby. The wine waiter then turned up allowing Arthur to show off by indulging in a little banter and a discussion on the best red Burgundy that might take the chill out of their bones. A 2009 Moulin de Vent was chosen and with much theatricality, tasted and approved by the host. Once left to themselves they all started talking at once. Arthur raised his right hand and with a twinkle in his eyes announced, "Dear friends, first, club rules, no talking business at lunch in the members dining room. Next, these walls have ears and are something like the whispering gallery at St Paul's Cathedral. Don't look now but that lonely old man sitting behind me in deep concentration reading his menu used to be head of MI5 and the two gentlemen sitting at the table in earnest conversation just behind Olive, *don't* turn round my dear, are the Egyptian Ambassador to the Court of St James and one of his senior diplomats. I suggest we stick to the weather and discuss the quality of the food and wine. I have booked the card room for a private tête-à-tête after lunch."

They nodded agreement and in fact enjoyed the hour chatting about the weather, abysmal; the food, not bad but a bit like school dinners; and the wine, superb. Although as Sanjay, Ishmael and Abdullah didn't drink it was left to Arthur to take on that burden on behalf of them all. After lunch they ordered coffee and mint chocolates to be sent up to the card room on the first floor. The room was musty and slightly damp and the green leather armchairs distinctly uncomfortable but at least they knew they wouldn't be disturbed once the coffee had been delivered and they had about 90 minutes before the meeting on the Strand. Arthur started off with his account of the extraordinary findings in the Olga Tufnell archives and they all shared a shiver down their spines, which was unrelated to the draft slipping through the cracks under the card room windows, at the mention of the name of the last person to access the archive. They all agreed that the timing was right and that this event was in someway responsible for triggering the murder of Joshua Black. They were also all anxious to see the copy of the Starkey cryptogram but no one had the vaguest clue to what it might mean.

The next to report was Abdullah who informed them triumphantly that he had just got engaged and that they were all invited to his wedding in Jeddah next winter. "Why wait so long?" asked Sanjay. "Well two reasons", replied Abdullah. "First none of you could survive the weather between April and September and secondly because by then my father's donation to establish a new department of surgical oncology will be in place, Sanjay will be appointed a full professor and he will appoint me as a senior lecturer and consultant surgeon so that I could keep my new wife in the comfort we offer our servants in Saudi Arabia!" After much laughter and joshing he turned deadly serious and the story he delivered convinced them that they were way out of their depth.

" After the ceremonies associated with the betrothal between me and Fatimah, I arranged to meet uncle Ali at his Office in the Exxon Oil Company. He assumed that this was a meeting to discuss Fatimah's dowry. He was so shocked when I explained my plans to blackmail him with my knowledge about his, how shall I put it, his sexual peccadilloes, that I almost felt sorry for the old man. However, when I put it to him that it related to a conspiracy against Saudi interests by a sleeping cell in London, he blustered a bit but agreed to cooperate as a good patriotic citizen. Saving face in this way made it a little easier for us to work together although, had he been found out saving his head, might have taken higher priority. I provided him with the key words that we think make up the algorithm and within 24 hours he came back to me by a coded email exchange, very excited and suggested a second meeting in his office. Within an hour we were sitting face to face again. He explained that the task was much easier than he had expected as the Mabahith was already monitoring some inexplicable traffic that carried at least three of the names we had suggested but with that limited amount of information even their limitless resources were insufficient to narrow things to less than 50,000 cyber-sphere dialogues. With the complete set of names they were indeed able to build an algorithm to secretly monitor the suspect cluster of names and narrow down the search. In fact the results came fast and furious and yet the final nexus they uncovered was almost unbelievable. Paradoxically the head of his division was so pleased with uncle Ali that he has been promoted to section head of the service in London were one of the nodes in this conspiratorial web seems to lurk." Everyone then spoke at the same time with Arthur's voice booming over them all, "For God sake Abdullah tell us about the whereabouts of the other nodes as I can't stand the suspense any longer!" Abdullah repeated his wolverine grin and continued, "Not surprisingly one node was in the central offices of VEVAK, the Iranian intelligence Ministry in Tehran, linking with a notorious cell of Hezbollah in an underground complex in the south of Lebanon. But the real surprises were the links with nodes in Crown Heights in Brooklyn New York and a roving wireless receiver in an apparently unpopulated barren area in the south western sector of the Palestine Authority, located south of Route 1 that runs eastwards out of Jerusalem and route 90 that runs north south alongside the west bank of the Dead Sea. None of which can have anything in common with a wireless receiver in of all places, Stamford Hill London, the centre of the web."

Before they had time to absorb or speculate about these new observations, Arthur interrupted to remind them that they had an appointment in 20 minutes in the Strand with just time for a comfort break and a brisk walk across Trafalgar

Square in the direction of Charing Cross Station. However, they were unanimous in agreeing not to say anything about the Olga Tufnell file or the links to the Iranian intelligence service. They were yet to figure out how best to handle such dynamite whilst Abdullah thought it might be safest to leave the Mabahith and VEVAK to slug it out amongst themselves whatever it was all about.

* * *

As they stepped outside the club the weather had turned for the worse and a thick haze obliterated the view of the London Eye across Horse Guards Parade and Whitehall to the southeast. As they walked across the pedestrian plaza on the north side of Trafalgar Square a bitter easterly wind was blowing right into their faces. They hunkered down into their scarves and heavy topcoats and by the time they arrived at 438 Strand they were covered in a dusting of snow that evaporated along with the sense of well-being they had enjoyed at lunch with Arthur Templeton at the Athenaeum. Their mood took another downturn when faced by the frigidity in the council room of Barnet, Peacock and Schecter's suite of offices.

Sitting on one side of the long table were Rachel and her two sons and on the other side three men in dark suits. The first of these men stood up to greet them and introduced himself as Seymour Barnet, senior partner. He was small and pompous man, with the red veined face of someone too partial to his liquor, wearing a three-piece suit with an old fashioned gold chain stretched across his considerable girth. He then indicated the man on his right as Aubrey Cartwright, the Black family's lawyer. Neither smiled or attempted to shake hands. The third man was an enigma. In spite of the fact he remained seated his height remained apparent. He was gaunt looking, with a lantern jaw; a grey military moustache and matching iron grey closely cropped hair. Rachel Black managed a wintery smile directed at Olive whilst her sons look down at their clenched fingers clearly embarrassed by the encounter. Obviously they had only been expecting four visitors so Seymour Barnet fussily buzzed his secretary to bring in an extra chair with his body language suggesting that this was an extreme inconvenience.

Once they were all seated and as Olive had already established some kind of rapport with Rachel Black, it seemed natural for her to take the lead.

Olive started off by introducing her brother and the three young surgeons, then set about delivering a narrative in chronological order with only an occasional glance at her notes. One by one Sanjay, Ishmael, Abdullah and Arthur, contributed their first hand accounts of the extraordinary story but, as agreed, made no mention of their new findings from the Olga Tufnell archive or the activities of the Saudi secret service. Whilst they were talking, Olive noticed that the two lawyers were busy writing notes in their yellow legal pads whilst the mysterious military looking man was writing notes in a black bound pocket book. Throughout this time much to Olive's dismay, Rachel Black was weeping softly with her head bent down whilst her two sons glared with ill disguised contempt at the five of them. In then occurred to her that the tone of the meeting was quite the opposite of what she had expected after the visit to the Black household. This wasn't an open-minded hearing but in someway they had been prejudged and the hostility of their audience was almost tangible.

They were heard out in stony silence during the best part of the hour that it took to tell their tale.

Silence then descended as the lawyers completed their notes during which time the third unnamed man stared at them with contempt. Once Seymour Barnet had completed his notes he looked up and addressing himself to Olive stated, "I've invited chief inspector Quatermaine of the counter terrorist command of the Metropolitan police force to sit in on this conference and I respect his patience for sitting quietly whilst listening to this cock and bull story." Then turning to the police officer, who by this time had risen from his chair to a commanding height of 6 foot 4 inches, " What do you make of all this chief inspector?" His response was surprising. Instead of passing any opinion he turned to Rachel Black and said, "Mrs. Black, was your late husband's bank account hacked into last year?" At this point it was obvious that the whole set up had been stage managed as Rachel Black shuffled through some bank statements before she replied, "Yes, on two occasions last summer my bank alerted me to the fact that £1,000 had been withdrawn from my husband's account without authorization," "How did the bank know these were unauthorized withdrawals?" continued chief inspector Quartermaine. "Because he was already dead by then!" sobbed Rachel. Stony faced, the policeman turned on the five outsiders and in an dry and emotionless voice began to tear them apart in the most vulgar terms, "Mrs. Hathaway I can find some forgiveness for you as a batty old lonely widow with nothing better to do." At this point, with difficulty, Olive succeeded in restraining Arthur from jumping up and involving himself in grievous bodily harm, although in spite of Arthur's intimidating bulk he looked no match for the lean and fit looking chief inspector. "As for you three qualified surgeons, I've no idea what kind of fantasy world you occupy, you're not living in Bongo Bongo land now and God help the NHS if they have to rely on the likes of you. As for professor Templeton, you must be suffering from the early stages of dementia. Your whole conspiracy theory is based on the assumption that only some foreign power with enormous resources would be able to insert the keystroke virus into someone's hard drive. The villains out there raiding our bank accounts all employ professional hackers and this particular virus that's deeply embedded in some jpeg file even has a name, they call it 'cash register'. It's a pity you didn't disable it before the Black family's account was raided. You then have the gall to challenge the verdict of a police enquiry and a properly conducted inquest. Of course the original

130

police procedures weren't up to scratch but in spite of the rather sloppy note keeping of the investigating officer at the time, my officers have reviewed all the evidence and can find nothing that might affect the outcome of the enquiry. Finally to suggest that the death of inspector Ramsay was anything but an unfortunate accident merely reinforces my opinion of the sick minds of conspiracy theorists." At this point Sanjay's demeanor suggested that he was about to explode but a sharp kick on the shin from Olive sitting on his right caused him to look round in astonishment. Olive fixed him with a steely glint and a short sharp shake of her head.

Chief inspector Quartermaine then sat down at it was then the turn of Aubrey Cartwright to speak.

In an oleaginous tone of voice he first addressed Rachel Black, "My dear Rachel I am so sorry to have had to put you through this terrible ordeal and I can imagine how much easier it might have been for you to believe that Joshua's death was murder rather than suicide but as you've seen the facts speak for themselves and we must thank the chief inspector for his sterling efforts." Then turning to the gang of five his tone changed to a theatrical restrained fury. "You can consider yourselves lucky that we have decided not to bring charges against you for wasting the time and resources of the police force but, in order to protect the peace of mind of the Black family, we will take out an injunction against you so that you must never approach Mrs. Black or her sons again either directly or by email or other forms of communication." Without further ado Olive and her companions were shown to the door.

As they arrived at street level the weather had worsened and an inch of snow covered the pavement. For want of anywhere better to speak they ducked down the stairs leading to the Charing Cross underground station next door. To avoid the arctic wind they instinctively turned right into a lobby with a small group of boutiques one of which happened to sell fancy dress costumes and props for magicians. For some reason

Olive thought this was strangely appropriate. They looked at each other in dismay until Olive stated in a graveyard tone, "We made no mention of our suspicions about the death of inspector Ramsay."

★★★

Chapter 16

January to March 2016

After the debacle in the offices of the Black family lawyers the group of five were left stunned and dispirited. As they were already at the entrance to the Charing Cross tube station it seemed sensible for each of them to return home. Arthur Templeton bade them farewell and made for the Bakerloo line going north towards St Johns Wood whilst the other four boarded the Edgware branch of the Northern Line. Sanjay, Ishmael and Abdullah disembarked at the Belsize Park stop to make their way back to the Royal Free Hospital leaving Olive to continue her journey alone for two more stops along the line to Golders Green. By the time she was outdoors again the snow had settled into a uniform pristine carpet about one inch in depth. Big fluffy snowflakes driven by a bitter easterly wind were beginning to build drifts against the walls outside the precincts of the station. As the H2 "Hoppa" bus was nowhere in sight she started to trudge the ten-minute walk home. Sadly her smart and sensible shoes were not waterproof and in any case, in places localized drifts of snow allowed her feet to sink into a depth where the snow began to infiltrate the gap between ankle and shoe. She felt the cold and damp climb upwards through her body as if by some capillary action. What was normally a pleasant brisk walk turned into a prolonged nightmare and by the time she placed her latchkey in the lock she was chilled to the bone and had begun to cough. She slipped off her coat and changed her shoes into her thick sheep skin Ugg slippers, turned up the central heating and made herself a hot mug of "Lemsip" sweetened with a teaspoon of honey. In spite of that over-the-counter remedy, her cough got worse and she started sweating and shaking with the rigors. As the wise widow of a skilled GP, she diagnosed herself as suffering with bronchitis or even pneumonia and texted Christobel asking her to look in that evening. By the time her daughter arrived three hours later, Olive was running a high fever and was hallucinating. Christobel phoned the family doctor who made an urgent home visit out of respect for his late colleague's wife and with a quick and slick clinical examination diagnosed pneumonia with consolidation determined via percussion, at the base of the left lung. Christobel was then sent off to the night chemist on Golders Green High Street to collect a prescription of Amoxicillin leaving Doctor Murphy to administer aspirin and to cool down the patient with tepid sponging. Christobel stayed with her mother all night leaving her husband to put the children to bed and continued where Dr. Murphy left off. By 6 a.m. Olive's fever had dropped from 101degrees to a less alarming 99 degrees and the rigors had passed and her mother appeared to be sleeping peacefully so at this point Christobel slipped out quietly and made her way home to the north side of the suburb. Dr. Murphy called round before his morning surgery at 8.30 am and was satisfied with Olive's progress but insisted that she stayed in bed for a few days and drank plenty of hot fluids whilst continuing the course of antibiotics for a full week whilst Christobel was given the task of ensuring that the fiercely independent elderly women fulfilled his instructions.

Over the next five days Olive slept fitfully and whenever her fever rose was plagued by dreadful dreams from which she woke drenched with sweat and terrified. These dreams had no discernable narrative, surrealistic or otherwise, it was if the texture or fabric of her sense of self was being distorted or torn apart. Before waking on each occasion, the sardonic expression of chief inspector Quatermaine seemed to float in front of her field of vision like the disembodied grin of the Cheshire cat from "Alice in Wonderland". On the 5th day of her sickness

134

she woke up feeling better and sat up in bed drinking a cup of tea and eating an oatmeal biscuit, the only solid food she had been able to keep down since she took to her bed. She sat there reflecting on the extraordinary sequence of events the previous week. True to her character, she analyzed the chief inspector's description of her as a "batty old lady" and felt some sympathy for that judgment by someone on the outside listening to her tale of murder most foul and a conspiracy involving some foreign terrorist organization. She repeated to herself a line from one of Robert Burns' poems, "*O, wad some Power the giftie gie us, to see oursels as others see us!*" She then decided to turn the tables on the chief inspector and suddenly saw him in a completely different light.

This man was no fool, the gleam in his eye of bright intelligence matched her own, so there was little doubt left in her mind that the rudeness of his words and the slip of his tongue was deliberate, perhaps meaning to capture her attention or to deliberately mislead someone at the table.

She chewed this over for a few minutes before sending a coded text on her disposable mobile phone to her brother and the three wise men. "When shall we three meet again, in thunder lightening or in rain?"

★★★

On their arrival back at the Royal Free Hospital the three surgeons walked up nine floors to the department of surgery partly for the exercise and partly to avoid the terrible delays and unseemly crushes of the lifts from the main concourse. It had often been said that whoever designed the software that was meant to run the eight lifts in the hospital tower block was also likely to been the same genius tasked with designing the IT system for a paperless patient records initiative, as both had come close to driving the hospital to a standstill. It was only when the medical staff threatened to go on strike that the IT system for the records was abandoned, the £25M costs of the debacle was cleverly disguised as a efficiency saving scheme and the man responsible promoted to be director of information responsible for the three biggest teaching hospitals in the University College group. Having won that battle the medical staff chose to make a virtue out of necessity and used the stairs instead of the elevators as part of a keep fit campaign. On arriving breathless on the 9th floor, Ishmael and Abdullah turned left to the wards to check out the patients for the operating lists of the next day, the first of the new year, whilst Sanjay turned right to his office to set to work on the backlog of emails and correspondence that would no doubt have flooded in that day, as everyone had returned to work after nearly two weeks enforced idleness. He was right on that score and it took him until 9 p.m. that evening to deal with just the urgent material. He had already warned his wife that he would be late back for dinner but he still paused for a moment whilst stretching his aching body before setting off home. All this time the image of the Starkey cryptogram had kept floating up from his subconscious. Sanjay prided himself on his mental agility in solving riddles and deciphering crossword puzzles, but this one defeated him. He couldn't begin to get a purchase on any internal logic of a code or play on words central to most of the puzzles he could crack within 20 minutes. He then concluded that the solution would have to be context or geography dependent. He then set off for a late dinner where he would have to fake a voracious appetite so as not to disappoint his wife, although to tell the truth he was still full of the stodgy vegetarian lunch he had eaten at the Athenaeum.

★★★

After completing their ward rounds, Ishmael and Abdullah retired to the seminar room in the department of surgery and helped themselves to coffee from the machine that offered freshly ground coffee fuelled by a hopper full of coffee beans.

For some reason or another, like every cup of coffee in any hospital in the United Kingdom, it tasted foul but at least gave them the caffeine kick to keep them going. They were in no hurry to go home as they were both on call and in any case Ishmael was waiting for the result of a CT scan before deciding to operate on a young woman with severe pain and tenderness in the right iliac fossa. This was a notorious trap and only the uninitiated would assume the diagnosis to be appendicitis. From the rather shifty way the patient answered his questions about her periods he began to think this might be an ectopic pregnancy and when she flew into a temper tantrum of denial, after he asked whether she could be pregnant, he was pretty sure that his hunch was correct.

Once they had both settled down in the comfy cinema style seats of the mini auditorium balancing their coffee cups on the fold out desk tops, Ishmael turned to Abdullah with a grin and with a put on thick oriental accent declaimed, "Welcome oh Sultan from Bonga Bonga land to my harem, please help yourself to the concubines of your choice!" Abdullah was not amused and replied, " Piss off Ishmael, I'm still smarting from the insulting language of that bastard police officer. How dare he speak like that to us and how come we meekly accepted the insults and left with our tails between our legs?"

" You're right of course old friend but there was something else going on here that I didn't understand and there was also something in the expression and body language of Olive that made me zip my mouth. Leaving that aside Abdullah I've been thinking hard about the nexus of wire taps you described and I've come up with a theory that might explain those links. The connection between Tehran and Southern Lebanon, the zone virtually controlled by Hezbollah is self-evident. You may not know this but the connection between Crown Heights Brooklyn and Stamford Hill in north London is also self evident. Both are major centres of ultra Orthodox Jews also known as Charedi. My initial reaction was that no way in the world could these two groups have common cause but then it occurred to me that the old aphorism might apply here, my enemy's enemy is my friend. Believe it or not there is an extreme Charedi sect, known as *Netueri Karta*, who are antipathetic to the State of Israel because the founding fathers were secular and were too impatient to wait for the arrival of the Messiah. They go so far as to campaign against the State as a creation of the devil and can be seen joining in anti Israel demonstrations in Trafalgar Square. I've even seen a picture of two of their leaders meeting the Ayatollah *whatsisname* in Tehran attending a conference on Holocaust denial. I wouldn't put it past these buggers to collaborate with the Islamic Republic in an attempt to destroy the country." "You know Ishmael you're not so stupid as I thought you were," joshed Abdullah in return "but can you account for the roving wireless receiver in the Dead Sea valley? I forgot to mention that this source only squirts out signals in millisecond bursts so it has been difficult to accurately locate their area of activity by triangulation." " I admit I can't figure that one out but I think I know a man who could" "And who might that be?" Replied Abdullah suddenly looking very alert. "My cousin Rafi who works as a junior attaché at the Israeli embassy in Knightsbridge and with your permission I intend to consult with him." Abdullah looked startled at first then thought for a moment before responding, "Using the same principle of my enemy's enemy is my friend I think our two countries have common cause and equal existential fear of those Shia lunatics in Iran developing nuclear capability. You have my blessing Effendi but I suggest for the time being we keep this a secret between the two of us" Just as Ishmael nodded his assent a young lady house officer bustled in with the report of the CT scan. He read the report whilst smiling to himself then turning to the house officer ordered her to cross match two units of blood and book an operating theatre and anaesthetist as soon as possible. As he left the room he called out to his friend, "it's another one of those immaculate conceptions but this time it's lodged in the right Fallopian tube."

Arthur Templeton arrived home at his bachelor pad in a modernist apartment block only a short walk from St Johns Wood tube station, in a foul mood. He was still fretting that he failed to stand up for his beloved sister's reputation yet at the same time bewildered by her tight lipped head shaking and shin kicking he had endured. His mood was not helped by the fact that his shoes had leaked on the short walk from the tube station to his flat one block away from Lords Cricket ground. On entering his cozy but disorganized modest home, he changed his shoes and socks for a pair of warm slippers, threw off his topcoat and jacket and replaced them with a cardigan and an old fashioned smoking jacket. He didn't smoke in fact but shared something in common with Sherlock Holmes under similar circumstances. Sherlock Holmes when faced with a difficult set of clues to unravel, would slip on his smoking jacket and smoke two pipe's full of tobacco. Arthur in his turn would drink two fingers of one of his favorite single malt whiskeys. Because he was cold and dispirited and wasn't sure what to make of the day, he thought it called for a two drams of his *Bruichladdich* 19 Year Old – Coopers Choice. He settled down in front of his gas fuelled coke effect fire, pored his scotch and gazed at the bottle as if for inspiration. As the familiar warm tones of ground almonds, cocoa and oak, teased his palate, he began to enjoy a sense of calm and purpose replace his previous mood of agitation and anger. After the first draft he looked again at the pale amber liquor and enjoyed the play of light from the flames of the gas fire that appeared to set the contents of the bottle alight. He turned the bottle lovingly in his left hand whilst holding his cut glass whiskey tumbler in his right hand and nearly chocked as the last drop of the amber nectar slipped down his throat as inspiration was suddenly delivered by the bottle's label—ne-ne-ne-nineteen. He had been so carried away by finding the Starkey cryptogram that he almost forgot the other contents of the Olga Tufnell letter. She had described the 19th Lachish letter, yet there were only 18 recorded in the official records of the dig and in the inventories of the British Museum and the Harvard Institute; the 19th ostracum, if it truly existed, must have been plundered by Flinders Petrie for his personal collection. He jumped out of his chair prepared to return to his office at the museum, took one look out of the window and thought better of it, as the snow continued to fall as if with deadly intent. Settling down again in his armchair glass still in hand, he determined to follow up this clue the next day as his top priority.

On waking the following morning he put on his slippers and dressing gown and shuffled to his bedroom window from which he could see a corner of Lords cricket ground. The storm of the night before had abated and the view of the low sun reflected off the futuristic white, egg shaped commentary box, against a pale eggshell blue sky, made him catch his breath in delight. Oh how he yearned for the summer cricket season when he could wear his MCC blazer and tie with their characteristic stripes of mustard yellow and red in the amiable company of other members of the exclusive Marylebone Cricket Club. Yet at the same time this view of the birthplace of cricket made him wince at the thought of England's disastrous performance in the "Ashes" series down under in the last couple of weeks. Parking that matter deep in his subconscious he briskly returned to the unfinished business from the night before. Within 30 minutes he was already at Warren Street tube station crunching through the virgin crust of snow across Tottenham Court Road and down Gower Street past the cupola of University College London towards his office at the back of the Petrie Museum. On the way he had bought himself fresh croissants for his breakfast and he then brewed a fresh pot of coffee before seriously settling down to think. If Petrie had indeed taken the 19th "letter" for his own collection then it must be of some great importance, if he was to hide it then the best place would be amongst more than a thousand such shards of ancient pottery and where better than in his own museum. All the artifacts in the museum were now on an electronic data base open to all scholars who could access the list at any desk top computer in the museum yet he would bet good money that he would not find anything filed under "Lachish ostraca", confirming this with two clicks of the mouse. Arthur then theorized that although the labeling of the artifact would be misleading it would still be hidden in full view. If that were indeed the case then he would have to look out for something that was somehow out of place and in a category of its own. Following that line of reasoning and following nearly two hours of searching he thought he had found the odd man out.

In spite of all the years of excavation that Petrie had carried out at Elephantine Island, there was only one artifact registered with that provenance in the museum, all the others having been distributed around the British Museum, the UCL department of archaeology and some American institutions who had in part funded one or more of the seasons in Upper Egypt. The odd man out was an ostracum that was identified with the index code *UC 32053*. He found it without much difficulty amongst 30 or 40 other ones in a long sliding draw under a glass display cabinet holding materials from the New Kingdom, XVIII dynasty, Thebes. It looked quite unremarkable and beneath the layer of dust appeared the pen strokes of demotic script as one might expect for this period. He took it back to his office for closer study under a strong light with a magnifying loupe.

The layer of dust was so thick that he pealed off a medical antiseptic wipe from a handy pack he always kept nearby and started to clean the surface. To his astonishment the ancient ink started to come off with the dust confirming that the old fox had not only stolen the ostracum, but also disguised it before hiding it away. With increasing excitement Arthur delicately removed the last of the dust together with the layer of early 20th C pen strokes. Following that he was just able to make out words in Aramaic written in delicate square Hebrew letters of the type one might expect between 700 and

300BCE, in other words cotemporaneous with the other 18 Lachish letters. With great difficulty he was able to roughly translate the message that read "*...of the covenant together with... rod ...salvation beneath Golgotha*" He shot back in his chair with a sense of *déjà vu,* he felt sure he had read these words before. He wracked his brains and paced up and down his office like a caged animal reading the titles of his book collection for *aide memoires.* It came to him in a flash when his eyes fell on a book that contained photographs of all the Dead Sea scrolls together with the ancient Hebrew lettering translated into English. After searching backwards and forwards in frenzy, he finally hit upon it. It was a fragment from cave 3 found on the floor amongst other litter close to the hiding place of the Copper Scroll. The Dead Sea scroll version had been better preserved with additional words scattered here and there that made little difference to his understanding. That scrap had been dated to some time after the crucifixion and had been used as evidence that the Essenes who dwelt near the Dead Sea caves were indeed proto-Christians. Arthur chewed on this for a while when he suddenly had another flash of inspiration and laughed out loud in appreciation of his own cleverness. The place of crucifixion on that first Easter in history was a on a hill known as Golgotha from the Hebrew word for skull that was an approximation to the shape of the mound. James Starkey's important discovery was found under a mound of skulls and he must have immediately linked this finding to the writing on the shard of pottery that now sat on professor Templeton's desk. If that was indeed the explanation then how come the same words were found on a scrap of parchment deep inside cave 3 at Qumran 60 km due east of Lachish and bearing a style of script that was at least 550 years before the crucifixion of Jesus in 31 CE?

He was so excited by this find that he phoned his sister on her covert mobile number. When he got no answer from that he phoned her regular mobile number and again was invited to leave voice mail. Finally he rang Olive's home number and became really alarmed when once more he was invited to leave a message after the bleeps. In desperation he phoned his niece Christobel who answered her mobile phone at the second ring. She then went on to explain that her mother was ill in bed with suspected pneumonia. Concerned for her health yet relieved that she hadn't been kidnapped by an Islamic fanatic, Arthur locked away the "19th letter", mumbled something to the receptionist at the exit to the museum and caught the Northern line from Warren St to Golders Green pausing only to buy a bunch of grapes from the little fruit stall outside the station.

When he let himself in with his latch key he called out a cheerful hallo which was met with a grunt from Olive tucked up to her chin in bed. He was alarmed to find her flushed and shivering and confused.

★★★

Ten days later on the first Sunday afternoon once Olive felt up to it, the three young surgeons together with her brother met at the Hathaway cottage on Hampstead Way. After tea and dainty smoked salmon sandwiches, they began to debrief each other. Arthur felt a sense of triumph after pulling an ostracum out of his capacious jacket pocket like a rabbit out of a hat and then captivating his little audience with the details of his search, the translation of the Aramaic text and the as yet unsolved mystery about a similar passage of text being found in one of the Dead Sea scrolls.

He had to confess that even if he was right, then who in heaven or in hell could have hidden the message whatever it was, under the pyramid of skulls and survived to tell the tale?

Ishmael then recounted his theory to explain the nexus between the Iran, Lebanon and two centres noted for being populated by extreme orthodox Jewish sects. He said nothing about his visit to his cousin at the Israeli embassy. Olive had little new to offer other than the fact that there was something dodgy about chief inspector Quartermaine that did little to advance the understanding of the situation they found themselves in. "So has anyone any idea what on earth we should do next short of dropping the whole matter?" she concluded. The five of them hung their heads and studied their feet totally bereft of ideas when suddenly Ishmael's phone started to shake and buzz indicating an incoming text message. He lifted his i-phone from its pouch on his belt and clicked it on. His faced drained of blood and reflected back the light from his smart phone the colour of stainless steel. "What's the matter, Ishmael?" They asked in unison. "It appears that what we do next has been suggested by a third party. We have been invited for coffee with the deputy head of security at the Israeli embassy. His name is Yossi Goldfarb but I can vouch for the fact that he is the station chief of Mossad in the UK".

Chapter 17

A morning with Mossad

When the group learnt of Ishmael's visit to his cousin at the Israeli embassy that had provoked the invitation for coffee and biscuits, the recriminations followed fast and furious but were equally quickly extinguished. First Ishmael reminded the others that he was a citizen of the State of Israel and a reservist in the IDF therefore he had a duty to inform his country's agents of any threat to security of his homeland; secondly he mentioned that he had consulted Abdullah who shared this viewpoint and finally he asked whether anyone had a better idea because he had come to the conclusion that there was nowhere else to go. After a short discussion they agreed to accept the invitation but to follow Olive's guidance on how much of their knowledge, above and beyond that uncovered by Abdullah, they would share depending on how the "coffee morning" progressed. After all it was Olive who set them off in the search for a conspiracy surrounding the death of professor Black and she was more than ever determined to demonstrate that she was not the batty old lady described by a chief inspector of special branch. So the following Sunday morning they presented themselves clutching their passports at the security gate inside the Israeli embassy just off Kensington High Street. To get that far they had to run the gauntlet of a mob of young men and women many of who were wearing checkered keffiyehs although few looked as if they were of Middle Eastern stock. Many of them also carried placards promoting an academic boycott of Israel, so it was easy to deduce that they were students at the School of

Oriental and African Studies at the university of London with more important matters on their minds than attending classes.

They handed in their mobile phones, showed their passports as ID and then passed through an airport like screening device before entering a surprisingly gracious lobby with a grand staircase a vestige of the past when the embassy had been a mansion belonging to an Edwardian railway magnate. Once inside that were warmly welcomed by Ishmael's look alike cousin Rafi, and shown into a comfortable sitting room that was laid out with cups and saucers a thermos jug of coffee and Lebanese pastries. Within a few minutes Rafi returned with a short stocky gentleman of about 50 years of age wearing smart but casual clothes. His open neck shirt displayed a bull neck and his short-sleeved shirt exaggerated his bicep muscles. The deeply suntanned shaven head, completed the picture of a senior Mossad agent from central casting however the big surprise was when he introduced himself with a perfect educated English accent. His friendly smile and charming manner put them all at ease and he paid particular attention to Olive obviously seeing straight through her cloak of invisibility. The only one who seemed Ill at ease was Abdullah whose country had never recognized the State of Israel.

Once the formalities were complete and everyone had been served coffee and pastries, Yossi Goldfarb opened the conversation.

"Mrs. Hathaway, gentlemen, thank you so much for taking the trouble to visit us at such short notice, but what I've already learnt from Rafi here, is potentially of enormous significance to the security of my country and as you will soon learn, to the United Kingdom as well.

I noted your surprise at my accent, well it shouldn't surprise you because I was born in London and studied archaeology at Oxford University about 30 years ago before making *aliyah* to the land of Israel. In fact professor Templeton's reputation precedes him into this room as I've read his masterly textbook on the Jews of Elephantine Island" At that Arthur's chest

146

swelled and he beamed with delight. Olive meantime couldn't help but admire the social skills of this dangerous looking secret agent. "Professor Templeton knows as well as I do what a powder keg the Middle East is at the moment and I have sources who confirm that he himself has been in some sticky situations and even spent a short periods in a rather unsavory prisons for crossing the wrong line or saying the wrong thing in countries that have little time for Israel or for that matter the United Kingdom. I'm sure you all must be following the tragic story of how the Arab spring has descended into deepest winter. Libya is a failed state run by armed militia, Egypt has just avoided a civil war and is now virtually run by a military junta but with the Muslim Brotherhood cowering but not defeated. The Sinai almost a no-go zone in the clutch of Al Qaeda jihadists; Iran is close to developing its own nuclear weapons whilst supplying weapons to Hezbollah in Southern Lebanon and Hamas in Gaza with the aim of destroying Israel in a three pronged attack. Whilst against this background the so-called Islamic state is running riot as a multi-headed serpent in the badlands at the Syrian and Iraqi borders whilst extending its grasp into northern Nigeria. Even Tunis, the birthplace of the Arab Spring has enjoyed visitations from ISIS. This very day our navy in the Red Sea intercepted a ship flying the Panamanian colors, discovering a large supply of sophisticated missiles with a range of over 100 miles en route to Gaza from Iran. Iraq is falling apart again, Jordan appears stable yet our agents there tell us that the masses of refugees from the disastrous civil war in Syria also conceal many jihadists sympathetic to the Palestinian plight not to mention the Palestinians and their descendants who have been living in refugee camps in Jordan since they fled their homes in 1948.

The Kurds have emerged as major players with an eye on a homeland for themselves that might extend across the borders into Syria, Iraq and Turkey.

Paradoxically (this with a nod to Abdullah) the only major player in this very dangerous neighborhood that we can trust is Saudi Arabia, and this is not because we love each other but because we have equal fear and much to lose if Iran and her client terrorists groups have their way. The West having failed miserably in Syria, are now somewhat preoccupied with events in Eastern Europe and looking the other way. All sorts of unlikely alliances are being forged in these multi-faceted battles, even to the point that even Mossad has difficulty with deciding who are our friends and who are our enemies. For these reason any hint of the building of a coalition amongst these fighting factions, who see Israel as a common enemy, is of great importance to our tiny nation State, and you my dear friends may have stumbled upon something whose importance you could not have imagined." At this point Yossi Goldfarb paused in his long speech to catch his breath and take a drink of coffee whilst holding up a finger to indicate he didn't want any interruption at this juncture.

"Our security services have also been monitoring the four way coded wireless chatter between Tehran, Lebanon, London and New York but we had not picked up the shorts bursts of activity in the West Bank close to the Dead Sea, kindly detected by our brethren in Jeddah. This really worried us as it suggested that the epicenter of this activity is very close to home and a mere 30 miles from our major centers of population. The links between the Islamic Republic and Hezbollah in Southern Lebanon I have already explained and the new links with the dense population base of Charedi Jews in North London and Brooklyn New York, are intriguing and suggest, as you rightly deduced Ishmael, the finger print of *Naturei Karta*. What frightens us is that even amongst this sect there are extremists who go beyond denying the right of Israel to exist as a Jewish homeland but find common purpose with Iran in advocating its destruction. You can understand therefore why we have become a little nervous at the detection of a fifth node in the nexus so close to our borders at a time when the whole of the Middle East is close to melt down. How we came to discover this evil axis is our business but how

148

you, a bunch of amateurs, stumbled on it truly intrigues me as your route to this discovery might contain the missing piece of the jigsaw that would allow us to see the whole picture. Please enlighten me." At that point Goldfarb looked directly at Olive with a twinkle in his eye almost as if he was flirting with her. Olive felt herself blush as she was overcome with mixed emotions. After a moments hesitation she returned his steady gaze and with a hint of steel in her voice replied. "Mr. Goldfarb, thank you very much for that fascinating account of your version of events in the Middle East. I have to confess that I find the whole historical tangle of the Israel/Palestine conflict very difficult to unravel in my mind. There is much I have learnt to admire about your State and I for one have no time for those who demand an academic boycott of Israel making a nuisance of themselves nearby in Kensington High Street. I take no sides in this complex geo-political conflict but like you my prime loyalty is to my country. I understand why you feel threatened by I see no reason why I should share all my knowledge with you unless I thought it might involve the security of the United Kingdom. It came as a surprise that Ishmael had shared with you the secrets that Abdullah learnt from his uncle in Jeddah but then he is an Israeli citizen, however even he agreed that the route that lead us to this discovery was not necessarily relevant to your cause. I'm afraid that my brother and I, together with Sanjay have persuaded Ishmael and Abdullah to provide you no further information unless we can be convinced that it serves my country as much as it serves yours." After that scolding from an elderly English widow the tough Mossad agent slapped his thighs with delight and burst out laughing. " Mrs. Hathaway, Olive if I may? You are wonderful and your response was exactly as wagered by my contact in the foreign office. So having prepared for this contingency I've asked my British counterpart to make himself available to persuade you to share all your knowledge with us. Rafi would be so good as to invite Commander Quartermaine to join our meeting."

Olive, her brother Arthur and the three young surgeons, turned their heads to the door of an adjoining room as one and all five jaws dropped south at the same instant and made as if to stand up from their seats as the senior police officer entered the room. However on this occasion all 6 foot 4 inches of Scotland Yard authority was relaxed in demeanor and smiling ear to ear. He flapped his hand to urge them to be seated before helping himself to a cup of coffee and settled comfortably in a vacant armchair. " Lady and gentlemen, I believe you have already met my dear friend Alan Quartermaine, recently promoted from Chief Inspector to Commander at the Met." Said the bull necked Mossad man with a chuckle. Before any of them had a chance to reply, the senior police officer quickly chipped in. "Mrs Hathaway, Gentlemen, I owe you all a sincere apology, please forget the unkind words I said about you in the lawyers office. You Mrs. Hathaway are one of the shrewdest and wisest women I have ever met and your brother Arthur is a credit to his profession and has for sometime been on our radar for recruitment to a special unit we have in mind. As for you three medical gentlemen, we know a lot more about you than you may credit, please forget my insults, the NHS is much in debt to you and your adoptive country takes pride in your achievements. I hope by now you will have guessed the meaning of the little charade I was playing in the offices of Mrs. Black's lawyers. However before I can go any further I must ask you each to sign a copy of this document as I'm about to share with you some very sensitive information. People working with sensitive information are commonly required to sign a statement to the effect that they agree to abide by the restrictions of the Official Secrets Act. This is popularly referred to as 'signing the Official Secrets Act'. Signing this has no effect on which actions are legal, as the act is a law, not a contract, and individuals are bound by it whether or not they have signed it. Signing it is intended more as a reminder to you that you are all under an obligation not to repeat what you are about to learn outside the group within these four walls. Before doing so let me reassure you that, using the very words of Mrs. Hathaway I picked up whilst eavesdropping on your conversation next door, what I'm going to ask of you does indeed serve the security of the United Kingdom." With a flourishing of pens and a rustling of papers, five pairs of eyes studied the document as if their lives depended on it and after about five minutes signed the dotted line almost in unison before looking up expectantly in the direction of Commander Quartermiane who cleared his throat and continued. " Mrs. Hathaway, Olive if I may, I couldn't help noticing your body language when I let drop the fact that we didn't believe that DI Ramsay's death was murder knowing full well that the subject hadn't been raised by you. This was intentional with the idea of sending out a signal. I'll return to that matter in a moment. The reason for my unkind charade was to avoid reopening the inquest on the death of professor Black and as a result bringing up the evidence in favor of it being murder, however cruel that might be in the short-term for the Black family. We have good reason to believe that Joshua Black's death is linked to a major ongoing and covert investigation of a cell of Islamic jihadists in London. As you know London has become a viper's nest of such unwelcome guests to the extent that our American counterparts call it Londonisthan. We have to thank the idiotic political correctness of our immigration officers at London Heathrow for that. We were closing in on one of the leaders of this cell, a Dr. Al Mazri, when the killing took place and when we learnt that this young surgeon was working for the deceased, our suspicions were raised even though we could think of no motive. However when we learnt of the death of DI Ramsay under suspicious circumstances and then realized he was the officer investigating the death of Joshua Black, we instigated the paper trail that led us to believe that we had a mole high up in the ranking of the Met. This made it all the more serious as it suggested that the integrity of our whole program of counterintelligence against Islamic terrorists that I head up, might be at risk. Yet we still have no clue as to how professor Black could be linked into some plot involving these enemies of the State.

You now bring us new evidence that supports some of our own intelligence that Al Mazri and his cell, might be linked to some unholy alliance between Iran, Hezbollah, and an extremist group of Charedi Jews operating in Stamford Hill in my own back yard, who together might be plotting the destruction of Israel, one of our most important allies in the Middle East. So yes it seems we all have common purpose. Thank you Mr. Kadir for bringing this matter to our attention and thank you Mr. Ibn Sharif for sharing your intelligence with us. I can reassure you that you have acted correctly and my colleagues in Jeddah, although embarrassed by the leak, will treat you fairly should you return home. Now Olive, Gentlemen, please share with us the intelligence that allowed you to arrive at out own conclusions and how this could have lead to the professor's untimely death, start from the beginning because Mr. Goldfarb did not have the pleasure of sitting in with us at the office of Rachel Black's lawyers,"

Before responding Olive and friends put their heads together in a huddle and after a short period of muttered conversation, during which time the two anti-terrorist officers smiled at each other and shared a mutual wink, raised their heads and nodded to Olive to begin. She then launched into the whole story in chronological sequence with meticulous attention to detail and clarity of speech that reflected a well organized and highly tuned intelligence. At every step along the way wherever appropriate she invited one of her collaborators to deliver their part in unraveling the plot. Throughout this dissertation that took more than an hour Goldfarb and Quartermaine listened intently without interruption and without taking a single note. Olive had little doubt that the whole disclosure was being taped and transcribed. Once they had finished their audience of two remained silent for a few minutes deep in thought until Alan Quartermaine broke in to ask permission to fill his pipe. "This is a remarkable story and I'm at a loss on how best to express my admiration to the five of you. Like Sherlock Homes I think better with a pipe in my mouth so I hope you'll forgive me if I light up." They all nodded in assent whilst the Commander performed a complex ritual of filling and lighting his pipe, filling the room with pale blue and pleasantly spicy smoke and then appeared to go to sleep. After a few minutes whilst they looked on in disbelief and Yossi Goldfarb smiled back at them in tolerant good humor, Commander Quartermaine suddenly sat up straight, knocked out his pipe in a handy ashtray and started to speak again.

"Thank you for tolerating my tobacco habit but it helps me to think clearly and I believe I see the whole picture as it is today but I have little idea where it is all heading although Armageddon might be on the cards. Thanks to the translation of Joshua Black's grandfather's diaries, we can start the story from the meeting in Hitler's office in 1937 and relate that back to the Olga Tufnell archives.

Clearly the source of the row between Starkey and the others was the morphometric measurements of the ancient Judean skulls that refuted the pet beliefs of the eugenicists present. Starkey must have insisted on publishing the data that would deny the suggestion that the ancient Israelites, the forbears of the modern day Jews, were somehow an inferior race to the ancient Egyptians or the ancient Greeks. As a result the expedition lost a major source of funding and Petrie and Starkey would never trust each other again. Starkey's distrust was vindicated when Petrie helped himself to the 19th Lachish letter, disguised it and hid it in his museum. Arthur Templeton's decoding of that item suggests that it is the odd man out. The fact that the text resembles something uncovered in Qumran in the 1950s is way beyond my powers of deduction to explain. Starkey then makes another discovery under the pile of skulls about a year later and only Tufnell and the foreman of the dig, Al Mazri, knew what it was. Whatever it was must have been of seismic importance to one or other side because of the political situation of that time.

This was one year before the Second World War was to erupt and close in time to the troubles between the Jewish and Arab Palestinians at the time of the Mandate. Starkey suspects Al Mazri of disloyalty and hurries to hide the artifact shortly before he was murdered. That, in all likelihood was carried out by Al Mazri or his agents. The outcome of the war and the partition of Palestine in 1948 could not have been predicted at that time and whatever it was this ancient relic remains hidden to this day. 77 years later, another Al Mazri, murders Joshua Black having been recruited by a shadowy organization who had the know-how to monitor the world's traffic in the cyber sphere using an algorithm to detect the keystrokes that suggested someone else was on the path of the missing relic of Lachish. But that won't work because the spyware would not have been embedded in Black's computer unless he was already suspected, so something else must have alerted the conspirators. I would like to shelve that for the time being. Although Al Mazri, literally meaning the Egyptian, is a common name I would bet good money that our prime suspect is the grandson of the foreman at the Lachish dig who has been entrusted with the task of continuing the search for the missing object ever since it remained out of reach in the State of Israel. He also turns up at the PEF archives but misses out on the Starkey cryptogram that was only discovered by the forensic skills of professor Templeton. Having failed at that point our prime suspect decides to do away with Black because he was getting too close to the long buried secret as judged from their embedded spyware in his computer. Al Mazri and his henchmen then lure their victim to the ambulance bay outside the A&E department at the Royal Free, bundle him into a waiting van disguised as an ambulance and whisks him off to the Heath after midnight to stage his suicide. DI Ramsay reports his suspicions to someone senior he knows at the Met and for that sin is killed by a hit and run driver. There is one other detail that hints at corruption at a high level in the security service, that is the fact that the elaborate hoax that supported the suicide note's confession of scientific fraud and reported

154

to SCOPE was not followed up even after Mr. Kadir here had demonstrated that the results had been tampered with by person or persons unknown. It is possible that this one lapse will eventually lead us directly to our mole. That again I wish to shelve.

Now let me tie this all in with the recent discovery of a nexus of secret cyber communications between Iran and her proxies that appeared on our radar round about the time Joshua Black uncovered the Lachish story. We have only just found out that there is a fifth node close to the Dead Sea sending out short bursts of coded information from a mobile source in the Palestinian territories. Yossi and I have been pouring over maps and satellite pictures of this area before you came to visit and we have concluded that this area encompasses the Essene archaeological sites at Qumran and the Dead Sea caves. We conclude that Starkey's important find at Lachish must in some way be linked to the Dead Sea scrolls and there is something yet to be discovered that could tip the balance in the region and might indeed lead to a nuclear Armageddon. What this might be, we have not a clue!" Only then did Alan Quartermaine pause for breath and a drink of mineral water. Yossi Goldfarb then took this moment to intervene. "Alan, my dear friend, once again you impress me with your powers of recall and analysis, none of which I can fault but I would go even further and state than in addition to having no idea what this dangerous relic might be I have no idea what the specific threat to the security of our country might be. Unlike the UK, we have been facing existential threats to our country ever since the partition of Palestine and the 1948 war of independence. We have resisted four attempts to drive us into the Mediterranean Sea in full blown wars and multiple other attempts to undermine our integrity from civil unrest and rocket fusillades from Gaza and the south of Lebanon. We know that Iran is close to developing a nuclear ability thanks to Obama's pussyfooting around, and their leaders make no secret of their intentions to wipe us off the map. Yet there is something more sinister in the plot that seems to be unveiling itself as we speak and that is the putative collusion between our sworn enemies and members of extremist sects amongst our co-religionists. Like most members of my faith I have a very good long term memory and this takes me back to the fall of the second Temple in 70CE when more harm was done to our cause by infighting amongst the Zealots, the Sicaari, the Sadducees and the Pharisees, than by the Romans themselves who more or less stood by as our lot fell upon themselves like mad dogs. This is what really frightens me. I can therefore add to your analysis that part of the plot might be to destabilize the State from within by mobilizing our extremist Israeli Charedim some of whom are represented in the Knesset. This might provoke a civil war in the name of delegitimizing our secular state, turning their back on all we've achieved since 1948. Naturei Karta are in the business of postponing the re-creation of the Kingdom of greater Israel until the Messiah turns up when they will rebuild the third Temple in place of the Dome of the Rock and restore the priesthood and animal sacrifice. The timing of all this is critical as the Knesset has just repealed the law that young Charedi men need not serve their three years national service in the IDF whilst they are sponsored by the state to study the Talmud full time. The black hat community is not pleased and we have endured some violent demonstrations already and I predict worse is to come." "Indeed Yossi" Quatermaine continued, "but some might say, so what concern is this to the interests of the United Kingdom? To which I would reply, forgetting the plight of the Palestinians for a moment as their suffering merely provides a *causus belli* for the belligerence of Israel's hostile neighbors. Our fear concerns the Islamization of the south eastern seaboard of the Med from Latakia to Tripoli that will lead to a fight to the death between the Sunni and the Shiite sects and a closure of our trading routes as well as an escalation in oil prices throughout the Western world. Our intelligence suggests that the sideshow of the Israel/Palestine conflict is a distraction from the main event plotted in Teheran in league with Assad and the Syrian ruling elite, Hezbollah and Hamas. Teheran has persuaded the USA that they have a common enemy with ISIS as a result the sanction on Iran has been lifted and Iran has been allowed to continue its work on developing nuclear energy. Our agents have reason to believe that covertly ISIS and Iran share the common goal in establishing a global Caliphate but one piece of the jigsaw is missing. What is the cement that will bind together their disparate religious ideologies? We suspect that the conspiracy we've unearthed is something to do with this missing link. The fact that one of the groups involved in this plot hangs out in my patch is the least of our security services' concerns. This matter is of such importance to us that I was advised by the foreign office to brief the Prime Minister. By chance she has just returned from Israel where she delivered a speech to the Knesset. She is aware of this meeting and suggested I quote these words from her speech when soliciting your help in uncovering this plot." Quatermaine then referred to a note in his little black book for the first time and read; " *I share your deep skepticism and great concern about Iran. I am not starry eyed about the new regime. A nuclear-armed Iran is a threat to the whole world – not just to Israel but all our allies, Britain will ensure that is never allowed to happen. Islamist extremism is a warped and barbaric ideology that tries to set our societies against each other by radicalizing young Muslims all across the world including London the capital city of the United Kingdom*".

"What do you mean by soliciting our help in uncovering this plot?" piped out Olive in a quiet voice.

"Simply by reporting to us this morning has been of enormous help to our efforts but having listened to you all very carefully you may be able to help us much more than I originally considered. Before I go any further may I have another quick look at the Starkey cryptogram that professor Templeton copied out from the original?" Arthur rummaged in his notes and dutifully drew out the slip of paper and handed it to Commander Quartermaine. The policeman studied it carefully for a while shook his head and handed it across to the Mossad agent. Goldfarb repeated that exercise and turned enquiring eyes to his guests. "Can you guys make any sense of this?" Arthur speaking on behalf of the others confessed that they had no idea of its meaning and had not a clue where to start with deciphering the enigmatic scrap left by James Starkey. Quartermaine then continued. "The fact that none of us can even begin to make sense of this coded message in spite of our combined prodigious deductive skills suggest that out of context, we are missing the key and my guess is that the key is somehow linked to the topography of the area where the events of 1938 took place. If this is the case you could help us further by taking a short vacation all expenses paid in the land of Israel." This suggestion was greeted by a sphinx like smile from Yossi Goldfrab, a muted squeal from Olive and spluttering indignation from Arthur Templeton whilst the three young surgeons leaned forward with intense interest carved across their faces. "Please hear me out and postpone judgement. Let me assure you we would not be asking you to do anything illegal or put yourselves in harms way, but it turns out, that apart from Mr. Ibn Sharif for obvious reasons, the rest of you make for a perfect coterie of under-cover agents with the intelligence and commitment to decipher Starkey's last message and lead us to the missing artefact and then leave the rest to us professionals. What could be more natural than Olive, a churchwarden, wanting to make a pilgrimage to the Holy Land and what could be more natural than her brother, a distinguished professor of archaeology wishing to join her and visit some of Israel's biblical archaeological site? Professor Manchandra could join the tour group as a lone traveller as a side trip from giving a lecture at the school of medicine in Jerusalem and finally Ishmael is soon to be recalled to Israel to carry out his annual reserve duties in the IDF. Unfortunately Abdullah, you would have to stay behind and look after the shop as your entry into Israel on a Saudi passport could raise suspicions and we might end up with the farce of Shin

Bet, the Israeli internal security apparatus, spying on a low profile Mossad operation." Once Quartermaine had finished and exchanged glances with Goldfarb it became obvious to all, that this collusion between the two intelligence services had been plotted in advance. After a few moments thought Ishmael agreed that it was his loyal duty to comply, Olive agreed it would be quite an adventure and that she could write up her visit to the Holy Land for the St. Jude's parish magazine and Arthur thought why the hell not and eventually it might give him a head start to publish the discoveries in a leading archaeological journal once the dust had settled and the embargo had been lifted. The only one they had difficulty in persuading was Sanjay but even he gave in when he learnt that his wife would be allowed to join him all expenses paid on receiving the invitation to lecture at the medical school of the Hebrew University on the Mount Scopus. Even as they spoke that invitation was on it's way and appeared in the in box of his G mail account when he logged in that evening after returning to his office. Once the dates were agreed they were told to expect packages of travel documents in a couple of day's time and were then politely ushered to the door by their host. Before leaving Olive turned to Quartermaine and said, "There are two unresolved matters that I can't understand, what first triggered the cyber attack on Joshua Black's computer and how come this precious relic was buried under a mountain of skulls?" Her questions were received with a blank look but continued to niggle her all the way home.

★★★

Unknown to this assembly, events in the labyrinthine allegiances in the Middle East took a turn for the worse even as they spoke. A few days later this report appeared in the Jerusalem Post,

Changes in region have led the to the rearrangement in the relationship between Iran, Hezbollah, and the Muslim Brotherhood.

Following the fall of Muslim Brotherhood from power in Egypt, Iran and Hezbollah are seeking closer relations with the Brotherhood, the Lebanese newspaper As-Safir reported. Recent changes in the region including the restarting of Israel-Palestinian negotiations, the fallout related to the Syrian civil war and opposition to the Brotherhood in various Arab countries, have led the "resistance axis" to "rearrange the relationship between Iran and Hezbollah, and the Muslim Brotherhood."

The Islamic Republic and the Lebanese terrorist organization both identify with the Shi'ite sect of Islam while the Brotherhood is a Sunni movement. Iran's Supreme Leader Ayatollah Ali Khamenei, in a meeting of the Iranian National Security Council, deemed what happened in Egypt as distressing and dangerous and that it would have negative repercussions on the Islamic reality. He said that no matter what mistakes the Brotherhood has made during its time of leadership in Egypt, it should not lead to the end of the Islamic revival in the region, referring to the Arab uprisings. Iran must support this revival and reengage, he said according to sources quoted in Tuesday's report.

Iranian officials have already begun holding intensive meetings with prominent leaders in the international Brotherhood organization to deal with outstanding issues.

In recent weeks, meetings were held between Iran, Hezbollah, and Hamas in Beirut and Tehran in order to come to an agreement to strengthen political and military cooperation despite differences over the conflict in Syria. These efforts are being made to outline a new strategy that will look for points of convergence between the parties of the resistance and newly re-elected President Hassan Rouhani will promote unity among the resistance forces and try to stop sectarian strife in the region. Of even greater concern is that this new emerging alliance might find common purpose with ISIS also known as Islamic state in spite of its Sunni allegiance.

So perhaps Arthur Templeton was not too far off target when suggesting the authorship of the conspiracy bore the fingerprints of the Moslem Brotherhood and the reach of the Grand Mufti of Jerusalem beyond the grave.

★★★

PART 2

Palestine 1938-1948

Chapter 18

"The Egyptian"

Following the death of James Starkey and in spite of the leadership skills of Olga Tufnell, the excavation at Lachish rapidly came to an end. With almost unseemly haste, Flinders Petrie declared that the archaeological expedition be closed down, explaining that he judged Starkey's death as an adumbration of the dangers ahead, as the security of the British Mandate in Palestine was beginning to unravel. In this respect he showed much wisdom, as the British authority was being challenged on three fronts. The Jewish population of Palestine was becoming more and more troublesome, demanding the implementation of the Balfour declaration and the establishment of their own state. Their demands were also being fuelled by the desperation of Jewish illegal immigrants, escaping the clutches of the Nazi government of Germany, yet being denied safe haven in Palestine because of the infamous MacDonald "White Paper". Jewish terrorist groups such as the Stern gang and the Irgun, were beginning to harass the Mandate police and the British army. Not to be outdone, Arab terrorist groups were doing all they could to stymie the ambitions of the Jews, and atrocities were committed on both sides, with the British policemen, "Bobbies" and infantry, "Tommies", caught in the cross fire. As if that wasn't sufficient, German bellicosity and expansionism, threatened the stability of the Middle East. This was as an indirect response to the importance of the Suez Canal for the transport of oil and maintaining the integrity of the British Empire. Jerusalem and Cairo, under the "protection" of the British, became hubs in the field of espionage, whilst British and German agents pitched their wits against each other, recruiting local agents and double agents from amongst the native populations. Although the British were notionally at war with Jewish terrorist groups, when it came to picking sides in the likelihood of war with Germany, they felt confident of the support of the majority of the Jewish population, however they were not so sure of the Arabs. The Grand Mufti of Jerusalem made no secret of his sympathy for the Nazi ideology, and the majority of the Arabs believed that perfidious Albion had reneged on her promises, after the concessions won for their support against the Ottoman army in the First World War. It was against this background that Sultan Al-Mazri, erstwhile Foreman of the Lachish dig, planned his future.

Sultan was born at the turn of the century into a dirt-poor family scratching a living in Al-Jiza, a village West of Cairo, lying in the shadows of the great pyramids. Like many other villagers, the pyramids themselves were the source of their livelihoods. Some acted as guides, others offered camel rides, whilst others carried out illegal digs searching for ancient Egyptian artifacts to be sold to the English, German and French travelers; many of whom had broken their journey at Suez on a P&O liner heading for the Indian Ocean and the far flung extremities of the British Empire. Still others hired themselves out for a pittance, as labourers working at legitimate archaeological digs, authorized by the Egyptian department of Antiquities, but funded through generous donations from charitable foundations in London, Berlin and Paris. It was in this role that the young Sultan Ibn Fahoud, then aged 11, fell in with Flinders Petrie. Petrie and his crew were exploring an area 15 miles south of Cairo on the West Bank of the Nile, thought to be Memphis, the ancient capital of the Old Kingdom from 2575-2130 BCE. They had just uncovered what they believed to be the Great Temple of Ptah, but the colonnaded passages and anterooms where full of the sand and rubble accumulated over nearly four millennia. All this debris hid the relief carvings and hieroglyphics on the walls, that had to be dug out carefully, sifted and searched for precious artifacts or fractured pottery. The latter would help Petrie accurately date the archaeological site, according to the techniques described in his classic works. In order to help with this delicate task, Sultan together with a pack of other village children, were hired en masse to sift the rubble from the dig for fragments of pottery, or more important "finds" missed by the elders, working as unskilled labourers. The children were paid *backshish* on a sliding scale, depending on the importance of the find. Sultan was both nimble of foot and nimble of mind. He outshone his entire peer group by his remarkable powers of observation and rapidly mastered knowledge of detail, which allowed him to distinguish ancient shards of pottery from modern detritus. Unfortunately his success bred jealousy and jealousy bred violence. It was only when the Foreman of the dig broke up a fight amongst the village children that the blooded and bruised young boy came to Flinder's attention. He learnt of Sultan's exceptional gifts as a finder of buried treasure and was charmed by the bright sparkly brown eyes and cheeky smile, of the feral young boy. However the most endearing attribute of the lad was his comical attempts to speak the English he had acquired by eavesdropping on the British contingent. In November 1913 shortly before the end of Petrie's last season at Memphis, Sultans' father was killed when a trench he was digging at the nearby necropolis, collapsed and buried him alive. The young orphan was then taken under the patronage of Sir Flinders and Lady Hilda Petrie, who with typical arrogance renamed him Al-Mazri, "The Egyptian". Sultan travelled everywhere with the Petrie expeditions, acting as houseboy, general factotum and spy. Lady Hilda treated him almost like a son and taught him to read and write English. Astonished at the natural gift for language Sultan exhibited, Flinders taught him how to read hieroglyphics and ancient Aramaic inscriptions. As a loyal and gifted assistant, the Petrie's came to trust him with secrets, so that he could run errands throughout their veritable empire of ancient Egyptian and Levantine archaeological sites, extending from the cataracts of the Nile to the South and Gaza to the North. Amongst these errands, Sultan was tasked to look out for figurines or bas-relief carvings, which illustrated the facial characteristics of the ancient races that populated the Fertile Crescent of the eastern Mediterranean and the fertile belt that ran alongside the Nile. Those objects that could be bought or stolen were taken back to the Petrie encampment and those that were engraved on walls or door lintels, were to be sketched or taken as an imprint molding in tin foil and then used to make a plaster casting. This way Sultan played a key role in creating one of Petrie's most important works, "The Ancient Races of Man". By the time General Allenby entered Jerusalem on horseback, in 1918, at the head of the victorious Imperial army, Sultan had grown into a tall and handsome young man, fluent in English and knowledgeable about the languages and customs of his ancient forbears, their satraps and trading partners. He held his head high as one carrying the perfect physiognomy of the elite of the pre-dynastic Old Kingdom, who drove out the inferior races and repopulated the Nile valley in ancient times. From the very same collection of plaster castes he had made for Sir Flinders, he was able to contrast his own noble profile, to the ugly hook nosed and fleshy lips of the Hebrew traders and slaves. In this way Sultan was taught from an early age to literally look down his nose at the Jews of the Levant and to share the racist ideology of his master and benefactor. After the war when it was judged safe to restart his archaeological campaign, Petrie turned his attentions to the ancients of the Levant and set up shop in Gaza. He had embarked on the study of Biblical archaeology in Palestine, now cleansed of the Turks at the final collapse of the Ottoman Empire, "the sick man of Europe". His "mission statement", had such things been known in those days, was to study the physiognomy and morphometrics of the ancient Israelites, to confirm his theory that the Hebrews were an inferior race, only one rung higher on the evolutionary scale of Homo sapiens, than the Negroid races. He was also looking for evidence to flesh out his nascent theory that Jesus and the early Christians could not have been of Israelite stock, but most likely immigrants from Ancient Greece in the golden age of Pericles. By this time Petrie had taken on a first assistant, a young Englishman named James Starkey whilst at the same time Sultan was promoted to Foreman in charge of the hired help of the local unskilled labour force. Sultan Al Mazri was proud of his new position of authority but resented the weedy new first assistant to his master. He was jealous of the attention Petrie lavished on his latest protégé, whilst at the same time being convinced he knew more about the science and techniques of digging for the buried remains of ancient civilizations, than the new boy. However Sultan was smart enough to hide his feelings and always greeted Mr. Starkey with a brilliant smile, showing his perfect set of gleaming white teeth. He couldn't ignore the fact that James Starkey treated him well without any suggestion of patronisation, yet he never trusted the man. His mistrust was fuelled by the fact that he often eavesdropped on heated debates between Petrie and Starkey, when the young upstart dared to challenge the theories of his master.

In 1932 Petrie and Starkey's relationship fractured when the latter received a grant from the Wellcome foundation, to excavate Tell Ed-Duweir in the Shefela, the hilly country south west of Jerusalem. This mound was suspected of hiding the remains of the ancient Judean city of Lachish, mentioned in the Bible as one of King Rheoboham's fortified outposts, protecting Jerusalem and its Temple. To add insult to injury, James Starkey purloined Olga Tufnell, archivist and bookkeeper, from Petrie's archaeological dig at Gaza. This was facilitated by the fact that Miss Tufnell had been bullied by Hilda Petrie, to the point that Olga had formally complained in writing to the governing authorities in London. As Petrie's second season of excavations at Gaza was coming

167

to an end and as he and Lady Hilda were planning to return to Hampstead Village in north west London, to put their affairs in order before the start of the third season, they thought it might be a clever step to allow Sultan to offer himself, on a pretext, to support Starkey's work. This way Flinders and Hilda would have a spy in the camp to keep an eye on the Lachish excavations and alert them to any significant findings.

Once the blistering heat of the Palestinian summer was over in the early Autumn of 1932, Starkey and his team set up camp on a flat grassy plain to the west side of the Tell making good use of some empty stone built structures left over from the time of the Ottoman Empire. These structures once cleared of debris and swept clean, provided good cover from the heat of the midday sun, yet the thick walls and small windows made sure that they were warm and cozy in the cold nights as winter approached. This time of year the hills and meadows of the Shefelah looked beautiful with abundant wild flowers, olive trees and citrus groves bearing oranges, lemons and esrogim as well as the late flowering pomegranate trees that were soon to bear fruit in time for the Jewish New Year, Rosh Ha'Shana. The stone building was used for the offices of the dig, with two small rooms set aside for the camp beds of Miss Tufnell and Mr. Starkey. The rest of the crew was housed in ridge tents or tepees. Olga even planted out and English flower garden in anticipation of the Spring to come, whilst the workers on site, helped dig out furrows in the fertile ground, to plant vegetables to enhance their diet. Supplies for the expedition were dropped off at the port of Gaza, and brought up on an old First World War Bedford truck, along the main road that went to Jerusalem via Hebron through the valleys and canyons along the way. This route from ancient times, explained the strategic importance of Lachish in the time of the Kingdom of Judea.

The identity of the site and its strategic importance was hinted at by Biblical sources in the book of Jeremiah and Kings II, together with a spectacular if somewhat stylized pictorial representation of its fortification provided by the bas relief frieze discovered in Nineveh, by Austin Layard in 1845, then on display in the British Museum. An inscription cut into a corner of the frieze made its identification unquestionable.

"Sennacherib, the mighty king, king of the country of Assyria, sitting on the throne of judgment, at the entrance of the city of Lachish. I give permission for its slaughter"

The expedition was well organized and adequately equipped. They worked from dawn till dusk, with a one hour lunch break and every Sunday was considered a day of rest and recreation.

To start with their cartographers and surveyors, made accurate plans of the undisturbed site sketching in stone-works, the remains of fortifications or large building, that penetrated the surface in places, providing the first tangible clues to the layout of the ancient city.

Before digging the stratographical trenches, the workmen were ordered to uproot all the vegetation on the surface of the Tell and then rake out the amorphous debris; the accumulation of more than two millennia of neglect. In the unlikely event of ancient artifacts being included in the rubble, this early phase of working was controlled, in so far as to limit the accumulation to the lower slopes of the mound, on the northern and eastern flanks. This was to facilitate the work of the tribe of young urchins from local villages and farms, who had already been attracted to the site by the disturbance of so much unusual activity. These children, aged five to eleven, were quick to understand that they might enjoy the sometimes-fruitful experience of sifting through the rubbish for ancient treasure.

At all times, Sultan, foreman of the dig, diligently supervised the work of laborers and village children alike, leaving the professional architects to get on with their planning, surveying and mapping, but always taking time out for afternoon tea.

The first important finds of the expedition occurred surprisingly early. One morning a few days before Christmas 1932, Sultan was making his rounds supervising the hired labor force and the freelance corps of the rubbish sifting children, when, out of the corner of his eye, he caught sight of a boy behaving suspiciously. He was strolling along the grassy footpath, fashioned by the naturally seeded debris that filled the space between the remains of the inner and outer defensive walls of the ancient city, and had just turned the corner that allowed him an unobstructed view of the eastern slope of the Tell. Suddenly he witnessed a boy of about eleven years old, lifting something from the rubble and slipping it into his pocket after looking shiftily side to side, making sure that no one was watching. Unfortunately for the boy, he didn't look up. Sultan continued walking nonchalantly along his way and then poised just above where the boy and his ragamuffin companions were grubbing in the dust, announced in a sardonic voice. "Good morning my little helpers, have we found any gold coins today". The groups of boys were taken totally by surprise and then with the speed and accuracy of a cobra, he leapt down the incline and grabbed the neck of the hapless young fellow with a secret to hide. "Empty out your pockets" screamed Sultan in mock fury, making the poor boy wet his pants in terror. Sure enough Sultan had not been mistaken, the boy had pocketed hidden treasure. At that moment neither the boy nor his foreman had any idea of the importance of the find. Holding the boy's ear with his left index finger and thumb, Sultan flipped the heavy fragment of terracotta pottery over in the palm of his hand. He immediately recognized that it was a segment of the handle of a very large vessel still attached to the rim of what must have been a storage jar. He had seen many such objects working with the digs near Giza and Gaza but there was something special about this object. Just were the handle flared out to make contact with the jar, there was the imprint of a seal bearing four letters in paleo-Hebrew text arranged symmetrically around the outstretched wings of a bird. He slapped the boy fiercely about his head and unceremoniously sent him on his way with a kick up his backside.

Feeling pleased with himself, Sultan retraced his steps and set off to the encampment in search of James Starkey. He found him outside the stone hut studying a map on a trestle table alongside Olga Tufnell. With mock ceremony and a deep bow he said, "Effendi, I bring you treasure from ancient times that I have just discovered amongst the debris on the eastern flank of our Tel." Starkey looked up with a start, irritated by Sultan's constant habit of creeping up on him without warning, but without disclosing his inner feelings indicated that Sultan had his full attention. The foreman placed the object on the surface of the map they had been studying and stood aside with a smirk of self-satisfaction. It only took a moment or two before James and Olga understood the significance of the find. James looked and with a smile of genuine gratification blurted out, "I say, well done old man, jolly good show. This, as I'm sure you've guessed already, is part of the handle of a large pottery jar, but these are commonplace, however this specimen has a seal with ancient Hebrew lettering." Sultan nodded as if this was news to him and Starkey continued, "Lookie here, these letters have to be read right to left and are as clear as the day they were fired in the kiln. They read Lamed Mem, Lamed, Kaph." Sultan nodded again with an expression combining awe and admiration, knowing full well how the letters were pronounced. Unfortunately he had not a clue as to their significance. This was where James Starkey had the advantage. Although Sultan was steeped in the history of ancient Egypt and could read the ancient languages of those times, that included Aramaic written in Hebrew characters, he was new to the work of Biblical archaeology and carried a very rudimentary idea of the history of the ancient Israelites apart for their links with the putative period of slavery under the Pharaohs. By this time Starkey had a pretty good idea about the provenance of the artifact and dashed indoors to fetch his much fingered and battered copy of the Old Testament. He rushed back out again and breathlessly riffled through the pages of the black bound Bible. "Got it!" he exclaimed in triumph. "The letters spell lamed lamelech, which can be translated as 'belonging to the King' and this is the personal seal of King Hezekiah, King of Judea at the time of the sacking of Lachish by the Assyrian King, Sennacherib. This is what we are looking for; this is the evidence that proves beyond doubt that we have identified Biblical Lachish. Thank you Sultan, you will get a bonus in your pay packet this Sunday and you will be mentioned in dispatches."

Sultan bowed again and with a glow of satisfaction, backed away in another display of mock ceremony.

Over the duration of the dig many such examples of LMLK seals, as they had come to be known, were discovered in strata from the 8th, to the 6th centuries BCE, suggesting that the Babylonians reused those, which had survived the conquest of the Assyrians, following the conquest of 587.

On the Sunday after his success, and with a large cash bonus burning a hole in his pocket, Sultan borrowed the Bedford truck in order to travel to Jerusalem to buy further supplies in the Souk but also to indulge a secret habit of sharing a bottle of Arak with an old friend who had given up working as a laborer for Flinders Petrie in Egypt, in order to open up a little curio shop on the Via Dolorosa in the old city. He sold religious icons and ancient Egyptian scarabs and statuettes, stolen from the digs at Memphis in the same manner as the hapless lad who pocketed the seal of Hezekiah.

Climbing through the steep canyon on the narrow road up to mount Scopus, the truck started over-heating and when steam started hissing through the side slats of the engine cover, Sultan was forced to stop and wait for the engine and radiator to cool down.

He sat on the tailgate of the truck and lit up a Pall Mall cigarette whilst looking round for a possible source of water to fill up the radiator. High above him he spotted a village on the eastern edge of the ravine and assumed there would be a well nearby. Having finished his smoke, he climbed up the rocky escarpment nimble as an Ibex, and with his natural stealth, strolled to a well on the outskirts of the village and startled a young girl who was transferring water from a zinc bucket into her terracotta amphora. The girl, probably aged about 18, was furious to have spilt the water dragged up from the deep well and boldly turned on the stranger whilst her veil slipped to reveal large dark luminous eyes, flashing with anger. When she realized that the intruder was a strange man, it was too late to attempt to protect her modesty by covering her face, but in any case Houriya Abbas, for that was her name, was not by temperament, the demur young lady that one expected to be found in these parts. "How dare creep up on me like that?" She demanded with hate in her eyes. For Sultan it was love at first sight but for Houriya, the initial hatred took about two weeks to mutate into reciprocal feelings.

Sultan eventually persuaded the beautiful young lady to draw water for him to top up the radiator of his truck. He then skipped down the side of the ravine, watched in awe by the girl, emptied the jug of water into the radiator and glided back up to the well to return the jug. She was about to leave when he begged, "Please stay a while so that I might offer my thanks". This time covering her face, Houriya turned to listen, somewhat intrigued by this handsome stranger who had interrupted the achingly predictable passage of the day.

He then captivated her with tales of his adventures in Memphis and Giza and explained his new role in nearby Lachish. He went on to explain that he was off to the souk in Jerusalem to purchase stores for the expedition, but whilst he was there, would like to buy a beaded necklace for her as a reward for her help. She was about to protest but Sultan interrupted, knowing the traditional ways of Palestinian village lives, and explained that before visiting her again, he would obviously do so with the approval of her father and only in the company of her mother or an aunt.

And thus did the courtship of Sultan and Houriya begin.

Whilst in the old souk in town, Sultan did indeed purchase a beautiful beaded necklace made of topaz, lapis lazuli and amber and indeed many of the stones were in truth semi-precious, and indeed he ended up only paying half the asking price. In this way he blew all his weekly pay, plus the bonus for finding the handle with the royal seal. This left him penniless, so his leisurely afternoon drinking Arak with his friend was forgotten as he hastened back to the village of Deir Yassin.

Sultan was received with the elaborate courtesies of an Arab village, that involved drinking three thimbles of sweet dark coffee flavored with hel, in the company of Houriya's father, uncles and two brothers. He was only then allowed to present his token of gratitude to the only daughter of the household. There was a hiss of indrawn breath from the women of the Kazim family. They had quickly estimated the cost of the gift and having made those calculations, silently agreed with each other, with much raisings of eyebrows behind their veiled faces, that this tall handsome man was a suitable suitor for the girl. Houriya's father, Nassim, agreed that Sultan would be welcome any time he was passing, to drop in for a visit.

Sultan, who never had time or wealth sufficient to consider marriage, drove back to Lachish with his head in a whirl. Thereafter he settled into a routine of visiting Deir Yassin every Sunday to conform to the courtship rituals and to win the none too reluctant heart, of Houriya. Beyond the pleasure of meeting up with his bride to be, he enjoyed the company of Nassim and the other men folk, because in all truth, they were closer in age to him than Houriya. In particular he enjoyed talking politics. Once he had secured the trust of the men of the household they ventured to test out his ideas about the Moslem brotherhood. In fact Sultan had no thoughts on the matter and had only the vaguest idea of what they stood for. The brotherhood had been founded in Egypt five or six years earlier, as a Sunni pan-Arabic organization. Their motto summed up its intentions in an unambiguous manner:

"Believers are but Brothers; Allah is our objective; the Qur'an is the Constitution; the Prophet is our leader; jihad is our way; death for the sake of Allah is our wish."

174

This heady brew of brotherly love, absolutism and certainty of purpose suddenly intoxicated Sultan, who had never held a political or ideological concept in his head before. It took little effort to convert him to the cause and like many new converts, he rapidly became a zealot even up to the point of giving up drinking Arak and beer. He rapidly rose in the ranks to become an executive officer in the regional branch of the organization, with the dual role of managing the local football club for the young men of the neighborhood whilst recruiting them to the cause.

An almost unspoken aspect of "the cause", was hostility to the British Mandate and the promotion of an ugly campaign of anti-Semitism directed to the Jewish settlers in their kibbutzim. Their hatred was most intense for the black hatted, heavily bearded, ultra-orthodox Jews in the Old City of Jerusalem; they who had gathered there since time immemorial, to live and pray in proximity to the "Western Wall" of King Herod's Temple.

All of Sultan's covert activities mostly took place on Sunday, the day of rest for the archaeological dig, and on the occasional pretext of having to take equipment for repair at a forge in a nearby village. His movements gave no reason for suspicion by the leaders of the expedition as Sultan made no secret of his courtship of a young woman in a nearby village.

Sultan and Houriya were married with great ceremony, in the spring of 1934 with James Starkey and Olga Tufnell as honored guests. Thereafter the Al Mazri couple, set up house in a modest stone hut close to the compound of Houriya's family home. As a wedding gift Sultan's father-in-law gave him a new BSA 650cc motorbike that took him to and from his work at Lachish each day, in record time. This also incidentally, facilitated his work as an agent of the brotherhood in the heartlands of the Palestinian Mandate.

Within a year of their marriage, Houriya presented Sultan a healthy baby boy they named Abdullah and a year later a little girl that she named after her recently deceased grandmother, Fatimah.

Against this happy domestic background Sultan continued his work as the Foreman of the Lachish excavation at last coming to terms with the fact that he could never expect further promotion in the hierarchy of the archaeological establishment. This frustration and more than compensated by the fact of his rapid promotion up the ladder of the Muslim Brotherhood.

★★★

Chapter 19

The Lachish Letters

In the spring of 1935, Starkey and his team, made a discovery of such importance as to go down in the annals of the history of archaeology alongside that of the Rosetta stone. By this time the remains of the two encircling defensive walls had been clearly identified. In addition the remains of a paved inclined approach road to the double defensive gates on the western approach to the city had also been cleared. A second inclined ramp leading up to the southernmost point of the Tell was also identified, but it was only confirmed as the siege ramp of the Assyrian conquest some years later.

Like most cities of this era, that were constantly at risk from marauding armies coming up from the coastal plains, the gates were enormous and complex structures. To enter the city one had to pass through two sets of gateways via a passage set at right angles to the direction of the main approach road. Each of these gates included blockhouses that were occupied by heavily armed guards, and every visitor had to explain and prove their motive for entering the city: a primitive form of border control experienced these days of heightened alert, at our airports.

The gateways and blockhouses were carefully cleared of rubble down to the pavement level. At this point an aqueduct system was discovered. A further detail, that pleased the archaeologists although considered of little interest to the workers, was the discovery of countersunk cylindrical holes within the stone lintels of the gateways, demonstrating the wear and tear of bearing the weight of stout reinforced wooden doors, that had swung on spindles sank into these housings. The laborers, followed by their flock of little sharp eyed scavengers searching for buried treasures, were close to completing the clearance of one of the inner blockhouses, when one of these urchins spotted some large fragments of glazed clay broken off from some pitcher of sorts. As was the routine when any "finds" were spotted, the work was halted so that the professional archaeologists might photograph and log the findings in situ. After which each fragment had to be carefully removed intact, with the object of reconstructing the pottery at a latter date. However on this occasion the sharp eyed little boy thought he saw an inscription in black ink on the surface of the fragment, so Starkey was summoned urgently to supervise the logging and removal of the ostracon.

Surrounded by curious members of his team, James got down on his hands and knees and working carefully with trowel and brush, he eventually freed up 18 ostraca bearing the pen strokes of ancient Hebrew script. Judging from the stratum of their discovery, supported by the evidence from the design of the handles and lips of pots discovered at the same level, there was little doubt that these dated from the reign of King Zedekiah and were probably the first examples of paleo-Hebrew from this époque ever discovered.

The ostraca were numbered in the order they were retrieved, measured and photographed in situ and carefully transported to the office on site. They were then each washed with clean spring water using a pipette and slowly the ancient script came to life. James and Olga were beside themselves with excitement, but Sultan would come to regret the fact that this was one of those few occasions he had taken the truck to collect supplies from Gaza during a working day. With the aid of a textbook containing the images of the ancient alphabetical forms of the Levant, the archaeologists slowly began to decipher what would go down in history, as the "Lachish letters".

The letters appeared to be duplicates of correspondence

sent by the commander of the military forces of Lachish to his superior, probably in Jerusalem. It seemed somewhat unlikely that none of these communications had left the fortress, as they described more than one event and some were even written as humble supplication for additional resources to do the job, reading almost like the complaints of a subaltern at the front in 1914. However the most striking and forthright of them all was letter number 4 that read as follows.

"Let my lord know that we are watching over the beacons of Lachish, according to the signals which my lord gave. For Azekah is not seen."

This immediately rang a bell with Olga, who was even a greater authority on the Old Testament canon of literature, than James Starkey. "I'm sure this reads like something in the book of Jeremiah. Hang on a minute whilst I search my books." In a flash she was in and out of her cubbyhole in the stone office block, bearing her own battered copy of the book of Prophets, and rapidly started riffling through the pages. "Here it is", she cried in triumph, and then started reading aloud from Jeremiah chapter 34, verse 7.

"Then Jeremiah the prophet spoke all these words to Zedekiah, King of Judah in Jerusalem when the army of the King of Babylon was fighting against Jerusalem and against the remaining cities of Judah, that is Lachish and Azekah, for they alone remained as fortified cities among the cities of Judah."

At a stroke the Wellcome expedition lead by Starkey and Tufnell, had found first hand confirmation of the veracity of the ancient scriptures describing the Babylonian conquest of the Kingdom of Judah in 587 BCE. For the ostracon, logged as the 4th letter of Lachish, bore witness to the soldier who saw the beacon signals of Azekah extinguished, no doubt shortly before the life of the man himself was extinguished. The whole gathering shivered as if a ghost had wandered through the camp.

By the time Sultan had returned to base, the news had travelled like wind through word of mouth.

Olga had already composed a letter to her mother describing her excitement at the find and then went on to compose a formal letter written on her typewriter, to their financial backers in London.

James supplemented this report with photographs developed in the dark room on site, together with hand drawn copies of the "letters". These would then allow other experts in the ancient languages of the Levant, based at the Wellcome Institute and University College London, to double check their interpretation of this momentous discovery. On his return, Sultan was furious to have been taken off guard but restrained his anger and charmed his way into Starkey's confidence. As the expedition director showed the ostraca to his site foreman, explaining the identity of each inscribed letter, Sultan was able in his own way to covertly confirm the findings and memorize their translation. Feigning fatigue he excused himself and set off northeast in the direction of his village, but in spite of the late hour, redirected his BSA motorbike westward once he had hit the main road and returned back to Gaza in search of Flinders Petrie. As he rode at top speed along the near empty highway, it suddenly dawned on him that this find had enormous political implications as well historical interest.

The intermediate ambition of the Muslim Brotherhood, was to recreate the Umayyad Caliphate from its apogee in the 7th century CE, when it extended as a crescent surrounding the Mediterranean, from the Iberian peninsula, across the straits of Gibraltar, around supra Saharan north Africa, including Egypt and the Sinai peninsula, the fertile crescent of the Levant, into Syria and up to the borders of Turkey. This extended eastwards to cover the whole of Arabia. With the Iberian Peninsula as a foothold in the southwest and Turkey as a foothold in the southeast, the whole of Europe could be caught in a pincer movement in the fullness of time, as was foreseen by the Prophet Mohammed. Critical to that way of thinking, was possession of the narrow fertile plain that ran from Gaza in the south and Lebanon in the north, bracketing the land known as the British Mandate of Palestine. In this land there would be no place for the Jews and once the British were kicked out, the native Muslim Arabs of Palestine would automatically accept the governance of the Caliph. Furthermore, the third most holy site in the Islamic world, after Mecca and Medina, was the so-called "Temple Mount" from which the Prophet on his white horse, leapt into the eternal embrace of Allah. Jerusalem would then become one of the three epicenters of the ummah.

If it came to be accepted that the Old Testament Biblical story of the first Temple was true, then it would follow that the Hebrew people had pride of place in occupying these lands, 1,200 years before the birth of the Prophet. He must therefore do all in his power to subvert the interpretation of the findings at Lachish, and in this he knew he would enjoy the support of Flinders Petrie.

He found Petrie at breakfast the following morning and recounted his tale. The great English professor listened without interruption and then agreed that he should visit the site later that day.

Sultan then sped off on his BSA and returned to the camp from a direction that suggested his was journeying back from his village below Mount Scopus.

★★★

That afternoon, just as James Starkey was settling down for tea with his colleagues, when much to his dismay, he looked up to see the large bearded form of his immediate superior, bearing down on him with black cape billowing out in his wake.

"What's this I hear Starkey?" bellowed the old man. "Found yerself something of importance for a change?" "My God, Flinders, news travels fast in these parts. Yes indeed I think we have found something of importance, come and see for yourself." Lead by Starkey; Flinders Petrie, Olga Tufnell and Sultan Al Mazri went into the offices of the dig to examine the 18 ostraca. After carefully examining each of the "letters",

Petrie stood up and grunted; "Look like bloody forgeries to me. In my experience anything that's too good to be true, aint true. I shall have to take these in person to the museum in Jerusalem to be looked over by better qualified specialists than you". "I'm afraid you can't do that as I have a contract with sponsors in London that all finds on this dig belong to them and it's up to folk at the Wellcome Institute to select the experts to evaluate our initial observations." Replied Starkey. After bickering and blustering for five minutes or so, Petrie had to accept that the matter was outside his control but demanded to see the precise spot were the ostraca were unearthed, together with any of the surrounding pottery fragments, so that he at least might confirm the dating of the specimens. "You needn't bother yourself James, finish your tea. I'll ask your foreman to show me around." Without waiting for an answer Flinders Petrie strode off guided by Sultan Al Mazri.

On arriving at the interior gatehouse, the old professor got down on his knees and with the help of a magnifying glass inspected all the pottery remnants. He reluctantly had to agree, that according to his own published classification, this stratum of the excavation belonged to the 6th century BCE.

As he was shuffling along the outer edge of the doorway of the blockhouse, he came across a segment of the aqueduct that drained into the main channel running under the pavement of the main roadway entering the gates of the ancient city. Something caught his eye. Sitting in this channel was a segment of curved clay pottery whose concave side was uppermost and whose convex surface, by chance, fitted the curvature of the tributary of the aqueduct system. Taking out a penknife, he slipped the blade under the edge of the clay fragment and eased it out. On the glazed convex surface were clearly inscribed letters in ancient Hebrew spelling out words he could recognize as the lingua franca of the 6th century BCE, Aramaic. Nodding to Sultan, who nodded back as a signal of complicity, he slid the fragment of pottery into the pocket of his cape and straightened up his back with a groan.

182

The pair of them strode back towards the encampment meeting James Starkey who was on his way up to find out what was going on. Petrie greeted him with a degree of coolness, yet his undoubted professionalism forced him to agree with the conclusions of his protégé. "Well James, old chap, I have to agree with your dating of these ostraca. Your finds will no doubt generate quite a lot of interest in the journals, but please in future, any finds of such importance must be reported to me first before being broadcast to the world. Incidentally I think you have been a little lax in the exploration of the nesting place of those ostraca, as I think I've identified a 19th specimen." With a flourish, like a stage magician, Petrie whipped the ostracon out of his pocket and without allowing Starkey to reply, strode off with the words of a playground jibe, "Finders keepers; losers weepers". Just before he drove off, he wound down the window and beckoned to Sultan. "You did well to draw my attention to this matter, I will need to study this one at leisure as it might hold the key to more than just the signal fires of Azekah".

★★★

Chapter 20

1936 The Valley of Dry Bones

The hand of the LORD was on me, and he brought me out by the Spirit of the LORD and set me in the middle of a valley; it was full of bones. He led me back and forth among them, and I saw a great many bones on the floor of the valley, bones that were very dry. He asked me, "Son of man, can these bones live?"

Ezekiel 37:1-14

The third dramatic discovery at Lachish was during the fifth season of the dig in the spring of 1937. The "finds" were about 200 yards outside the protective walls at the northeast sector of the Tell. The chance discovery had an element of drama combined with comedy. It was early evening just before supper, when a bunch of young boys were kicking a ball around and one suddenly disappeared as if the earth had swallowed him. The others looked on in amazement until galvanized into action by terrified screams that seemed to come from below where they stood. On closer inspection it appeared that a sinkhole had opened up under the feet of the unfortunate lad. As the others peered over the edge, they could just make out their teammate yelling his head off and begging them to save his life. Two of the older boys lay flat on their stomachs and gingerly wriggled to edge of the grassy edge of the hole, reached in and grabbed one hand each and then pulled him out like a cork from a bottle. He was white with terror and kept gabbling on about dead bodies and skeletons. Once they had calmed him down, the two older boys looked over the edge again and could just about recognize what looked like a rib cage reflecting the oblique rays of the setting sun. Whilst the gang stood guard around the perimeter of the sinkhole, the leader of the pack ran off to summon one of the grown ups from the expedition. As luck would have it, the first adult he encountered was Andrew Fleming. Andrew was a Scotsman studying osteology in the department of anatomy in the medical school at University College Hospital. He was carrying out fieldwork for his PhD in paleo-osteology as part of Starkey's team. So far he had not much luck in finding human remains, but he had already collected sufficient material to deduce that the diet of the Ancient Israelites contained fish, sheep, goats and beef. That was hardly surprising, so he assumed the boys had stumbled on the remains of an ancient abattoir that for reasons of hygiene and discretion, had been built beyond the limits of the city walls. As night was falling, Andrew collected his flashlight and followed the boy back to the hole guarded by the other children. When he shone the beam into the pit he confirmed that these were animal bones but that a more thorough examination would have to wait until the next morning. He gave the boy, who had inadvertently made the discovery, a shilling for his pains, who then skipped off happily to tell the tale of his terrifying experience to his family, in a nearby farm on a hillock due south of the Tel.

★★★

The following morning, after an early breakfast, Andrew Fleming accompanied by James Starkey, strolled along the meadow from their encampment to the pit containing the bones, followed by an excited gang of local young boys.

The young osteologist took out his trenching shovel and cleaned the turf around the hole in the subsoil until him came the edge of the chalk rock that formed the roof of the pit. They were a bit disappointed to find that this was simply a burial pit for animal carcasses, rather than a built structure that might have represented an abattoir.

Fleming extended a makeshift ladder down the pit, manipulating it through the pile of bones until it found a solid purchase on the floor, of what appeared to be a cavity that had been carved out of the soft rock. The cavity extended outwards to form a bell shaped cavern from the access portal, accidentally discovered by the hapless lad the previous evening. He then gingerly stepped into the cavern and made his way down to the top layer of skeletons. After a rather superficial examination he found something surprising and called up to Starkey above him, "I say James, I found something very odd, let me pass up these bones so I can be sure of my initial guess." After a few moments sifting through the bones, he passed up a femur, half a pelvic bone and a near intact animal skull, to the waiting hands of his boss. He then climbed back out of the hole and sat cross-legged on the grass, and examined the skeletal remains in the clear sunlight. "Any idea what these are James?" Starkey shook his head so Andrew continued; "These bones come from a pig, not part of a kosher diet for your ancient Hebrews you'll agree. How old do you reckon this charnel house might be?" "Well from what I've seen of the structure so far, it reminds me of the underground complexes we unearthed in Maresha a few years back and those certainly antedated the Hasmonean Kingdom by a long way." Replied Starkey. "My guess is that it is an 6th century BC structure from before or around the time of the Babylonian conquest. Let's clear out the bones for you to log and examine properly and then see what clues we might find at the bottom of the pit below these carcasses."

Starkey, who by now had lost interest, went about his business leaving Andrew Fleming to carefully supervise the removal of the bones with the eager help of a band of local boys. He set up a trestle table and camp chair at the edge of the pit and carefully logged and described each bone as it was passed up to him by the chain gang of cheeky young men who thought this was the most interesting day of their lives. For Andrew it was a rather tedious job after the original excitement, once he was sure that the vast majority of bones were of porcine origin. Why this was the case, could be debated with the other members of the expedition, over a gin and tonic at sundown that evening.

After the lunch break during the heat of the noonday sun, the osteologist and his little helpers returned to work. By this time Fleming had estimated that he could account for about three hundred dead pigs, by simply counting the remains of pelvic bones and skulls. Just before the anticipated afternoon tea break, a long bone was pocked out through the hole in the ground and carried over to Andrew, who took it from the boy barely giving it a glance, his eyes still on his notebooks. Suddenly he recognized that the bone was significantly much heavier than anything else he'd handled that day.

He turned his head to look at what he was holding in his left hand and noted with a start, that it was the femur from a human skeleton. On closer looking he then noticed an iron arrowhead bedded in the shaft of the bone. His heart leapt with excitement and he immediately dispatched one of his urchin helpmates to fetch the boss, James Starkey. Starkey arrived within minutes breathless with exertion having captured the excitement displayed by the little message boy. Fleming wordlessly handed him the femoral bone and Starkey whipped out his magnifying glass to study the arrowhead muttering to himself, "Mmm, mid-iron age, Mesopotamian design, near perfectly preserved by dry chalk cavern with narrow mouth, could only be Babylonian Empire period." Then turning to Fleming he continued, "Well Andrew, glad you joined us now? This bone almost certainly comes from a Judean defender of Lachish just before the taking of Jerusalem. You've got a gold mine here. If I'm correct this might be the burial ground for all the defenders of the city before the Babylonians overran it. I would guess the pig carcasses thrown on top of the Judean soldiers was meant as the final insult to their faith. Let's set up some floodlights powered by a generator to get a quick idea of the size of the task ahead. This find is too precious to barge in upon without careful planning."

Two hours later under the unforgiving brilliance of floodlights, James and Andrew cautiously stepped down a ladder in the cave that was anchored on the hard virgin rock deep below an ossuary of human remains that stretched as far as the eye could see. They were reluctant to test their weight on this cavern of dry bones but at least they could estimate the enormity of the task ahead.

They decided to organize a chain gang of the village children, with the smallest and lightest standing on the bones and passing them up to helpers at ground level. These would be divided into two teams, one selecting and organizing the human skeletal remains, to be logged and later examined in detail by Fleming and the other to collect up any artifacts like arrowheads or bronze scales from a coat of mail. Any intact skulls were to be carefully preserved for detailed morphometric examination by James Starkey once the clearance was complete. These rare specimens would then be used to either corroborate or refute Flinders Petrie's theories of race.

On the face of it Starkey's plans made good sense and once work re-started human remains went one way to Andrew and all other artifacts went the other way to Starkey to be classified and logged. The bones piled up and were arranged logically into sets of right and left femora, tibia, clavicles, skulls and so on.

On the other table remnants of ancient armor, arrowheads, beads and leather straps soon piled up.

It took nearly three days to clear down to the virgin rock around the perimeter of the bell shaped cavern before an extraordinary pyramid of about 100 human skulls was discovered. Witnessing this bizarre arrangement suggested that the first 100 Judean captives were killed by decapitation and their heads organized in a ritualistic manner, before the bodies were dumped without ceremony on top. The final insult was then to bury the remains of hundreds of Judean captives under a layer of the carcasses of pigs.

Andrew and James estimated that the total number of

skulls accounted for 1,500 brutally murdered defenders of Lachish an adumbration of Stalin's massacre of Polish officers in Katyn in 1940.

The task at hand was huge and Starkey needed to increase his number of volunteers to carefully log and classify the artifacts on the one hand whilst logging and organizing the skeletons into the equivalent human units. Only once this repetitive work had been completed would he allow himself to start work on the treasure trove of human skulls. This resource would be the ultimate test of Petrie's predictions about race and cranial capacity.

He then summoned his foreman Sultan to ask him to recruit some more nimble fingered boys from the neighboring villages to help with the task and to then let professor Petrie know about this remarkable find. Unknown to Starkey, Flinders had been well aware of this discovery a couple of days earlier and was trying to contact the sponsors of the dig in London to allow him to take control of the cataloguing human remains. Telegrams had been sent but replies were as yet not forthcoming.

The next afternoon professor Petrie ambled on to the site of valley of dry bones as if only hearing of the discovery that morning. Starkey showed him around whilst Petrie exuded avuncular charm and complemented the team on their excellent work. Having inspected the crudely reconstructed human skeletons, early iron-age arrowheads and other such artifacts, he was then guided to the pit where he could look down on the pyramid of skulls that were left to last. He was clearly taken aback but refused the offer of a descent through the narrow aperture at the apex of the cavern, apologizing that his weight and girth might on one hand leave him stuck like a cork in a bottle or on the other hand destroy the rickety hand built ladder leading down. Starkey found Petrie's good humor unnerving and completely out of character. That evening over dinner served by the light of a campfire the great professor politely asked James Starkey if he might have a hand in the classification and intra-cranial measurements of the skulls. James' heart sank as he could think of no gracious way of refusing the professor's polite offer.

Either by divine intervention or a low pressure system drifting in from the Judean hills, a torrential storm hit the encampment that night. The burial pit flooded and much damage was done to the excavations. They worked half the night bringing the new finds from the pit into the safety of the stone built offices of the dig, but there was no question of continuing their work until the weather improved. Petrie went back to Gaza in a huff and renewed his efforts to try and get Starkey's sponsors to hand over the skulls for his safekeeping. In any case the season was coming to an end as the first khamsin of the late spring followed on the tail of the low-pressure system, with its excoriating hot and dry winds.

After the rainy season ended in February 1938 work restarted on the collection of skulls. They were each numbered with Indian ink on the frontal bone, and measured with calipers along the classical diagonals of cranial morphometry. These numbers were then correlated with museum specimens described in textbooks of eugenics in order to allocate them to racial sub-types. Each skull then had the cranial bones removed by a circular saw so that in cerebral volume could be estimated. Along the way Andrew came across three skulls bearing the stigma of trephination. In other words holes had been drilled into the skull as a primitive act of surgery. Even more remarkable was the evidence that the victims had survived the procedure to fight another day. This was deduced by observing the cribriform fringe of new bone formation surrounding the edges of the circular defect. One could only speculate, but these trefinations suggested that a Judean doctor had released the pressure of an extra-dural blood clot from three of the defenders of Lachish who had been struck on the head by Babylonian missiles.

From this point onwards Starkey, supported by Andrew Fleming, engaged in a furious battle of wills with Flinders

Petrie. James and Andrew demonstrated unequivocally that the skeletons belonged to the Judean soldiers and were therefore descendents of the ancient Israelites who had populated the fertile plains of the eastern Mediterranean coast. Yet against all the predictions of Petrie's theory of race, these bones belonged to a race with a cranial capacity equivalent to a modern day European of Caucasian lineage. Petrie couldn't accept this refutation of his precious theory. He couldn't challenge the morphometry of the skulls, as the team was using his methodology and instruments. He therefore argued that these soldiers could only be mercenaries from Sparta or ancient Greece.

Matters came to a head when out of the blue James Starkey was summoned to attend a meeting with Flinders Petrie in Berlin. He was instructed to bring Sultan Al Mazri with him together with all the morphometric calculations made on the skulls so far. They were to meet with professor Eugen Fischer at the Kaiser Wilhem Institute of Anthropology, Human Heredity, and Eugenics, who was to provide a second opinion on the interpretation of Starkey's calculations. Apparently Eugen Fischer had developed his own methods for designating race following measurements of the skull that was known as the Fischer-Saller scale. James thought that this was a complete farce because the man was a notorious racist who would only reinforce Petrie's prejudices. At the same time he couldn't simply decline because the Kaiser Wilhem Insitute, via the Rockefeller Foundation, was one of the most important sources of funding for excavations throughout the Holy Land.

Strongly resenting the interruption of his fieldwork, James and Sultan met up with Petrie at Atarot airport near Jerusalem and from there flew to Cyprus and then caught BEA flight to Berlin.

The three men were met by professor Fischer at Tempelhof airport and whisked off to Kaiser Wilhem Institute in the professor's huge Mercedes convertible. No sooner were they settled in Eugen Fischer's office than the professor was summoned to the telephone. He returned white faced and shaking. "Gentlemen," he said in a portentous voice, "The Fuehrer has demanded an immediate audience. I briefed him about your visit and he went into a tantrum over the suggestion that the skulls of ancient Israelites suggested a level of intelligence and cultural evolution that might match the Aryan race. Mr Starkey, I advise you most sincerely to keep your mouth shut and leave the talking to professor Petrie and me. It's a shame I wasn't allowed the time to correct your calculations but there is no doubt in my mind that either you have made a series of basic errors or that professor Petrie is correct and that the skeletons belonged to Spartan mercenaries."

All that James Starkey remembered of that fateful meeting with Adolf Hitler was the Fuehrer screaming at them as he marched up and down in a petulant rage. Starkey to his credit refused to be bludgeoned into submission and considered himself lucky to have been allowed to leave without a quick visit to Gestapo HQ. Meanwhile Sultan watched the pantomime with carefully disguised grim satisfaction. However for him the most memorable event of the whole encounter occurred as they were leaving the anteroom of Herr Hitler's office. Ignoring the bickering amongst his own company he turned to take in the view and noticed that they were not alone. Huddled in a dark corner on the other side of the lobby was a Jew. He had never knowingly set eyes on a Jew before but he recognized the yellow star on the lapel of the man's pocket. The hunched over old man corresponded to the stereotype he had helped to create as a result of his contributions to Petrie's masterwork, "The Races of Man".

★★★

In spite of that ugly row in Berlin, Starkey's work continued systematically once he was back on site. However work came to an abrupt end shortly after James and Andrew had removed the last set of skulls at the base of the pyramid. As it happened Sultan Al Mazri was assisting them at that time when the last and most remarkable find of the expedition was uncovered. Hidden amongst the last layer of skulls was a capped clay jar of the type that was traditionally used to store scrolls. James carefully examined the jar sealed at one end with the mark of King Hezekia. The three-line inscription on the surface of the jar in the neat calligraphy of ancient Hebrew text, confirmed that it held a scroll of extreme antiquity and extreme importance.

Such was his excitement that for the first time in his career he acted in an unprofessional way and broke the seal at one end of the cylinder in order to see what it contained. To his surprise, instead of the expected papyrus or parchment, a well-preserved copper scroll slid out. The writing on the exposed surface of the scroll was hard to decipher but the inscription on the jar he had seen enough to confirm that this object might be the most important find of his career if not in the whole history of biblical archaeology so far.

Assuming that the others in his company would not be able to translate the early Aramaic runes on the surface of the jar or the embossed letters on the copper scroll, Starkey slipped it in his back pack muttering that he we need to study the artifact at leisure and then nonchalantly completed the final stages of clearing the hill of skulls.

★★★

Chapter 21

The death of James Starkey

January 10th 1938

"Not for the greed of gold not for the hope of fame.
Nor for a lasting heritage not for a far-flung name
Rather for making history and for some lore of old
This is our aim and object not for the greed of gold"

As the last words of the campfire song, echoing off ancient walls, faded into the twilight of a still winter evening in the Judean Shephelah, J.L. Starkey sat smoking his pipe contemplating the significance of the week's remarkable discovery. Seated alongside him in companionable silence was his good friend and ally, Olga Tufnell. That morning as on every Sunday, they counted up the finds and rewarded their workers according to the standard tariff as a kind of formalized *baksheesh*. The going rate was 2 shillings a day for the skilled workers and a shilling a day for the children from the local villages who eagerly scavenged through the debris and rubble dug up from the trenches, looking for fragments of pottery or other artifacts that had been overlooked by their elders. For these children it was an exciting game as well as a treasure trove as there were additional cash rewards for important finds that included coins or ostraca bearing the inked runes from a civilization that was destroyed more than 2,500 years in the past.

1938 was the 6th season for the expedition and was to be Starkey's last.

His troubles began the previous year when they had discovered approximately 1,500 skeletons that had been carelessly dumped through a hole in the roof of a chalk cavern just outside the perimeter wall of the ancient citadel. On first inspecting this ossuary Starkey could not help recalling Ezekiel's valley of dry bones. These demonstrated savage wounds of battle where the Babylonian invaders had literally cut through to the bone of the Judean defenders of Lachish. It didn't take a forensic pathologist to reconstruct the ferocity of the slaughter of the last defenders of the last important outpost guarding the approach to Jerusalem. There was no doubting the identity of these human remains as judged by the broken weaponry and remnants of body armor that were characteristic of the ancient Israelite fighting man. Apart from the mutilation of the skeletal remains there was a further macabre aspect to these finds. The floor of the ancient tomb carried a pyramid of skulls of the Judean defenders who had been decapitated by the merciless Babylonian victors.

This week's find was of even greater importance because of the recent Arab uprising brutally put down by the British army, the exile of the Grand Mufti of Jerusalem, the Peel Commission considering partition of Palestine between the Arabs and the Jews, not to speak of the threat of war with Germany on the horizon. The Middle East was a tinderbox and any spark might set it alight. There was no way he would let Flinders Petrie into the secret because of his lightly disguised sympathy for the Nazi cause and so far, apart from himself, only two others knew of the find. The first was Sultan Al Mazri who was with him when they finally removed and inspected the last few skulls at the base of the pyramid in the ancient tomb and the second was Olga Tufnell. He had long since doubted the loyalty of Sultan, so Olga was the only one he could trust.

As dusk fell to night, Starkey finished his pipe and came to a decision. Turning towards his companion he said, "Olga I've decided. I told Sultan that I'm taking the scroll jar to the new museum of antiquities in Jerusalem as an appropriate gift to celebrate its opening. But, only known to you, I've transported it to Maresha this morning whilst Sultan was enjoying his day of rest. I found a secure hiding place for it there; it's been hidden underground for well over two millennia, so for as long as it takes until we know more about the possibility of the partition of Palestine and threat of war with Nazi Germany, it can remain dormant."

"I think that makes sense JL, when will you leave for Jerusalem?" replied Olga.

"Now!"

"Are you mad James? The road from here to Jerusalem via Hebron is notorious bandit country. You cannot possibly travel by night."

"I have no choice Olga. I suspect that as we speak Sultan is on his way to Gaza and it's even a greater danger to us all should the jar and the copper scroll fall into Flinders' hands. Anyway our sturdy old Bedford truck would be difficult to ambush, I'll carry my service revolver and my driver, Ahmed, is loyal and handy with a knife. However, just in case anything happens to me, I have written this cryptogram which will give you the exact coordinates of it's hiding place in the subterranean vaults of Maresha."

Without giving Olga any further time to remonstrate with him or even open the envelope that he'd placed in her hand, Starkey picked up an old canvas hold-all he used for transporting his field-work tools, strode to his quarters in the camp, slipped on his bush jacket that covered the belt carrying his sheath knife and a holster for his Webley 0.455 mark II, and made his way to the Bedford truck. Ahmed fired up the old truck without a problem and they bumped out of the encampment area until it met the main road between Gaza and Hebron. The following morning his body was found about 100 m from the ransacked Bedford motor on the bend in the road 3km out of Hebron just where you can turn back to look at the best view in the country. There was no sign of his driver.

★★★

Chapter 22

Sultan 1939-1948

After the closure of the dig, Sultan Al Mazri returned to his village to continue his work for the Muslim brotherhood. By this time his little boy was a boisterous and beautiful five-year old miniature of his father, whilst Aisha his pretty little daughter had just turned three and Houryia was expecting his third child. The mood in the village was somber as the storm clouds of the forthcoming war gathered. For the men of Dier Yassin the enemy was twofold, the officers of the British Mandate and the perfidious Jews. It therefore made sense to find common purpose with Hitler and the Nazi party. When war eventually broke out Sultan was co-opted to work on the staff of Haj Amin al-Husseini, the Grand Mufti of Jerusalem. He was given the task of organizing fedayin into operational groups to carry out attacks on British supply routes and isolated kibbutzim in the sector south west of Jerusalem that extended to Gaza and the coastline from Jaffa to the Egyptian border. He was as familiar with this terrain as with the lines on his face, having navigated the land by motorbike for many years serving two masters. To preserve an innocent face to the authorities he was also appointed as the English teacher at the local school. With this front and at the covert recommendation of Flinders Petrie dining in his club in London with the head of the SIS, he was even recruited as a British asset making him all the more valuable to the brotherhood as a double agent. Shortly before the end of the war in 1945, his cover was blown and he just escaped the hangman's noose with a moonlight flit across the border into French mandated Lebanon where he found refuge in a safe house belonging to the Muslim Brotherhood.

Here he cooled his heals until the end of the World War at which point the British had lost patience with the feuding in Palestine and let the Muslims and the Jews fight it out between themselves.

In November 1947 the United Nations had voted in favor of partition and the creation of a Jewish state. A civil war broke out between the Jews and Arabs of Palestine and on the 14th of May 1948 when David Ben Gurion announced the unilateral declaration of independence and the State of Israel. The Arabs called this the Al-Nakba, the disaster, and a coalition of Arab armies from Lebanon, Syria, Trans-Jordan and Egypt invaded the nascent state with the intent of driving the Jews into the sea.

Sultan was jubilant and made his way via the Golen Heights, into the west bank region of the Arab sector of divided Palestine and from there began his trek home in the wake of the victorious Arab Legion. He arrived home in Dier Yassin on April 12th at the time of the siege of Mount Scopus, the home of the Hadassah hospital, north east of Jerusalem. He was warmly greeted by his wife who proudly showed off his two year old second son, Emir, who was born whilst he was in exile. Whilst Abdullah and Aisha looked on in silent awe at their father as he embraced the little boy before turning his attention to them. He had barely two hours with his family before he was summoned by the village elders to take command of a band of irregulars who had been ordered by the Jordanian Arab legion, to tighten the noose around the sole remaining corridor leading to Mount Scopus running through the ravine to the south of the village.

What happened over the next 48 hours is fiercely contested to this very day in the two narratives of the Israel war of liberation or the Palestinian Arab version of Al-Nakba. There were two massacres by terrorist organizations, one from each side of the divide. They happened close in time and close in proximity. Who was responsible and whether one was a reprisal for the other depends on which narrative you choose to believe but the facts on the ground were beyond dispute.

A convoy of doctors and nurses running the gauntlet to the Hadassah hospital on Mount Scopus were ambushed in a ravine carrying the road as it snaked its way up the hillside. Machine gun fire and mortar shells poured down on the on the lightly armored lorries and command cars killing 79 innocent civilians. During this offensive the British army looked on but did not intervene.

Meanwhile two extremeist Zionist para-military groups, the Irgun and the Stern gang, invaded Deir Yassin, blowing up many of the village houses and leaving more than 100 innocent women and children dead. Other versions of the narrative include finding the bodies of many armed Arab irregulars. Whatever the facts leading up to the massacre, there was no doubt that the Jewish terrorists murdered many innocents.

Two massacres close in time, many innocents murdered on both sides, two historical narratives including various versions of self-justification, yet the memories of those events echo to this day.

As one enters the ravine on the main highway half way up to Jerusalem, the burnt out shells of the armored cars from the Hadassah relief convey, are preserved as a monument, on the hard shoulder of the north side of the road. From the Arab point of view the massacre at Deir Yassin has taken on an even more potent memorial as a focus of hatred of the exiled Palestinians in Gaza and the occupied territories of the West Bank.

Sultan Al Mazri returned to his village after those terrible events to find his home destroyed and the bodies of his wife and his two youngest children lying dead in the rubble.

Later that day he discovered his son Abdullah, whimpering and blooded, hiding in the roof of his father in law's house. Sultan's hatred for the Jews became incandescent and he vowed one day he or his son would take revenge. Picking up his boy, Sultan with the remnants of their village joined the flood of refugees following the retreat of the Arab Legion beyond the eventual armistice line between the old and new cities of Jerusalem. As well as his hatred Sultan carried as secret weapon that one day he hoped would help him take his revenge on the Jewish usurpers of his land.

The inscription on the scroll jar that James Starkey had discovered at the base of the pyramid of skulls might one day help him and the Moslem brotherhood to unite the Arab race to renew the Caliphate of old.

Sultan and Abdullah made there way in stages to Amman where covertly he continued working for the Brotherhood whilst continuing to teach English in a local high school.

Sultan died at the early age of 55 having been burnt out by his hatred but not before he had time to brief his son with his mission. Abdullah qualified in medicine in Amman, as did Sultan's grandson Saleh in 2001.

★★★

Sultan's grandson shared his good looks and Islamic zeal. Whilst in medical school in Amman, he was recruited by the Muslim Brotherhood but this was no mere radicalization as he was pre-programmed by his heritage to continue the work of his late grandfather. With the premature death of his father whilst acting as a medical officer in the Yom Kippur war of 1973 he inherited his father's confidential papers including the narrative of the Lachish dig. As a teenager he made a solemn vow to avenge his father's death at the hands of the Israeli army as well as to continue his grandfather's quest to continue the search for the lost scroll hidden somewhere in the Land of Palestine somewhere between Lachish and Hebron. On qualification he trained as a surgeon that included a year as a resident in Boston at the Deaconess hospital. His mastery of the English language was perfect and along with that was his value as an agent for the Brotherhood.

In 2012 he was sent to complete his postgraduate training

in England, which was by no means remarkable but was in part inspired by the fact that London had become the central hub of covert activity of the Brotherhood in Europe. He spent two and a half years specializing in vascular surgery at Kings College Hospital in southeast London without once being called upon as a secret agent when suddenly, out of the blue he was advised to leave his post and apply for the job as a locum senior registrar at the Royal Free Hospital in northwest London. That again was not seen as anything remarkable as he had nothing more to learn in his chosen specialty at Kings and claimed that 6 months at the Royal Free might allow him to work with the new materials for arterial replacement being pioneered in the department of bio-technology at University College London.

With his experience, charm and command of the English language, he had no difficulty being appointed to that post. Shortly before starting his new job he was summoned to a meeting with the regional director of the Muslim Brotherhood at Dulwich Art Gallery, not far from Kings College Hospital. Whilst strolling round and ostensibly admiring the works of art on display, Saleh's controller briefed him about the job in hand. Apparently a sophisticated computer program had picked up a sequence of Internet searches using an algorithm to alert the Brotherhood that someone outside their closed circle was close to uncovering a closely guarded secret of great importance. Furthermore this secret had something to do with his grandfather's quest. Another agent, who by chance was serving as a night care nurse for an elderly Jewish couple in Hampstead, had happened upon a script written in German that was being translated into English on behalf of professor Joshua Black who worked at the Royal Free Hospital. This provided the intelligence that allowed them to pin point the computer responsible for this worrying sequence of searches. One of their IT experts was then able to gain access to professor Black's computer through embedded malware in one of his downloaded programs that enabled accurate monitoring of his key strokes. From this they discovered that professor Joshua Black was altogether too close to this secret and needed to be taken out. Once he was settled into his new job he would be alerted when an opportunity arose for professor Black to be abducted. At this he was handed a mobile phone to be used once only following a command by text and then disposed of. Once that mission was complete he was to leave the country immediately using a false identity and passport they would supply, and return home.

In the meantime he could be of further service by joining the Palestine Exploration Fund to undertake searches of the archive as directed. He would then learn how this mission was closely aligned to his grandfather's work.

A few weeks later he checked in at the PEF and signed for the archives of the Lachish dig for the years 1937 and 1938. It took him only a couple of hours search to find the letter he was looking for dated January 12th 1938. He copied out the letter from Olga Tufnell to her mother and on returning the letter to its envelope spotted the slip of paper bearing the code. Again he copied this out and swapped identical buff envelopes from 1937 to hide this exhibit so that no one else could trace it in the future. He returned the box files and signed out of the office without drawing attention to himself.

In June he received the text on his disposable cell phone and immediately phoned professor Black to tell him that his wife had been involved in a serious accident. He then destroyed the phone and made haste to Heathrow to catch the 17.05 departure on the Royal Jordanian Airline bound for Amman.

★★★

PART 3

Olive in the Holy land

Chapter 23

Jerusalem June 2016

Olive and Arthur were comfortably settled in business class of flight BA167 as it gently lifted off the runway at London Heathrow at precisely 14.40. As the seat belt sign went off and the stewardess started her round, Arthur ordered a double scotch whilst Olive ordered a tomato juice with Worcester sauce. Arthur then got out a fat novel with a story about a courageous and handsome young archaeologist searching for legendary treasures in Upper Egypt, seeing this hero as his avatar. Meanwhile Olive opened her guidebook on Israel but found she couldn't concentrate.

Unlike her brother who had made this journey many times, her emotions were tumultuous, swinging from excited anticipation to sweaty armpit terror. She wasn't frightened of flying but she was frightened of flying into a war zone. Like most of her peer group, who tended to read the "Guardian" or "Independent" newspapers, she had read nothing but bad news coming out from this sliver of land on the Eastern coast of the Mediterranean. Yet her enquiry of the Foreign Office reassured her that there was nothing to worry about and any hostilities were way beyond the borders. Furthermore, the itinerary that the Israeli tourist board organized, endorsed by her minder at New Scotland Yard, included all the biblical sites she had always wanted to visit, from the Church of the Holy Sepulcher and the *Via Dolorosa* in Jerusalem, all the way north to the Basilica of the Annunciation in Nazareth and "The Jesus Boat" on the Northern shore of the Sea of Galilee.

She was to give Bethlehem a miss as this involved crossing

into the West Bank and although this was considered safe they daren't risk any disturbance of their real mission resulting from some mishap at the border crossing. Eventually she calmed down to a state of excited anticipation at the thought of the great adventure ahead. At which point she fell asleep in the comfort of a business class fully reclining seat. Arthur carefully placed a bookmark in his novel and stowed it in the seat pocket. He glanced at the menu of films on the in flight entertainment booklet but decided they were all selected for the benefit of little toddlers or teenage assassins. He then drifted into a reverie recalling his first visit to the Holy Land in 1963. He was a 19-year-old divinity student at the time and decided to volunteer for the Masada excavation on the western shore of the Dead Sea. His motives were complex. Firstly he fancied the adventure but then this was also a rare opportunity to visit all the sites mentioned in the Bible and literally to walk in the steps of Jesus. Finally he was not having much success with girls at Oxford and he had heard that Israeli girls were hot. As things turned out he fell in love with the land, fell in love with archaeology and fell in love with a girl. He never forgot that moment. He was shoveling up rubble and debris whilst doubled up in an underground water cistern, when he stood up too quickly and cut his scalp on the sharp edge of some ancient plasterwork. The bleeding from his scalp was so profuse he was almost blinded. He was then rushed to the camp hospital on the western side of the plateau close to the foot of the Roman invasion ramp. He felt lucky that the surgeon on duty was English born and trained. The surgeon whose name he could no remember, staunched the bleeding by getting his nurse to press on the edges of the wound whilst he scrubbed up and began to close the wound with deep sutures under sufficient tension to control the haemorrhage. All this time the nurse assistant comforted him smiling through her eyes above her facemask. He would never forget those beautiful emerald green eyes framed by long black lashes. It was love at first sight but sadly unrequited. After the end of his term as a volunteer he said fond goodbyes to the girl with the evergreen eyes and decided that he would devote his life to the archaeology of the Bible once he had qualified as a Doctor of Divinity. With those memories in mind he drifted off to sleep and together with his sister, woke with a start as the plane put down at Ben Gurion airport.

They were met at the gate and given VIP service that facilitated their transition through border control and baggage retrieval. Olive, who was expecting the chaos of a third world country in a combat zone, was delighted with the beautiful terminal built out of Jerusalem golden stones, bright and airy with everything working efficiently with none of the misery she had experienced flying into Gatwick in the days she went on holiday to Italy with her late husband. A chauffeur driven limousine was waiting for them outside the terminal and they were whisked off to Jerusalem. Arthur who was an old hand at the game acted as a guide. The road was beautiful as it ran eastward across the fertile plain and Olive was enchanted with the views of fig tree plantations, olive groves and vineyards. As they left the plain and started the climb through the Judean hills the road changed its character and when they entered a ravine Arthur pointed out the russet painted wrecks of the last convoy trying to relieve the siege of the Hadassah hospital on mount Scopus in the 1948 war.

On entering the outskirts of Jerusalem the famous "City of Gold" lived up to its name as the street lights illuminated the stone walls of the modern apartment blocks and civic buildings the bordered the route. After the tortuous twist and turns around the fabled seven hills, they arrived at King David Street just by the Montefiore Windmill and half a mile later they reached the perfect exemplar of art deco, the Jerusalem International YMCA building right opposite the King David hotel. They climbed the steps to the arched doorway and checked at the Three Arches Hotel.

Awaiting them was a thick envelope containing a welcoming letter and a map of Jerusalem that happened to contain an invitation to breakfast on the terrace of the King David hotel at 08.00 am the following morning with a scribbled note that read, "If you see a familiar face don't acknowledge him but take the table next to where he is sitting."

★★★

To maintain the fiction of an invitation from the Hebrew University of Jerusalem, Sanjay was submitted to the indignity of flying El Al economy out of Luton on LY312 departing at 09.40. It was scheduled to arrive at 16.40 the same day as Olive and Arthur. Before he could step up to the check-in desk in departures, after standing in line for 45 minutes, a petite black haired Israeli girl who looked about 16, subjected him to the third degree. He was quite unprepared for this interrogation and broke out in a sweat. When asked the purpose of his visit he was at a loss to say. At this point the girl summoned her tough looking supervisor and with frequent glances over in his direction they engaged in a rapid rat-a-tat conversation. Her supervisor broke off and started an urgent conversation with his wristwatch nodding his head all the time. Sanjay started looking for a way to escape until the supervisor nodded at his timepiece for the last time and returned to the girl and restarted the rat-a-tat-tat.

He then stormed off and the young girl turned back to Sanjay offering him a radiant smile, apologised for the delay and stamped his passport and baggage before beckoning him through.

The tough guy was waiting for him and with a blank face ushered him to the business class counter.

Having checked in his luggage and received his boarding card he was also offered an invitation to wait in the King David lounge until his flight was called.

On boarding the flight he was disappointed to be directed in the tail end of the Boeing 737 and to make matters worse he found himself squeezed between two enormous, malodorous fat men wearing black gabardine long coats, full beards and big black hats.

The black hats were placed in hatboxes and then stowed in the overhead locker taking all the available space so that he had to make do with putting his carry on computer bag under the seat in front. These large men were accompanied by very large families that included screaming babies.

After they took off the nightmare was somewhat relieved by the fact that these ultra-orthodox Jews, as soon as the seat belt sign went off, got out of their seats and started walking around. For most of the five and a half hour of the flight, his companions gossiped with others of their kind, with frequent breaks for prayers. The first prayer session before breakfast was served appeared to include a ritual that involved checking one's blood pressure with a strange device carried in a velvet bag. During the time Sanjay was on his own he was able to read his Kindle where he had downloaded the two volumes of Simon Schama's "The Story of the Jews". Before they touched down, not a moment to soon for his sanity to survive, he had managed to read and inwardly digest the Biblical history and the post Biblical episodes that recounted the époque of the Elephantine Island settlement of the Jews that was Arthur Templeton's specialty. His passage through Ben-Gurion immigration and baggage retrieval was mercifully uneventful as if supervised by a guardian angel, which was closer to the truth than he might have imagined. It was also with great relief, that he spotted his name on a board held up by his driver the moment he entered the spectacular arrival's hall.

He enjoyed the view from the car window during the 40 minute drive up to Jerusalem where he was to be housed in a guest house for distinguished guests of the Hebrew University called the almost unpronounceable, Mishkenot Sha,ananim. Sanjay had no idea what to expect but was pleasantly surprised when the silent driver stopped just by an old stone built windmill. The driver helped him out and carried his case down some steep steps between pretty gardens and the golden glow of Jerusalem stone reflecting the late afternoon sun that shone brightly on his back.

They entered a modern foyer through smoked glass doors that enhanced the intrinsic beauty of an ancient stone built hall. The driver left him and he was immediately warmly welcomed by an attractive lady of middle years. She insisted taking his case and escorted him down another steep set of stairs that confirmed his suspicion that the complex was built into a cliff face.

Along the way to his rooms the walls were covered with photographs of the great and the good from the artistic and scientific disciplines from all over the world. Separating the doors to each apartment were little gardens of cacti and archaeological artifacts lit from above, all of which added to the charm of this delightful building. The nice lady showed him into his apartment and threw open the shutters that displayed a breathtaking view across a valley to the ancient Ottoman embattlements of the Old City. Whilst he was taking in the view the receptionist quietly slipped out without giving him a chance to ask questions. He appeared to be standing in a Spartanly furnished sitting room with two easy chairs, a desk and a coffee maker. Facing the window was a desk and chair and behind that a door that lead to a small bathroom. There was no message waiting for him on the desk and he was at a loss what to do next. Suddenly he heard muffled noises from behind a curtain on a sidewall that covered another doorway. He opened the door and was surprised to find a maid making up his bed. She turned at his entry and executed a perfect Namaste greeting. Surprised Sanjay took a closer look into the shadows and saw a beautiful Indian looking young woman. He instinctively returned the traditional greeting but was flabbergasted when the young women addressed him in his native language of Malayalam. "Welcome Professor Manchandra, I hope your journey was comfortable and uneventful". He was about to reply in the same tongue when a thought came to him that this might not be a simple housemaid, so he replied in English.

"Yes thank you all the arrangements worked perfectly, now tell me how come you speak my language?" Flashing him a big smile she continued in perfectly accented English. "First of all Professor Manchandra it would be more seemly if we continued this conversation on the terrace." She lead him back into the sitting room, drew back another set of curtains alongside the windows and opened up a double door leading on to a delightful shady terrace overlooking the Kidron valley and the Old City beyond.

Just beneath the window ledge was a rattan table bearing fruit juice in a decanter and pastries, with two comfortable rattan chairs alongside. She indicated a chair and pored him drink and then sat down alongside him. "Well professor I suspect that by now you might have deduced that I'm not really your housemaid. My name is Miri Cohen and my parents came here when I was 5 years old in 1995. We were one of the last Jewish families to leave Cochin and that is how I come to speak your language. I work for Shin Bet the equivalent to your MI5, and act as a liaison officer between the two agencies. All this I share with you knowing that you have signed State Secret's act. I am to act as your controller for this mission and whenever we in a public area we will behave as if we were husband and wife" With this Sanjay blushed so deeply that it shone through his nut-brown skin. Miri continued without a break. "Your instructions are as follows. Tomorrow morning at 07.30, I will be waiting outside your door. This institution is a safe house because all guests are screened and the management has top security rating. We will then walk hand in hand up to the windmill and then along King David Street to the King David hotel just 10 minutes away. We continue walking through the lobby to the terrace where I have booked a table. Your friends, Arthur Templeton and Olive Hathaway will then appear and sit at a table nearby but have been ordered not to recognise you. I will then strike up a conversation as if we were meeting for the first time and invite them to our table. From that point on I will brief you all on how we will be managing this mission. The only additional thing you need to know at this point is that you will be picked up from here tomorrow at 12.00 and driven to the university where you will deliver your first lecture. Later on you will deliver your second lecture at the Hadassah Medical centre and in the evening there will be a reception and dinner in your honour in the restaurant upstairs. The conversation will no doubt be mostly about the content of your talks but if asked how you intend to spend the rest of your time in Israel, stick as close as possible to the truth and say that your joining a tour group to visit some famous archaeological sites near Jerusalem and in the Galil." With that she shook his hand turned left on the terrace and before disappearing round the far side of the building turned to execute a Namaste greeting with a mischievous grin on her face.

Stunned by this turn of events, Sanjay plonked himself back in his terrace chair, took out his Kindle from his computer flight bag that had so far never left his hand and returned to "The Story of the Jews" constantly looking up to the Old City of Jerusalem hardly believing that he was playing some kind of role in the continuing history of these old stones and perhaps even in the continuing story of the Jews.

★★★

Chapter 24

Breakfast at the King David Hotel

The following morning, precisely at 08.00am, Olive and her brother crossed the road and entered the magnificent foyer of the Kind David hotel. They literally followed in the footsteps of the world's leaders of the previous 90 years as illustrated by illuminated tiles on the floor. Directly ahead of them they could see brilliant sunlight radiating through an array of French windows. Wending the way past a huge arrangement of lilies, bird of paradise flowers and twigs of blossom, they walked out onto the terrace. For a moment they were blinded by the low sun just rising over the battlements of the Old City, but once Olive's eyes adjusted there was sharp intake of breath.

Her whole field of vision was filled with the golden walls, minarets and church towers along with the iconic Tower of David, that marked the western extent of the Old City of Jerusalem from the Jaffa gate on the left to the Armenian cathedral on the right. Whilst she stood there transfixed her brother was already shuffling to a table by the far wall next to one with an Indian couple. At first she didn't recognise Sanjay because she had fixed in her mind that his wife had declined the invitation to join them. She joined Arthur at the table and studiously ignoring the couple on her right began to study the menu. After a few minutes the Indian lady turned to Olive and said, "Is this your first visit to Jerusalem?" "Yes" Olive replied, "Isn't it wonderful". They chatted on for a while as strangers in a strange land. After Olive and Arthur had ordered their breakfast the nice Indian lady invited them to join their table. Introduction and handshakes all round completed the charade until they were seated comfortably and breakfast was served. At this point the nice Indian lady continued in the same soft tone of voice. "My name is Miri Cohen and of course you know my companion." Shy smiles were exchanged and Miri continued, "First of all remember that you are still signatories of your State Secret act. I am to be your controller for this mission and I work for Shin Bet, the Israeli internal security agency. Sanjay and I will act as if we were a married couple who have just made your acquaintance, whenever we are in public places. I will now describe your itinerary, which you will have to memorise. Sanjay will spend the day giving lectures and acting the part of a visiting professor at the Hebrew University, meanwhile you will act the part as Christian tourists visiting the holy sites in Jerusalem. At 11.00 you will meet a guide in the lobby of the YMCA. You will recognise him by his neat beard and seaman's cap. He is a genuinely humble man and his name is professor Uri Barzilai and happens to be professor emeritus of archaeology at Tel Aviv University. He followed professor Ussiskin as the director of the excavations of Lachish and he was the one who finally identified the Assyrian siege ramp. He was also the one who had the bright idea of sifting all the rubble from the southeast corner of the temple mount and discovering pottery from the time of the first temple including seals of king Hezekiah from the 8thC BCE. He understands your mission and has very high-level security clearance. You'll be doing a lot of walking so remember to wear sensible shoes." Olive smiled inwardly at that comment.

"Tomorrow, the four of us will be joined by two American tourists to make up a party of six. Professor Barzilai will be our guide. The American couples, Mr and Mrs Schapiro from Detroit, are in fact both agents of Shin Bet and will provide proximal security. They will be carrying Uzi 9 mm machine pistols in their backpacks along with water and sandwiches."

At this Olive blanched and made as if to interrupt but Miri Cohen held up her hand and continued, "Mrs Hathaway you have no need to fear, there have been no security breaches or alerts for the areas you will cover tomorrow, this is simply a procedural matter for a Shin Bet mission" Hazel nodded coolly as if this was familiar territory for her, yet to tell the truth she had never been so thrilled in her life. A secret agent with an armed guard, you couldn't make it up.

Miri continued, "I must now make you understand the complexity of this mission and the complex chain of command. Our operation is now endorsed by the foreign offices of Israel, the United Kingdom *and* Saudi Arabia. The command structure is as follows. I will liaise with our embassy in London who will liaise with MI5 and the Metropolitan police anti terrorist unit. Your colleague in London, Abdullah Ibn Sharif, will be liaising with his uncle who is station head of intelligence in London and will be instructed to keep in touch on a secure line with Mr. Schapiro who as well as being handy with an Uzi speaks near perfect Arabic. Your other colleague, Ishmael Nadir, is a reserve in the IDF and will be riding point with a company of infantry on maneuvers with a security battalion belonging to central command. His cover for this is rock solid as he was due for his regular call up for a few weeks as a reserve officer with the rank of major."

Olive couldn't contain herself any longer, "Miri, you say there is no danger and Commander Quatermaine together with Mr Goldfarb in your embassy reassured us that we would be safe, yet now you tell us we will be protected by two agents with machine guns and a battalion of the IDF *riding point!* are you playing cowboys and Indians with us?" "Dear Olive, you have nothing to fear. The moment we learn of a security breach or pick up cyber chatter from our listening centers, the mission will be aborted. The level of security I describe is an insurance that if you find anything of importance, then you will be immediately evacuated from the area and the mission will continue with the professionals alone who will already be in place. Talking about chatter in the cyber sphere, our agents have just had a fix on the current position of that mobile node in the matrix of chatter between the centers in Brooklyn,

Stamford Hill, Lebanon and Tehran. It happens to be in the wilderness just north west of Qumran. We guess that our mysterious friends are searching for caves with other missing Dead Sea scrolls.

So tomorrow a large SUV will pick you up outside the YMCA at 08.00. Sanjay and I will already be on board and we'll then drive a short way to the David Citadel hotel to pick up the Schapiros. Professor Barzilai will be driving."

Turning then to Sanjay she said out loud, "Come on Darling we taken up enough of these good people's time let's go back to our lodgings and get you ready for your big day."

Smiling and bowing the charming Indian couple left the terrace with Miri calling over her shoulder, "Enjoy the rest of your stay".

★★★

Sure enough at 11.00am on the dot, Olive and Arthur made the acquaintance of professor Barzilai in the lobby of the YMCA. Olive was wearing sturdy walking shoes but had abandoned the Harris Tweed in favor of a lightweight linen skirt and bush shirt as the heat began to settle over Jerusalem.

She had covered her head with a Panama hat and carried a water bottle in a canvas bag thrown over her shoulder. Arthur wore his usual uniform as an archaeologist that was pretty much the same outfit her wore in London apart from an old sweat stained forage cap. Professor Barzilai, as allerted in advance wore an old navy blue sea dog's peaked cap, a neatly trimmed beard and twinkly eyes. He politely introduced himself and welcomed them to Jerusalem and explained that today they would explore the Old City by foot and lead the way out of the building.

Turning right along King David Boulevard they walked about 400 yards and turned east towards the Montefiore Windmill and then walked down a steep street made up of steps running through Yamin Moishe. They then strode out across the Sultan's pool and up a winding path that lead directly to Zion gate at which point they entered the Armenian quarter of the Old City. Following the ancient Ottoman walls now on their right hand side they soon entered the Jewish Quarter. Professor Barzilai then took them down some steep steps to the Roman Cardo, with the original paving stones leading precisely north south. Here he pointed out the pillars and cubicles that marked out the main shopping centre of Jerusalem at the time of Jesus. Coming up for air again he took them via a network of narrow allies until they reached a beautiful courtyard facing due east where they enjoyed their first breath taking view of the Temple Mount and the golden domed Islamic shrine, the Dome of the Rock. The rock inside he explained, was traditionally believed to be the site of the binding of Isaac where God stayed the hand of Abraham who was about to offer his son as a human sacrifice.

The Muslims venerated this rock because they believed that it was from this point that the prophet Mohammed spurred on his mount Buraq and in one mighty leap entered heaven.

Leaving that viewpoint they made their way down another steep lane, passed through a security checkpoint and strolled across a huge plaza the blazing sun directly above their heads, following a crowd of ultra orthodox Jews wearing their traditional black suits and black hats in spite of temperatures now in the 80's. Looking to their right it was obvious were this crowd were heading. There it was, the "Wailing Wall" or more correctly the Western Wall of the Temple Mount, standing 20 meters high and constructed out of huge limestone blocks. Packed two or three deep, were lines of nodding men facing the wall with their heads covered in prayer shawls. Young men in sun bleached army fatigues, wearing crocheted skullcaps, punctuated these lines like a piano keyboard. As it was a Thursday morning, several groups standing away from the wall were parading elaborately dressed scrolls of the Old Testament. In addition young boys were reading from other scrolls on mobile lecterns because Thursday was also the opportunity for the families of Bar Mitzvah boys to start the count down to the forthcoming ceremony on the Sabbath. Olive was surprised to her women's voices ululating from behind a screen at the southern extremity of the wall. Professor Barzilai encouraged her to walk down the plaza and join the women. When she got close she witnessed a strange sight. Hundreds of women wearing a variety of exotic head coverings were crowded by the screen trying to get a good view of their son's or grandson's coming of age. Others who were praying facing the wall, were inserting folded pieces of paper between the cracks. This she had already learnt from her guide book, were hastily written prayers for good fortune or the healing of loved ones. On a whim, Olive scribbled the enigmatic code guiding them to the place were James Starkey had hidden the find that had sparked this mission. She then said a quick prayer and slid her note into a crevice alongside hundred's of others. She had no idea why she had been so impulsive but in truth she was already suffering from the contagious disease known as the "Jerusalem Syndrome".

Feeling a little giddy in the heat she was glad of the break when Barzilai suggested that they sat on the cool shaded steps leading out of the plaza at its northwest corner. She was dehydrated already and greedily sucked ice-cold water from her thermos flask.

After a short rest they were guided up this set of steps, through another security barrier, under a series of deeply shadowed Roman arches and into the noisy souk of the Christian quarter.

★★★

As they climbed narrow covered alleyway, their feet had to negotiate a flight of narrow steps, hollowed out and polished by the thousands who had passed this way over two millennia. The steps were split into three cascades by parallel concrete

220

strips that provided a tramline for the constant and hazardous wheeled handcarts carrying produce and merchant's wares supplying the little boutiques that ran the full length of the souk as far as the eye could see. Exotic colors, exotic smells and exotic vendors on all sides assailed Olive's senses as she made her way timidly along the narrow thoroughfare, terrified of losing sight of her companions. Arthur was an old hand at the game and told her to ignore the merchants. Olive however was an innocent abroad and her natural English way of conducting herself, slowed them down as she very politely declined the offers of crucifixes, rosaries, heavily encrusted orthodox religious icons and authenticated wood fragments from the true cross. Instead of her polite rebuttals silencing the clamor of the vendors it appeared to inflame their generosity of spirit to the nice English lady with offers of, 40%, 50%, OK just for you madam special price 60% discount! In the end professor Barzilai had to intervene with a rapid exchange of Arabic to put an end to harassment of his charge. Somewhat chastened, Olive quickly caught on that is was foolish to make eye contact and followed the bulky backside of her brother until they made a sharp right turn into an alleyway that was a good deal quieter. They paused for a moment as their guide pointed out the Vth station where Simon of Cyrene carried the cross for Jesus. Olive paused for a moment to silently recite the Lord's Prayer. She then heard the sound of gospel song from further up the slope where a group of colourfully dressed African pilgrims had rested their feet by the VIth station, known as the Veil of Veronica.

They continued their slow ascent until station IX where the signs pointed off to the right in the direction of the Church of the Holy Sepulchre. The final stations leading to the entombment of Jesus were to be played out in the church itself. On reaching the small plaza packed full of pilgrims in front of the church, Olive confessed to herself a bitter disappointment. The church, said to be the epicentre of her faith, was blacked with soot and looked thoroughly unkempt.

On mentioning this to professor Barzilai, he explained that the constant squabbling amongst the Catholic, Greek orthodox and Armenian Church custodians constantly inhibited the upkeep of this Holy site. There was so little commonality of purpose amongst these three branches of the Christian faith that the doorway and keys to the door of the Holy Sepulchre were by tradition, entrusted to two Muslim families.

On entering the Church there was a scene of bedlam. Four separate services seemed to be going on at the same time in churches within churches and side chapels within side chapels. Multiple groups of pilgrims attended by the priests of their particular denomination in their own peculiar garb and headgear, were either kneeling in prayer or walking in awe the last few stations of the cross.

Everywhere was incense, gold and bejeweled icons of Mary and Jesus, Jesus on the cross, Jesus being laid to rest and Jesus' resurrection. The heat and smell were insufferable and the noise was like something from the Tower of Babel. Olive started climbing a narrow set of steps clutching a brass hand rail, that ran round a huge misshapen rock that was said to be Golgotha, the place of the crucifixion of her Lord. She then came over faint and would have fallen all the way down if it wasn't for the kindly attention of a group of Irish nuns who caught her as she stumbled and with the help of Arthur, propelled her through the crush to a stone bench in the plaza outside.

Uri Barzalai showed real concern and expressed sentiments of guilt that he had over-stretched her.

With a wan smile Olive fluttered her hands and said, "I wouldn't have missed that for the world. A pilgrim has to suffer a little but I think that's enough for one day." Once she had recovered strength to walk again, professor Barzilai gently ushered Olive and her brother the relatively short walk to the Jaffa gate where he flagged down a taxi that took them back to the pristine white, perfect art deco building, that housed the three arches hotel deep in the cool interior of the YMCA.

All agreed that this was enough for one day and as Uri Barzalai left he reminded them to convene in the lobby at 08.00 the next morning. As Olive went to sleep that night she suddenly realised that this had been the best day of her life since her husband had died. She also felt at peace with herself and as she drifted off the words of John Bunyan came to mind:

He who would valiant be 'gainst all disaster, Let him in constancy follow the Master. There's no discouragement shall make him once relent His first avowed intent to be a pilgrim.

★★★

Unknown to Olive, when she passed through immigration at Ben Gurion airport, her name on the manifest triggered an algorithm on a computer in Crown Heights Brooklyn, as a "person of interest". The hackers in New York had little difficulty with this break in security helped as they were by sympathisers working at Ben Gurion airport. Olive Hathaway's name had been stored on the hard drive as a "person of interest" ever since her name had been picked up from DI Ramsay's notebook.

The fact that she had now entered Israel made her even more interesting. Their agents on the ground reassured their masters that Mrs Hathaway was yet another sentimental Christian pilgrim.

However their masters thought it advisable to put a tail on her next time she left the YMCA.

Had Olive known that, her peace of mind might well have been shattered, yet ignorance is bliss and she enjoyed the slumber of the innocent.

★★★

Chapter 25

Tel Lachish and Tel Maresha

Rehoboam lived in Jerusalem and built up towns for defence in Judah: Bethlehem, Beth Zur, Adullam, Gath, Mareshah, Adoraim, Lachish, Azekah and Hebron. These were fortified cities in Judah and Benjamin. He strengthened their defences and put commanders in them, with supplies of food, olive oil and wine. He put shields and spears in all the cities, and made them very strong.

Chronicles 2, Chapter 11

Friday morning Olive was woken up by the bright sunlight filtering in through the slats of the Venetian blinds covering the arched windows of her east facing room. She felt refreshed and raring to go. She swiftly showered and dressed in her lightweight clothes and met her brother for a quick breakfast of freshly baked rolls, olives and strong black Turkish coffee flavoured with *hel*.

Having learnt her lesson from the day before, she tanked up with fresh water. They were waiting on the front steps of the YMCA as the black SUV driven by Uri Barzilai drew up. Miri Cohen and Sanjay were seating on the back row of seats so Olive and Arthur settled themselves and their back packs in the middle row of the SUV seating arrangement. They turned left out of the drive of the YMCA and about 200 yards further on turned into the drive of the David Citadel hotel.

Waiting on the pavement were Mr and Mrs Schapiro. It was easy to spot these middle aged American tourists by their choice of summer garb. They both wore unflattering

Bermuda shorts decorated with tropical fruit and palm trees. Their tee shirts of a similar design were covered by sleeveless jackets with many pockets and festooned with photographic equipment. Neither looked particularly fit and only those in the know were have judged that the effort of lifting their backpacks into the vehicle was a shade more than might have been anticipated.

Polite introductions were made all round. Mr Schapiro insisted they called him by his first name, Melvin and likewise Mrs Schapiro insisted they called her Betty. Driving north to the next set of traffic lights at the Mamilla shopping mall, they took a left turn and headed off west towards route 1, the main highway to Tel Aviv. The Schapiros were charming and garrulous and they chatted happily away like any other band of tourists in the Holy Land.

After about 40 minutes they turned due south on highway 6 in the direction of Beersheba. At this point Miri called for order and explained the details of the day's assignment to her three British charges.

"Today we will be visiting Lachish and Bet Guvrin also known as Maresha. Uri will explain some of the archaeological relevance of these sites but before that I will remind you of some operational details. I act as your controller and liaison officer and have radio connections on secure wavebands to Shin Bet and MI5 HQ. Melvin is ranking officer as a Major in the IDF intelligence service. He has radio connections with Central command HQ as well as Ishmael Nadir's company. In the highly unlikely event of any unfriendly activity you will do exactly as Major Schapiro orders. There is one other thing I can now advise you. You might be still be questioning how you came to be on this expedition so let me explain in full. First of all without your exceptional observations and deductions we would not have uncovered a plot of what we now think is of exceptional importance to regional peace in the Middle East. Secondly, as much as by chance as by design, the three of you provide perfect cover as a regular tourist group; a Christian brother and sister on a pilgrimage to the Holy sites and an Indian couple on a lecture tour taking a day off. Finally, and here I must apologize to Olive, we need Arthur's unique knowledge of some of the Biblical archaeology relevant to the mission and in addition professor Templeton happens to be a secret agent who has been working for us for some years as part of a covert Anglo-Israeli collaboration."

Arthur then turned to his sister and muttered, "Sorry sis, couldn't share this with you, mum's the word". Miri continued, "Finally if we find something of significance, it will be transferred immediately to professor Barzalai's safe keeping, but we will continue our tour as if nothing out of the ordinary had occurred. Any further inspection of a find will have to be performed under laboratory conditions. Uri will you take over now?"

"*B'seder motek. (For sure sweetheart)* Lachish and Maresha were two of many small garrison towns decreed by King Rehoboem King of Judah, to form a protective circle to cover the northern and western approaches to Jerusalem. What most people forget is that he was defending himself from his brother Jeroboam, King of the northern state of Israel. The two had a bitter struggle for the spoils after the death of their father, King Solomon. As a result Solomon's Kingdom was split in two with the tribes of Judah, Benjamin and the Cohenim remaining in Judea, which included the Holy Temple, the sanctuary and its treasures in Jerusalem. The other 10 tribes occupied the northern Kingdom that extended up to what is now the Lebanese border. The most powerful of the tribes was Dan, whose authority reigned in the far north.

Jeroboam was inflamed by losing the Temple to his brother and set up in competition his own sanctuary in the tribal lands of Dan. The remains of this alternative altar for ritual sacrifice can be now seen on the archaeological neighborhood known as Tel Dan in the foothills of Mount Hermon. Scholars of the sources of the Pentateuch, claim that there are two voices with much duplication of the text, suggesting that much later, perhaps during the Babylonian exile, two version of the Old Testament text were woven together as one. Legend also has it that Rehoboem was instructed by Ha'Shem to make peace with his brother and that was achieved when a share of the Temple treasure was transferred to the Northern Sanctuary.

The Assyrians, led by Sennacherib, attacked the Northern Kingdom in about 700 BCE and conquered the land advancing as far as Lachish en route to the capture of Jerusalem. There was a ferocious campaign but for some reason the Assyrians withdrew. The Bible claims this was a miracle but a more prosaic and likely explanation suggests it was an outbreak of typhus that decimated Sennacherib's legions. All the Jews of the northern Kingdom of Israel went into exile and are remembered as the fabled lost 10 tribes.

About 100 years later, round about 580-590 BCE, the Babylonians led by Nebuchadnezzar, finally conquered the Southern Kingdom of Judea and sacked Jerusalem taking Lachish and Maresha on their way. Lachish never really recovered but Maresha was to some extent rebuilt, but as you will learn today, much of it was an underground city built in the soft chalk rock of the shephelah.

Now that you have a sketchy idea of the Biblical history of the area, I will ask my friend and colleague, professor Templeton to let you into a secret."

Arthur then took his cue, "Olive, Sanjay, I'm sorry to have kept secrets from you but I hope you'll understand. Uri Barzalai and I have worked together in the past at digs on Elephantine Island and Maresha. Our work suggested that the community on the island in the Nile had built a sanctuary ready to take into safe custody, the Ark and other treasures from the first Temple in Jerusalem following the threat by the Assyrian hordes. That aside we are both of the opinion that our visit to Lachish will reveal little, as you will soon see, but that the likely hiding place for Starkey's important discovery must be in Maresha and here's why. The clue James Starkey left behind read as follows, 'Complex 2, System B, E wall, QB6'. Complex 2, System B is the archeological nomenclature for a set of caves that in Hellenistic time were used as a columbarium or dove coop.

Doves were much in demand in those days for paying homage to the Phoenician Goddess, Astarte, the Goddess of love. All women of this period offered up a pair of doves for sacrifice after giving birth as a token of thanks. In classic iconography you will often see a pair of doves associated with pictures of Venus another incarnation of Astarte. I think that is where we will need to concentrate our efforts."

After a few minutes silence Olive spoke out, "Arthur I don't understand, why and how you become involved with covert activities of a foreign power." To which Arthur replied, "Well first of all I was an obvious asset as someone who could legitimately travel from country to country in the Middle East because of my profession, digging up history in the rich subsoil of this Fertile Crescent. Next I was appalled of the iconoclastic activities of the Islamic extremists, destroying some of the richest archaeological sites in Iraq and Syria. Finally as a devout Christian I was deeply concerned about the welfare and security of our co-religionists in countries with Islamic fundamentalist regimes. I happened to be at a dig in upper Egypt when the Muslim Brotherhood took control and personally witnessed the destruction of Coptic Christian churches. The only country in this region that jealously guards the religious monuments of all faiths and protects all religious minorities is Israel. An old friend from my University days eventually recruited me at a lunch date in the Athenaeum Club. I always thought he was some kind of civil servant but now I know he works in the higher echelons of MI6 at Vauxhall Bridge. Our own government, like that of the USA, is concerned about Iran's nuclear ambitions and has a network of agents like me who have an ear to the ground. I can easily play the role of the bumbling British tourist in the fashionable clubs and dining rooms of the Levant without anyone guessing that I have command of the Arabic language.

Also at remote digs in Sinai or Iraq I can even witness military maneuvers. This mission is different as I also have some specialist knowledge about what I think and hope we might find and how this ancient artifact might resonate with modern concerns about the dangerous world we live in today. Finally there is a precedent. Nelson Gluek, one of the greatest Biblical archaeologists of all time, worked for the OSS, the for-runner of the CIA, during the Second World War and even tracked Rommel's movements in the North African campaign. "

Shortly after this speech Uri turned sharply eastwards onto a narrow minor road and 10 minutes later they were bumping over a poorly maintained and empty car park that served the ancient remains of Lachish.

Olive and Sanjay's initial response was one of great disappointment. This monument to the ancient Kingdom of Judea looked nothing more than a grassy mound that you might see from a train window passing through the South Downs in Surrey. The others in the party had of course visited before. Never the less under Uri's expert guidance, the footprints left in the sands of time, were quite remarkable. The car park was situated on the south side of the Tel and the first thing that Uri pointed out was the cut section of what was claimed to be the Assyrian siege ramp. To the untutored eye it just looked like a badly constructed wall. Professor Barzalai then led them up the well-preserved road made up of paving stones that were at least 2,500 years old, and up an inclined plane running alongside the western limits of the Tel. This was the remains of the original road leading up to the fortified double gates. Nothing much was left of the gate complex other than a truncated wall rising to the height of about one meter made up of three or four building blocks. Uri then pointed out the remains of the gatehouse where Starkey had discovered the "letters" that had started them on this quest.

Continuing through the remnants of the double curtain walls that fortified the whole garrison town, they entered a rocky but picturesque meadow full of wild flowers, covering the surface of Tel Lachish. Up here, apart for themselves, the only living creatures they could see were a dozen or so long eared shaggy goats that were contentedly nibbling the long grass. From this vantage point they could make out the double walls that encircled Lachish and appreciate the size of this ancient city. Professor Barzalai pointed to the north west of the Tell to some grassland where once there was an ossuary representing the remains of two generations of Judean defenders, the victims of both the Assyrian and Babylonian conquest. To clarify this point Uri Barzalai explained that James Starkey was killed before he had a chance of writing up his finds. Olga Tufnell eventually completed that work. However in the 1970s his team had reclassified the finds and discovered that the amour plates and remnants of weaponry were in fact from both sieges separated by about 100 years.

Finally standing on the ancient walls of the southernmost limits of the Tel, Uri mapped out for them the counter siege ramp built by the Judean defenders fighting the Assyrians. Looking up across a narrow valley the professor pointed to some farm buildings and with attempt at theatrics explained that the vantage point facing them was the seat of Sennacherib as illustrated on the bas-relief sculpture in the British Museum that was looted from it's the ruins of Nineveh that bore the inscription,

"Sennacherib, the mighty king, king of the country of Assyria, sitting on the throne of judgment, before the city of Lachish. I give permission for its slaughter"

That completed the tour and they agreed that no new insights had come to mind. However something had been said that lodged in Sanjay's memory and served some purpose as their adventures unfolded. On the way back to their SUV Olive noticed that they were no longer alone and that a battered flat bed truck was parked in the trees at the top end of the car park where two young goatherds were ushering their flock from the lush pastures above into the farm buildings on the ridge that once was the seat of the mighty King of the Assyrians.

★★★

The tourist party of six plus their driver clambered back into the SUV and drove out of the car park took the first exit on the side road, turning north east to drive 10 km to the archaeological park of Bet Guvrin-Maresha. Unlike Lachish this was a very welcoming, well-maintained and beautiful leisure facility. As it was Friday afternoon and most families were on the way home to prepare for the Sabbath, it was relatively quiet. They parked outside the visitors' centre and walked to a picnic area laid out with wooden refectory tables and benches protected from the blazing sun by a canopy of trees. The party pulled out their sandwich packs and flasks of ice-cold water and quickly satiated their thirst and hunger. The only other visitors sharing this space were a party of school children from a nearby Arab village who gawped at the foreign visitors. A few of the braver ones walked over to try out their rudimentary knowledge of English. Olive was charmed by these unexpected companions. Once the children had left, Miri again called them to order. "Right, we will continue as tourists. First we will visit the Bell caves, then the Sidonian burial caves and olive oil plant and finish off with the Columbarium cave. Make sure you drink plenty of water as we will be walking in the sun between the attractions and take plenty of photographs." The Bell caves were huge ancient quarries in the chalkstone with the quarrying carried out through a narrow opening at their apex and broadened out to the perimeter as the quarrymen dug out the building blocks. This provided building materials for the cities of the Coastal Plain. The caves were awesome, 40-50 feet in depth connected by a labyrinth of walkways inscribed with graffiti of workman from more than 2,000 years in the past. The Sidonian burial caves dated from the 3rd and 2nd

231

centuries BCE. The burial niches and walkways underground, illuminated by shafts of light shining in through narrow slots in the roof, were covered in beautiful Hellenic inscriptions and murals of mythical beasts.

The underground dwelling houses and the olive oil plant were reached via spiral staircases carved out of the soft chalkstone substratum. The oil plant and its presses were so perfectly preserved in every respect that they will still in use for demonstration purposes for visiting school children.

Although the visit was all things bright and beautiful, there was so far nothing observed that was relevant to their mission. Finally having nearly completed the visitor's trail in a clockwise direction they arrived at an unremarkable hole in the ground with the signpost reading, "The Columbarium Cave". They began their decent into the hole 6 feet in diameter via a spiral staircase, as before, but as they reached the roof of the underground complex a modern set of stairs looking like a New York fire escape, took them downwards into a vertiginous cavern the size and shape of the nave of Salisbury Cathedral. Apart from Uri and Arthur, no one else had visited this cavernous structure before. The central aisle was about 40 yards long with side chapels every 20 feet along the way. The height of the ceiling was uniformly 20 feet high so that the whole complex had a pleasing symmetry. Inset into every wall, well out of arms reach, were thousands of square holes that presumably were the nesting boxes of the sacrificial doves 2,000 years ago. They were dazed by the spectacle lit from apertures in the ceiling that gave the impression of rows of halogen lights. As they turned slowly round to marvel at the spectacle, Sanjay calculated the points of the compass as suggested by the sun's direction in the early afternoon. He judged that their entrance had been down the staircase set against the eastern wall to which the sunrays were pointing. Suddenly he knew with precision beyond doubt, where the object of their hunt was buried. Before he announced this fact he needed to learn one further detail about the excavation of this site. He politely turned to professor Barzalai and spoke in a hushed voice, "Uri, when your team excavated these caves was there much debris to remove?" "Indeed" he replied, "The interior of the Columbarium was full of debris made up of plaster falling off the wall, brick fragments, terracotta pottery and bird droppings. It took a year to clear. You can get an idea how full it was by the fact you could easily reach the dove coop holes in the highest sections of the complex." "I guessed as much" said Sanjay, "I now know without a shadow of doubt where the hidden scroll is to be found. The route we came down is from the eastern side of this cave. If you look at the highest set of dove coop holes you will note a perfect square with made up of 8 x 8 nesting boxes. That happens to be the configuration of a chessboard. I used to play chess for my school's first team and I know which square is QB6. That stands for Queen's bishop 6. There is a white and a black QB6 and my guess for rapid access it would have been easiest for Starkey, when standing on all that debris, to have slipped the object into white QB6 that is three along and three down from the left hand corner. Sanjay made as if to run up the steps and reach into the hole he indicated when professor Barzilai shouted, "Stop him!" The Schapiro couple then each grabbed an arm and turned the surprised culprit to face the archaeologist.

★★★

Chapter 26

The Golgotha Scroll

There was a deafening silence in the Columbarium after Uri's outburst. Barzalai then calmly opened his backpack and withdrew a pair of leather gloves and a telescopic walking stick with a sharp tip. For one irrational moment Sanjay had the impression that he was about to be tortured by the Shin Bet. However all Barzalai did was to wave the stick at Sanjay and then in a tone as if telling off a naughty schoolboy he said, "Never, ever, put your bare hand into a deep dark hole in this part of the world. You have no idea what might be nesting there." Everyone laughed with relief and Sanjay was released from his protective custody. Uri Barzalai then clattered up the iron ladder to the point where QB6 was within easy reach. He extended the walking stick to its full length and rummaged around in the hole. As if on cue a family of yellow scorpions, with tails raised in readiness for a strike, marched up the stick towards Uri's hand. Uri nonchalantly knocked the venomous creatures off his walking stick with his gloved left hand, whilst Olive responded with a high-pitched shriek.

"The yellow scorpions although somewhat smaller than their black cousins, carry a sting in their tail that can kill a child and might even lead to an amputation if an adult is stung in the hand" said Uri, whilst Sanjay wiped the sweat from his brow and took a long draw at his thermos of iced water.

Uri rummaged around a bit more with his stick and then gingerly reached into the cavity with his gloved hand. He then started brushing out debris and bird droppings along with worms and a millipede the size of his index finger.

Having completed that task he picked out a flashlight from his backpack and inspected the interior. All waited with baited breath until he let out a triumphant,

"*Kol ha'kavoed koolum, yaish lonu matmon.* (Honor to you all, we have found treasure)"

He then slipped his arm into the cavity up to his elbow and carefully withdrew a white clay cylindrical jar with a terracotta cap. Carrying it like a newborn baby, Uri carefully backed down the iron steps until he was at ground level. He beckoned the others to gather around as he laid the cylinder on the soft cushion of his backpack and knelt down. The jar was about 24 inches in length with a diameter of about 6 inches and carried some kind of inscription scratched deeply on its surface.

He then took some photographs of the find and stood up to photograph its nest. Without another word he slipped it in his bag and the gathered in a circle when Uri spoke again. "The inscription is in ancient Hebrew lettering and I think the language is Aramaic. I must get this to the department of Archaeology at the Hebrew University as quickly as possible and once we are on the road I will call ahead to my friend, professor Daniel Cohen to alert him of our discovery. We shall now walk out of this cavern and pose for a group photograph at the top before walking slowly back to our vehicle."

After the photograph had been taken the company strolled back to their SUV. Just as they were about to leave the site Olive noted something out of the corner of her eye. Half hidden under the trees at the other side of the car park was a battered old truck that caught her attention. The fact that the near side door was rust red confirmed that it was the same flatbed truck she had spotted at Lachish. Turning to professor Barzalai she said, "Uri, I think we are being followed. Check your rear view mirror, the truck at the other side of the parking lot was at Lachish when we left. I maybe paranoid but I find it hard to believe that a pair of goatherds would be interested in an afternoon in an archaeological park." Uri looked at his rear view mirror and cried out, "Fasten your seat belts and hold tight, Olive is right and I have to outrun this unwelcome intruder. Fortunately I know all the back routes into Jerusalem" With that Uri set off at high speed and entered a confusing network of minor roads running in all directions in the south east approaches to Jerusalem. To be doubly secure he made a loop into the PA controlled west Bank zone that entailed passing through a heavily guarded checkpoint. It was highly unlikely that their tail would risk following them any further.

Along the way Uri made radio contact with his colleague in the department of archaeology at the Hebrew University. His spoke rapidly in staccato Ivrit that his guests could not follow but later explained their plans. They were going to enter Jerusalem from the direction of Bethlehem and take back Olive, Arthur and Sanjay to their hotels. They were to freshen up and rest but be prepared to meet up again that evening with himself, Miri and professor Cohen. In the meantime Miri would communicate with her higher command in Tel Aviv and London. He then went on to say, "Olive, Arthur and Sanjay, you are a remarkable trio and your combined skills, powers of observation and analytical intelligence, have allowed us to reach this point. You have served your purpose and if I could have my way I would advise Shin Bet to recruit you all as agents for our State. Miri and her supervisors would probably wish you out of the country as quickly as possible in case the balloon goes up. The suspicion that we had a tail is sufficient to send the three of you back home. I think it only fair though that you should at least see whatever we found this afternoon so I'm hoping that professor Cohen will allow us all to hear his initial analysis of the cylinder and its contents this evening". Melvin Schapiro who had also been busy on his secure line then chipped in, "I've just been in conversation with your friend Ishmael Nadir. I alerted his company who have been close by on route 6, and they immediately set up a checkpoint on the slip road that is the quickest link from Maresha to the main highway. Even though he knew we were taking the scenic route to Jerusalem via Bethlehem, he argued there would be nothing to lose. Firstly our tail would guess they'd been rumbled if they encountered the roadblock and secondly this would suggest to them that we had indeed taken the fast route home. There was also a half chance that the registration plates of the truck might teach them something. Ishmael notified me 30 minutes ago that a truck resembling the one Olive spotted came within sight of the checkpoint and made a rapid u-turn and returned in the direction they had come from. The number plate on the truck was one stolen from an Opel sedan a couple of days ago. I'm afraid that some details of our mission have been leaked or our communications have been intercepted. I support Uri's suggestion that Olive, Arthur and Sanjay, should be booked on the first convenient flight to London tomorrow out of Ben Gurion. As it is Shabbat, El AL will not be flying so you will have to fly BA."

Once they were back in Jerusalem, entering the city from the east, the passengers were dropped off in reverse order, the Schapiros, Arthur and Olive and finally Sanjay. The last three were reminded to rest and freshen up and await further instructions. It was 5.30pm when they got back to their rooms and Olive was exhausted. She collapsed onto her bed and fell asleep. 90 minutes later there was a knock and two envelopes were slipped under her door. She awoke with a start in the midst of a terrifying dream feeling sweaty and dirt encrusted. One envelope contained her flights tickets on BA 164 leaving Ben Gurion airport at 16.50 the next day with a check in time two hours earlier. The other was an invitation to dinner at the home of professor Daniel Cohen at 7.30 pm that evening at an address in Yamin Moshe that was said to be a short walk away. They were to meet Miri in the lobby at 7.20 pm. Olive remained calm and took a quick bath and changed into a fresh white linen dress, deciding there would be plenty of time in the morning to pack for their departure. On the dot of 7.20 pm she met up with Arthur and found Miri waiting in the lobby but without Sanjay. Miri explained that the Cohen's home was very close to the guesthouse where Sanjay was staying and they would pick him up along the way. They turned right out of the YMCA towards the windmill. Miri asked them to wait at the top of a broad stone staircase and within two minutes she returned with Sanjay in tow.

They then turned left along a series of terraces each overflowing with beautiful flowering plants cascading down towards the Sultan's pool. Each terrace was bordered by low-rise villas built of Jerusalem stone that reflected back a miniature version of the Ottoman battlements that faced them on the other side of the valley.

They arrived at a cobalt blue door just as the carriage lamps on either side were switched on and just as the first four stars that announced to start of the Sabbath, appeared in the Prussian blue sky above the Old City.

Chapter 27

Friday night dinner in Yamin Moshe

The door was opened by a tall, bronzed, handsome man wearing tortoise-shell glasses who introduced himself as Daniel Cohen and showed them into a comfortable sitting room with a spectacular view towards the Old City. Uri Barzilai was already there and stood up to shake hands in a formal manner. Glasses of wine were handed out and then Daniel turned at the sound of his wife entering from a back room. Everyone stood up again to be introduced to Daniel's wife who insisted they called her by her nickname, Jessie, short for Yehudit- Esther. Jessie was tall and slim and walked like a gazelle. She had a preternatural beauty with emerald green eyes that seemed to be trans-illuminated. She was probably in her early 40s but it was difficult to judge. Arthur, who had been in close conversation with Uri, was the last to turn round to greet his hostess. As he shook hands with Jessie Cohen, his face turned deathly pale and he broke out into a sweat. He collapsed in a heap on a strategically positioned armchair. Jessie was embarrassed and confused yet kept her composure and said, "Professor Templeton you look like you've just seen a ghost." "Indeed you are right Mrs. Cohen, I thought I had." Arthur replied. "About 50 years ago when I was a young student aged 19, I was working as a volunteer on Masada when I cut my head. A young English surgeon sewed me up assisted by a nurse, the most beautiful woman I had ever seen, it was love at first sight, and you my dear are her spitting image." Jessie blushed and laughed at the same time and turned to her husband who joined in with her laughter. "Professor Templeton, Arthur if I may, that young woman was my mother and the surgeon who stitched you up was my father." Olive then joined in, " But Mrs. Cohen, how come you have a perfect English accent?" "Mrs. Hathaway, please call me Jessie, I have a perfect English accent because I have dual nationality and was educated up to the age of 18 in London. My father, Martin Tanner, went on to become professor of surgery at the Royal Marsden hospital." "Well I'll be damned" Arthur interjected, "I know your dad, he and I are both members of the Athenaeum, yet the young doctor who stitched my scalp had a beard. Perhaps that's why I never recognized him. How is the old man?" "Well sadly he passed away earlier this year. This was his last home and he bequeathed it to me in his will. In fact we only moved in a few weeks ago." "I'm so sorry my dear, what a faux pas, my sincere condolences," said Arthur, quickly trying to gather himself together. "Oh please don't fret, there was no way you were to know and he had a long and fulfilling life that we celebrate rather than mourn. Here let me show you some photographs of my parents. Sadly I never knew my mother who died when I was a baby," With that Jessie took Arthur's hand and lifted his considerable bulk out of the chair and conducted him around the room. When Arthur saw the pictures of Jessie's parents he had to choke back his tears. Mother and daughter were like identical twins. "My father was a great man, Arthur and in this cabinet you can see a display of his medals collected for his scientific contributions plus this one, the 'The Israel Prize' for services to archaeology." Arthur was just about to ask her about this surprising honor when Jessie took his hand again and announced to all that dinner was ready but first she must light the Shabbat candles and Daniel must recite the *Kiddush*.

They moved over to the dining area in the L shaped room where a table, covered in a brilliant white cloth, was set out for seven. At one end of the table were twin candlesticks, a silver goblet and what looked like a table fountain with little spouts leading to 8 petite silver cups. Arthur and Sanjay were handed crocheted skullcaps and all the men covered their heads. Olive looked on wide-eyed not understanding what was to happen. Jessie lit the candles, covered her eyes with the palms of her hands and chanted a short blessing. Daniel then lifted up the goblet full of wine and in a beautiful baritone voice sang a blessing to welcome the Sabbath and bless the wine. He took a sip and poured the remainder into the mouth of the table fountain allowing the eight cups to fill simultaneously.

Each of those standing at the table were handed a silver cup and encouraged to sip the sacramental wine leaving one cup behind. Jessie took that cup and placed next to the picture of her parents. Daniel then washed his hands with a jug and bowl on the sideboard and then lifted an embroidered linen cloth that was hiding two twisted choler loaves. He lifted the loaves and blessed the bread that was then torn into small pieces, salted and passed round to all his guests.

They then sat down to an exotic dinner of traditional Jerusalem Sephardic cuisine.

With the rituals out of the way and the first plates served, Daniel opened the conversation.

"Olive, Arthur and Sanjay, you have to be the three most remarkable and tenacious people I've met in my long career. What you have led us to, if my initial suspicions are correct, is the equivalent to a treasure map pointing out the precise resting place of the Holy Grail. Miri and Uri have done their best to explain how you all got involved and what led you to this find, but before we go any further please can you be troubled to repeat your story from the start because there are many things I still don't understand." Sanjay and Arthur turned to Olive, who acknowledged the unspoken compliment with a nod, then replied. "Daniel, I might start with the question, how long have you got? As our flight isn't until tomorrow afternoon I could go on all night but as you know the outline of our story I'll give you the shortened version but I can assure you that there are many things *we* still don't understand." Olive then embarked on an abbreviated version of their story as first told in that unpleasant occasion with the Black's family

241

law firm. Throughout this time the others nodded and she was left without interruption. Once her story was complete Daniel spoke again. "Mrs. Hathaway, you have a remarkably well organized mind to repeat all that without referring to notes.

As you imply there are many things that are difficult to understand, but the most puzzling to me and professor Barzalai, is how this scroll jar came to be buried under a pyramid of skulls that were under more than 1,000 human skeletons that in turn were buried under the bones of about 100 pigs."

Olive shook her head with a downward grimace of her mouth but then to everyone surprise Sanjay raised his hand like the smartest kid in the class and called out, "I know!"

They all turned to him with expressions of deep skepticism but he continued unabashed. "It was a throw away remark that professor Barzalai made at Tel Lachish, that left me pondering that puzzle. There can only be one explanation. The Assyrians never completed their conquest probably as a result of a breakout of some highly infectious disease like typhus. They withdrew without bothering or for that matter risking the burial of their Judean captives who had already been decapitated, assuming quite reasonably that the rotting corpses of their foes were the source of their curse.

Once it was safe, the Judean survivors buried the remains of their fighting men in the manner of their tradition. Not in a grave as in modern times but in a temporary shelter waiting for the bodies to rot away and then for the skeletons to be reburied in a group ossuary at a later date. Fast forward 100 years and this time the Judeans were defending themselves against the Babylonians. This time their masters in Jerusalem must have seen the writing on the wall and decided to hide their most precious treasures as far away from capture as possible. In the same way that during the second world war, the contents of the National Gallery were hidden in disused mines in south Wales. These treasures must have included

242

ancient documents that were always prized by the People of the Book, together with the treasures from the Sanctuary in the Temple. Arthur Templeton's work has suggested that the Jews in Elephantine were already prepared to accept the Ark of the Covenant and who knows were the rest of their stuff was to secreted? My guess is that the contents of the scroll are effectively a treasure map that was also on its way for safe keeping outside the country. When it looked that Lachish might fall one of the guards was given the task of hiding the scroll. He then hit on the brilliant idea of burying it under a pyramid of skulls and then covering the skulls with remains of those killed by the Assyrians. He or his senior officer then transcribed the clue to its hiding place onto an ostracum similar to the other Lachish letters. They probably made two copies, one to be sent by courier as far away as possible and the other kept in the guardhouse.

Once the Babylonians had conquered Lachish they had time to dispose of all the bodies of its Jewish defenders in the same burial pit and for good measure, to add insult to injury, included the remains of their celebratory feast." Sanjay said all this without drawing a breath, leaving his audience stunned. Then as an afterthought he added, "Of course I have to thank professor Barzalai for that insight as he pointed out that their were remains of two types of armor in the burial cave, one that was fashionable in 700BCE and the other that was all the rage 100 years later."

Everyone collapsed with laughter and once Daniel had recovered he said, "What is it you said you did for a living? – Seriously though, that has to be the explanation." Jessie Cohen backing her way out of the kitchen bearing steaming dishes of rice and spicy lamb stew then interrupted the conversation. "What's all this I've just missed whilst slaving away in the kitchen?"

"Nothing to bother your pretty little head about darling," joshed Daniel in return. Jessie made as if to throw a dish at him but he redeemed himself immediately. "Ladies and

Gentlemen, allow me to introduce professor Yehudit, Esther Tanner, co recipient of the Kettering prize for cancer research and daughter of the man who discovered the Third Tablet of the Holy Covenant now on display in the Israel Museum." "Oh my God", exclaimed Arthur, "I followed that story in the journals but never made the link to the Tanner I knew in London. Well it's a great honor to meet you professor Tanner, I wish we had time to visit that exhibit but sadly we are booked on the early afternoon flight back home." Jessie laid down the serving bowls and dished out the spicy lamb stew, whilst Daniel described the "Manchandra Hypothesis" that was the explanation of the laughter that preceded her entry. Jessie was quiet and thoughtful for a moment and then spoke up, "I think that all makes sense Sanjay so now I can't wait to hear what Daniel made of the scroll jar and its contents."

"*B'seda motek,* (of course sweetheart); the jar itself is ubiquitous throughout this region and invariably contains a scroll of antiquity. The shape of the stopper at the open end is even reflected in the architecture of the Shrine of the book that houses our collection of the Dead Sea scrolls. In fact the one I handled today was very similar to the jars that held the intact scrolls that first came into the hands of professor Yadin, one of my predecessors, in 1947; the only difference being the inscription on the outside and of course the contents of the clay tube. As Uri has already deduced the inscription on the surface is in ancient Hebrew lettering but in the lingua franca of that period, Aramaic. The period in question as Sanjay has guessed, was about the 7th C BCE. I could not trust my initial translation because I thought too far fetched so I got my colleague, Bernard Naftalin, an expert on ancient Semitic languages, to confirm. And yes Sanjay, the inscription, using the modern idiom read as you predicted, '*The treasures of the Holy Temple and the Rod of Aaron*' and my bowels turned to water. The clay jar was opened in a dust free darkroom under ultra-violet light. The wax sealing the cap had almost decomposed so it came off easily. Looking inside there was indeed a tightly wrapped scroll but the UV light was not required because I was not looking at parchment but looking at copper. I'm sure my heart stopped beating for a moment because I knew exactly what you had found." Intentionally to maintain the excitement, Daniel paused to catch his breath, take a couple of fork-loads of stew and compliment his wife on her cooking skills.

" Copper scrolls like this are rare and the scribe's decision to inscribe on copper rather than papyrus or parchment suggests that the contents are considered very important, so important that whoever dictated the text to the scribe wanted it to outlive many generation of mere mortals. The most famous copper scroll so far discovered was the one discovered in Qumran cave 3, in 1952. Cave 3 is the northern most cave in the Qumran complex. The numbering of the caves is simply the order with which they were discovered. So far 11 such caves have been identified but cave 3 is the furthermost one from the archaeological site of the Essene colony. The Qumran copper scroll is also different to all the others in a number of ways, first it is thought to be of a different époque as judged by the manner of writing and secondly because of the nature of the inscribed text. All of the other Dead Sea scrolls contain recognizable extracts from the Pentateuch, the Prophets and the Kings. In addition others provide details of religious observances and the smallest of them all are the tiny transcripts of the *Shema* prayer from within the boxes attached to phylacteries. The Qumran copper scroll is literally a coded treasure map minus the key to help with its decifer. Imagine the enigma code without the computing skills of Alan Turing. Many experts since its discovery have suggested it was a hoax but most now agree it is authentic, yet even amongst those there remains uncertainty as to whether it dates from before or after the fall of the second Temple. If my hunch is correct then you have discovered, proof positive, that it dates back to the fall of the first Temple. That by itself is a key to understanding the nature of the treasure. It must be the gold bullion of the tithes collected from the people of Israel at the command of the Torah to support the Temple and its priesthood, the Cohenim. In addition it might also include the golden artifacts from within the sanctuary, including the candlesticks that lit the Holy of Holies and the fabled candelabra. Finally of course it might also refer to relics more valuable than gold that of course include the Ark of the Covent, the tablets inscribed by the Decalogue and Aaron's rod.

The candelabrum is already accounted for as it can be clearly seen on Titus' arch in Rome in a relief of Roman soldiers carrying away loot from the remains of the Temple. The golden candlesticks were recently discovered in a vault in southern India near Sanjay's hometown, how they got there is another story for another night. You can view them in an exhibit in the Israel museum alongside the third tablet that was recovered from the far north of Israel near the Lebanese border. So from those examples we can judge that the ancient Israelites were prepared to hide their treasures far and wide in the then known corners of the globe. This should not be surprising if you remember that during the Second World War, some paintings from the National Gallery in London were hidden in Carnarvon castle in north Wales "

Daniel paused again to swallow another mouthful of his dinner and to take another sip of wine.

"Let me now read an extract from the copper scroll from cave 3 to convince you that I'm not making this up." Daniel stood up and walked across to his well-stocked bookshelves that covered nearly all the available space on the walls between the windows of the L shaped room. He was the kind of bibliophile who probably knew the exact place of every volume he might be looking for in this great expanse of books. He found the book without hesitation and found his place amongst the well-thumbed pages at the first attempt and then started reading.

" 'In the cave that is next to the fountain belonging to the House of Hakkoz dig 6 cubits there are six bars of gold.'

246

Hakkoz was the name of a priestly family that traced back it time to king David. The Hakkoz estate was in Jordan valley not far from Jericho. The book of Ezra 8:33 describes how the Temple treasure, including the 7th year tithe, was entrusted to Meremoth son of Uriah son of Hakkoz. There are similar descriptions of 64 locations of hidden treasure, mostly of gold and silver but some relate to items that might be linked to religious practices. Finally there were 7 locations were the code to their whereabouts not only include Hebrew numbers and letters and that do not make words but with couplets of ancient Greek letters written in a style closer to their Phoenician origins, for example, delta epsilon or sigma kappa. The way those letters were inscribed again supports that the scrolls belong to the period just before the fall of the first Temple.

If my hunch is correct then the intact copper scroll you've discovered might contain the missing key we've been searching for in order to break the code of QT3."

Olive the interrupted this discourse with a query, "Excuse me but what is QT3?"

"Oh sorry Olive, this is the standard nomenclature for identifying the individual scrolls, it simply means Qumran, Treasure, Cave 3". "Is there a scroll indexed as QB6?" asked Sanjay.

"Let me think," said Daniel as he turned to the index at the back of the book, "Yes here it is, QB6, B for benedictions found in cave 6 in 1955, deep in the upper part of Wadi Qumran west of Khirbet Qumran. Why do you ask?" "Can it just be a coincidence that Starkey's clue to the pigeon hole where we found the clay jar was QB6-Queen's Bishop 6? " There was a communal sharp intake of breath by all those round the table.

At that point Miri Cohen's mobile phone beeped and the checked the incoming SMS. Lifting her head she said, "Ladies and Gentlemen, Hamas has chosen this evening to fire 30 missiles in the direction of Tel Aviv, most were taken out by the "iron dome" anti-missile defense system but two landed just inside the perimeter of Ben Gurion airport. All flights in and out have been suspended until further notice. Olive, Arthur and Sanjay, your stay in the Holy Land has just been extended"

In the hubbub that followed Sanjay's question was soon forgotten. Hotels were called to extend the stay of the visitors and plans made for the following day. By then it was past midnight and the eventful evening came to an end.

That night, unusual for him, Uri Barzalai couldn't sleep. Something just out of reach was bothering him. When he eventually fell asleep he had a nightmare very much like "Alice through the looking glass". In the dream he was a white pawn and the black queen knocked him over so that he fell down a steep flight of stairs that had opened under his feet. He woke in a sweat and knew exactly what had troubled him. In the excitement of the previous afternoon he had forgotten one of the basic rules of archaeology. Once you have finished at a dig tidy up and leave the site as you had found it. He had left the columbarium with the debris he had scooped out of the pigeonhole QB6, scattered on the floor and the cleaned out cavity was conspicuous when compared with all the others. He wasn't sure why that troubled him, but it did.

Chapter 28

Sabbath in the Israel Museum

Arthur also had a fitful night, partly because of overindulging in deliciously spiced lamb stew and partly from drinking too much Chateau Golan cabernet sauvignon. In addition something important linked to the notation of the Dead Sea scrolls was hovering just out of reach in his memory. He fell asleep and woke up an hour later suddenly remembering what it was. Not having any reference books with him, he logged into the hotel WiFi on his laptop and Googled "Dead Sea scrolls". He then clicked on the link that listed all the scrolls in the index and found what he was looking for. As anticipated there it was QG3, Qumran scroll found in cave 3 with G for Golgotha. The scrap of parchment discovered in the neighborhood of the copper scroll had always been assumed to be proof that the Essenes had scriptures describing the crucifixion of Jesus on mount Golgotha in 31CE, and were therefore proto-Christians. In fact that text had been written more than 500 years earlier and was a copy of the 19th Lachish letter. The circle was now complete and Arthur fell into a deep sleep looking forward to sharing this information the next day when the party was to reconvene in Daniel Cohen's laboratories at the Israel Museum.

★★★

The Israel museum is built up of a chain of glass cubes linked in a knight's move pattern. The whole complex had been reopened in 2011 after extensive refurbishment and was in pristine condition reflecting the early morning sun of the Judean hills off every surface. To reach the sloping underground entrance to the museum one had to pass through beautifully landscaped gardens with spectacular views over the seven hills of Jerusalem and each viewpoint is occupied with a piece of contemporary sculpture from the world's most famous sculptors. Because it was *Shabbat,* Olive, Arthur and Sanjay, enjoyed this vista alone apart from two security guards with little coils of cable exiting their shirt collars en route to their earpieces. Miri was waiting them as they entered the complex and pointed out the dome marking the roof of the Shrine of the book that did indeed resemble the cap on the jar holding the copper scroll. She promised them a visit once the formalities were complete.

They finally entered the building having passed through the equivalent of airport security and were issued visitor's passes to wear on lanyards round their necks and were then conducted to Daniel Cohen's office in the administrative block. The name of the door read, "Professor Daniel Cohen, curator biblical archaeology first and second Temple period." Daniel and Uri, who had been at work since before sunrise, rose to greet them and offered coffee and donuts all round. Daniel cleared some space on his desk and invited them all to sit down. "Sorry about the formalities but security is strict even on the Sabbath when we are supposed to be closed. I've had a tough time convincing the ministry to allow us to open up and Mr. Ben Tzadick, the minister responsible, was not pleased to be disturbed on Shabbat, but he is very quick on the uptake and recognised the importance of our work." He then opened a large cardboard box that contained the clay cylinder and its contents side by side. The copper scroll was tightly rolled and it was difficult to see anything other than one superficial surface covered in mysterious imprints. " We now have the task of unrolling this scroll without cracking it into segments. When the first copper scroll was discovered it

250

was sent to Manchester University to unravel. They merely sliced it into segments and photographed them side-by-side. The photographic technique was primitive and significant fragments of the fragile oxidized copper was lost along the edges making it very difficult to read sentences that crossed those fracture lines. Since then we have developed a much more sophisticated way of handling relics like this.

First of all we soak the scroll in dilute acetic acid and run a current through the bath to get rid of the superficial cuprous oxide. We then transfer to another bath that contains a resin that fixes the brittle copper in a soft matrix that allows us to gently unroll the scroll without too much risk of fracture.

The process takes about three hours and will be carried out in my laboratories on site. Although my chair is at the Hebrew University on Mount Scopus, I only go there to teach. The artefacts under my care are too precious to be *schlepped* backwards and forwards so the university funds my lab close to the museum and the scrollery." "Excuse me Daniel but what does *schlepped* mean?" piped up Olive. "Sorry Olive, it a Yiddish word with no English alternative; it sort of means carrying awkward or heavy objects all over the place whilst breaking into a sweat. Anyway whilst the scrolls are being prepared there is nothing to see so I suggest Uri shows you round the Museum and the shrine of the book, break for lunch and come back here at 14.00 when with any luck we might have unraveled the secret code of the treasure scroll."

★★★

The Israel Museum is one of the top five archaeological and anthropological museums in the world.

Sanjay had not visited the other four, nor when he came to think of it, any museum of any kind anywhere in the world. This realization came to him as a shock. Gazing in wonder and awe at the beautifully organized and illuminated exhibits in the first few rooms covering Ancient Egyptian and Biblical archaeology, he realized that he had missed something central to a cultured life, in his rapid rise to success in his chosen field. Uri was an excellent and enthusiastic guide and Arthur was in his element, exchanging esoteric banter with his Israeli counterpart. Olive was quietly absorbed with all she saw but became animated when she saw the exhibits linked to the Essenes and the other early Christian sects. There was a freestanding exhibit that had pride of place in an atrium at the centre of this wing of the museum. On a raised platform inside a perfect glass cube, illuminated in blue light, were the two reunited segments of the Third Tablet of the Holy Covenant flanked by the recently uncovered golden candlesticks that had illuminated the sanctuary for the High Priest once a year on Yom Kippur, the Day of Atonement. Uri described professor Tanner's role in the recovery of these priceless relics aided and abetted by his daughter and son in law Jessie and Daniel Cohen. He also described the act of near genius that allowed them to reveal the long lost inscription in the tablet of stone and its translation from the ancient Egyptian hieratic script.

After viewing the archaeological and ethnological wings of the museum they then went across to the older section of the building to view the remarkable collection of impressionist and post-impressionist art that were mostly acquired from legacies of rich Jewish families around the world many containing restituted works of Nazi looted art. So even in the art galleries the tragic history of the Jewish people was being retold for future generations.

After that they had a lunch break out of doors in the shade of a pergola festooned with bougainvillea before crossing the sculptor park to the Shrine of the Book. The entrance lobby was framed to reproduce the atmosphere of the Qumran caves and was lined with exhibits explaining the discovery and translation of the scrolls. However they were not prepared for the drama of entering the central circular room showing the original Dead Sea scrolls and facsimiles of those on display in the Rockefeller Museum in New York and the Archeological

Museum in Amman, Jordan. The circular gallery was built on two levels with the main display case supported on a central spindle built to look like the scroll of the *Sefer Torah,* the holy scriptures of the five books of Moses.

Pride of place was given to the scrolls found in cave 1 but the centerpiece, that wrapped around the glass fronted cylinder on its gigantic mahogany spindle, was the complete scroll of the book of Isaiah dating back to 100BCE.

Now marinated in the soup of biblical antiquity, the group of latter day scroll hunters, made their way back to Daniel Cohen's offices for their assignation with the copper scroll that might have been inscribed earlier than that of the prophet Isaiah.

★★★

Having been marinated in a soup of acetic acid and a polymer resin the unraveled copper scroll awaited them in Daniel's laboratory. As he welcomed his guests back his face carried a mischievous grin. He bade them to sit down alongside the scroll table and indicted a fresh cotton drape hiding something below its billowing surface. Then with a mock portentous voice proclaimed, "Behold, the treasure map of ancient days revealed! Well not just yet. The results are spectacular as far as the quality of preservation but as far as interpretation is concerned we haven't made a start. I want to keep it covered whilst we're talking and whilst we await the special emulsion photographs to be developed for close observation. Our breath and ambient moisture even in this controlled environment could lead to re-oxygenation of the surface. You will of course get to view it but beforehand, in order to help us interpret what we have discovered, we need to put it in its historical context. Remember if the scroll does indeed lead us to the hidden treasures of King Solomon's Temple, these might have been moved a number of times between Holy sites as well as being hidden at times of threat. I therefore want to give you a brisk review of Biblical history, as it might be relevant to our understanding of this scroll. Remember the further back in time we go the greater the margin of error in dating we can expect.

In approximately 1,300 BCE, the children of Israel complete their 40-year sojourn in the desert and enter the Promised Land. The Ark of the Covenant is then set up in a temporary Sanctuary at Shiloh, near modern day Beth El in the West Bank. The tribes are then allocated regions in the land they have conquered, literally from Dan to Beersheba, the extremities of the land of Canaan.

Joshua 19:47 describes how the tribe of Dan, dissatisfied with their portion on the coastline turned north and conquered Laish a city populated by Phoenicians. I'll return to the city of Dan shortly.

King David's reign was in the region of 1,100 to 950 BCE. He was followed to the throne of the United Kingdom of Israel, by his son Solomon who is remembered for his idea of justice, his harem of countless concubines, but mostly for building the first Temple in Jerusalem. Once complete, the Ark, the altar, and the treasures of the Sanctuary were taken from Shiloh and housed in glory in the Holy of Holies on the Temple Mount. After the death of Solomon in about 930 BCE, a fight breaks out between his sons, Jeroboam and Rehoboam. Rehoboam was the anointed monarch but his brother disputed the title and the civil war was closely avoided but the Kingdom was split between Israel to the north and Judea to the south. By way of diplomacy some of the wealth of the Temple treasury was apportioned to the northern Kingdom. Not only was the Kingdom of man split but also there was a split in the worship of the Kingdom of God. Judea retained the traditional practices of Temple worship but Jeroboam was something of a heretic and returned to some pagan modes of worship that reflected the influence of his unruly neighbors. In Kings 2, 10:29, you can read that Jeroboam established a religious sanctuary in the city of Dan, which included the worship of a golden calf. In about 870 BCE King Omri, built a new capital city for the Northern Kingdom that was known as Samaria and the northern Temple and its treasures were moved south from Dan to Samaria. Finally, in 722 BCE, in the reign of King Hoshea, the Assyrians conquered Israel and the 10 northern tribes were scattered all over their Empire.

As you know full well, the Assyrians marched south and failed to conquer Jerusalem although they did some serious damage to Lachish on their way. The final destruction of Jerusalem and the first Temple was left to the Babylonians in 587 BCE, who as an aperitif razed Lachish to the ground.

Any questions yet?" His small audience shook their heads in unison although Sanjay did that funny thing with his neck that was a bit ambiguous. Daniel continued, " One last thing, we must remember that the lands of the two kingdoms were surrounded and influenced by other Empires and cultures. Of note of course was the Ancient Egypt. The Biblical period we are considering was between the 21st and 25th dynasties and they had problems of their own at the same time. Although the period we are interested in pre dates the Hellenic Empire, Athens was already established as a centre of culture and scholarship and was spreading its influence in the eastern Mediterranean. The relevance of the that will soon become apparent." At that point the door opened and Professor Barzalai entered carrying a large buff envelope. "Ah your timing is perfect Uri, here are the photographic prints for you to study, but first …voila!" Daniel then whipped the linen cloth away like a magician and the others went "Ahhh" again in unison. The copper scroll was about two feet long and 18 inches in width. It reflected light with a bright reddish hue, engraved notches and glyphs looked like new and apart from the corners on the curling lateral margins, the scroll was in perfect condition. Just before it was covered again Arthur could be heard muttering, "I see why you mentioned other cultural influences." Daniel then withdrew the plates from the envelope and spread them out. "Arthur, we've barely made a start on this, so what's your first impression?"

"Well apart from marveling at your skills my first impression is that this ancient Hebrew scroll contains not a word of Hebrew!"

"Exactly, and what do you deduce from this?"

" A quick glance shows me early Greek style lettering, Ancient Egyptian hieratic script and hieroglyphics. Only the most learned would be able to make sense of this and that could only be the priesthood."

"My reaction as well. So this is a secret that could only be shared by privileged few. Now let's look at the photographs which are easier to read than the scroll itself. "

They all looked closely at their copies and Daniel once more placed the ball in Arthur's court.

"In all due modesty, this is the period of Egyptian history in which I specialize. It looks like a simple list running from alpha to omega in early Phoenician/Greek letters. Each is followed by what looks like a place name in Egyptian hieratic script of round about the 25th dynasty, whilst each line ends with a hieroglyphic of the same era. Mmm very interesting."

"Go on Arthur, try and read it for us as best you can."

"OK here goes. Now remember that Hebrew reads from right to left, this text seems to read from left to right. Running down the left hand margin we have the letters of the Greek alphabet as I've already said but something odd here, all but 5 are in lower case. Alongside them all are one or two words in hieratic ancient Egyptian that I'll try and read from the top. H'mm, akko, bersheba, gaza. Hang on a bit this looks like a list of cities. Acco, Beersheba, Gaza and now Dan. Theta is linked to Tyre. Many of the others I can't make out yet at a cold reading, but wait a minute it gets easier lower down the list, must be something to do with the was the scroll was rolled. Errr here's a triplet against Sigma- Samaria, Shilo and Sela and against chi I can make out Hazor. Hazor was an important fortified city in the reign of King Jeroboam and if I remember correctly, Sela was the capital city of the Edomites at the time of interest. The five letters engraved in upper case are Dan,

Hazor, Samaria, Shilo and Sela. At the right hand side of the scroll are Ancient Egyptian hieroglyphics that I would need to study with a magnifying glass at leisure. Another thought that has just occurred to me, let me double check," Here Arthur took out a magnifying glass from one of his many pockets and looked closely half way down the list then lifted his head again, " Yes I'm right, Jerusalem is conspicuous by its absence, it should be alongside Lamda for Lerousalem in ancient Greek, but whatever this inscription names its not that. I suppose that is indirect evidence that if we are indeed looking for treasure, it is indeed treasure moved from its original home in Jerusalem"

"Any further ideas?" Daniel addressed to the whole group.

After a pause with everyone in deep thought, Sanjay was first to speak.

"Do you have a map showing the principle cities of this period with their precise geographical position?"

"Indeed I do, it's on the wall behind you."

Sanjay stood up and took a close look and turned round with a beaming smile.

"Those cities with the upper case letter are precisely in a line running north south on longitude 35 East. Except for Beersheba, the other cities run down the coastline. West of Beersheba no coastal town is shown but this is the southernmost point of the Holy Land. I think we have discovered an ancient version of geographical coordinates!"

The rest of the group stood up and gathered round Sanjay to look at the map.

"I think he's right Daniel," said Uri.

"I agree. Whilst we are waiting for an understanding of the hieroglyphics let's have a look at the transcript of the Q3 copper scroll now in Amman." Daniel left the room and after a few minutes returned with a limited edition of a scholarly book containing the scroll inscriptions and transliterations. "If your hunch is right Sanjay, and as I said already, my intuition supports you, then let's find transcript of the Amman scroll and the section where the seven alleged treasure hiding places are identified simply by two Greek letters, representing longitude and latitude."

Daniel then riffled through the book and stopped at the relevant page. "Here it is, Eta Nu; Theta Epsilon; Delta Iota; Tau, Rho; Sigma Kappa; Sigma Theta; Kappa Epsilon. Any matches?"

" How frustrating, there's only one of the couplets where we have both coordinates translated and that's Sigma, Theta," said Arthur. They all rushed back to the map with Daniel arming himself with a setsquare. Two Sigma; Samaria and Sela, were aligned with longitude 35 East, whilst Theta, Tyre, sat on 33 North for latitude, and their intersection was slap bang in the centre of ancient Dan.

"For the time being we have no option but to concentrate on this hit. Now let's see what the first copper scroll has to say about it," said Daniel finding his place again in the reference book. "Here it is, '..beneath the other, eastern corner and buried at a depth of 10 cubits 40 talents of gold and the rod of Ha'Cohen Ha'godal'. Let me do some quick calculations." Daniel took out his smart phone and touched the app, keyed in some numbers and turned back to his audience. "Bingo! Somewhere on Tel Dan, buried approximately 5 meters in the ground lies 1,400 kg of gold as well as the rod of the High Priest; that probably refers to Aaron. Not bad for a day's work?" Everyone clapped. "Arthur perhaps you could focus on focus on the hieroglyphics for both ∑ and Θ." Arthur took out his magnifying glass again, adjusted the light and started drawing with a fine stylus an exquisite sketch of two cows, with elaborate horns and a disc on their heads. The Sigma cow faced to the left and the Theta cow faced to the right.

"Those cows are symbols of the Goddess Hathor, who carries the sun disc on her head. She is my favorite of all the ancient Egyptian Gods. She is the Goddess of the sky, love, beauty, joy, music and fertility. As such she is considered the adumbration of Aphrodite and Venus. She was also deemed the mother of Ra and the disc carried on the head of her depictions represents the daily rebirth of Ra as the rising sun in the east. Why there are mirror images of this glyph in Sigma Theta, I haven't a clue, and their relevance to treasure-trove would need a lot of thought. Sanjay your good at solving puzzles, any ideas?" Sanjay put on his deep thinking face and then gave an alarming nodding of his head that implied he had no ideas to offer.

Daniel then decided to wrap up things for the day. "The scroll and its contents will demand years of scholarly research. I cannot take this matter any further without discussing it with the director of the Israel museum, the chairman of my department at the Hebrew University and the Minister responsible for antiquities. For the time being I suggest that we all take a day trip to Tel Dan tomorrow and who knows the clues might make sense in the right geographical context."

Miri who had kept quiet until then, spoke, "I have just received a text message that flights out of Ben Gurion will restart the day after tomorrow, so with your agreement I will rebook your returns to London. Tomorrow will be hot so remember to bring hats and water bottles. I suggest pick up at your hotels early tomorrow morning as we have a long drive. Let's say 6.00 am." There were groans all round but they were a happy band of adventurers as they left the Museum.

★★★

This happy band would not have been so happy had they been aware of the attentions of Selah Al Mazri. He was one of the goatherds on the rather conspicuous flat bed truck at Lachish and later on at Maresha. The conspicuous appearance of the truck was intentional as a feint in the monitoring of Mrs. Hathaway and the black SUV that carried her around the country. Her movements were in reality being closely watched by a spy in the sky of an orbiting satellite recently covertly launched by the Revolutionary Guards in a remote desert region of Iran. Of course the Americans were quickly onto it but short of initiating Star Wars there was nothing they could do.

The gambit served its purpose by hastening the departure of the black SUV so as to allow Saleh and his companion to retrace the steps of Mrs. Hathaway's party. When they climbed down the iron staircase of the columbarium, some fresh debris was to be seen at its foot. This enjoined Dr. Al Mazri to cast his eyes around the walls and ceiling in the vicinity to trace its origin. As by now the sun had sunk a little, the eastern wall of the columbarium was no longer spot lit and the empty pigeonhole was not obvious. In any case as Al Mazri had never learnt to play chess, the significance of that would have been lost on him. Although none the wiser he still had the gut feeling that somehow or other a little old Englishwoman and her coterie would lead them to the scroll. So nothing was lost she and her friends could still lead them to their goal thanks to the celestial eye above.

★★★

Chapter 29

A day trip to Tel Dan

To paraphrase the old Irish joke, if I wanted to drive to Tel Dan I wouldn't start in Jerusalem.

Although the distance was only 100 miles as the crow flies, the crow would need a visa and have to pass through check points entering and leaving the PA controlled West Bank. That could easily have been arranged but they were taking no chances. Instead they would have to take a nearly 50-mile detour around the border between Israel and the West Bank. To add to their problems it was Sunday morning, the first day of the working week in Israel, so traffic was expected to be heavy. That was the reason Miri suggested such an early start. Furthermore as the scroll had now been found and was in safekeeping the services of Mr. & Mrs. Schapiro were dispensed with and there was no need for Ishmael and his company to ride point.

They found themselves in heavy traffic getting out of Jerusalem going west towards Tel Aviv, but once they turned north on the Yitzhak Rabin Highway they were able to pick up speed. As the highway ran out near Tiberias to the west of the Sea of Galilee, they ran into traffic again on the network of minor roads and it was already 8.30 am as they entered the Hula valley and stopped for a coffee break in the pleasant early morning sunlight where they could enjoy the beautiful scenery.

They were sitting outside on a terrace of a roadside coffee shop just north east of Rosh Pinah. Uri had chosen that spot in order the witness the rising sun clearing the highest ridge on the Golan Heights due east of where they sat. To their northeast was mount Hermon's snow capped peak, already reflecting the morning sunlight. Behind them and a little to the north was mount Meron and the mountain ridges that marked the border with Lebanon. Between these two mountain ranges lay the lush green valley of the Hula. In the 1920s and 1930s Jewish pioneers set up collective farms here, and drained the mosquito-infested swampland. Many died of malaria. This was now some of the most fertile land in the fertile crescent of the Levant.

The birdsong was an extraordinary in its variety and volume but nothing like that to be witnessed in the early spring or early autumn. This valley, part of the great the rift, extending from Syria to North Africa, acted as bottleneck through which all migratory birds passed twice a year.

As they watched, the sun disc rose over the Golan Heights, and as it became momentarily bracketed by twin peaks on the horizon, it resembled the emblem of the Goddess Hathor. They took this as auguring well, but Uri was quick to point out, that this sight could be seen anywhere in the mountainous lands bordering the 35th latitude at this time of day. Uri mentioned that he had fought over this land in the 1967 war as a young officer in the Golani Brigade. It was a short but bloody battle to capture the highlands opposite from the Syrians and to this day the Golan was in Israeli hands, although the Syrians were determined to regain it one day. However they had other things on their mind at the moment as their civil war entered its fifth year, and they preferred having their backs protected by Israel rather than Islamic State.

Once the sun had cleared the heights they felt the fierce heat of its rays as they re-boarded their SUV for the last phase of their journey to the northeast tip of this finger of land. At this point the Hula valley was bordered by Lebanon to the west and north and Syria to the east, with Damascus just about visible from a look out on the highest point of the Golan.

They arrived at Tel Dan nature reserve and archaeological

park, nestling in the foothills of Mount Hermon, just as it was opening up for the first visitors of the day.

Olive and Sanjay were not quite sure what to expect but the Garden of Eden was not high on their list. The Tel Dan nature reserve was as close to the imagined *Gan Eden* of the book of Genesis as one could get, and very much reminiscent of paintings by Cranach, Breughel or even Hieronymus Bosch on a good day. In amongst the lush foliage and meadows studded with brilliantly hued wild flowers, scores of bubbling brooks feed into a running river. Tall trees reach for the sky and the shaded ground is refreshingly cool after the heat of the 10.00 o'clock sun in June.

Of the three sources of the river Jordan, the Dan River is most important. The drainage basin of the Dan is very narrow which means that all the springs bursting out of the rocks on the lower slopes of mount Hermon are channeled to this spot. The fact that the springs have their origin in the melting snow on the mountain peak accounts for the water and the refreshing air beneath the canopy of trees, being deliciously cool on the hottest of days. The water that seeps into the mountain 2,000 feet above, reappears as a vast network of little streams that eventually gather into a shallow lake called the "wading pool" before being discharged into the river Dan itself. Rare creatures including desert rodents and amphibious salamanders, that found their way here along the Syrian-African rift, add to the exotica of wild life and rare plant life such as *stinking St. John's Wort*, add to the sense of other worldliness. Colorful noisy Jays and warblers fly amongst the treetops and if you choose to cool off in the wading pool, the Damascus barbell or the Jordan loach might nibble your toes.

Little wonder the Israelite tribe of Dan preferred this heavenly place to the rigors of desert life or the hazards of living too close to the Philistines.

By way of recreation and inspiration, Uri determined to conduct them round one of the nature trails that would eventually take them to the summit of the Tel and the archaeological site of the ancient city of Dan. As they left the shaded glades and made their way to the ancient gate of the city, the noonday sun beat down on them without mercy. Sunhats were taken out of backpacks and sunscreen was applied to the necks of the white skinned Olive and Arthur.

The ramped cobbled road that leads to the entrance of the ancient city, its supporting walls and the architecture of the double gate was exactly as at Tel Lachish but with a big difference. The whole structure was much better preserved and much less damaged than Lachish, evidence that the city was left to decay rather than razed to the ground. The size of the stones used for the boundary walls was astonishing and the receiving room for dignitaries being welcomed by the King was almost intact apart from the throne. As if to make up for that deficit, the Israeli parks authority had mounted a picture of what might have looked like 2,700 years earlier, nearby under a shady oak.

The hike from there along the ancient paved highway free of shade was tiring but worth the effort. At the highest point of the Tell was the so-called "High Place" that was used for religious ritual, animal sacrifices and worship. This complex, thought to have been built by King Jeroboam in 930 BCE, was a forlorn looking spot. There was nothing much there to capture their imagination and they were reluctant to stand around in the hot sun. Before they left Uri wanted to show them some relics of more recent history. They turned northeast towards the steeply sloping flank of the Tel and their guide turned their attention to the metallic debris littering the plain below that had been the front line between Israel and the Syrians during the six-day war. There were two burnt out tanks in the distance and a half-track command car nearby. They then walked round the northern perimeter of the Tel following a line of slit trenches that had been preserved as a monument to that battle. Finally they stopped to admire the beautiful view of the green slopes of the Golan Heights to the east of the Tel.

By this time they felt they'd had enough. They'd been up and on the road since 06.00am. They were hot and sticky and had all but forgotten the purpose of their visit until Arthur suddenly reminded them. "Can we go back to the High Place for a short while? A need to look at something again because I think I now know where the treasure is buried." As it was in any case on the way back to their SUV no one complained but all felt a deep sense of skepticism. Once they were back at the shrine of the ancient Kingdom of Israel, Arthur spoke again. "All this while I've been looking for contextual clues to help us decode the enigma of the copper scrolls and of course my eyes have looked downwards at the excavated area. As it turns out, and I nearly missed it, the clue is at eye level as happens to be an artifact of very recent times." He then pointed at something in front of him and followed the direction of his index finger and were none the wiser. "Funny how against the bright sky it almost is invisible. Look at the central square marking stones, at each corner there is a zinc post, a the top of those four post are cross pieces making it look like the support for a marquee. If you look carefully each corner has a curved spike pointing outwards. I think I've guessed what it is meant to represent. Let's look at this diagram and legend kindly provided by the Israel Park authority." At this he directed the party to a yellow board standing nearby. He then continued with mounting excitement. "Yes exactly as I thought. That hideous structure is meant to represent the sacrificial altar that stood there two and a half millennia ago. Now yesterday when we were in the Israel museum you were shown a stone altar from this period. You will have noted stone horns at each corner. I have little doubt now that what we are looking for is buried 5 meters below the ground in the centre of that square. The horns on the two cows of Hathor must represent the four horns of an altar. If I remember correctly the exert from the Aman scroll that brought us here started '…*beneath the other eastern corner…*', that tells us there were two eastern and two western corners and each must bear a horn!" They were all struck dumb for a moment, then Daniel touched Uri shoulder and the two of them moved a little way from the group and went into a huddle. After a few moments Daniel turned to the others and said, "Professor Barzalai and I are both professional archaeologists, our profession is half science and half educated guess work or intuition. The two of us share Arthur extraordinary insight. We have no doubt that this is where the treasure is buried.

One small problem remains; we have to dig down through 5 meters of earth and rubble. An industrial trench digger we can easily hire but my dear friends you have no idea of the logistics involved in getting the agreement of the Israel Nature and Parks authority, the Ministry for antiquities, the Chief Rabbinate, the IDF and for all we know the Prime Minister and the President.

I don't speak Yiddish but I remember one phrase that will serve its purpose, *Oi vaiz myr,* in English that approximates to 'woe is me'. We have every intention of pursuing this goal but our guess it will take at least a year to set it up. Meanwhile Olive, Arthur and Sanjay, we owe you an enormous debt of gratitude and when you return home tomorrow you can bask in the glow of your success. I have no doubt you will also receive formal notice of our gratitude from our masters."

After all this excitement this was all a bit of an anticlimax but by now everyone was exhausted and looking forward to a hot bath and an early bed. Olive slept almost all the way back to Jerusalem whilst Arthur and Sanjay remained in silent contemplation of the day's events.

The next morning after a leisurely breakfast together on the terrace of the King David hotel, Miri drove her British guests to Ben Gurion airport, where all three took the BA flight home.

Meanwhile Uri remembered to return to Maresha to make good the mess he left behind and disguise the fact that one of the chessboard squares had been tampered with.

★★★

PART 4

The End of Times

Chapter 30

Olive returns to the Holy Land

May 2017

Over the best part of a year since her adventures in Israel, Olive had grown older and wiser but nothing much else happened to disturb her equilibrium or daily routine. The only event of note was the publication of an account of her travels in the Holy Land in the St. Jude's gazette. This account, it goes without saying made no mention of the search for treasure scroll or anything remotely that might be in breach of the official secrets act.

Her brother Arthur had also grown older but now doubted his own wisdom in having exposed his sister to the hazards of hunting treasure in the Middle East. His routine of watching cricket through the summer and drinking claret and fine malts through the winter at his club remained unchanged.

The only matter worth mentioning was the fact that he had started to write up his notes on the discovery of the hiding place of the Temple treasure in anticipation of the time when the secret could be shared with the world via the pages of the Palestine Exploration Fund quarterly.

As anticipated, Sanjay was appointed to the chair of surgery, making his temporary status permanent so that at last he was able to put the title Professor on his letter heading and bank account although his monthly income remained the same.

Along with this his friend and colleague, Abdullah Ibn

Sharif, was appointed senior lecturer with honorary consultant status in the NHS. His wedding was scheduled for later in the year once the infernal heat of the summer would begin to ebb.

Ishmael made the surprise decision to return to Israel where he had been offered a senior rank in the Medical Corps of the IDF based at Tel Ha'Shomer hospital just outside Tel Aviv. However there was a good reason for this. He had been betrothed to the girl he loved for two years but her father, the patriarch of a prominent Bedouin family, would not allow her out of the country. Like Abdullah, he would also be married later the same year.

Meanwhile in the background, all the diplomatic skills of Uri Barzalai and Daniel Cohen were put to test in their negotiations with the department of archaeology at the Hebrew University, the ministry of Israeli antiquities, the Israel Nature and Parks Authority and both the chief Rabbinates of the Ashkenazi and Sephardic traditions. Eventually it took a presidential commission to resolve their differences before they could even start planning the logistics for the excavation of the High Place at Tel Dan. All these deliberations were carried out in the utmost secrecy.

Of course in parallel with these activities they continued work on the copper scroll. They applied and were successful in winning a major grant from the Ministry of Antiquities, which allowed them to recruit staff to work with them on the decoding and interpreting the inscriptions.

The first and easiest question to answer was to establish in context, the provenance of their scroll.

They simply turned to be the translation, in the modern vernacular of the last item in the last column of the Amman copper scroll.

A copy of this inventory list, its explanation and the measurements and details of every hidden item are in the dry underground cavity that is in the smooth rock north of Kohlit. Its opening is towards the north with the tombs at its mouth

Without having any knowledge of the whereabouts of

Kohlit or its nearby dry underground cavity, there was little doubt that the scroll in their hands had been moved from its original hiding place and ultimately hidden under a pyramid of skulls outside the walls of Lachish just before the Babylonian conquest.

After that things became more difficult. As often happens they had been first time lucky with the discovery at Tel Dan, other inscriptions were tougher nuts to crack. Some of the geographical coordinates suggested locations outside of Israel mostly in lands that didn't even recognize the right of Israel to exist. Other locations were in Gaza and the West Bank. Gaza was now out of bounds and to start digging anywhere in the West Bank risked a diplomatic backlash unless, their secret was revealed. However there was one with the couplet of ancient Greek letters, beta/beta both in lower case, which was a source of great frustration. They had so far located only one beta that represented by Beersheba, so there had to be another beta to help determine the longitude or latitude coordinates bearing in mind that they weren't even sure whether Beersheba lay on the longitude or the latitude of this focal point. Furthermore the original copper scroll from Q3 carried a very intriguing paragraph in column 1 that read something like this:

In the tomb of the third section of stones there is one hundred gold bars. Nine hundred talents are concealed by sediment towards the upper opening, at the bottom of the big cistern in the courtyard of the peristyl. Priests garments and flasks that were given as vows are buried in the hill of Kohlit. This is all of the votive offerings of the seventh treasure that is guarded by the gold cherubim. The opening is at the edge of the river of blood on its northern side six cubits toward the immersed pool. [ββ]

What made this of spine chilling relevance was that in their own scroll the line identifying one of the betas as Beersheba was completed with an ancient Egyptian icon depicting a winged goddess:

This would have been the popular image describing the appearance of a *Cherub* carried out of the land of Egypt by the Children of Israel. The Ark of the Covenant as described Exodus 25:10-22, carried two golden *Cherubim* facing each other with wings outstretched as if to protect the Tablets of stone. Furthermore the line carrying the unidentifiable second beta also ended with the identical image but facing left. They couldn't trust themselves to believe that they had identified the hiding place of the Ark and the twin tablets of stone. So instead they decided to shelve this enigma until something else came up from their researches or until one or other of the team experienced divine inspiration. Anything was possible in the holy city of Jerusalem.

★★★

Olive received her invitation on the 5th May in a large cream and crisp envelope bearing the insignia of the State of Israel. Her hands trembled with excitement as she reached for her paper knife. The invitation written in Edwardian script read:

> *His Excellency the Israeli Ambassador to the Court of St James has great pleasure in inviting Mrs. Olive Hathaway*
> *to a reception at the Hilton Hotel*
> *Tel Aviv*
> *To celebrate the opening of a new wing of the Israel Museum at the Tel Aviv Institute of Art*
> *On Sunday the 4th June at 7.30 pm*
> *Lounge suits and cocktail dresses*
> *RSVP*
> *Embassy of Israel*

Included with the invitation was a letter explaining that all expenses would be covered including a club class ticket on El Al arriving on Thursday evening the 1st of June together with a week's stay at the Hilton Hotel. She immediately broke out in a sweat and phoned her brother who happened to be at home that morning. Arthur confirmed that he had received the same invitation and he had no doubt what this meant and was damned he wouldn't miss this show. He did however caution Olive that the political situation in that part of the world was much less stable than 12 months earlier and thought it might be wise if she declined the invitation. Olive's response to that came as a surprise, as it involved words of an explicit carnal nature somewhat uncommon in the vocabulary of a lady Churchwarden. In order to placate her outraged brother she did agree to consult to Foreign Office's web site carrying advise for British citizens abroad. The only warnings she found there were to avoid crossing into Gaza or the neighboring townships in south west Israel as well as exploring the high-ground of the Golan heights where stray mortar shells fired by ISIL militants, who had backed the forces still loyal to the Assad regime and his Iranian proxy militia, into a tight corner.

Olive then phoned Sanjay and he also confirmed the invitation. As this was addressed to professor and Mrs. Manchandra, his wife Savita, had got to it first. She had been jealous of his first visit and was ready for a holiday in the sun after such a long cold winter and a miserable wet spring. Sanjay could not think of a convincing reason for dissuading her short of breaking the official secrets act.

It should be noted at this point that Dr. and Professor Manchandra had been promoting their professional careers for so long that they had completely overlooked the possibility of starting a family. So in that respect felt unencumbered by the remote and theoretical risk of a third world war breaking out in the one week they happened to be in the Middle East.

★★★

Jerusalem is the city of peace and spirituality, fought over for three millennia, built and rebuilt out of the local currency of golden stone. In contrast Tel Aviv marches to the beat of a very different drum. It not so march marches as throbs to the boogie rhythm of a vibrant, secular city open 24/7 to all comers. Built out of the sand dunes north of the ancient port of Joppa, it is now conjoined with its upstart younger brother as Tel Aviv/ Jaffa and has only survived wars over the last 100 years. In place of golden stone its original buildings were hideous Bauhaus concrete blocks that were hot in the summer and cold in the winter. That is why most of the old real estate, is disfigured with rusting air-conditioning units and roof top solar panels. All that has changed now thanks to a booming economy of its silicon valley start up companies and multinationals.

On the Sabbath Jerusalem lives up to its name *Ir Shalom* (city of peace), whilst Tel Aviv lives up to its reputation- beach party time by day and clubbing all night.

When their limousine turned west on the highway out of Ben Gurion airport driving into the setting sun, Olive, Arthur and the Manchandras, were in for a big surprise. Entering Tel Aviv through the business sector they had not been prepared for the ultra-modern tower blocks on both sides of the road and the maniacal driving by the kamikaze pilots in their white Opels and Audis competing to overtake each other, just in case the city ran out of food before they got there. However once they entered one of the main thoroughfares running north south parallel with the beach, they were able to appreciate the main attraction of the city.

They checked into the Hilton Hotel, right at the northernmost part of the beachfront just as the sun sank below the horizon flooding the modernist lobby with a gold and orange glow. This boded well for the following day thought Olive, "Red sky at night, shepherds delight". Of course what she had forgotten was that in the eastern Mediterranean at sea-level, between the end of May and the end of September, most locals would have been delighted with a let up in the heat and a month of English summers. The four British travelers were booked into rooms on the concierge level with balconies looking over the beach and marina 12 floors below. A letter welcoming them to Israel included an invitation to breakfast in the penthouse club on the 14th floor the following morning where they were to be joined by Miri Cohen, Daniel Cohen, Uri Barzalai and their old friend and colleague, Ishmael Nadir.

★★★

Chapter 31

Saleh El Mazri

Such was the ring of secrecy surrounding the mission to reclaim some of the treasures from King Solomon's Temple, that even the nexus of conspirators who had been guilty of the murder of Professor Black were unaware of what was going on. Once Olive and her brother had left for home, Saleh Al Mazri was called to a debriefing session in Amman where he made his report to representatives from the Charedi fundamentalists from Crown Heights and Stamford Hill, together with their Islamic friends from Teheran and Southern Lebanon. This meeting however was not so secure and was noted by MI6 and Mossad. In addition it had been agreed by the main players that the CIA should be briefed and kept in the loop.

When Saleh made his report it was treated as something of an anticlimax. Mrs. Hathaway's visit to the Old city of Jerusalem's holy sites and the Israel museum were clearly on the tourist trail. The fact that an Indian couple and an American pair of tourists joined her and her brother for visits to archaeological sites was not that surprising. All in all she seemed an unlikely suspect with a perfectly reasonable explanation for her visit. They did however decide to keep her under some low level of surveillance. For his troubles Saleh was appointed as a liaison officer working between the Muslim Brotherhood and Islamic State, coordinating terrorists attacks in Turkey and the European capitals. Saleh's masters reinstituted their search for the Starkey scroll amongst the caves north of Qumran still convinced that QB3 pointed in that direction in spite of his protestations. However by now the intelligence services in

Israel and Jeddah were alert to the resumption of their futile search and were happy to allow them unmolested access but they as yet had no knowledge of Al Mazri's links to IS.

All that changed the moment that Olive Hathaway passed through immigration at Ben Gurion airport and triggered a sequence of events that ended with cataclysmic violence.

★★★

On the wider Geo-Political scene things were going from bad to worse. In May 2017, two apparently unrelated items were published synchronously on Arab language websites appearing to usher in the age of the apocalypse.

Harun Yahya

Hazrat Mahdi is amongst us

For hundreds of years now, the Islamic world has been awaiting for Hazrat Mahdi, who will be instrumental in people attaining salvation, restore the moral values of Islam and unite Muslims by dispersing the darkness over the Muslim world. Our Prophet has imparted the glad tidings of the coming of Hazrat Mahdi to the whole Muslim world through the hadiths. And he has described a great many highly significant phenomena that are portents of the coming of Hazrat Mahdi (as). And just about all of these have come about, one after the other, over the last few years. Muslims are now preparing to welcome this holy person they have been awaiting for the last 1,400 years.

According to the hadiths, the coming of Hazrat Mahdi will take place in this century. The whole Muslim world is experiencing the excitement of these great tidings, awaited for centuries, becoming a reality and of Hazrat Mahdi appearing in our own day...

Our Prophet's (saas) descriptions of Hazrat Mahdi (as) are so detailed and explicit that when Hazrat Mahdi (as) appears those who see him will immediately be able to recognize him.

Yet beyond recognizing his person the ultimate proof of his identity will be that he and he alone will carry Aaron's rod. The power of the rod will unite all the Muslims of the world for the common purpose of establishing the Caliphate in the lands held by the blasphemers and heretics of all other religions leaving the one true religion to rule this world and the world to come.

In the End Times in which we are living Hazrat Mahdi (as) will assume the spiritual leadership of all Muslims…

Iran's Revolutionary Guard Sepah News:

Successful launch of new intercontinental ballistic missile
Major General Mohammad Ali Salasi, the commander of Iran's Revolutionary Guard Corp (IRGC) warned on Tuesday that Israel could expect a "destructive" response for its role in the explosions that they claimed had destroyed the uranium enrichment plant at Natanz. The fact that this was not an empty promise was emphasised by the successful launch of a new intercontinental ballistic missile capable of carrying a nuclear warhead at a secret site in Semnan province.

The missile is a modification of the Shahab 3 that extends its range to the capability of hitting the East coast of North America.

"We cannot imagine the Zionist regime starting a war without America's support," he said. "Therefore, in case of a war, we will get into a war with both of them and we will certainly get into a conflict with American bases. … In that case, unpredictable and unimaginable things would happen and it could turn into a World War III and hasten the End of Times."

"The new missile has been dignified with the name 'Aaron's Rod' and insha'Allah, this will extend the reach of militant Islam across the whole of the infidel world."

President Obama's "legacy" on nuclear arms control in return for lifting sanctions on Iran was considered a disaster in Jerusalem and that was why they took the risk of bombing Natanz in spite of provoking the USA to vote in favour of the motion condemning Israel at the UN for the first time in history. Only Canada voted against the motion but curiously the United Kingdom abstained.

By this time Iran had consolidated its reach through its proxies in Syria, Lebanon, Gaza, North Africa, Sub Saharan Africa, Sinai, Yemen and Parts of Iraq. All of this expansionism was funded by the generous largesse of the Western world in return for Iran's promise to postpone the development of a nuclear capacity. Their activity in such an enterprise was to be closely monitored by an international committee with representatives from the USA, the EU, UK, France, Germany, Japan, Russia and Iran herself. Iran also had active cells in Jordan in spite of the crack down by the Jordanian Special Forces, covertly aided and abetted by the partnership of Israeli and Saudi Arabian intelligence agencies. Standing back to take a look at the map of North Africa, the near East and the Levant, it was simple to note a geographically huge crescent of Shia Muslim influence surrounding the Mediterranean and the world's major suppliers of oil. Standing firm against the hegemony of Iran was the unlikely alliance of the Military government of Egypt, Israel, Saudi Arabia and the Gulf States. Even the new leadership of the Palestine Authority in the West Bank understood which side its bread was buttered on. Meanwhile the Sunni brotherhood of Islamic fanatics, known as Da'esh, the bastard son of ISIL and Al Qaida, covertly aided and abetted by the Muslim Brotherhood, was locked in mortal combat with a ragtag alliance of Syrian, Iraqi, Kurdish and tribal militia aided by bombing raids by a western alliance and not so covert activities of American, British, French, Canadian and Nordic Special Services.

Effectively there was a three-way stalemate, with the legions of Western Liberal democracy facing the legions of Sunni and Shiite Islamic fundamentalists. Short of an all out mobilisation of ground troops or the nuclear option, there appeared no way for the Western alliance to break the deadlock.

Matters were not helped by a succession of Left wing, risk adverse, leaders elected to high office in Europe and North America.

Against this background the successful launch of Iran's new intercontinental ballistic missile was considered a serious escalation of the level of threat by all the intelligence agencies of the Western world and there allies in the middle east.

★★★

Chapter 32

Breakfast at the Hilton Hotel Tel Aviv

Breakfast in Israel is the best meal of the day and unlike the "full English", is healthy as well.

The buffet table in the concierge lounge on the penthouse floor of the Hilton looked like a cornucopia or symphonic rhapsody, of good things to eat arranged in a color scheme that looked like homage to Matisse. Against the ultramarine of the eastern Mediterranean, reflecting the rising sun as it crested the white Bauhaus blocks on Ben Yehuda Street, the buffet table looked a feast for the eyes as much as a feast for the mouth. Huge bright red tomatoes and peppers were the first thing to catch the eye. These were laid out, as if obeying the rules of a complimentary color chart, alongside brilliant green peppers, salads and other exotic vegetables and fruit unknown in northern Europe. All of this provided a framework for a large variety of dairy products; cream cheeses, humus, tehina, sour cream, smetanna, goat's cheese, hard cheese, yoghurts and varieties of milk and soya products. Eggs were in abundance; boiled, scrambled, fried eggs, bespoke omelets and hot spicy Yemenite deviled eggs in cast iron skillets. The pita breads, crisp breads, bread sticks and black breads; were piled up in baskets at each corner of the table. There were six different varieties of pickled cucumber keeping company with all sorts of olives including large green variants stuffed with spices. The centerpieces of the display were the smoked fish and herring platters. Nowhere in the world could match the abundance of smoked salmon, marinated salmon in thin slices, smoked mackerel, smoked herrings, pickled herrings, schmaltzed herrings, herrings pickled in wine, herrings pickled in brine, herrings in oils and herrings in coils, known as roll mops. In keeping with all other Israeli Hotels, the food at the Hilton was kosher; so conspicuous by their absence were meat products because of the prohibition of eating meat and milk at the same time, not to mention any sign of a crustacean that was prohibited at all times.

So much salt and herring made you thirsty, so there were also ample supplies of freshly squeezed citrus fruit, apple juice and cranberry juice.

Olive delayed her attack on the breakfast buffet to admire the view of the beaches and marina below. She would not have been aware of the fact that just below her, discreetly sheltered from any cross contamination, were the gay beach, the dog beach and the orthodox Jewish beach, that this morning was restricted to men only. The orthodox women in their modest swimming gear would have sole access to that beach in the early evening.

Arthur in contrast made an immediate frontal attack on the buffet, filled two plates to overflowing and then sought out the table where Miri Cohen, Daniel Cohen, Uri Barzalai and Ishmael Nadir were waiting. He was joined shortly afterwards by the Manchandras who were delighted to find so many dairy and vegetarian dishes to suit their Hindu dietary restrictions.

Olive sat down last with a generously laden plate and glass of orange juice.

A waitress served hot coffee and warm greetings were exchanged all round. For once Olive's forgot her English reserve and indulged in the hugging and kissing; genuinely delighted to be meeting up with old friends whose friendship had been forged through extraordinary shared adventures. Savita was the odd one out and looked perplexed at this show of camaraderie. Miri smiled across at Savita noting how close in appearance they looked. Sanjay looked from one to the other with a blush that penetrated his dark brown skin. All the visitors looked admiringly at Ishmael in his crisply ironed officers uniform with a single oak leaf on each epaulet denoting his rank as colonel in the medical brigade of the IDF.

Once breakfast was complete and Arthur finally sated, Miri called the group to order for briefing. At this point the visitors suddenly became aware that the room had emptied and deeply bronzed bald young men stood engaged in reading newspapers at each entrance to the lounge.

Savita looked round in alarm sensing that something in the atmosphere had changed.

Miri again looked across at Savita and began with an elaborate sequence of apologies before starting to explain what she described as "their little secret" with no attempt at hiding her note of irony. Sanjay had been dreading this moment and had no idea how his wife might react. They had never rowed and as far he knew, never kept secrets from each other. Her reaction could ruin the thrill of their discovery or more importantly, become a stain on the fabric of their marriage for evermore.

Miri then launched into a well-rehearsed, chronological explanation of the events leading up to this meeting. Certain details concerning the collaboration between MI6 and Mossad were left out of the discourse but nevertheless Miri concluded with these words. "Once again Savita, please forgive us and most of all your poor husband, for keeping you in the dark about all this, but I hope you understand that these are sensitive issues with a potential for further destabilizing the tinder box of geopolitics in our troubled corner of the globe. Your husband had no choice but to sign the State Secret's Act, you of course cannot be made to do so, but I'm sure you can now understand why we would prefer you not to discuss these events outside this tight circle. Fortunately there have been no leaks concerning our findings and the enemy is still chasing a wild goose up the canyons on the Northwest shore of the Dead Sea. I no longer feel concerns for our safety but I'd like to keep security tight until we've finished our searches at Tel Dan. After that, who knows, Sanjay, Olive and Arthur might become as celebrated as Lord Carnarvon in the Valley of the Kings."

Throughout this long speech, Savita never opened her mouth but maintained an icy silence whilst fixing her lustrous brown eyes on Miri. Sanjay was terrified, he had never seen Savita look like this before and the spark of intelligence she always carried in her eyes appeared to be ratcheted up by a megawatt or two. Once Miri had stopped talking there was a full minute of deathly silence until Savita's mouth broke into a huge smile with a full display of her perfect, brilliant white teeth.

"To think all this time I have been thinking that Sanjay was having an affair during his visit last year to Israel. When he came home he wouldn't meet my eye and kept changing the subject when I asked him how the trip turned out and how he spent his time when not working. Oh goodness gracious me, his answers were so evasive; I assumed he had fallen for a beautiful Israeli girl. Looking at you Miri, I could easily understand how this might happen, but looking at my poor pot-bellied husband, who in their right mind would want him apart from me." She then turned to face her husband with a mock stern expression, before collapsing with laughter at the look of dismay on his face. With the tension relieved the whole party joined in the laughter at Sanjay's expense.

Miri then continued to map out the rest of their stay. "This evening we will send a limo to pick you up at 6.30 pm, for the reception at the new wing of the Tel Aviv art museum for the opening of the branch of the Israel museum. These new galleries will house the collection of European Judaica from the 19th and early 20th C up until the rise of Hitler. This is to make way for the huge influx of Biblical artifacts being dug up all over the land of Israel. Needless to say there is always a political dimension to these decisions."

Savita then raised her hand, "Miri what is the dress code this evening?"

"Good question. Although this country is very informal,

as this is a function attended by the President of the State, men for once are expected to wear suits and ties and women cocktail dresses."

"Would a sari be OK?"

"More than OK, most appropriate, if I may continue? For the rest of the day please free to enjoy all that Tel Aviv has to offer. I might suggest that you walk or cycle along the paths of the beautiful promenade all the way from port to port. That is starting just north of here at the old port of Tel Aviv all the way to the ancient Biblical port of Jaffa in the south. Tomorrow, Friday, we would like you to come and visit Daniel Cohen's laboratory in Jerusalem to see how far they've got with decoding the copper scroll. Friday night and Saturday are our Sabbath so that can be a day of rest for you as well. Sunday we will pick you up at 7.00am for our drive up north to Tel Dan and later that day we hope to make the breakthrough into the chamber holding the treasure hoard. Daniel will now tell you some more about that next and then Ishmael will have a few words to say about health and safety."

"OK, my turn. After our experiences last year it took all our powers of diplomacy and patience trying to balance the interests of the department of archaeology at the Hebrew University, the ministry of Israeli antiquities, the Israel Nature and Parks Authority and the chief Rabbinates of the Ashkenazi and Sephardic traditions. In the end the President intervened and established a commission that reached a compromise that satisfied all parties. First we had to satisfy the religious factions that we would not desecrate a holy site and if anything of religious significance were found they would determine were eventually they might rest. Minor finds of treasure of no religious significance would be housed in the Israel museum but any artifact directly linked to the Biblical narrative would be housed in a new built shrine in Jerusalem close to the Temple mount. After the excavation was complete and rendered safe, the remaining areas of the site would be made good and the chamber itself would be protected and opened up as an attraction for visitors to Tel Dan. Finally everyone was pledged to secrecy until the dig was complete and any significant findings were in safekeeping. Throughout this time the whole area around the high place of the Tel would be cordoned off with out of bounds notices posted with the legend 'area closed because seismic activity have rendered walls and pathways subject to collapse'. All heavy equipment such as trench diggers and rock breakers are in position having been driven up on the military roads that run along the borders between Israel and Lebanon to avoid curiosity.

We started excavating two weeks ago, first of all removing the flagstones covering the site of the sacrificial altar built by Jeroboam. We slowly excavated a rectangle 15 by 20 meters subjecting all the sub soil to a careful search including sieving of the debris. The small artifacts and potsherds confirmed that we were working in an area that was once occupied by mankind in the 9th and 10th century BCE together with a further layer from the 6th century BCE. Paradoxically the deeper stratum carried the objects from the more recent era. This added confidence that we were on the right track. Then precisely at a depth of 5 meters we struck solid stone. After cleaning the surface of the pit we found a floor of perfect blue marble slabs covering an area 5 by 7 meters. Sonar and radar scanning of this surface demonstrated that we were standing on the roof of a chamber within which were free standing objects of enigmatic shapes and sizes. You can imagine our excitement and you can now understand why you were summoned for the uncovering of the secret chamber. Ishmael your turn."

"Dear friends, I have the honor of being ranking officer in the IDF on site. As well as having a small field accident an emergency unit as is routine for major archaeological digs, we will also have a battalion of 12 infantry men from C Company of the Golani brigade responsible for security. Captain Amos Barzalai, Uri's grandson, is in command so as to keep it in the family. They will guard the perimeter from incursions by nosy passers by. You may wonder why this is so important.

What you may not fully appreciate is just how politically sensitive Biblical archaeology is in the ancient lands of Judea and Samaria. Anything that links the ancient Israelites directly to the modern land of Israel strengthens our claim to the land and weakens the arguments of the revisionists, who deny these claims and claim that the Bible is simply the stuff of legend. So even the remote chance of a breach in security might lead to the sabotage of our mission."

Sanjay then raised his hand for attention. "Ishmael, I've brought Savita with me almost under false pretences and it would be irresponsible to put her in harms way. Can you guarantee our safety?"

Miri then chipped in before Ishmael could comment, "Sanjay that is a fair comment. As I've said we have picked up no electronic chatter or other intelligence to suggest there might have been a breach of security. Any visit close to the border between Syria and the Golan heights would be foolhardy at this time but, short of a sudden rocket barrage from ISIL being misdirected by 30 degrees to the west, we can think of no need for concern. Hezbollah on the other side of the Lebanese border have been quiescent for a while and it looks as if we have cut of the routes by which Iran has been supplying them with ammunition. All that aside Shin Beit and Mossad are monitoring the situation with enhanced vigilance hour by hour because of the importance of the mission as judged by a Presidential commission. Well I think that's enough for now enjoy the rest of the day and we look forward to seeing you this evening."

★★★

After breakfast they went their separate ways. Arthur joined Uri to visit a mutual friend a colleague at Tel Aviv University department of Archaeology. Olive borrowed a bike from the hotel to ride on the cycle track all the way south along the promenade to Jaffa, whilst Sanjay and Savita decided to take it easier and stroll along the boardwalk due north to the old port of Tel Aviv that had now been reinvented as a tourist attraction with shops, restaurants and bars surrounding the now defunct harbor. They walked in silence all the way until Sanjay broke the ice with one word, "sorry".

Savita turned to him and at once he noted that she had been crying. "Oh Sanjay, I'm the one who should apologize. To think that for nearly a year I've allowed the green worm of jealousy to grow in my belly! I truly thought you had been unfaithful to me. Although I'm stunned by Miri's revelations, I have to confess that it's a great relief and now I feel very excited by this adventure you've allowed me to join in. I think I shall wear my peacock blue sari tonight but I've brought nothing with me that is suitable for an archaeological dig." At this point she spotted a sportswear shop overlooking the harbor and dragged Sanjay inside before he could protest. 30 minutes later they emerged with carrier bags bearing the latest fashion in camouflage fatigues with lots of pockets as well as lace up hiking boots. In the dressing room mirror she looked a bit like Angelina Jolie in her role as Lara Croft in "Tomb Raider", although a little heavier around the hips.

Meanwhile Olive was thoroughly enjoying her bike ride following the beach in the direction of Jaffa. The sun was bright, the sea was calm and a gentle zephyr from the west cooled her down in the ambient temperature of 27 degrees Celsius. Every so often she stopped to admire the beautiful and bronzed young men a women, playing beach volleyball or aimlessly hitting a rubber ball backwards and forwards with wooden paddles. Others were surfing or paddling boats close in on the water's edge, or further out windsurfing on boards powered by butterfly wings. She couldn't help noting that this blissful image was degraded when she saw that the young men and women on leaving the beach were clothed in military khaki carrying assault rifles on straps over their shoulders. Further along the ride she stopped to look at a memorial to the 21 teenagers killed by a suicide bomber whilst queuing to enter the Dolphinarium nightclub in 2001. Even more remarkable a little further south was a memorial to those who died in 1948 when the nascent Israeli army shelled the MV Altalena, as it tried to supply arms to the Irgun, a Jewish paramilitary group. This fratricidal killing was more difficult to comprehend than the atrocity at the Dolphinarium.

The closer she got to Jaffa the more Israeli Arabs she encountered noticeable by the significantly greater modesty of their dress as well as their head coverings.

The cycle track ran out at the sea wall just below the steep hill leading up to the centre of old Jaffa. Olive chained her bike and walked up a narrow flight of stone stairs that meandered through beautiful landscape gardens until she arrived at a large plaza baking in the sun. I front of her lay the Greek Orthodox Church of St Michael and to her left she could see the minaret of the mosque that had been visible from her look out at the Hilton hotel 12 Km to the north. It was too hot linger in the plaza so she started exploring the artist quarter and the old port itself by clambering up and down vertiginous narrow alleyways that dated back to the time of Jesus and beyond.

Hot and thirsty from her ride and exploration she sought out a fruit juice bar just inside the souk that was bustling with the local Arab Israelis and European tourists with red faces and long shorts.

After rehydration and a plate of hummus with peta bread, she wandered closer to the town centre and discovered a flea market and some antique shops. She suddenly thought it would be nice to buy something for her daughter Christobel and her three grandchildren. As she was inspecting a Yemenite mirror with a silver filigree frame she spotted a dark skinned man, who seemed to be studying her closely. He wore a short carefully trimmed beard and a red chequered keffiyeh that shaded his eyes. With a start she realized that this was the third time today she had seen him. He was certainly in the small crowd in front of the Dolphinarium memorial and she was pretty sure that he entered the fruit juice bar shortly after her.

There was no doubt in her mind that she was being followed, catching her stalker off guard by his chance reflection in the hand mirror. Keeping calm and acting normally, she made her purchases without haggling over the price for too long, retraced her steps to her bike, and peddled all the way back to her hotel without looking back.

She was exhausted, hot and sweaty by the time she dismounted her borrowed bike and returned it to the doorman. She took the lift to her room, took a cool shower and in a white fluffy toweling robe lay back on her bed to think through her recent experience and promptly fell asleep. She woke at 6.00 pm understanding with crystal clarity that their cover had been broken. She therefore decided to take the opportunity of discussing this further with Miri Cohen some time during the evening's reception at the gallery.

Chapter 33

A mixed reception

Exactly at the appointed time Olive and her friends gathered in the reception hall awaiting their car.

Savita look stunning in her peacock blue sari that exposed just enough of her brown midriff to be alluring but not vulgar. Sanjay stood proudly in attendance looking uncomfortable in a suit and tie with the suit jacket tightly buttoned across his bulging abdomen. Curiously enough Arthur looked splendid in a dark suit and white shirt, making no attempt at buttoning his jacket. His sheer bulk and beard gave him a magisterial aura. Yet the biggest surprise of the evening was Olive's appearance.

Her tight bun was replaced by a fashionable "hair do" care of the in-house stylist. She was wearing a demur but expensive looking dark blue cocktail dress, black patent court shoes and her costume jewelry that for once looked like the real thing. Arthur, for the first time in her memory, complimented Olive on her appearance.

The limo arrived on schedule and the little party was whisked off to the reception at the gallery.

President Reuven Rivlin in person welcomed them individually with a warm handshake and warm words. He even flirted a little with Olive who blushed with delight.

Sparkling white wine and canapés were served and thus encumbered they stood in respectful silence to hear the speeches. The speeches mostly in Ivrit went on and on until the four British guests started fidgeting and glancing at each other with raised eyebrows. President Rivlin spoke last and had the grace to repeat his oration in English whilst looking directly at the foreign visitors.

He then cut a ribbon and declared that the Tel Aviv annex to the Israel museum was finally open.

Hazel and Arthur wandered round the exhibits together whilst Miri held Sanjay and Savita in earnest conversation. They had to admire the wonderful architecture of the building designed Preston Scott Cohen. The extraordinary angles of the interior space and the unexpected shafts of light from hidden sources reflected off the gold filigree of the crowns and breast plates of the Sifrei Torah, gave the appearance of a modern Aladdin's cave, but to tell the truth the collection of 19th and early 20th Judaeica, left them cold. As soon as Miri was free of the Manchandras, Olive left her brother and hastened over to grab her attention.

Miri listened carefully and nodded as Olive explained her concerns and then summoned over a tall bronzed, tough looking guy with an earpiece emerging from under the lapel of his sharp suit.

She rattled off a few short sentences at him in Ivrit after which he left her and hastened to join the Praetorian Guard around the President who was firmly and politely ushered out of the museum.

Olive looked on in dismay and came over faint and had to sit down on a nearby red plush chair bearing a sign "Please do not sit on this chair". Miri then turned back to Olive, helped her out of the chair and proceeded to gather up the group and guide them into a limo that seem to materialize out of nowhere. The large black car set off at high speed leaving Miri at the curbside.

The limousine set off in the direction of the Hilton hotel but to their surprise, it stopped shortly after entering a wide boulevard lined by anonymous white three story blocks. Olive noted that the trilingual road names, written in Hebrew, Arabic and English, announced that this road was named Ben Gurion Avenue. The driver remained silent whilst, Olive,

Arthur, Sanjay and Savita, exchanged anxious glances and wondered what was expected of them. Arthur was just about to get out and throw his considerable weight around, when another black car drew up behind them. Out stepped Miri followed by two other figures that looked vaguely familiar. Miri opened the door and beckoned the occupants of the first car to accompany her as she led the way into a small glass lobby of one of the three story white buildings. In the bright lights of the lobby, Olive, Arthur and Sanjay immediately recognized the two strangers as their companions from last year's adventures in Lachish and Tel Maresha; Melvin and Betty Schapiro. They greeted each other warmly whilst Savita looked on with bewilderment. Olive was sensitive to the fact that the two Americans no longer looked like tourists and carried themselves with an altogether different and slightly sinister demeanor. In the lift up to the third floor all they could get out of Miri on demanding an explanation was, "This is a safe house and we can speak freely once inside". This of course meant nothing to anyone but Olive.

On arrival at the top floor they noted three doors leading off a narrow and featureless corridor.

One door carried an electronic keyboard and Melvin gained access for the company by pressing a six-digit code. The door opened onto a sparsely furnished room with blank white stucco walls.

As they entered two men stood up to greet the party, one was the squat bull necked Mossad chief Yossi Goldfarb, and the other was the tall, mustachioed, insouciant, Commander Quatermaine of Special Branch, Scotland Yard.

★★★

After they had all got over their surprise and Savita was finally let in on the secret, they sat down around a conference table generously supplied with laptop computers and jugs of coffee. Yossi Goldfarb was paying Savita special attention doing his best to reassure her about this sudden turn of events whilst at the same time turning on his manly charm. Out of the corner of his eye Sanjay was examining his wife wondering when this accumulation of surprises might finally crack her powers of endurance, yet to his relief she seemed to be enjoying every minute almost as if she were playing a role in an Agatha Christie thriller. Yossi then called the group to order and started to cross-examine Olive.

"Olive, if I may? We are very sorry to alarm you in this way but when Miri here alerted us to your suspicions we had to take it seriously. The excavations at Tel Dan are politically very sensitive, not just within Israel but with the potential of wider repercussions amongst our not so friendly neighbors. So please enlighten us to why you suspected you were being followed?"

"Yossi, if I may?" Replied Olive with a twinkle. "You might choose to put it down to feminine intuition which to some extent I do, but I'm a pragmatic type of person with little patience for metaphysics. My sense of being followed was tangible and I've been thinking it over since I woke up from my nap earlier this evening. In retrospect I think my suspicions were first alerted when I spotted the man paying close attention to the plaque bearing the names of the murdered teenagers on the memorial to the atrocity at the Dolphinarium. Subliminally it must have registered as surprising that a man wearing Arabic clothing should be demonstrating so much interest. To see him again soon after, closely observing my activity in the curio shop seemed too much of a coincidence."

"How could you be so sure it was the same man? Surely all brown men, with beards and red chequered head coverings must look the same to an elderly woman from North West London."

Olive had the wisdom to recognize that Yossi Goldfarb was intentionally trying to provoke her, so turning her steely gaze at her inquisitor she responded. "Surely Mr. Goldfarb you can't be that familiar with gentile women living in Hampstead

Garden Suburb to make such sweeping generalizations." That provoked laughter all round and Yossi grinned and turned to Commander Quartermaine muttering, "Touché"

"True, most Arab men in traditional garb look the same to me and are commonly to be seen in Knightsbridge where I go to buy my trinkets, but this one just happened to have a minor degree of strabismus in his left eye. Strabismus Mr Goldfarb is probably what members of the security services call a squint. In other words it was difficult to judge which eye he was using whilst spying on me."

"Well I think you've put my friend from Mossad in his place Olive," Interjected the man from the Met. "…and I think you have convinced us that your suspicions are worthy of our concern."

"Yes indeed Olive and forgive my apparent rudeness, it's just my training as an interrogator for the Israeli secret service overcame my British sense of gallantry. Do you think you might recognize the man again if we showed you some pictures?" Olive nodded furiously. Yossi continued, "Now turn you attention to the computer by your chair. I'm going to flash hundreds of headshots of known terror suspects operating in our country that we are monitoring at the moment. If you spot him shout stop and I will hit play-back one image at a time until you think you've identified him."

The images flashed by on Olive's computer screen until she shouted, "Stop!" Yossi then played back the file of images pausing at each one until Olive quietly replied, "Yes that's him"

Yossi and Miri then put their heads together and searched some electronic files, nodded to each other and Yossi turned back to Olive. "The man who you suspect was following you is indeed a credible threat. His *nom de guerre* is Abu Jihad and he is a low level operative paid by Hamas although living legally in Jaffa under the name of Ahmed ibn Hassan. Now tell us why Hamas might have an interest in you?"

"I've no idea why Hamas in particular might be interested in my whereabouts but I've always had the fear that I might be the weak link in your chain of security. If you remember right at the start of my adventures, I informed a certain D.I. Ramsay of my suspicions that Professor Black had been murdered. Ramsay recorded my statement and not long after was killed in a hit and run accident.

Commander Quatermaine has reason to suspect that there is a mole in the chain of command within the Met. From that point on I must have been a person of interest to whoever is running this conspiracy. I suspect that the first time I entered Israel last year I automatically triggered an alert but that our movements during that visit were adequately camouflaged by me acting out the role of the Christian pilgrim. My second visit within such a short period, and our VIP treatment must have triggered a second alert, and that is why I'm now being watched."

The two security experts studied Olive silently with ill-disguised admiration, exchanged knowing glances and were about to speak in unison when Arthur butted in.

"I think our security has been compromised and I fear for my sister's safety as well as that of my traveling companions so I suggest that we leave Israel at the first opportunity."

"I think you are right professor," responded Yossi Goldfarb, "I don't think that Shin Beit can any longer guarantee your safety if our suspicions are correct."

" NO, with respect, I think you are wrong. If we cut and run now the suspicions, and they can only be suspicions, of our enemies, will be confirmed. This will then compromise the security of your excavation at Tel Dan. I remember that when I signed the State Secret's act in your embassy in London Yossi, it was after the assurances of Commander Quatermaine that *my* country's best interests were being served. If that is still the case we should carry on as if nothing had changed." Said Olive with a challenging look at her brother.

Before anyone had a chance to respond this challenge Savita quietly intervened and with a sweet and consolatory tone of voice came up with a suggestion. "Why don't we try and make a virtue out of necessity? As the new girl on the block I can see how all your attempts at secrecy can only fuel the interests of your enemies, if indeed your conspiracy theory is true. Why not run a front-page news item on the excavation, with photographs of this famous British archaeologist, Professor Arthur Templeton and his sister, meeting the President at the reception this evening? Then going on to explain that thanks to the professor, important new finds, linked to the Assyrian conquest of the Northern Kingdom, might explain what happened to the 10 lost tribes of Israel. That would make a good story and explain the two visits of Mrs. Hathaway acting as a consort to the great man." This with a mischievous smile directed at Arthur. Olive nodded with enthusiasm whilst Alan Quatermaine started to fill his pipe and slipped into a reverie. The others waited expectantly as if understanding the Commander's rituals. Once the pipe was lit and the fragrant smoke began to drift across the room, Quatermaine sat up straight and muttered to himself, "That just might work". Then in a louder tone of voice directed at Savita, "Jolly good show old girl, splendid idea, what do you think Yossi old chap?" Yossi stood up and beckoned Miri, Melvin and Betty to join him in the next room. Quartermaine continued puffing away at his pipe leaning back in his chair in a new state of relaxed bonhomie, whilst the others looked at each other with mystification. Sanjay's look at Savista also included notes of surprise and admiration.

10 minutes passed until the four Israeli agents returned. Yossi had a large grin on his face as he addressed the room. "I've just spoken to the chief who wasn't much pleased at having been called out of a production of Madam Butterfly. He agrees with Olive and Savita's analyses of events and suggestions for our next move. He would also like to offer the two ladies honorary status as members of Shin Beit, but to keep that secret. Meantime for operational purposes, you lot will be referred to as the "Gang of Four". I suggest that's enough for one day you all must be exhausted. Tomorrow

morning we will continue as planned but the Commander and I would like to join you in professor Cohen's office in Jerusalem tomorrow at 10.00 am."

★★★

Chapter 34

Friday morning in Jerusalem

The Israeli secret services had clearly been busy all night as judged by the front pages of the Jerusalem Post and the English edition of Ha'Aaretz. With some light touches of "Photoshop" magic, both newspapers carried pictures of Arthur Templeton shaking hands with the President, with Olive standing dutifully by his side. The caption to the picture in both publications read, "Famous English archaeologist, Arthur Templeton, greeted by President Rivlin at the opening ceremony of the new Israel Museum building in Tel Aviv." The banner headline in the Jerusalem Post read, "The 10 lost tribes of Israel found! English Professor unearths stele in Tel Dan dating from the Assyrian conquest, listing the depositions of the conquered tribes across the Assyrian Empire. " The headline in the Left wing Ha'Aaretz took a different tone altogether, "Likud government racist propaganda exploits new findings at Tel Dan dig to justify its continued illegal occupation of Samaria. (*See page 12 opinion piece by Professor Chaim Ben Tovim on why Biblical archaeology is being subverted to support a political agenda.)*" Both newspapers also contained a photograph of an ancient stele covered in Assyrian cuneiform writing purporting to be a list of the lost 10 tribes.

At breakfast in the executive lounge at the Hilton, the gang of four fell about laughing on seeing the headlines. Arthur didn't know whether to be flattered or furious at first but ultimately settled on the former particularly when other guests reading their papers started pointing him out. Olive in her turn was quite pleased with her appearance in the front-page photograph. It was probably for the first time since her husband died that she became visible again to the wider world. Sanjay confessed to jealousy for not coming up with the idea ahead of his wife, whilst Savita wasn't sure what to feel.

She had never been so excited in her whole life. On being questioned by the others as to how she came up with the idea so quickly, she explained that on the flight coming over she had read an old Hercule Poirot novel where a stolen diamond was hidden in full view as a crystal tear-drop in a chandelier.

Their chauffer-driven car arrived at 8.30am and a little after 10.00am they were dropped off at Daniel Cohen's office in Jerusalem. What they would not have noticed on the road up to the Holy City was that they were merely the front vehicle of a veritable motorcade. Two unmarked supercharged, battered looking old Opels, flanked them on either side about two car lengths behind.

One carried Miri, Melvin and Betty and the other carrying a back up team of Shin Beit agents.

Almost boxed in between these three cars was an old Renault driven by a dark skinned, bearded man with a slight squint accompanied by two other Arab looking hard cases wearing blue overalls. Whilst bringing up the rear at a discreet distance further back was a smart new, brilliant white, Lexus town car, driven by a uniformed police officer, carrying Yossi Goldfab and Alan Quartermaine in the rear.

As the gang of four disembarked through the rear entrance of the Israel Museum via a security barrier, the shabby looking Renault disappeared into a warren of streets in the rundown Nachloat district of West Jerusalem, closely followed by one of the battered looking Opels.

The second Opel carrying Miri and her colleagues followed the gang of four through security and a minute or two later were joined by Goldfarb and Quartermaine.

Daniel Cohen was waiting for them in his office flanked by Uri Barzilai and Ishmael Nadir. He was not expecting such a crowd so he suggested that they all moved to a nearby tutorial room equipped with an overhead data projector and screen. Additional jugs of coffee, mugs and donuts were sent for and by the time they had all settled down professor Cohen's incandescent rage at the newspaper headlines had to some extent been assuaged by a brief and reassuring few words with the two Shin Beit officers.

Yossi Goldfarb asked Daniel permission to address the small gathering that now amounted to 12 souls. He introduced Commander Quartermaine of the London anti-terrorist squad and then explained in detail the breech in security and the sudden decision to use the bait and switch dodge to wrong foot the opposition. Their decision had been vindicated by the fact that an old Renault car carrying a bearded Arab man with a minor degree of strabismus had followed Mrs. Hathaway's car but had turned off in another direction once its final destination had become obvious.

"They in their turn had been followed by my men, who have just informed me that brother Strabismus and his friends, were now drinking Turkish coffee and having a smoke in Café Beersheba, Rechov Nachalot."

Daniel thanked Yossi and turned on the projector.

"Dear friends, a lot has happened since you last sat in my department and once again I want to thank you from the bottom of my heart for helping us to find the copper scroll and for leading us to the site of the hidden treasures of King Solomon's Temple. I will now show you some pictures of the site as we first left it (*click*) and now the site as you will find it on Sunday morning (*click*)"

There was a deep sigh as the second slide showed a large rectangular trench with a pavement of perfectly cut and aligned blue marble slabs.

"The next few slides show you the scans we've made of the cavity below the paving stones. They may look to you like a barn in a snowstorm at first but using modern ultrasound and radar scanning analysis techniques developed for the Israeli Dolphin class sub-marines we've come up with this (*click*)"

At this click there was another sharp intake of breath as what appeared to be a teenager's cluttered bedroom filled the screen.

"You see a fair sized room measuring about five by three meters filled with a haphazard collection of boxes of different shapes and sizes but of particular interest is this magnified and enhanced image of the north-east corner of the room (*click*). Here you see a container that has cracked along a seam spilling its contents. What looks like a collection of chocolate bars are the correct size and shape of one *mina* biblical gold bullion. There are 60 *mina* to a *talent* and a *talent* has been estimated as weighing approximately 60 kilograms. So each of those chocolate bars are likely to be one kilogram of purest gold. So forgetting any conspiracies or even archaeological hubris, this appears to be a treasure trove of unimaginable value and we must have very tight security and armed protection for bringing so much gold into the light of day. So the main reason for gathering all you very privileged folk who will witness this historical event, is for us all to be briefed on our plans for the opening of the vault under the watchful eyes of Shin Beit and the IDF.

Captain Barzilai of C company Golani brigade will join us in about 30 minutes so to fill that time I want to show some of our new observations regarding the copper scroll."

Daniel then closed his first PowerPoint file and started searching his computer desktop for the next file. There was much background murmuring, slurping of coffee and further donut selections made by Arthur, before Daniel was able to continue.

"This first picture shows you the copper scroll after it was unrolled (*click*). This magnified line shows you the clues we solved to lead us to Tel Dan (*click*, click). These rows of text and icons have led us, with some degree of confidence, to three or four sites well outside our zone of jurisdiction (*click*). This one though is proving a problem and is tantalizing because of this pair of winged angels.

The coordinates are *beta, beta,* but so far we only have one *beta* and that is Beersheba and we don't know if that indicates longitude or latitude. Any thoughts?"

After a few moments deep thought, Sanjay raised a hand as if he was still in high school.

"Daniel can you project that map that you had in your office when we first made our deductions."

After a few more minutes whilst Daniel shuffled PowerPoint virtual folders on his virtual desktop, the map of the ancient Levant appeared on screen. After another pause for thought Sanjay asked,

"Can you expand the view to take in Egypt and North Africa?"

"That'll take a minute or two but why do you ask?"

"Well maybe the second *beta* is somewhere to the west of the first map. After all weren't the ancient Israelites equally aware of civilizations to their west? We might have got lucky with the first map but who's to say the second *beta* has to be confined to the original geographical zone we explored."

"Your right of course Sanjay, I think I've been rather stupid about this. It's always a good idea to have fresh input, h'mm let's see what I can find."

After a few minutes another map appeared on a larger scale that this time took in ancient Egypt and ancient Greek civilizations. They all gazed on this with ferocious attention until Sanjay spoke again.

"Can you magnify the Delta region of Egypt please?"

"There's another *beta* for you. What's Bubastis?"

"Oh my God" blurted out Arthur, "That was the capital of ancient Egypt during the 22nd and 23rd dynasties that coincide with the period of the Babylonian conquest."

" By Jove you've got." Sang Daniel, impersonating the voice of Rex Harrison in My Fair Lady.

"Let's check the coordinates. Someone please write this down. Beersheba is 31 degrees 15 minutes North and 34 degrees 47 minutes East. Bubastis is 30 degrees 36 minutes

North and 31 degrees 30 minutes East. So we are looking for a landmark that is 30/36 North and 34/47 East."

Taking a cursor on the screen maneuvered by a mouse, Daniel traced the longitude and latitude coordinates to a point where they crossed in the northern Negev of modern day Israel.

He then brought up an ordinance survey map of the region and focused down on what seemed to be a featureless area of desert before looking back at Sanjay.

"I think you've discovered the hiding place of the Ark of the Covenant and its golden cherubim.

It's buried somewhere in the Ramon crater in an underground cistern fed by a river of blood! Maybe that's some reference to the affliction of the Nile as one of the plagues that persuaded Pharaoh to let the Children of Israel go. I suggest we go after that with the blessing of the Chief Rabbinates of course, one we've sorted Ten Dan".

At that everyone stood up and cheered. That is apart from Goldfarb and Quartermaine who thought that this discovery had nothing to do with the matter in hand.

Things turned serious again when the young IDF captain, Amos Barzalai, was shown in and the security briefing started in earnest.

★★★

Chapter 35

Return of the Caliphate

Saleh Al Mazri had been keeping a low profile whilst growing a long Islamic beard, at his safe house in Amman for the best part of a year, before being summoned for his first meeting with the Caliph, Ibrahim Abu Bakr al-Baghdadi, in Al-Raqqah. Such was the reputation of this hard line bloodthirsty cleric, that Saleh literally wet his underpants on decoding the signal. He was not an observant Muslim even though he had adopted the outward appearances of a true believer.

He only had a week to prepare for the visit and for that period gave up alcohol and female companionship. He also tried to memorize the most important prayers and rituals by daily visits to the nearby Sunni Mosque.

Amman was close to the southern border of Syria about 100 miles south of Damascus. That stretch of the journey was fairly routine and safe, still being the stronghold of troops loyal to Assad. His passport with a new identity that matched his new beard was the best that the Brotherhood could provide. However the onward journey via Homs and Aleppo was treacherous yet a well-worn "underground" route used by his associates and lone wolves volunteering as fighters for the new Caliphate. The last stretch to Al-Raqqah was cross-country through the desert and then along the north bank of the Euphrates. This area was a war zone where his armoured truck bucked and swerved to avoid the somewhat desultory bombing raids from high-flying unidentifiable stealth bombers. Arriving exhausted and filthy in the capital of the Caliphate he was dismayed to see not a single building intact, no one walking above ground and the roads empty apart from the occasional truck like his, with rear mounted light anti-aircraft guns. They stopped at an anonymous cross road with the remains of a clock tower at its centre. The width of the avenues on each side, and the marble slabs left coating the remnants of walls and road level, suggested that this was once a centre of commerce in the city. He was marched to an intact doorway that apparently led nowhere until his dark adjusted eyes gave him sight of a flight of stairs leading downwards. Once the steel reinforced doors were closed behind him, the lights above the cellar stairs were turned on. After walking down two flights of unremarkable grey slabs he turned a corner to be greeted by the most remarkable sight he had ever seen. Laid out before him was a replica of the matrix of roads above his head; a virtual underground city worthy of the Caliph of Baghdad. He was later to learn that for the last four years whilst the Western allies were bombing away above, Ibrahim Abu Bakr al-Baghdadi, had decreed an underground city to be built by the thousands of slaves captured from the neighbouring infidel communities. The infidel wives and daughters were conscripted to fill the harems or if over a certain age act as servants to the senior clerics or officers of the regime.

In the apparent centre of this complex, boasting a shallow pool with a tinkling fountain, was a grand archway fashioned out of crossed scimitars leading to a wide marble staircase carrying him down to the quarters of the Caliph himself and his Praetorian Guard. Saleh was ushered into a grand receiving room, invited to sit down on an Ottoman cushion and served fruit juice and figs. With knees trembling he waited and waited as a line of supplicants and dignitaries arrived and departed through the thick curtains leading to the inner sanctum. After about two hours it was his turn and as he was about to enter into the presence a guard whispered in his ears, "Be sure to prostrate yourself in front of the Mahdi, kiss his toes and wait till he tells you to rise." Keeping his eyes modestly downwards he made his way across the tent like room and did as instructed half expecting a scimitar to fall and dislodge his head. After a brief moment he felt a soft hand tap him on the shoulder and a soft voice instructing him to rise.

Seated on a cushion in front of the Caliph he had no time to take in his surroundings before

Abu Bakr al-Baghdadi began to speak. At first site he was an unimpressive man, looking very much like any other fundamentalist Muslim cleric it had ever been his misfortune to meet. But the soft voice, that of a man of such power that he never had to raise his voice to be heard, and the intensity of his gaze through fathomless black eyes, rapidly held Al-Mazri in thrall.

After a brief formal welcome the Caliph launched into a monologue.

"Over the past several months Islamic State has made significant gains. We control a huge expanse stretching in Iraq from Ramadi west of Baghdad across the Syrian border to Palmyra. And, at the same time, we have consolidated our hold on the entire northeastern region of the disintegrating Syrian state. Already the Caliphate has been able to spread out from the Fertile Crescent and penetrate the other half of the Arab world, as evidenced by our attacks on the Egyptian army in Sinai. We were responsible for bringing down a Russian airliner in the Sinai and the hugely successful attacks on the infidels in Paris in November 2015. We are represented by Boko Haram in Nigeria and have well embedded branches in all Muslim states including Malaysia and Indonesia. We needed some time to digest all the territory we have taken in Syria and Iraq and that accounts for the relative lull in our activities over the last 12 months. We are now planning a concerted push for Baghdad; a drive into Kurdistan, a move on Aleppo and Homs in northern Syria together with gaining a foothold in Jordan. A successful thrust northward into Kurdistan capturing the oil fields in and around Kirkuk would be a major coup, enabling us to run an independent state on oil revenues alone. The Jordanian population is homogenously Sunni, and we could easily pick up popular support against the Hashemite monarchy. Success would then open up the road to Saudi Arabia, the glittering prize including the holy cities of Mecca and Medina. This is what we dream about.

So what thwarts this dream?"

Saleh assumed that this was a rhetorical question, so remained silently attentive until he nearly chocked on his spittle when the Caliph roared, "Are you deaf or are you stupid? Answer my question" With a weak and shaky voice, Al-Mazri replied, "Err-Iran" with an upward inflection as if to leave it ambiguous whether his answer was a statement or a question.

"Exactly, along with all their Shiite puppets like Hezbollah on the Lebanese border. Now imagine we had common purpose with the Shiites and persuaded them that I am the true Mahdi and the harbinger of the end of times, then we could realise our dreams. Yet how do we achieve this miracle?" Assuming that he was expected offer an opinion at this, Saleh opened his mouth as if to speak when once again Al-Baghdadi roared. "Silence, you foolish man. There is no way you could guess the answer. The first part of the question is easy. We both want to see the end of the great Satan, the United States of America and the little Satan, that Zionist entity occupying our lands. That is our common purpose but to unite all Muslims, Shiites and Sunnis, under the banner of the true Caliph, the *Hazrat Mahdi,* requires a sign from Allah that all will recognise, and that is why I summoned you to my presence. I have agents embedded in the Muslim Brotherhood, in Teheran, with Hezbollah in Lebanon, Hebron in the West Bank of Palestine, New York and even in the Metropolitan Police of the cesspit of sin, London. The English jokingly refer to their Capital City as Londonistan, if only they knew how true that was going to be. We have been closely following your searches for the copper scroll and allowed your masters to foolishly disregard your sound advice. We now know that the copper scroll is in the hands of the department of Archaeology in Jerusalem as our agents in the Zionist entity have been tracking the movements of those English fools you had been following for over two years. We also now know with certainty that the copper scroll will lead us to Aaron's Rod and whoever has control of that holy relic, will be recognised as the *Hazrat Mahdi*. Your role is now act as my liaison offer making use of your Muslim Brotherhood network helping our military commanders coordinating a two pronged attack on Tel Dan in the northern most finger of occupied Palestine at the time that the Rod is retrieved from its hiding place in the vault of the heretics Temple in ancient Samaria.

Timing is everything in this campaign. We must allow the archaeologists to complete their work in uncovering the underground sanctum holding the treasures of King Solomon's Temple and then we strike. We will surprise the Satanic Zionists by simultaneously attacking this region with Shiite forces from the northwest and our Sunni army from the northeast and the Golan Heights. The ferocity and surprise of this joint expedition will allow our land forces to sweep through occupied Palestine whilst 30,000 ground to air guided missiles, concealed in bunkers beneath Hezbollah controlled territory, will take care of any air force trying to frustrate our holy war.

Our forces will then sweep through the Negev and fork East and West. To the West we will take the Sinai Peninsula and the whole of Egypt on both sides of the Nile and then link arms with our North African allies based in Sirte and occupying most of the failed state of Lybia. To the East we will invade that corrupt and decadent and heretical Islamic nation, Saudi Arabia. Finally Jerusalem, Mecca and Medina will be in the hands of the *ummat al-Islamiyah* and then in the world will be wiped clean of heresy and sin, *insha'Allah"* The Caliph stopped speaking and a deathly hush filled the tented walls of his underground encampment. Time stopped for Saleh as in awe he suddenly began to appreciate the enormity of what he was hearing and vowed there and then to carry out any duty assigned by his new master even if it lead to his death. Then surely he would be greeted as a *shahid* as he entered Paradise and received the rewards granted to a martyr in the cause of Islam. As if reading his thoughts Al-Baghdadi broke the silence.

"Once you've completed your work in helping us retrieve Aaron's Rod, you will be sent on another mission that will distract and dismay our enemies whilst we re-conquer the Arab world that was once the Empire of the Prophet. You will be trained and granted the ultimate distinction being sent to Paradise as a *shahid* when you boldly carry a suicide vest carrying radioactive shrapnel, to the epicentre of that viper's nest, the City of London. The time and place has already been chosen and you will only be informed at 24 hours notice lest you fall into the arms of the enemy and they torture you to learn of this plan. Now begone and may Allah be your guide." At that Saleh was dragged to his feet as the blood drained from his face, and frogmarched out to the waiting armoured truck.

★★★

Chapter 36

King Solomon's treasure

In Tel Aviv, Saturday was a day of rest. As the beach and promenade were full of young men and women enjoying a day off at the sea side, Olive, Arthur, Sanjay and Savita, decided to spend the day lounging and reading round the Hilton pool that nestled on the cliff overlooking the beaches and marina. Olive and Savita, who had more or less kept their youthful figures, appeared in brand new swimming costumes bought especially for the occasion. Arthur looked like a beached whale in huge Bermuda shorts of radiant hue. Sanjay had given no thought to the matter so he had to buy shorts in the hotel boutique and modestly cover up his midriff with a short-sleeved linen shirt.

Olive and Savita passed the time with books of a romantic nature they had bought at Heathrow on the way out whilst Arthur started reading a textbook on the archaeology of Samaria and the Northern Kingdom but fell asleep before long. Meanwhile Sanjay who was ill versed in the art of relaxation, paced up and down, paddled in the shallow end, dried off in the sun and finally settled down with his Kindle to read "A suitable boy" by Vikram Seth. They gathered for lunch under the awning outside the main restaurant and shared a rather good bottle of Sauvignon Blanc from a winery on the Golan Heights. Shared in this context meant one small glass for Olive and the rest for Arthur, as Sanjay and Savita were teetotal. Daniel Cohen and his charming wife joined them in the evening for dinner. As they were leaving for the most northerly point of Israel at dawn the following morning they all opted for an early night.

★★★

Daybreak on Sunday morning was balmy with a gentle warm wind coming from the southwest and as the group gathered in the forecourt. As soon as they showed themselves, they were besieged by the press corps anxious to learn about their forthcoming dig. Daniel and Arthur had prepared a joint statement that was half true in that their treasure was buried in an underground vault at Tel Dan, but described the treasure as a stele listing the names and dispersions of the lost 10 tribes of the ancient Israelites. They were both interviewed for the local channels, Sky News and the National Geographic TV station, before setting off in convoy again. The first three SUVs carried the archaeological team leaders, the English adventurers and agents from Mossad, Shin Beit and MI6. Taking up the rear was a battered looking truck carrying workmen in charge of the heavy-duty hoists and drilling equipment. They were in truth a platoon from C Company of the Golani brigade led by Captain Barzilai; the genuine workers were already in place and had already completed their work leaving the final breakthrough to the director of the excavation, professor Cohen.

At Friday morning's briefing they were somewhat alarmed to hear that security levels in the country had been raised to amber implying that something was going on as judged by the chatter in the cyber-sphere and reports from agents embedded amongst their hostile neighbours. For these reasons the foreign visitors were given a second chance to change their mind with the predictable response. Therefore another platoon from B Company from the Golani brigade had travelled through the night and deployed themselves at the northern rampart of the Tel, making good use of the slit trenches left in place since the 6-day war of 1967. This way the civilians were protected in the vanguard and the rear.

Sunday was a normal working day and the roads were busy but most of the traffic was entering Tel Aviv from the north.

They reached the outskirts of Tiberius in under three hours and stopped for Turkish coffee, olives, humus and pita bread at a popular Arabic restaurant with views of the *Kineret* reflecting the newly risen sun high above Ein Gev on the eastern shore of the inland sea.

After a short rest they drove around the western shores of the lake and then due north towards Kyriat Shmona. From there they branched northeast on a minor road and within a few kilometres they arrived at a checkpoint manned by border guards and a smattering of journalists. Without much of a delay they were ushered to a car park within easy access to the mount and the site of the excavations. Whilst the others were unloading all their equipment, the gang of four, strolled up to the cordoned off zone where a year ago they had deduced the meaning of the horns of Hathor. In an encampment nearby they were delighted to meet up with Ishmael who was in process of setting up a small field first aid unit. He proudly showed them round and then took them on a tour of the slit trenches left over from the armistice line at the end of the 6-day war nearly 50 years in the past. The visitors were not sure to be alarmed or reassured to find this defensive line once again occupied by members of the IDF. On balance the sight of machine guns and mortars pointing north heightened their growing sense of anxiety.

Ishmael then tried to explain the extraordinary complexity of the topography, national borders and occupied territory, surrounding them. Due north was a tongue of land pushing south into Israel from Lebanon, whilst due west was a reciprocal tongue of land belonging to Israel pushing into Lebanon with the town of Metula at its tip. The Israeli border to the west ran southward all along the boundary of the Hula valley along a mountain ridge for about 20 kilometres before turning west and running all the way to the sea. The other side of this mountain ridge was Lebanon proper but mostly controlled by Hezbollah militants, clients and beneficiaries of Iran's largesse. Imediately in front of them was the Bekka valley. Wrapping round them to the east and northeast were the Golan Heights and occupied lands taken from the Syrians at the time of the 6-day war; burnt out tanks and field guns were still on display in the meadows facing them to mark that occasion. Out of sight and just beyond the crest of the hills, ISIL were well dug in having completed the encirclement of president Assad's forces and beginning to threaten Damascus, 40 kilometres to their northeast. Olive felt a little vulnerable standing on this patch of high ground encircled by forces with malign intentions to their hosts and subconsciously back away to the flimsy protection of the first aid tent where coffee was being handed out.

After about 30 minutes the various parties involved were requested to make their way to the perimeter of the excavation that was marked by a yellow and black striped tape.

From the surface a collapsible aluminium ladder was in place, cables snaked their way to and from the command centre and trenching equipment on caterpillar tracks waited its turn. In addition a scaffold bearing two block and tackle pulley systems, arched over the pit.

One of the technicians was already in the pit standing on four large blue marble slabs that fitted each other with perfect linear proximity. He carried a scanning device and was waiting instructions from above. Sanjay couldn't help noting that by his estimation each slab had the perfect dimension of the golden ration of 1.62. Daniel Cohen then popped his head out of the command centre tent and beckoned his four visitors inside. Once their eyes had adjusted to the gloom, Daniel called the technician with the scanner on his Walkie-Talkie whilst turning on one of the video-screens sitting on a trestle table. Immediately the screen came to life and flooded the dark interior of the tent with a pulsing blue light. The images on the screen then began to move as the underground cavity was scanned under the verbal instruction of professor Cohen. Sanjay and Savita were familiar with this technique as it was virtually the same of the ultra-sound scans they often used in their clinical practice but they had to remind themselves that the womb being studied was scaled up to the dimensions of the tent in which they stood. The other difference was that the edges of the acoustic shadows in the cavity were much sharper than their clinical equivalent. With another command and some adjustments to a control panel the images suddenly became three-dimensional just like the latest version of the scanners used on a foetus in-utero. The visitors were then taken a tour of the underground sanctuary that was cluttered with boxes of different shapes and sizes, some spilling their contents and others of strange shape that defied the imagination to deduce their contents. Strangest of all was a long narrow rectangular box that seemed to have pride of place in the centre. It reminded Arthur of the carrying box for his personal snooker cue that he kept in the billiard room at the Athenaeum.

Having drunk their fill of the images of this gravid underground storeroom, Daniel then gave the command for work to commence on prising off the roof. Once again they all gathered round the lip of the deep pit and watched as two technicians gently drilled holes at the midpoint of each side of the slab lying in the southeast quadrant. As these holes were completed there was a sigh of relief that the ancient marble hadn't cracked. In addition Olive imagined she heard the sigh of stagnant air being released into the atmosphere having been imprisoned for more than 3,000 years.

The technicians then passed malleable rods through the holes and then threaded two sturdy ropes running crosswise. These were then linked to the two block and tackle complexes on the assembly above the pit. Then using a diamond tipped circular saw, cut away the edges of the marble slab from were they joined the stone edges of the underground room and the neighbouring other two slabs. Whilst this was going on the ropes on the pulleys were kept tight to steady the target and to avoid the cut marble collapsing onto the treasures below.

Once that process was complete the marble slab was

slowly winched up to the surface, swung laterally and lowered to its rest on a prepared cushioned pallet. An arc lamp was then turned on that illuminated the underground chamber brilliantly and was reflected back by the brilliant gleam of polished cedar wood boxes and the even more dazzling shine of gold bullion. This was greeted with oooos and ahahs from the assembly above and even Daniel Cohen lowered his carapace of *sang-froid* for a brief moment. A fibre-optic 'scope was then lowered into the cavity and the team leaders retired to the tent to check the images beamed up from below as the snake like instrument explored the vault. More than satisfied by what they saw, Daniel was about to give the team the go ahead to raise the remaining three slabs when Arthur intervened. "I say old chap, you see that long box just showing in the top right hand corner of the screen, the one that leaning at about 45 degrees against that wooden chest, can you get your man to give us a closer look because I think I can see some lettering." Daniel called out some instructions and as if like magic the long narrow box floated into view. Along one side were what looked like Egyptian hieroglyphics whilst along the other visible side were some runes of another archaic writing system. Arthur then cried our barely able to control his excitement. "Holy Mary and all the saints! That's ancient Aramaic and I can read it: *'Hinay Ha'Yad shell Aaron Ha'Cohen Ha'Godal'*, roughly translated it reads 'here is the hand of Aaron the High Priest!" There was a deathly hush that was only broken when Olive burst into tears.

★★★

The continuation of the work that involved the removal of the three remaining slabs of marble, went without a hitch but as the word went out that the likely resting place of Aaron's rod had been uncovered, the assembly on the summit of the Tel gradually drifted to the edge of the pit to witness the historical event. Even the majority of the platoon from Company B of the Golani brigade manning the trench at the northwestern perimeter of the cordoned off zone, couldn't resist the temptation. However Captain Amos Barzilai and his platoon were unaware of the excitement above, as they were guarding the southeastern approaches to Ten Dan were the main access roads merged into the hiking trails. The hiking trails themselves branched into a complex network that followed the tributaries of streams and waterfalls draining off the water from the melting snow on Mount Hermon.

The explosion took everyone by surprise. Some of the party were thrown off their feet, many were wounded by shrapnel and Sanjay nearly lost an eye as a flying metal object cut a slice in his left cheek. As the dust settled, in the still aftermath, the shredded corpses of three members of the IDF were noted with their body parts littering a crater that interrupted the straight edges of the Command Post trench. The exact sequence of events emerged following witness statements at the public enquiry six months after the event. Whilst the majority of those standing on the plateau of "The High Place" of the Tel were distracted by the uncovering of the treasure hoard from the first Temple, four soldiers remained at their post sitting on the edge of the trench facing northwest. One got up to stretch his legs and lit a cigarette. He then turned round as one of his squad suddenly started jabbering away in Arabic into a field telephone. The remaining two soldiers started remonstrating with their neighbour in the trench and at that point the suspect pulled a lanyard and detonated his suicide vest. This witness was lucky only to lose a leg but lived to tell the tale.

After the explosion time seemed to stop as all those involved tried to process what was happening to them. The eerie silence that was in part the consequence of the impact of the detonation on the eardrums was amplified as the birds stopped their chatter and song. When the natural adrenaline surge took place, each responded according to their age, experience and training. The four English visitors threw themselves to the ground and searched for cover. Most of the

317

others on the plateau if not actively serving in the IDF were reservists. The ranking officer was Daniel Cohen, director of the dig and a reservist with the rank of Major in the military intelligence service. Having regained his composure Daniel was just about to order everyone off the plateau, when a volley of rockets roared overhead with their trajectory clearly defined by their smoke trail that pointed directly back to the high ground to their northwest marking the border with Hezbollah occupied Lebanon. The explosions as the rockets landed to their southeast rocked the ground on which they stood.

With explosions coming from front and rear Daniel was at a loss what to do, however the second salvo made it clear what their assailants were up to. A curtain of rockets described a 45-degree sector behind them was clearly designed to cut off any land access to Tel Dan.

At the foot of the Tel, Amos' battalion watched in awe as the rockets rained down behind them. Captain Barzalai wasted no time in getting into radio contact with the Brigade HQ, demanding back up and requesting the IAF to fly a sortie to silent the barrage incoming from the Lebanese border. He then ordered his men to move away from the road and set up a defensive position uphill in the first line of trees. He then tried to make contact with his comrades from Company B without success.

Back on top of the hill everyone had taken shelter in amongst the ruins of ancient Dan whilst Ishmael swung into action having just finished setting up his first aid station. One of the first casualties he attended to was his friend and colleague Sanjay who was bleeding heavily from a face wound. Olive and Savita were sitting on the ground nearby in a state of shock being comforted by one of the army nurses whilst Arthur was sitting on a nearby stonewall 3,000 years his senior being comforted by swigs of Cognac from his hip flask.

The members of Daniel's team gathered round the HQ tent together with the unharmed or walking wounded of Company B, waiting instructions from their leader whilst his radio operator was desperately trying to contact someone in Tel Aviv. Standing aside in a private huddle were the members of the security services trying to make sense of what was going on whilst Miri was shouting obscenities to some poor underling at Shin Beit central command.

The silence was broken by the sonic boom of three IAF F-16 fighting Falcons that had been scrambled from Ramat David airbase near the ruins of Megiddo that prophetically took its name from Armageddon. A cheer went up from those watching on the Tel but that soon turned to groans as a barrage of ground to air missiles hunted the fighters before they could reach their targets. Hunted was the word; these missiles latched on to their prey with uncanny precision whatever avoidance tactic was attempted. One F-16 was hit and they watched the pilot eject and float slowly down hitched to his parachute to an unknown fate in the hostile territory below him. The other two fighters banked right and left. One flew out to sea before returning to base and the other flew low overhead forcing the observers to duck as it also returned to base.

At that point the jaws of darkness opened and the apocalypse unfolded before their eyes.

A chain of explosions ran up and down the softly rolling grasslands that were to foothills of the mountainous regions to their northwest and northeast. Huge black smoking cavities appeared on each side and as the smoke cleared countless trucks with mounted field guns together with hundreds of smaller vehicles bearing black shrouded fighters, charged towards each other. Just when it looked as if these two armies from the depths of Hades would smash into each other, with almost balletic precision their vanguards turned south in the direction of Tel Dan. As they got closer those on the plateau of the Tel began to pick out the black flags of Jihad and pick up the shouts of "Allahu Akbar - Allahu Akbar!"

Thinking their end of days had arrived, the group of friends remained frozen on the spot composing their last words. Daniel Cohen was distracted from this task when a young corporal, slipping through the trees at his rear, tapped him on his shoulder. Rapidly he explained that Captain Amos Barzilai had sent him up the mound as a scout to find out what was happening since they lost radio contact. "This is what has been happening," explained Daniel making a sweeping gesture towards the oncoming harbingers of death. The young man, probably an 18-year-old conscript, went deathly pale at the sight. Pulling himself together Daniel then fired of a series of orders. "Keep out of sight on the slopes behind us, there are many hiding places amongst the trees and ravines. Get on the field telephone and explain what you've just seen. I will order surrender and fashion some white flags to wave. I suspect we will be more value to them alive as hostages than killed on the spot, but who can tell what these lunatics have in mind. I'm sure that you've already contacted brigade HQ but from this vantage point I think our best chance of turning back this tide is with a squadron of Apache assault helicopters flying in low from the south." The young soldier gave a perfunctory salute and scuttled back into the woodland and charged down one of the hiking tracks back to his commander.

Things then moved very quickly. Within about five minutes the northwest circumference of the Tel was completely surrounded at its base and probing manoeuvres into the almost impregnable mixture of craggy ravines and lush foliage, were being attempted by the invading forces at each flank. As the amorphous hoard approached individuals began to stand out. They were all heavily bearded and heavily armed. As irregular militia they wore no identifying uniforms and if it wasn't for their fearful reputation, might have been judged a ragtag army. However apart from the black flags of the Jihad, the trade mark of IS, the green on yellow flag sporting a hand clutching a Kalashnikov, the symbol of Hezbollah, was notable amongst the legions swarming in from the northwest. On reaching the base of the Tel instead of exploiting their momentum, the conjoined armies came to a halt. This gave Daniel and his team just enough time to improvise white flags from the clean sheets in Ishmael's field hospital. There was no immediate need for flag waiving as all went still and quiet. The point where the rearguard of the ocean of fighting men had halted then began to split in two like the parting of the Red Sea, to make way for a white painted command car to approach the Tel. Daniel raised his binoculars to his eyes to focus on this oncoming vehicle. Just behind the armoured cab were two benches running along the sides of the flatbed. On each side were six heavily armed men wearing smartly pressed camouflage combat uniforms. They held themselves aloof is if they were a chosen elite. Standing behind the cab and controlling a mounted heavy machine gun with a belt of ammunition running through the breach block, was an impressive figure dressed from head to toe with a brilliant white thawb and a turban of similar material wrapped around his head. Seen through the binoculars the face was instantly recognisable as the self-declared Caliph, Abu Bakr al-Bagdadi.

★★★

Erect, slow of pace and with great dignity, the Islamic Cleric, climbed up the slope of the Tel flanked by his praetorian guards. As he reached the summit everyone raised their hands as sign of surrender. He paused at the edge of the slit trench a gazed expressionless at the carnage scattered at his feet. The disembodied head of the suicide bomber gazed back. He then turned to study the throng in front of him and broke the silence with a voice that was little more than a whisper, speaking in almost perfect English, "Who is your leader?" Daniel stepped forward and declaimed, "I am their leader"

"And who might you be?"

"My name is Daniel Cohen, professor of archaeology at the Hebrew University Jerusalem and director of this dig."

" Major Daniel Cohen of the Israeli military intelligence service if my memory serves me correctly?"

"The very same"

"Well thank you very much *Major* Daniel Cohen for leading us here and saving me so much effort"

"As you elect to use my military rank in the reservists then I demand that you treat me and my colleagues as prisoners of war under the Geneva Convention."

"My dear *Major* Cohen you are in no position to make any demands. You are surrounded by 10,000 fighting men and we do not respect the Geneva Convention we are governed by the rules of warfare as laid down by the Prophet, *alayhi as-salam*. You are all formally declared hostages and you have one minute to contact the authorities of the Zionist entity to dismiss any idea of a counter-attack in which case you will all die on the spot." At this point he nodded at his armed guard who lifted their Kalashnikovs and ostentatiously released the safety catches and raised their guns to firing positions.

Daniel then nodded to his radio operator and who handed over the handset of their transmitter. He then spoke in rapid fire *Ivrit* to whoever happened to be at the receiving end. Miri obeyed the orders by speaking calmly and slowly into her smart phone whilst staring insolently at Al-Bagdadi.

He responded with a wide smile, "You young woman must be Miri Cohen although you photograph does not do justice to your beauty. I think I will take you as a concubine as one of the spoils of war as described by our own code of conduct." He then nodded to the senior officer of his retinue, a tall fierce looking Pashtun, who ambled over and picked up Miri as if she were weightless carrying her kicking and screaming to the side of his leader.

Al-Bagdadi continued, "Please step forward Olive Hathaway and Doctor Manchara"

Olive and Sanjay gasped in unison to hear their names called out by this complete stranger from another planet but had no option other than to step forward meekly.

"Well, you two have caused us no end of trouble but, *al'amdulill'h,* you too have served your purpose in bringing us to this place so your lives will be saved providing your protectors obey our instructions." Olive and Sanjay were then beckoned to join Miri alongside Al-Bagdadi.

At that point a platoon of the advance guard of the Caliph's army breasted the crest of the Tel and positioned themselves in a circle with guns raised to cover all of those on the plateau. At the same time unseen by those from above, a full Company of the Caliph's army had worked their way round to encircle the southeastern perimeter of the mound.

"Now to get down to the business in hand; as the Mahdi, the Caliph of Allah, I have come to claim what is rightly mine. With the Rod of Aaron in my hand I can prove that I am the true descendant of The Prophet and unite the world of Islam in the service of Allah and herald in the End of Days. Please conduct me to the burial site of the Rod, the Temple treasure will be of much less relevance but will help to finance the completion of my God-given mission."

Encouraged by a nudge in the back from a Kalashnikov, Daniel led the way to the edge of the excavated pit.

Al-Bagdadi gazed upon the treasures exposed below shining in the reflected glow of arc lights his black eyes reflecting his ill-disguised avarice.

"You, Major Daniel Cohen, will have the honour of climbing down and bringing up the receptacle of this holy relic. You drop it at your peril!"

Urged on by the gun in his back, Daniel clambered down the steep ladder and made to lift up the long timber box with the name of the first High Priest running down each side. To his dismay he found it rooted to the spot. Going to the end of the box that was propped up on a wooden chest, he was just about able to tilt it forward a few degrees but it was simply too heavy for him to handle.

"I think this box must be lined with lead, I can barely move it an inch", he shouted up. "We will have to use the block and tackle."

Taking Miri by her neck and holding a handgun to her temple Al-Bagdadi shouted back.

"If this is trickery or you are playing for time I will have no hesitation in killing this young woman, so bring it up in any way that will avoid damage to the contents"

Daniel gave out the orders and the assembly with the block and tackle was re-located over the pit and one of the technicians scrambled down to join Daniel to help secure the long box to the end of the rope that was reeled down to them. Very slowly and with considerable muscular effort the box was winched up to the surface and gently lowered to the ground close to the feet of the Caliph.

Pushing Miri back into the assembled crowd Al-Bagdadi started barking out orders to his men in Arabic and then returning to English said, "From now on none of you infidels must come near me, only my own men can provide my needs." As two of his men grabbed crowbars from a pile of the workmen's tools nearby, another dressed as a cleric wearing a black turban wrapped round his head, approached with a bowl of water in a stainless steel bowl taken from the field first aid centre. Opening a sterile pack of surgical swabs the mullah cried out a prayer and then knelt before Al-Bagdadi to wash his hands and feet. The two men with the crowbars turned the box so that the surface displaying a junction in the wood panels suggesting a lid. With some difficulty they were able to prise off the lid without significantly damaging the wood and then the contents were visible for those in the Caliph's company closest to him. At once it was noted that the cedar wood box was indeed lined with lead that provided an explanation for its weight but at first sight the contents were a disappointment.

All that could be seen was a long, gnarled, wooden staff with a bulbous end. Al-Bagdadi bent down with a show of great dignity and veneration and gently lifted out the staff and placed the narrow end at his right foot. The staff was exactly his height that the nearest onlookers took as a good omen.

On rotating the rod it became apparent that the bulbous end had been hollowed out to provide a cavity that held a grayish metallic looking rock about the size and shape of a pomegranate. The rod and stone took on the appearance of a large blunt sewing needle or an old fashioned bodkin.

With his hand two-thirds up the length of the staff, Al-Bagdadi waved it above his head and with a voice designed to carry to his cohorts below, cried out, "Behold the Rod of Aaron!"

He then bent forward to kiss the stone at which, as if by divine intervention, the miracles began.

★★★

Chapter 37

Armageddon is postponed

Olive thought she had witnessed a miracle of Old Testament proportions whereas Sanjay rapidly deduced a rational explanation for what played out in front of their eyes.

Al-Bagdadi's kiss of the stone mounted on Aaron's Rod lasted longer than polite society would consider decorous. In vulgar teen-age slang he appeared to be "snogging" the stone and wrestling with the rod. It then became clear to his attendants that the attachment of the rod to the Caliph's lips was more physical than emotional. In spite of screams from their leader, two of his men tore the rod away accompanied by a large chunk of his lower lip. As blood spurted out from his mouth, Al-Bagdadi continued screaming and then started clawing at his eyes that had become veiled by a milky white opaque film. The victim then started to stagger around like a drunk and as his two attendants grabbed his arms to control him, with apparent super-human strength he dragged them along the ground to the edge of the excavated pit where they let go for fear of their lives. With that the self-declared Mahdi plunged head first to his death with his skull smashing against a box of gold bullion from King Solomon's hoard. Everyone stood aghast trying to understand what they had just witnessed and the first to give voice to this extraordinary turn of events was the Mullah with the black turban. In Arabic he shouted out, loud enough for those at the foot of the Tel to hear, "Al-Bagdadi the false Messiah is dead. The rod of Aaron destroyed him. This is the sure sign that he was not our Caliph but a fraud!" Some of those surrounding him tried to shut him up whilst others tried to pull him free. The skirmish between the Islamic invaders grew wilder as punches were exchanged and then the first shots were heard and some in the melee fell to the ground.

At that point two snipers from Amos' platoon who were perched unseen in the branches of neighboring trees, took advantage of the moment to take out the militia men holding Olive, Miri and Sanjay hostage. Brief bright red sunflowers seemed to replace the heads of the erstwhile praetorian guards before their corpses dropped to the ground.

Pandemonium then broke out amongst the members of Islamic State and Hezbollah. Some tumbled down the hill into the arms of their comrades below whilst others started fighting amongst themselves unaware of the source of gunfire. The confusion below developed into hand-to-hand fighting between the rival bands of Sunni and Shiite militants.

Meanwhile about 150 well-armed men, some encumbered with rocket-propelled grenades, started advancing up the approach road from the southeast perimeter of Tel Dan. As they fanned out into the plaza at the entrance to the ancient walled city, they were taken by surprise by Captain Barzilai's platoon waiting in ambush, hidden in the thick foliage at each side. After about half the invading force were accounted for the remainder fled downhill only to face the frenzied fighting amongst their own side that had spilled round the left flank of their advancing army.

In quick succession, half a dozen IAF Apache attack helicopters rose up from the south and started to harry the invading army on the northern perimeter of the Tel. Then a squadron of F-16s that had flown out to sea towards Cyprus from their base at Ramat David made a sudden U-turn and flew back east to take out the Hezbollah rocket launchers in Lebanon from the rear.

The tanks of the Golani brigade on the Heights then rumbled forward into Syria and took on the well dug in forces of Islamic State.

At long last, having kept their heads down for four years, the Israeli forces were at war with the terrorist groups threatening them from the northwest and northeast. All reservists were called up and Southern command was at full strength keeping a close watch on the borders with Gaza and along the border with Sinai. Hamas agents witnessing the carnage in the north sent urgent messages to their cells in Gaza, the West Bank and Jordan, suggesting that now was not a good time to get involved. However the ISIL forces in Sinai had already been given notice to attack but were rapidly driven back underground by the combined air forces of Egypt from the west and Israel from the east. As the hydra headed snake of IS became decapitated, their offshoots in North Africa were at a loss how to react as news from the north trickled back to them.

Meanwhile in the beautiful verdant Bekka valley turned red as the forces of IS and Hezbollah, were locked in mortal combat. Those on the summit of Tel Dan took little pleasure in witnessing this slaughter of young men who had been brain washed into death cults from an early age. The four English tourists turned their eyes away and took refuge in the First Aid tent. Together with Miri they were in a state of shock. The symptoms were those of a panic attack, sweating and shaking and with a sense of impending death. Ishmael who had witnessed the whole drama, issued instructions that all five should have intravenous diazepam. Once they had calmed down and were sitting in a circle with hot cups of coffee in their hands, Olive was the first to break the silence.

"Dear friends my faith is restored, we have just witnessed a miracle, should we pray together?"

Sanjay was the first to respond, "Olive dear friend, I would do nothing to undermine your faith that no doubt has given you the strength to complete this journey with us but what we have just seen has a natural explanation. The rock in the head of the staff must have been radioactive and by the look of it could only have been Radium. Radium 226 has a half-life of 1,600 years. This must be the largest sample of the element ever discovered." Arthur concurred and added another insight from his encyclopedic knowledge of the ancient history of the Levant. "As you may remember from your childhood readings of the Old Testament, only the High Priest was allowed into the Holy of Holies and then only on the Day of Atonement. To break this commandment the Bible says, would be at the pain of death. I think we've just witnessed what that meant. No wonder Aaron's rod was kept in a lead lined box." Outside the tent Daniel's technicians had reached the same conclusions and treated the unearthed relic with great respect. Gingerly approaching it from two sides where it had fallen from the Bagdadi's hands, Daniel's technicians were carrying Geiger counters. The readings reached 100-200 cps of gamma radiation within a circumference of one meter. It was decided that the rod should be returned to its lead lined casket once someone had fetched protective clothing.

The battle of the Bekka valley and the Golan Heights lasted about 24 hours. ISIL and Hezbollah had thrown all their combined men and materiel into this suicidal mission and from that day forth were spent forces. The aftermath of their failed mission reverberated round the globe.

★★★

Chapter 38

Aftermath

The geo-political fallout from the Battle of the Bekka valley was profound and broadly favourable.

ISIL and Hezbollah were effectively defanged. As a result the official Lebanese government were able to reclaim control of the badlands south of the Litani River. A rapidly called general election consolidated a left of centre secular democratic coalition and Hezbollah, as a political force became a thing of the past. Events in Syria and Iraq took longer to settle down and were of great complexity. The warring factions, even with the destruction of ISIL, were hard to reconcile. The Assad family regime, with loyalty to the Alawite sect, remained in control of the western central part of Syria. The north west of the country was in the hands of an unholy mix of so called freedom fighters from all extremes of the political spectrum ranging from secular democrats to extreme Islamic fighting groups linked to tribal and religious sects. The Kurds had more or less carved themselves out a self-governing mini state from the borders of Turkey crossing eastward to northern sections of Syria and Iraq. Iraq itself became a hotbed of strife again with fighting renewed between the Sunni and Shiite tribal groups. After another year of instability in the region the UN at last decided enough was enough and for the first time did something useful in the cauldron of the Middle East. They effectively reversed history and tore up the Sykes-Picot agreement of 1916. This was a secret pact between Great Britain and France that defined their proposed spheres of influence should the allies succeed in defeating the Ottoman

Empire. Imaginary straight lines in the sand created in 1916 eventually created Lebanon, the Palestine mandate, Syria and Iraq after the Versailles conference in 1919, when the victors divided up the spoils. Religious and tribal feuding ever since was the long-term price paid for this promiscuous expression of Imperial power.

In its place the overwhelming majority of the UN voted for three new nations determined by tribal, racial and religious uniformity, namely Kurdistan, the Sunni republic of Mohamedstan and the Shiite republic of Alistan.

Further south in the Sinai desert, Egyptian forces in hot pursuit of ISIL operatives, entered Gaza. The citizens of that benighted strip of land welcomed the invaders and rebelled against their hated rulers. Egypt then returned Gaza to the *status quo ante* the 6-day war, to the relief of everyone in the neighbourhood. The Palestinian authority in the West Bank exploited this event by rounding up all the militants in Hamas cells. Israel and the Palestinians on the West Bank settled down for a period of peaceful animosity whilst waiting for another miracle.

Wider afield, Saudi Arabia and Iran became more concerned about internal affairs than international adventurism, as the crash in oil prices led to civil strife. That aside all stake holders agreed that militant Islamicism had a great future behind it and the "Caliphate" was better conceived as a global spiritual convocation of believers rather than a geographical entity.

★★★

At a more parochial level the failure of the conspiracy to take possession of Aaron's rod led to a remarkable chain of events. Chief inspector Alan Campbell-Norton, a senior member of the anti-terrorism team at New Scotland Yard, was found dead in his office with a single bullet hole in his right temple and a Colt revolver in his right hand. Seeking an explanation for his suicide, a search of his home led to the discovery of a laptop computer hidden in his attic. A search of the hard drive revealed 3,000 plus images of paedophile pornography. In addition was another heavily encrypted file that took the experts at the Met five days to hack into. Amongst the e-mail exchanges with an unidentified correspondent was a detailed description of the confidential plans for security covering the coronation of King Charles III. As that was only a few days away a high level meeting in Cabinet Briefing Room A, commonly known as COBRA, attended by the prime minister, the leader of the opposition, the home secretary, representatives of the armed services and heads of all the security and relevant police departments, was convened. They had to make a tough decision as to whether or not to cancel the Coronation at Westminster Abbey. Whilst they were in conclave an operative working at GCHQ, by chance picked up a transmission from the html 5 address of the correspondent linked to Campbell-Norton's suicide.

The message read, "Arrived London rendezvous 22.30". Fortunately the recipient of the message was amongst the list of terrorist suspects under active surveillance. COBRA was informed and a squad from the Metropolitan police SCO 19 SWAT team was rapidly deployed to encircle a house in a non-descript row of semi-detached properties in a ribbon development running alongside the south circular road in the Brixton area. At precisely 22.30 that evening a suspect with a NIKE sports bag slung over his shoulder was seen entering the building. Wearing gas masks and goggles, the SWAT team battered down the front door and in quick succession, stun grenades followed by smoke bombs were lobbed through every window at the front and rear of the house. All the suspects, who had been gathered in the front room, surrendered without a fight and were whisked off in unmarked black vans to a secure holding place in an apparently abandoned warehouse close to the river at Nine Elms. A search of the buildings revealed an arsenal of combat rifles, small arms and grenades together with a suicide vest that was almost complete in its assembly.

The newly arrived suspect seemed to be relieved to end up in the hands of the security service and the contents of his sports back contained a number of passports. The one he had used to get past the border police at Gatwick carried the name Selah Al Mazri.

Al Mazri seemed happy to divulge all his secrets having decided he would prefer to spend the rest of his life in a British jail for the murder of Jonathan Black rather than the promise of eternity in the company of 70 virgins. He was therefore transferred to the HQ of MI6 nearby on the southern end of the Vauxhall Bridge. As a result of his "spilling the beans" MI5 agents raided houses in London's Stamford Hill area and FBI agents raided homes and offices in New York's Crown Heights district and arrested many members of the extreme Charedi sect known as Naturei Karta, or Jews United against Zionism.

In December 2015, the then Prime Minister David Cameron, had laid before parliament of a report on the Muslim Brotherhood that opened with this statement:

I have today laid before both Houses the main findings of the internal review I commissioned in the last Parliament to improve the government's understanding of the Muslim Brotherhood; establish whether the Muslim Brotherhood's ideology or activities, or those of individual members or affiliates, put at risk, damaged, or risked damaging the UK's national interests; and where appropriate inform policy.

Following on from Al Mazri's confessions the government then had the smoking gun to justify rounding up all known members of the Brotherhood in the UK who were either imprisoned or deported to their countries of origin to meet whatever fate they might expect. It goes without saying that this was accompanied by howls of protest from those "progressives" amongst the extreme left wing polity, who accused the government of breaching the human rights convention of the UN.

In parallel with these events the home office gave out

instructions for a second inquest into the death of professor Joshua Black. The new evidence made it clear beyond doubt that he was murdered and that his suicide note was a forgery. With his reputation restored the University organised a memorial service at Senate House, in his honour proudly attended by his wife and two sons.

★★★

It took the best part of a year to complete an inventory of the treasures from King Solomon's Temple. The first job was for a team wearing protective clothing to retrieve Aaron's rod and replace it in its lead lined receptacle and then transport to the vaults of the Israel Museum in Jerusalem for further detailed analysis and study under controlled conditions. What to do with it afterwards was a complex decision that required a Presidential committee to be convened.

The gold bullion was of course worth its weight in gold! Yet its true worth was beyond calculation because of its 3,000-year-old provenance. Tel David was protected by a ring of steel and armed guards whilst the individual ingots were catalogued and divided up into manageable aliquots before being driven in armoured vehicles to add to the gold reserves of the country. Of course some choice specimens were kept for display in the Museum along with examples of the goldsmith's skills dating back to the time of Bezalel the chief artisan of the Tabernacle.

Apart from the rod itself perhaps the most extraordinary finding of the excavation was not so much the contents of the vault but the walls themselves.

Once Olive and her compatriots had recovered from their ordeal and shortly before their return to the UK, they were taken back for the last time to Tel Dan. By this time to vault had been made safe as well as secure and a wooden staircase was in place that made descent into the pit relatively easy.

The archaeologists at work stood aside out of respect and they were allowed to inspect the findings at their leisure. Of the four, Arthur, being an experienced archaeologist, was as much interested in the structure of the vault as to its contents. Wandering round the walls with a flashlight, he carefully inspected the cracked and flaking plaster on each surface. In one corner a large fragment of the plaster had come loose. Taking out his pocketknife he carefully prized it off and to his astonishment encountered a deeply engraved line of characters presumably of an ancient language with which he was not familiar. With great excitement he summoned over Daniel Cohen who agreed that this looked like an ancient tongue and perhaps a variant of Assyrian cuneiform. They both agreed that the finding was of such importance that it would have to wait until the contents of the vault had been removed and specialist staff recruited to examine the walls in detail.

By the time Olive and her brother together with the Manchandras were ready to go home a whole month had passed. As they waited in the departure lounge at Ben Gurion airport Ishmael and Aisha, his shy fiancée with beautiful large brown eyes modestly showing through the gap in her hijab, joined them. They formally invited the four friends to attend their wedding in the autumn. They each made their excuses but in truth the thought of returning to this tumultuous corner of the globe so soon, was too much to contemplate. As it was Ishmael and Aisha had decided to spend their honeymoon in London, a legendary and exotic venue in Aisha's imagination who had never travelled further than Beer Sheba in the past. So plans were hatched for a great reunion party in November. By the time they disembarked at London Heathrow the full story of their adventures had got out into the popular media and they were greeted like celebrities by a wolf pack of journalists and television crews. Waiting patiently at the back of the crowd was Abdullah Ibn Sharif with his fiancée in tow, the beautiful, tall and fashionably dressed, princess Layla bint Abdul Rahman Al Saud. A further wedding invitation was offered for the relatively cool month of January in Saudi Arabia but again this politely declined. Abdullah then decided that part of the formal wedding celebration, the Valima, would be extended for an additional two days at his father-in-laws' mansion on the outer circle of Regent's park. Honour was satisfied and each went their own ways as life slowly returned to normal.

★★★

Epilogue

Tablets of Stone and Rivers of Blood

A year has passed and Savita is expecting her first child. After their near death experience at Tel Dan, Sanjay thought it best they started a family before it was too late. As a result they reluctantly refused the invitation to a free holiday as guests of the department of archaeology of the Hebrew University. Along with Arthur and Olive, the invitation was offered, half in jest, to begin the search for the Ark of the Holy Covenant at the coordinates described in the copper scroll somewhere near the Ramon crater in the northern Negev.

Olive by this time was suffering from withdrawal symptoms and was seeking further adventures.

Arthur meanwhile was recuperating from a minor heart attack that had demanded emergency coronary artery stents. His cardiologist recommended a week's holiday in the sun chilling out by a swimming pool and this was exactly what on offer. They were to travel out to Jerusalem and spend the first night with Daniel and Jessie Cohen at their house in Yamin Moishe, before travelling south to a five star hotel perched on the edge of crater. Whilst they were to be in Jerusalem, Daniel wanted to exploit Arthur's expert knowledge of ancient languages in making sense of the inscriptions on the walls of the underground vault that held King Solomon's treasure.

It was a bright fresh early summer morning with cloudless blue skies as Arthur and Daniel made their short drive from Yamin Moishe to the offices at the Israel Museum. After coffee and doughnuts they settled down in Daniel's seminar room whilst a technician set up the data projector and ran through the images of each of the twelve individual stone slabs that had been affixed to the walls of the symmetrical cubic space of the vault. Each upright engraved stele had been cleaned of its surface plaster to reveal ten lines of differing scripts. The ancient Egyptian hieratic script, the Sumerian and Assyrian cuneiform runes and the paleo-Hebrew lettering resembling that of the Lachish letters, were readily recognised by Arthur. He thought he recognised Phoenician and Cretan Linear B but the other six stone slabs contained symbols and inscriptions that were alien to him. He had no difficulty in recognising the 10 commandments carved into the Aramaic column and assumed that all the others were translations of the same.

"Well Arthur, what do you make of this? So far we have kept the discovery of these twelve inscribed stones a secret until we could make sense of their provenance."

Arthur gazed on in awe and suddenly bellowed out, "I think I know. Do you have a copy of the Art Scroll edition of the Chumash?"

Without a word Daniel popped back into his office and came back with a beautifully bound volume that contained the Torah and its commentaries.

Arthur rapidly riffled through the papers until he found what he was looking for but obviously someone had been here before as there was a bookmark between the same pages.

"Here it is. Deuteronomy, chapter 27, verses 1-12. This is the point where Moses in standing on the heights overlooking the Promised Land and issuing his last commands. *'Observe the entire commandment that I command you this day. You should set up great stones and you shall coat them with plaster. You shall inscribe on them all the words of the Torah when you cross over. It shall be that when you cross the Jordan, you shall erect these stones on Mount Ebal and you shall coat them with plaster. You shall inscribe all the words of the Torah, well clarified'*; Rabbi Shlomo Yitchaki, better known as RASHI, writes a commentary as follows, *'Well clarified means it should be clear to all who read it i.e. that it be inscribed in all seventy primary languages of the time.'* I think RASHI exaggerated about seventy languages but I'm more than content to have twelve. What we've got here is of greater importance than the Rosetta stone but Daniel I think you knew that already."

"You are of course right in that assumption but it is always of value to have a second opinion from an authority such as you. You may have forgotten but I was given the responsibility of decoding what is now referred to as 'The Third Tablet of the Holy Covenant' that was discovered by professor Yigael Yadin aided and abetted by Jessie's parents, Martin and Sara Tanner. Martin's brother, Joseph, made the same leap of imagination for identifying the object as you have just now. These twelve tablets of stone are the companion pieces to the one already on show that has pride of place in the Museum that houses these offices; let's go upstairs and pay homage once more before we leave for the Negev.

★★★

The road to Beer Sheba went due south off the main Jerusalem-Tel Aviv highway and in no time the green foothill of the Judean mountain ridge gave way to the parched landscape of the desert regions of the southern half of Israel. They then passed into the region occupied by scattered Bedouin encampments. These were not the exotic tented oasis villages of the western imagination but more like shanty towns with rubbish dumps, sheds covered with corrugated iron roofs protecting live stock, chicken pens and the black tents providing living quarters. The shepherds with their flocks of long eared goats and the occasional hobbled camel provided a reassuring biblical backdrop to their drive. After an hour they made a detour on the ring road bordering the city of Beer Sheba and entered the Negev desert proper. After another hour driving through featureless scrub- land they arrived at the township of Mitzspe Ramon. This little town in the middle of nowhere was founded as an encampment for workmen building the road to Eilat in the 1950s. It's spectacular position on the lip of the Ramon crater and its hot dry climate allowed it to grow as a tourist resort. The Ramon crater is strictly speaking a *makhtesh,* is 38 km long, 6 km wide and 450 meters deep.

A *makhtesh* is a very rare geological feature. Unlike craters formed by meteorite impact or canyons resulting from rivers eating their way into the earth's crust, a *makhtesh* is the remnant of an inland sea where an earthquake allowed all the water to drain into a deeper trough in the earth's crust. In this case the body of water decanted into the deepest declivity on earth, namely the Dead Sea. As a result this barren land provides a rich harvest of ammonite fossils and shark's teeth to this day.

The hotel *Beresheet* sits on the very lip of the deepest section of the crater and affords astonishing views that were set in place during the earliest phases of the earth creation. The very name of the hotel explains the view, as it is the first word of the first book of the Old Testament: *Beresheet-* In the beginning.

The hotel comprises a central complex of pools, recreation facilities, restaurants and a synagogue.

The large "infinity" pool, the centre piece of the attraction, is perched on the edge of the crater and provides vertiginous views of the Cambrian era of the earth's surface as it looked 4 billion years ago. What really makes this hotel so special is that all the guest suites are built in the manner of a Nabatean village arranged around a network of lanes bordered by cacti, sculptures and families of wild goats with long curved horns, the Ibex. Legend has it that a male Ibex was the replacement sacrifice when God decided to reprieve Isaac from death at the hands of his father Abraham. To this day, the horn of an Ibex is crafted into the *shofar* whose notes can be heard in the synagogues all round the world on the Day of Atonement.

If you are lucky your holiday villa will include its own miniature infinity pool overlooking the crater where the Ibex will come to visit for a drink in the cool of the evening. Olive and Arthur enjoyed that privilege.

On their first evening, Daniel and Jessie met up with

Olive and Arthur in the bar of the hotel where they sat around an open log fire. Although the midday temperatures rose to the low 30 degree Celsius, in this desert area, once the sun had set it became distinctly chilly. With the flickering light of the log fire and a glass of fine red wine in hand, the company felt mellow and relaxed. Arthur looking across at Jessie, whose beauty was enhanced by the firelight, wistfully recalled his first unrequited love of her mother, Sara Zinati, over 50 years in the past. Conversation then moved on to recalling the near fatal experiences of their adventures at Tel Dan the previous year. Thereafter and continuing over dinner, the two men discussed the clues in the copper scroll that brought them to this place whilst the two women settled down to discuss family affairs and the contrasting life styles in Jerusalem and northwest London.

The following morning the four of them found themselves in the large infinity pool in the central complex and stood, with elbows resting on the pool's edge, chins resting on the backs of their hands, looking across the almost featureless crater extending thirty kilometres in front of them. In the early morning light the main attraction of the view was the remarkable variety of colours that ranged from russet coloured iron ore to the verdigris green of the copper deposits. They had just agreed, that in this vast expanse of desert with little to go on but map coordinates that could at best be accurate to the nearest ten square kilometres and the vaguest of clues from the copper scroll, the task of tracking down the last and greatest treasure of King Solomon's Temple, was close to impossible, when Olive suddenly screamed.

"I know where to look!" They turned to her in astonishment.

"We always assumed that the 'river of blood' referred to the plague when Moses turned the Nile into blood." She then stood on tiptoes in the pool and pointed downwards. "There is your river of blood right under where we are standing." For a moment or two the others couldn't make sense of what she was saying until they realised that the wadi bed below, one of many draining from the escarpment, was so rich in iron ore content as to look like dried blood in this light.

They all climbed out of the pool, quickly dried off and dressed before running over to the concierge desk to enquire if they might hire a Jeep and a driver who knew the terrain. As luck would have it there was one waiting outside looking for customers. Following their instructions the Jeep driver took them down the narrow switch back paved road that led into the depths of the crater and then cut back along unmarked bumpy paths until they were placed directly below the hotel's pool.

Sure enough, with the aid of the guide's binoculars, a dried out tributary of Wadi Ramon could be traced up to the mouth of a cave hidden by the overhang of the escarpment. The red iron ore, bright in the morning sun coming from behind their backs, did indeed look like a river of blood.

The Jeep's driver couldn't understand why his party was in such a hurry to get back to the hotel but happily pocketed the price of a four-hour tour of the crater's base for a drive that lasted no more than thirty minutes. The hotel manager was well aware of the distinction of his four guests and without any questions was happy to dig out the documents regarding the design and building of the hotel. One of the surveyor's reports described an underground dry riverbed leading to a cavern that they were careful to avoid when digging the foundations of the hotel. The report contained an accurate map of the underground survey. Pointing to the site of the cavern, Daniel asked the manager if he could estimate the position this might occupy beneath the hotel. As the map carried a line drawing of the proposed "footprint" of the hotel, this wasn't too difficult. They followed the man down the polished wooden stairs to the sub ground floor level. Then looking at the map and orienting himself with the points of the compass, the hotel manager pointed at the door marked Synagogue.

"How can you be so sure?" asked Daniel. "Because the

ark bearing the scrolls of the law in a synagogue always faces Jerusalem," replied the man.

Daniel offered his sincere thanks and without another word the group of four reconvened in the bar but this time sitting on a balcony looking out to the east where they could just make out the mountainous area at the opposite edge of the crater. Jessie then spoke for them all when she said, "If indeed we have found the resting place of the Ark of the Holy Covenant then we should let it rest in peace and take its secret to our graves." They toasted their pledge with a glass of sacramental wine brought up from the cellar by a bewildered waitress.

★★★

The resting place of Aaron's rod was another matter altogether and was the topic of hot debate within the Presidential committee for more than twelve months. The issue was finally resolved with the intervention of Rabbi Joseph Tanner, the ageing brother of Jessie Cohen's late father Martin. Rabbi Tanner served a modest congregation in Rosh Pinah a small town that overlooked the Sea of Galilee. His wisdom and rhetorical skills had made him the unofficial diplomatic voice of the Ashkenazi chief Rabbi in earlier times of political upheaval. His speech to the assembly is reported in full, an appropriate close to this story.

"Mr President, Prime Minister, Chief Rabbis, Colleagues and friends. For many months now I have listened to this complex and sometimes acrimonious debate. I have no doubt of the sincerity and scholarship of those involved and I have listened patiently because until now I had no solution of my own to offer but only a ghost of an idea. All this time we have been debating the final disposition of Aaron's rod, the most remarkable finding in professor Cohen's famous archaeological dig. Now some of us may know that professor Cohen is married to my niece so I had a little earlier notice than most of you about the discovery of another twelve holy objects, that until a few weeks ago had not been fully understood. We are now sure that these are twelve tablets of stone engraved with the Ten Commandments as decreed by *Moishe Rabenu* when first seeing the Promised Land from Mount Ebal. Each stone was inscribed with one of the known languages of those times. In other words these commandments were for the whole world not just the children of Israel. Aaron's rod is different yet is not ours alone for it is revered equally by the three Abrahamic religions, Judaism, Christianity and Islam. At the end of the 6-day war in 1967, under the command of general Dayan, the Old City of Jerusalem together with the Temple Mount, was in Jewish hands for the first time in nearly 2,000 years. Let me now remind you that Dayan's first act on the Temple Mount, only a few hours after IDF Chief Rabbi Shlomo Goren blew the *shofar* and gave the *Shehecheyanu* blessing beside the Western Wall, was to immediately remove the Israeli flag that the paratroopers had raised on the mount. Dayan's second act was to clear out the paratroop company that was supposed to remain permanently stationed in the northern part of the mount. General Narkiss, his CIC, reminded Dayan that Jordan too, had stationed a military contingent on the mount to maintain order, and that long ago the Romans had done the same, deploying a garrison force in the Antonia Fortress that Herod had built near the mount. But Dayan was not persuaded. He told Narkiss that it seemed to him the plateau would be best left in the hands of the Muslim guards and that sovereignty should be handed over to the Muslim Wakf. The same principle was applied to the control of the Church of the Holy Sepulchre. That act of magnanimity, for better or worse, remains the *status quo* today.

Let me suggest that we go one step further than Moishe Dayan. Let us erect a shrine on the Temple Mount and line its walls with the 12 tablets of the 10 Commandments facing the four corners of the earth and in the centre erect a lead lined glass cabinet to hold Aaron's rod. This will signify that the staff of the first High Priest belongs to all but that no one man may hold it for fear of death. In return we would request that the Temple mount and the shrine of the Rod will be open to those of all faiths and those of no faith, to pray as they wish or if they come not to pray then to marvel at the history of the Holy Land and Jerusalem, the City of Gold and the original resting place of the first code of conduct the north star of our moral compasses that points the way for all the tribes on earth who can trace back their origins to the 6th day of the creation."

And God said, Let us make man in our image, after our likeness: and let them have dominion over the fish of the sea, and over the fowl of the air, and over the cattle, and over all the earth, and over every creeping thing that creepeth upon the earth.

So God created man in his own image, in the image of God created he him; male and female created he them.

And God blessed them, and God said unto them, be fruitful, and multiply, and replenish the earth, and subdue it: and have dominion over the fish of the sea, and over the fowl of the air, and over every living thing that moveth upon the earth.

And God saw every thing that he had made, and, behold, it was very good.

And the evening and the morning were the sixth day.

And so it came to pass.

★★★

Author's notes and acknowledgments

It is conventional to divide literature into two simple categories, fiction and non-fiction although a third has appeared in recent years where the boundaries are less well defined, that is described as faction. I started carrying out research for this book in order to provide convincing background material against which the fictional narrative would play out. Yet along the way I made so many extraordinary findings, that the reader would assume are purely figments of my imagination, yet turn out to be factual. The cliché that fact is sometimes stranger than fiction or as some people put it, "you couldn't make it up", pretty much sums up my adventures.

This is my second foray in writing a novel relating to Biblical archaeology, the first was entitled, "The Third Tablet of the Holy Covenant" and was linked to events played out at the time of the fall of the Second Temple to the Romans in 70 CE. This was easy to research as the events in question were recorded in "The Jewish War" written by that renegade, Josephus, whilst these events described were still in living memory. Furthermore, as a young surgeon, I got dirt under my nails helping out with the excavations at Masada. I even uncovered bronze coins from the time of the third year of the siege dated 73 CE. A visit to Rome today will allow you to see the victorious Roman legions looting the Temple candelabra from the Temple carved in bas-relief on Trajan's arch. That was a *mere* 1,943 years ago. The intention of this novel was to explore events around the time of the Babylonian conquest of Judea and the fall of King Solomon's Temple about 600 years earlier in the period described in the Book of Kings in the Old Testament.

I thought that this would be a period lost in the mists

of time and described in legend and folklore similar to the authenticity of Nordic Sagas. Yet my deep skepticism concerning the actuality of the events described in the Books of Kings, in the words of the Prophet Jeremiah at the time of the reign of the King Hezekiah, was overturned as a result of my research. The first clues were close to hand in the British Museum in central London; in the Sackler galleries exhibiting artifacts from the Levant from the 7th and 8th centuries BCE. These included the bas-relief from the Assyrian Kingdom originally housed in Nineveh, that describes in brutal detail the conquest of Lachish along with the "Lachish letters" dating from the Babylonian conquest nearly 100 years later. The provenance of the "Lachish letters" then took me to the Palestine Exploration fund (PEF). With the support and encouragement of Felicity Cobbing, who was responsible for the collection at the PEF, I was given access to the archives and reports of the excavation of Lachish led by James Starkey between 1934 and 1938. From these archives I learnt of the discovery of 1,500 skeletons in a nearby burial pit and read the letters of Olga Tufnell to her mother where she described the murder of James Starkey. That gave me the idea for the central thread of the novel.

Whilst I was beavering away in the archives of the PEF, Miss Cobbing thought I might be interested in reviewing a new book about Flinders Petrie by Debbie Challis, (The Archaeology of Race: The Eugenic Ideas of Francis Galton and Flinders Petrie; Bloomsbury publishers, London, New York, 2013) This book revealed the repulsive ideology of the man and alerted me to the history of Eugenics as an academic subject at my own university, UCL. I also learnt about the macabre story of Petrie's head. This discovery then set me running to the Royal College of Surgeons (RCS), where I happened to be a fellow, and from the archives of my college I discovered the complicity of the Hunterian professor at the RCS in this vipers nest of racists.

The other fact that is stranger than fiction is the narrative in Dr. Bloch diary about his relationship with Adolf Hitler. That is entirely factual apart from placing him in London rather than New York between the years 1943 until his death in 1945.

I have one confession to make and that applies to the last chapter where Olive finally deduces the final resting place of the Ark of the Holy Covenant that is hidden under the foundations of the *Bereshet* Hotel. That idea was lifted from the conclusion of Lionel Davidson's novel, "A long way to Shiloh". This was not intended as outright plagiarism but rather as a token of respect for my favourite author of the genre of adventure stories linked to a dangerous quest in an alien land. Take it as a quotation rather than a theft.

Finally I owe a huge debt to Hazel Thornton and Jackie Gerrard for reading, correcting and some editing of my text.

★★★